Ex Líbris

VENUS, INC.

VENUS, INC.

THE SPACE MERCHANTS
by Frederik Pohl
and
C. M. Kornbluth

and

THE MERCHANTS' WAR
by Frederik Pohl

NELSON DOUBLEDAY, INC.
GARDEN CITY, NEW YORK

Printed in the United States of America

CONTENTS

THE
SPACE
MERCHANTS

one

· ◆ ·

As I dressed that morning I ran over in my mind the long list of statistics, evasions, and exaggerations that they would expect in my report. My section—Production—had been plagued with a long series of illnesses and resignations, and you can't get work done without people to do it. But the Board wasn't likely to take that as an excuse.

I rubbed depilatory soap over my face and rinsed it with the trickle from the fresh-water tap. Wasteful, of course, but I pay taxes and salt water always leaves my face itchy. Before the last of the greasy stubble was quite washed away the trickle stopped and didn't start again. I swore a little and finished rinsing with salt. It had been happening lately; some people blamed Consie saboteurs. Loyalty raids were being held throughout the New York Water Supply Corporation; so far they hadn't done any good.

The morning newscast above the shaving mirror caught me for a moment . . . the President's speech of last night, a brief glimpse of the Venus rocket squat and silvery on the Arizona sand, rioting in Panama . . . I switched it off when the quarter-hour time signal chimed over the audio band.

It looked as though I was going to be late again. Which certainly would not help mollify the Board.

I saved five minutes by wearing yesterday's shirt instead of studding a clean one and by leaving my breakfast juice to grow warm and sticky on the table. But I lost the five minutes again by trying to call Kathy. She didn't answer the phone and I was late getting into the office.

Fortunately—and unprecedentedly—Fowler Schocken was late too.

In our office it is Fowler's custom to hold the weekly Board conference fifteen minutes before the regular opening of the business day. It keeps the clerks and stenos on their toes, and it's no hardship to Fowler. He spends every morning in the office anyway, and "morning" to him begins with the rising of the sun.

Today, though, I had time to get my secretary's summary off my desk before the meeting. When Fowler Schocken walked in with a courteous apology for his tardiness I was sitting in my place at the foot of the table, reasonably relaxed and as sure of myself as a Fowler Schocken Associate is ever likely to be.

"Good morning," Fowler said, and the eleven of us made the usual idiot murmur. He didn't sit down; he stood gazing paternally at us for about a minute and a half. Then, with the air of a daytripper in Xanadu, he looked carefully and delightedly about the room.

"I've been thinking about our conference room," he said, and we all looked around at it. The room isn't big, it isn't small: say ten by twelve. But it's cool, well-lighted, and most imposingly furnished. The air recirculators are cleverly hidden behind animated friezes; the carpeting is thick and soft; and every piece of furniture is constructed from top to bottom of authentic, expertized, genuine tree-grown wood.

Fowler Schocken said: "We have a nice conference room here, men. As we should have, since Fowler Schocken Associates is the largest advertising agency in the city. We bill a megabuck a year more than anybody else around. And—" he looked around at all of us, "I think you'll agree that we all find it worthwhile. I don't think there's a person in this room who has less than a two-room apartment." He twinkled at me. "Even the bachelors. Speaking for myself, I've done well. My summer place looks right over one of the largest parks on Long Island. I haven't tasted any protein but new meat for years, and when I go out for a spin I pedal a Cadillac. The wolf is a long way from my door. And I think any one of you can say the same. Right?" The hand of our Director of Market Research shot up and Fowler nodded at him: "Yes, Matthew?"

Matt Runstead knows which side his bread is oiled on. He glared belligerently around the table. "I just want to go on record as agreeing with Mr. Schocken—one hundred percent—all the way!" he snapped.

Fowler Schocken inclined his head. "Thank you, Matthew." And he meant it. It took him a moment before he could go on. "We all know," he said, "what put us where we are. We remember the Starrzelius Verily account, and how we put Indiastries on the map. The first spherical trust. Merging a whole subcontinent into a single manufacturing complex. Schocken Associates pioneered on both of them. Nobody can say we were floating with the tide. But that's behind us.

"Men! I want to know something. You can tell me truthfully—are we getting soft?" He took time to look at each of our faces searchingly, ignoring the forest of hands in the air. God help me, mine was right up there too. Then he waved to the man at his right. "You first, Ben," he said.

Ben Winston stood up and baritoned: "Speaking for Industrial Anthropology, no! Listen to today's progress report—you'll get it in the noon bulletin, but let me brief you now: according to the midnight indices, all primary schools east of the Mississippi are now using our packaging recommendation for the school lunch program. Soyaburgers and regenerated steak"—there wasn't a man around the table who didn't shudder at the thought of soyaburgers and regenerated steak—"are packed in containers the same shade of green as the Universal products. But the candy, ice cream, and Kiddiebutt cigarette ration are wrapped in colorful Starrzelius red. When those kids grow up . . ." he lifted his eyes exultantly from his notes. "According to our extrapolation, fifteen years from now Universal products will be broke, bankrupt, and off the market entirely!"

He sat down in a wave of applause. Schocken clapped too, and looked brightly at the rest of us. I leaned forward with Expression One—eagerness, intelligence, competence—all over my face. But I needn't have bothered. Fowler pointed to the lean man next to Winston. Harvey Bruner.

"I don't have to tell you men that Point-of-Sale has its special problems," Harvey said, puffing his thin cheeks. "I swear, the whole damned Government must be infiltrated with Consies! You know what they've done. They outlawed compulsive subsonics in our aural advertising—but we've bounced back with a list of semantic cue words that tie in with every basic trauma and neurosis in American life today. They listened to the safety cranks and stopped us from projecting our messages on aircar windows—but we bounced back. Lab tells me," he nodded to our Director of Research across the table, "that soon we'll be testing a system that projects directly on the retina of the eye.

"And not only that, but we're going forward. As an example I want to mention the Coffiest pro—" He broke off. "Excuse me, Mr. Schocken," he whispered. "Has Security checked this room?"

Fowler Schocken nodded. "Absolutely clean. Nothing but the usual State Department and House of Representatives spy-mikes. And of course we're feeding a canned playback into them."

Harvey relaxed again. "Well, about this Coffiest," he said. "We're sampling it in fifteen key cities. It's the usual offer—a thirteen-week supply of Coffiest, one thousand dollars in cash, and a weekend vacation on the Ligurian Riviera to everybody who comes in. But—and here's what makes this campaign truly great, in my estimation—each sample of Coffiest contains three milligrams of a simple alkaloid. Nothing harmful. But definitely habit-forming. After ten weeks the customer is hooked for life. It would cost him at least five thousand dollars for a cure, so it's simpler for him to go right on drinking Coffiest—three cups with every meal and a pot beside his bed at night, just as it says on the jar."

Fowler Schocken beamed, and I braced myself into Expression One again. Next to Harvey sat Tildy Mathis, Chief of Copy Services and handpicked by Schocken himself. But he didn't ask women to speak at Board sessions, and next to Tildy sat me.

I was composing my opening remarks in my head as Fowler Schocken let me down with a smile. He said: "I won't ask every section to report. We haven't the time. But you've given me your answer, gentlemen. It's the answer I like. You've met every challenge up to now. And so now—I want to give you a new challenge."

He pressed a button on his monitor panel and swiveled his chair around. The lights went down in the room; the projected Picasso that hung behind Schocken's chair faded and revealed the mottled surface of the screen. On it another picture began to form.

I had seen the subject of that picture once before that day, in my news screen over my shaving mirror.

It was the Venus rocket, a thousand-foot monster, the bloated child of the slim V-2s and stubby Moon rockets of the past. Around it was a scaffolding of steel and aluminum, acrawl with tiny figures that manipulated minute, blue-white welding flames. The picture was obviously recorded; it showed the rocket as it had been weeks or months ago in an earlier stage of construction, not poised as if ready for take-off, as I had seen it earlier.

A voice from the screen said triumphantly and inaccurately: "This is the ship that spans the stars!" I recognized the voice as belonging to one of the organ-toned commentators in Aural Effects and expertized the scripts without effort as emanating from one of Tildy's English-major copywriters. The talented slovenliness that would confuse Venus with a star had to come from somebody on Tildy's staff.

"This is the ship that a modern Columbus will drive through the void," said the voice. "Six and a half million tons of trapped lightning and steel—an ark for eighteen hundred men and women, and everything to make a new world for their home. Who will man it? What fortunate pioneers will tear an empire from the rich, fresh soil of another world? Let me introduce you to them—a man and his wife, two of the intrepid . . ."

The voice kept on going. On the screen the picture dissolved to a spacious suburban roomette in early morning. On the screen the husband folding the bed into the wall and taking down the partition to the children's nook; the wife dialing breakfast and erecting the table. Over the breakfast juices and the children's pablum (with a steaming mug of Coffiest for each, of course) they spoke persuasively to each other about how wise and brave they had been to apply for passage in the Venus rocket. And the closing question of their youngest babbler ("Mommy, when I grow up kin I take *my* littul boys and girls to a place as nice as Venus?") cued the switch to a highly imaginative series of shots of Venus as it would be when the child grew up—verdant valleys, crystal lakes, brilliant mountain vistas.

The commentary did not exactly deny, and neither did it dwell on, the decades of hydroponics and life in hermetically sealed cabins that the pioneers would have to endure while working in Venus's unbreathable atmosphere and waterless chemistry.

Instinctively I had set the timer button on my watch when the picture started. When it was over I read the dial: nine minutes! Three times as long as any commercial could legally run. One full minute more than we were accustomed to get.

It was only after the lights were on again, the cigarettes lit, and

Fowler Schocken well into his pep talk for the day that I began to see how that was possible.

He began in the dithering, circumlocutory way that has become a part of the flavor of our business. He called our attention to the history of advertising—from the simple handmaiden task of selling already manufactured goods to its present role of creating industries and redesigning a world's folkways to meet the needs of commerce. He touched once more on what we ourselves, Fowler Schocken Associates, had done with our own expansive career. And then he said:

"There's an old saying, men. 'The world is our oyster.' We've made it come true. But we've eaten that oyster." He crushed out his cigarette carefully. "We've eaten it," he repeated. "We've actually and literally conquered the world. Like Alexander, we weep for new worlds to conquer. And *there*—" he waved at the screen behind him, "*there* you have just seen the first of those worlds."

I have never liked Matt Runstead, as you may have gathered. He is a Paul Pry whom I suspect of wiretapping even within the company. He must have spied out the Venus Project well in advance, because not even the most talented reflexes could have brought out his little speech. While the rest of us were still busy assimilating what Fowler Schocken had told us, Runstead was leaping to his feet.

"Gentlemen," he said with passion. "this is truly the work of genius. Not just India. Not just a commodity. But a whole planet to *sell.* I salute you, Fowler Schocken—the Clive, the Bolívar, the John Jacob Astor of a new world!"

Matt was first, as I say, but every one of us got up and said in turn about the same thing. Including me. It was easy; I'd been doing it for years. Kathy had never understood it and I'd tried to explain, with the light touch, that it was a religious ritual—like the champagne-bottle smash on the ship's prow, or the sacrifice of the virgin to the corn crop. Even with the light touch I never pressed the analogy too far. I don't think any of us, except maybe Matt Runstead, would feed opium derivatives to the world for money alone. But listening to Fowler Schocken speak, hypnotizing ourselves with our antiphonal responses, made all of us capable of any act that served our god of Sales.

I do not mean to say that we were criminals. The alkaloids in Coffiest were, as Harvey pointed out, not harmful.

When all of us had done, Fowler Schocken touched another

button and showed us a chart. He explained it carefully, item by item; he showed us tables and graphs and diagrams of the entire new department of Fowler Schocken Associates which would be set up to handle development and exploitation of the planet Venus. He covered the tedious lobbying and friendmaking in Congress, which had given us the exclusive right to levy tribute and collect from the planet—and I began to see how he could expect to get away with a nine-minute commercial. He explained how the government—it's odd how we still think and talk of that clearinghouse for pressures as though it were an entity with a will of its own—how the government wanted Venus to be an American planet and how they had selected the peculiarly American talent of advertising to make it possible. As he spoke we all caught some of his fire. I envied the man who would head the Venus Section; any one of us would have been proud to take the job.

He spoke of trouble with the Senator from Du Pont Chemicals with his forty-five votes, and of an easy triumph over the Senator from Nash-Kelvinator with his six. He spoke proudly of a faked Consie demonstration against Fowler Schocken, which had lined up the fanatically anti-Consie Secretary of the Interior. Visual Aids had done a beautiful job of briefing the information, but we were there nearly an hour looking at the charts and listening to Fowler's achievements and plans.

But finally he clicked off the projector and said: "There you have it. That's our new campaign. And it starts right away—*now*. I have only one more announcement to make and then we can all get to work."

Fowler Schocken is a good showman. He took the time to find a slip of paper and read from it a sentence that the lowest of our copyboys could deliver off the cuff. "The chairman of the Venus Section," he read, "will be Mitchell Courtenay."

And that was the biggest surprise of all, because Mitchell Courtenay is me.

two

· · ◆ · ·

I lingered with Fowler for three or four minutes while the rest of the Board went back to their offices, and the elevator ride down from the Board room to my own office on the eighty-sixth floor took a few seconds. So Hester was already clearing out my desk when I arrived.

"Congratulations, Mr. Courtenay," she said. "You're moving to the eighty-ninth now. Isn't it wonderful? And I'll have a private office too!"

I thanked her and picked up the phone over the desk. The first thing I had to do was to get my staff in and turn over the reins of Production; Tom Gillespie was next in line. But the first thing I *did* was to dial Kathy's apartment again. There was still no answer, so I called in the boys.

They were properly sorry to see me go and properly delighted about everybody's moving up a notch.

And then it was lunch time, so I postponed the problem of the planet Venus until the afternoon.

I made a phone call, ate quickly in the company cafeteria, took the elevator down to the shuttle, and the shuttle south for sixteen blocks. Coming out, I found myself in the open air for the first time that day, and reached for my antisoot plugs but didn't put them in. It was raining lightly and the air had been a little cleared. It was summer, hot and sticky; the hordes of people crowding the sidewalks were as anxious as I to get back inside a building. I had to bulldoze my way across the street and into the lobby.

The elevator took me up fourteen floors. It was an old building with imperfect air conditioning, and I felt a chill in my damp suit. It occurred to me to use that fact instead of the story I had prepared, but I decided against it.

A girl in a starched white uniform looked up as I walked into the office. I said: "My name is Silver. Walter P. Silver. I have an appointment."

"Yes, Mr. Silver," she remembered. "Your heart—you said it was an emergency."

"That's right. Of course it's probably only some psychosomatic thing, but I felt—"

"Of course." She waved me to a chair. "Dr. Nevin will see you in just a moment."

It was ten minutes. A young woman came out of the doctor's office, and a man who had been waiting in the reception room before me went in; then he came out and the nurse said: "Will you go into Dr. Nevin's office now?"

I went in. Kathy, very trim and handsome in her doctor's smock, was putting a case chart in her desk. When she straightened up she said, "Oh, Mitch!" in a very annoyed tone.

"I told only one lie," I said. "I lied about my name. But it is an emergency. And my heart is involved."

There was a faint impulse toward a smile, but it didn't quite reach the surface. "Not medically," she said.

"I *told* your girl it was probably psychosomatic. She said to come in anyhow."

"I'll speak to her about that. Mitch, you know I can't see you during working hours. Now please—"

I sat down next to her desk. "You won't see me any time, Kathy. What's the trouble?"

"Nothing's the trouble. Please go away, Mitch. I'm a doctor; I have work to do."

"Nothing as important as this. Kathy, I tried to call you all last night and all morning."

She lit a cigarette without looking at me. "I wasn't home," she said.

"No, you weren't." I leaned forward and took the cigarette from her and puffed on it. She hesitated, shrugged, and took out another. I said: "I don't suppose I have the right to ask my wife where she spends her time?"

Kathy flared: "Damn it, Mitch, you know—" Her phone rang. She screwed her eyes shut for a moment. Then she picked up the phone, leaning back in her chair, looking across the room, relaxed, a doctor soothing a patient. It took only a few moments. But when it was all over she was entirely self-possessed.

"Please go away," she said, stubbing out her cigarette.

"Not until you tell me when you'll see me."

"I . . . haven't time to see you, Mitch. I'm not your wife. You have no right to bother me like this. I could have you enjoined or arrested."

"My certificate's on file," I reminded her.

"Mine isn't. It never will be. As soon as the year is up, we're through, Mitch."

"There was something I wanted to tell you." Kathy had always been reachable through curiosity.

There was a long pause and instead of saying again: "Please go away," she said: "Well, what is it?"

I said: "It's something big. It calls for a celebration. And I'm not above using it as an excuse to see you for just a little while tonight. Please, Kathy—I love you very much and I promise not to make a scene."

". . . No."

But she had hesitated. I said: "Please?"

"Well—" While she was thinking, her phone rang. "All right," she said to me. "Call me at home. Seven o'clock. Now let me take care of the sick people."

She picked up the phone. I let myself out of her office while she was talking, and she didn't look after me.

Fowler Schocken was hunched over his desk as I walked in, staring at the latest issue of *Taunton's Weekly*. The magazine was blinking in full color as the triggered molecules of its inks collected photons by driblets and released them in bursts. He waved the brilliant pages at me and asked: "What do you think of this, Mitch?"

"Sleazy advertising," I said promptly. "If we had to stoop so low as to sponsor a magazine like Taunton Associates—well, I think I'd resign. It's too cheap a trick."

"Um." He put the magazine face down; the flashing inks gave one last burst and subsided as their light source was cut off. "Yes, it's cheap," he said thoughtfully. "But you have to give them credit for enterprise. Taunton gets sixteen and a half million readers for *his* ads every week. Nobody else's—just Taunton clients. And I hope you didn't mean that literally about resigning. I just gave Harvey the go-ahead on *Shock*. The first issue comes out in the fall, with a print order of twenty million. No—" He mercifully held up his hand to cut off my stammering try at an explanation. "I understood what you meant, Mitch. You were against *cheap* advertising. And so am I. Taunton is to me the epitome of everything that keeps advertising from finding its rightful place with the clergy, medicine, and the bar in our way of life. There isn't a shoddy trick he wouldn't pull, from bribing a judge to stealing an employee. And, Mitch, he's a man you'll have to watch."

"Why? I mean, why particularly?"

Schocken chuckled. "Because we stole Venus from him, that's why. I told you he was enterprising. He had the same idea I did. It wasn't easy to persuade the government that it should be our baby."

"I see," I said. And I did. Our representative government now is perhaps more representative than it has ever been before in history. It is not necessarily representative *per capita*, but it most surely is *ad valorem*. If you like philosophical problems, here is one for you: should each human being's vote register alike, as the lawbooks pretend and as some say the founders of our nation desired? Or should a vote be weighed according to the wisdom, the power, and the influence—that is, the money—of the voter? That is a philosophical problem for you, you understand; not for me. I am a pragmatist, and a pragmatist, moreover, on the payroll of Fowler Schocken.

One thing was bothering me. "Won't Taunton be likely to take— well, direct action?"

"Oh, he'll try to steal it back," Fowler said mildly.

"That's not what I mean. You remember what happened with Antarctic Exploitation."

"I was there. A hundred and forty casualties on our side. God knows what they lost."

"And that was only one continent. Taunton takes these things pretty personally. If he started a feud for a lousy frozen continent, what will he do for a whole planet?"

Fowler said patiently, "No, Mitch. He wouldn't dare. Feuds are expensive. Besides, we're not giving him grounds—not grounds that would stand up in court. And, in the third place . . . we'd whip his tail off."

"I guess so," I said, and felt reassured. Believe me, I am a loyal employee of Fowler Schocken Associates. Ever since cadet days I have tried to live my life "for Company and for Sales." But industrial feuds, even in our profession, can be pretty messy. It was only a few decades ago that a small but effective agency in London filed a feud against the English branch of B.B.D. & O. and wiped it out to the man except for two Bartons and a single underage Osborn. And they say there are still bloodstains on the steps of the General Post Office where United Parcel and American Express fought it out for the mail contract.

Schocken was speaking again. "There's one thing you'll have to watch out for: the lunatic fringe. This is the kind of project that's bound to bring them out. Every crackpot organization on the list, from the Consies to the G.O.P., is going to come out for or against it. Make sure they're all for; they swing weight."

"Even the Consies?" I squeaked.

"Well, no. I didn't mean that; they'd be more of a liability." His white hair glinted as he nodded thoughtfully. "Mm. Maybe you could spread the word that spaceflight and Conservationism are diametrically opposed. It uses up too many raw materials, hurts the living standard—you know. Bring in the fact that the fuel uses organic material that the Consies think should be made into fertilizer—"

I like to watch an expert at work. Fowler Schocken laid down a whole subcampaign for me right there; all I had to do was fill in the details. The Conservationists were fair game, those wild-eyed zealots who pretended modern civilization was in some way "plundering" our planet. Preposterous stuff. Science is *always* a step ahead of the failure of natural resources. After all, when real meat got scarce, we had soyaburgers ready. When oil ran low, technology developed the pedicab.

I had been exposed to Consie sentiment in my time, and the arguments had all come down to one thing: Nature's way of living was the *right* way of living. Silly. If "Nature" had intended us to eat fresh vegetables, it wouldn't have given us niacin or ascorbic acid.

I sat still for twenty minutes more of Fowler Schocken's inspirational talk, and came away with the discovery I had often made before; briefly and effectively, he had given me every fact and instruction I needed.

The details he left to me, but I knew my job:

We wanted Venus colonized by Americans. To accomplish this,

three things were needed: colonists; a way of getting them to Venus; and something for them to do when they got there.

The first was easy to handle through direct advertising. Schocken's TV commercial was the perfect model on which we could base the rest of that facet of our appeal. It is always easy to persuade a consumer that the grass is greener far away. I had already penciled in a tentative campaign with the budget well under a megabuck. More would have been extravagant.

The second was only partly our problem. The ships had been designed—by Republic Aviation, Bell Telephone Labs and U.S. Steel, I believe, under Defense Department contract. Our job wasn't to make the transportation to Venus possible but to make it palatable. When your wife found her burned-out toaster impossible to replace because its nichrome element was part of a Venus rocket's main drive jet, or when the inevitable disgruntled congressman for a small and frozen-out firm waved an appropriations sheet around his head and talked about government waste on wildcat schemes, our job began: We had to convince your wife that rockets are more important than toasters; we had to convince the congressman's constituent's firm that its tactics were unpopular and would cost it profits.

I thought briefly of an austerity campaign and vetoed it. Our other accounts would suffer. A religious movement, perhaps—something that would offer vicarious dedication to the eight hundred million who would not ride the rockets themselves. . . .

I tabled that; Bruner could help me there. And I went on to point three. There had to be something to keep the colonists busy on Venus.

This, I knew, was what Fowler Schocken had his eye on. The government money that would pay for the basic campaign was a nice addition to our year's billing, but Fowler Schocken was too big for one-shot accounts. What we wanted was the year-after-year reliability of a major industrial complex; what we wanted was the colonists, and their children, added to our complex of accounts. Fowler, of course, hoped to repeat on an enormously magnified scale our smashing success with Indiastries. His Boards and he had organized all of India into a single giant cartel, with every last woven basket and iridium ingot and caddy of opium it produced sold through Fowler Schocken advertising. Now he could do the same with Venus. Potentially this was worth as much as every dollar of value in existence put together! A whole new planet, the size of Earth, in prospect as rich as Earth—and every micron, every milligram of it ours.

I looked at my watch. About four; my date with Kathy was for seven. I just barely had time. I dialed Hester and had her get me space on the Washington jet while I put through a call to the name Fowler had given me. The name was Jack O'Shea; he was the only human being who had been to Venus—so far. His voice was young and cocky as he made a date to see me.

We were five extra minutes in the landing pattern over Washington, and then there was a hassle at the ramp. Brink's Express guards were swarming around our plane, and their lieutenant demanded identification from each emerging passenger. When it was my turn I asked what was going on. He looked at my low-number Social Security card thoughtfully and then saluted. "Sorry to bother you, Mr. Courtenay," he apologized. "It's the Consie bombing near Topeka. We got a tip that the man might be aboard the 4:05 New York jet. Seems to have been a lemon."

"What Consie bombing was this?"

"Du Pont Raw Materials Division—we're under contract for their plant protection, you know—was opening up a new coal vein under some cornland they own out there. They made a nice little ceremony of it, and just as the hydraulic mining machine started ramming through the topsoil somebody tossed a bomb from the crowd. Killed the machine operator, his helper, and a vice-president. Man slipped away in the crowd, but he was identified. We'll get him one of these days."

"Good luck, Lieutenant," I said, and hurried on to the jetport's main refreshment lounge. O'Shea was waiting in a window seat, visibly annoyed, but he grinned when I apologized.

"It could happen to anybody," he said, and swinging his short legs shrilled at a waiter. When we had placed our orders he leaned back and said: "Well?"

I looked down at him across the table and looked away through the window. Off to the south the gigantic pylon of the F.D.R. memorial blinked its marker signal; behind it lay the tiny, dulled dome of the old Capitol. I, a glib ad man, hardly knew where to start. And O'Shea was enjoying it. "Well?" he asked again, amusedly, and I knew he meant: "Now all of *you* have to come to *me*, and how do you like it for a change?"

I took the plunge. "What's on Venus?" I asked.

"Sand and smoke," he said promptly. "Didn't you read my report?"

"Certainly. I want to know more."

"Everything's in the report. Good Lord, they kept me in the interrogation room for three solid days when I got back. If I left anything out, it's gone permanently."

I said: "That's not what I mean, Jack. Who wants to spend his life reading reports? I have fifteen men in Research doing nothing but digesting reports for me so I don't have to read them. I want to know something more. I want to get the feel of the planet. There's only one place I can get it because only one man's been there."

"And sometimes I wish I hadn't," O'Shea said wearily. "Well, where do I start? You know how they picked me—the only midget in the world with a pilot's license. And you know all about the ship. And you saw the assay reports on the samples I brought back. Not that they mean much. I only touched down once, and five miles away the geology might be entirely different."

"I know all that. Look, Jack, put it this way. Suppose you wanted a lot of people to go to Venus. What would you tell them about it?"

He laughed. "I'd tell them a lot of damn big lies. Start from scratch, won't you? What's the deal?"

I gave him a fill-in on what Schocken Associates was up to, while his round little eyes stared at me from his round little face. There is an opaque quality, like porcelain, to the features of midgets: as though the destiny that had made them small at the same time made them more perfect and polished than ordinary men, to show that their lack of size did not mean lack of completion. He sipped his drink and I gulped mine between paragraphs.

When my pitch was finished I still didn't know whether he was on my side or not, and with him it mattered. He was no civil service puppet dancing to the strings that Fowler Schocken knew ways of pulling. Neither was he a civilian who could be bought with a tiny decimal of our appropriation. Fowler had helped him a little to capitalize on his fame via testimonials, books, and lectures, so he owed us a little gratitude . . . and no more.

He said: "I wish I could help," and that made things easier.

"You can," I told him. "That's what I'm here for. Tell me what Venus has to offer."

"Damn little," he said, with a small frown chiseling across his lacquered forehead. "Where shall I start? Do I have to tell you about the atmosphere? There's free formaldehyde, you know—embalming fluid. Or the heat? It averages above the boiling point of water—if there were any water on Venus, which there isn't. Not accessible, anyhow. Or the winds? I clocked five hundred miles an hour."

"No, not exactly that," I said. "I know about that. And honestly, Jack, there are answers for all those things. I want to get the feel of the place, what you thought when you were there, how you reacted. Just start talking. I'll tell you when I've had what I wanted."

He dented his rose-marble lip with his lower teeth. "Well," he said, "let's start at the beginning. Get us another drink, won't you?"

The waiter came, took our order, and came back with the liquor. Jack drummed on the table, sipped his rhinewine and seltzer, and began to talk.

He started way back, which was good. I wanted to know the soul of the fact, the elusive, subjective mood that underlay his technical reports on the planet Venus, the basic feeling that would put compulsion and conviction into the project.

He told me about his father, the six-foot chemical engineer, and his mother, the plump, billowy housewife. He made me feel their dismay and their ungrudging love for their thirty-five-inch son. He had been eleven years old when the subject of his adult life and work first came up. He remembered the unhappiness on their faces at his first, inevitable, offhand suggestion about the circus. It was no minor tribute to them that the subject never came up again. It was a major tribute that Jack's settled desire to learn enough engineering and rocketry to be a test pilot had been granted, paid for, and carried out in the face of every obstacle of ridicule and refusal from the schools.

Of course Venus had made it all pay off.

The Venus rocket designers had run into one major complication. It had been easy enough to get a rocket to the moon a quarter-million miles away; theoretically it was not much harder to blast one across space to the nearest other world, Venus. The question was one of orbits and time, of controlling the ship and bringing it back again. A dilemma. They could blast the ship to Venus in a few days—at so squandersome a fuel expenditure that ten ships couldn't carry it. Or they could ease it to Venus along its natural orbits as you might float a barge down a gentle river—which saved the fuel but lengthened the trip to months. A man in eighty days eats twice his own weight in food, breathes nine times his weight of air, and drinks water enough to float a yawl. Did somebody say: distill water from the waste products and recirculate it; do the same with food; do the same with air? Sorry. The necessary equipment for such cycling weighs more than the food, air, and water. So the human pilot was out, obviously.

A team of designers went to work on an automatic pilot. When it was done it worked pretty well. And weighed four and one half tons in spite of printed circuits and relays constructed under a microscope.

The project stopped right there until somebody thought of that most perfect servo-mechanism: a sixty-pound midget. A third of a man in weight, Jack O'Shea ate a third of the food, breathed a third of the oxygen. With minimum-weight, low-efficiency water- and air-purifiers, Jack came in just under the limit and thereby won himself undying fame.

He said broodingly, a little drunk from the impact of two weak drinks on his small frame: "They put me into the rocket like a finger into a glove. I guess you know what the ship looked like. But did you know they *zipped* me into the pilot's seat? It wasn't a chair, you know. It was more like a diver's suit; the only air on the ship was in that suit; the only water came in through a tube to my lips. Saved weight . . ."

And the next eighty days were in that suit. It fed him, gave him water, sopped his perspiration out of its air, removed his body wastes. If necessary it would have shot novocaine into a broken arm, tourniqueted a cut femoral artery, or pumped air for a torn lung. It was a placenta, and a hideously uncomfortable one.

In the suit thirty-three days going, forty-one coming back. The six days in between were the justification for the trip.

Jack had fought his ship down through absolute blindness: clouds of gas that closed his own eyes and confused the radar, down to the skin of an unknown world. He had been within a thousand feet of the ground before he could see anything but swirling yellow. And then he landed and cut the rockets.

"Well, I couldn't get out, of course," he said. "For forty or fifty reasons, somebody else will have to be the first man to set foot on Venus. Somebody who doesn't care much about breathing, I guess. Anyway, there I was, looking at it." He shrugged his shoulders, looked baffled, and said a dirty word softly. "I've told it a dozen times at lectures, but I've never got it over. I tell 'em the closest thing to it on Earth is the Painted Desert. Maybe it is; I haven't been there.

"The wind blows *hard* on Venus and it tears up the rocks. Soft rocks blow away and make the dust storms. The hard parts—well, they stick out in funny shapes and colors. Great big monument things, some of them. And the most jagged hills and crevasses you can imagine. It's something like the inside of a cave, sort of—only not dark. But the light is—funny. Nobody ever saw light like that on Earth. Orangy-brownish light, brilliant, *very* brilliant, but sort of threatening. Like the way the sky is threatening in the summer around sunset just before a smasher of a thunderstorm. Only there never is any thunderstorm because there isn't a drop of water around." He hesitated. "There is lightning. Plenty of it, but never any rain . . . I don't know, Mitch," he said abruptly. "Am I being any help to you at all?"

I took my time answering. I looked at my watch and saw that the return jet was about to leave, so I bent down and turned off the recorder in my briefcase. "You're being lots of help, Jack," I said. "But I'll need more. And I have to go now. Look, can you come up to New York and work with me for a while? I've got everything you said on tape, but I want visual stuff too. Our artists can work from the pix you brought back, but there must be more. And you're a lot more use than the photographs for what we need." I didn't mention that the artists would be drawing impressions of what Venus *would* look like if it were different from what it was. "How about it?"

Jack leaned back and looked cherubic but, though he made me sweat through a brief recap of the extensive plans his lecture agent had made for the next few weeks, he finally agreed. The Shriners' talk could be canceled, he decided, and the appointments with his ghost writers could be kept as well in New York as in Washington. We made a date for the following day just as the PA system announced that my flight was ready.

"I'll walk you to the plane," Jack offered. He slipped down from the chair and threw a bill on the table for the waiter. We walked together through the narrow aisles of the bar out into the field. Jack grinned and strutted a little at some ohs and ahs that went up as he was recognized. The field was almost dark, and the glow of Washington back-lighted the silhouettes of hovering aircraft. Drifting toward us from the freight terminal was a huge cargo 'copter, a fifty-tonner, its cargo nacelle gleaming in colors as it reflected the lights below. It was no more than fifty feet in the air, and I had to clutch my hat against the downdraft from its whirling vanes.

"Damn-fool bus drivers," Jack grunted, staring up at the 'copter. "They ought to put those things on G.C.A. Just because they're maneuverable those fan-jockeys think they can take them anywhere. If I handled a jet the way they—*Run! Run!*" Suddenly he was yelling at me and pushing at my middle with both his small hands. I goggled at him; it was too sudden and disconnected to make any kind of sense. He lurched at me in a miniature body block and sent me staggering a few steps.

"What the hell—?" I started to complain, but I didn't hear my own words. They were drowned out by a mechanical snapping sound and a flutter in the beat of the rotors and then the loudest crash I had ever heard as the cargo pod of the 'copter hit the concrete a yard from where we stood. It ruptured and spilled cartons of Starrzelius Verily rolled oats. One of the crimson cylinders rolled to my toes and I stupidly picked it up and looked at it.

Overhead the lightened 'copter fluttered up and away, but I didn't see it go.

"For God's sake, get it off them!" Jack was yelling, tugging at me. We had not been alone on the field. From under the buckled aluminum reached an arm holding a briefcase, and through the compound noises in my ears I could hear a bubbling sound of human pain. That was what he meant. Get it off them. I let him pull me to the tangled metal, and we tried to heave it. I got a scratched hand and tore my jacket, and then the airport people got there and brusquely ordered us away.

I don't remember walking there, but by and by I found that I was sitting on someone's suitcase, back against the wall of the terminal, with Jack O'Shea talking excitedly to me. He was cursing the class of cargo 'copter pilots and blackguarding me for standing there like a fool when he'd seen the nacelle clamps opening, and a great deal more that I didn't get. I remember his knocking the red box of breakfast food from my hand impatiently. The psychologists say I am not unusually sensitive or timorous, but I was in a state of shock that lasted until Jack was loading me into my plane.

Later on the hostess told me five people had been caught under the nacelle, and the whole affair seemed to come into focus. But not until we were halfway back to New York. At the time all I remembered, all that seemed important, was Jack's saying over and over, bitterness and anger written on his porcelain face: "Too damn many people, Mitch. Too damn much crowding. I'm with you every inch of the way. We *need* Venus, Mitch, we need the space . . ."

three

· ·◆· ·

Kathy's apartment, way downtown in Bensonhurst, was not large but it was comfortable. In a homey, sensible way it was beautifully furnished. As who should know better than I? I pressed the button over the label "Dr. Nevin," and smiled at her as she opened the door.

She did not smile back. She said two things: "You're late, Mitch," and, "I thought you were going to call first."

I walked in and sat down. "I was late because I almost got killed and I didn't call because I was late. Does that square us?" She asked the question I wanted her to ask, and I told her how close I had come to death that evening.

Kathy is a beautiful woman with a warm, friendly face, her hair always immaculately done in two tones of blond, her eyes usually smiling. I have spent a great deal of time looking at her, but I never watched more attentively than when I told her about the cargo nacelle near-miss. It was, on the whole, disappointing. She was really concerned for me, beyond doubt. But Kathy's heart opens to a hundred people and I saw nothing in her face to make me feel that she cared more for me than anyone else she had known for years.

So I told her my other big news, the Venus account and my stewardship of it. It was more successful; she was startled and excited and happy, and kissed me in a flurry of good feeling. But when *I* kissed *her*, as I'd been wanting to do for months, she drew away and went to sit on the other side of the room, ostensibly to dial a drink.

"You rate a toast, Mitch," she smiled. "Champagne at the least. Dear Mitch, it's *wonderful* news!"

I seized the chance. "Will you help me celebrate? Really celebrate?"

Her brown eyes were wary. "Um," she said. Then: "Sure I will, Mitch. We'll do the town together—my treat and no arguments about it. The only thing is, I'll have to leave you punctually at 2400. I'm spending the night in the hospital. I've a hysterectomy to do in the morning and I mustn't get to sleep too late. Or too drunk, either."

But she smiled.

Once again I decided not to push my luck too far. "Great," I said, and I wasn't faking. Kathy is a wonderful girl to do the town with. "Let me use your phone?"

By the time we had our drinks I had arranged for tickets to a show, a dinner table, and a reservation for a nightcap afterwards. Kathy looked a little dubious. "It's a pretty crowded program for five hours, Mitch," she said. "My hysterectomy isn't going to like it if my hand shakes." But I talked her out of it. Kathy is more resilient than that. Once she did a complete trepan the morning after we'd spent the entire night screaming out our tempers at each other, and it had gone perfectly.

The dinner, for me, was a failure. I don't pretend to be an epicure who can't stand anything but new protein. I definitely am, however, a guy who gets sore when he pays new-protein prices and gets regenerated-protein merchandise. The texture of the shashlik we both ordered was all right, but you can't hide the taste. I scratched the restaurant off my list then and there, and apologized to Kathy for it. But she laughed it off, and the show afterwards was fine. Hypnotics often give me a headache, but I slipped right into the trance state this time as soon as the film began and was none the worse for it afterwards.

The night club was packed, and the headwaiter had made a mistake in the time for our reservations. We had to wait five minutes in the anteroom, and Kathy shook her head very decisively when I pleaded for an extension on the curfew. But when the headwaiter showed us with the fanciest apologies and bows to our places at the bar and our drinks came, she leaned over and kissed me again. I felt just fine.

"Thanks," she said. "That was a wonderful evening, Mitch. Get promoted often, please. I like it."

I lit a cigarette for her and one for myself, and opened my mouth to say something. I stopped.

Kathy said, "Go ahead, say it."

"Well, I was going to say that we always have fun together."

"I know you were. And I was going to say that I knew what you were leading up to and that the answer still was no."

"I know you were," I said glumly. "Let's get the hell out of here."

She paid the tab and we left, inserting our antisoot plugs as we hit the street. "Cab, sir?" asked the doorman.

"Yes, please," Kathy answered. "A tandem."

He whistled up a two-man pedicab, and Kathy gave the lead boy the hospital's address. "You can come if you like, Mitch," she said, and I climbed in beside her. The doorman gave us a starting push and the cabbies grunted getting up momentum.

Unasked, I put down the top. For a moment it was like our courtship again: the friendly dark, the slight, musty smell of the canvas top, the squeak of the springs. But for a moment only. "Watch that, Mitch," she said warningly.

"Please, Kathy," I said carefully. "Let me say it anyhow. It won't take long." She didn't say no. "We were married eight months ago— all right," I said quickly as she started to speak, "it wasn't an absolute marriage. But we took the interlocutory vows. Do you remember why we did that?"

She said patiently after a moment: "We were in love."

"That's right," I said. "I loved you and you loved me. And we both had our work to think about, and we knew that sometimes it made us a little hard to get along with. So we made it interim. It had a year to run before we had to decide whether to make it permanent." I touched her hand and she didn't move it away. "Kathy dear, don't you think we knew what we were doing then? Can't we—at least—give it the year's trial? There are still four months to go. Let's try it. If the year ends and you don't want to file your certificate— well, at least I won't be able to say you didn't give me a chance. As for me, I don't have to wait. My certificate's on file now and I won't change."

We passed a street light and I saw her lips twisted into an expression I couldn't quite read. "Oh, damn it all, Mitch," she said unhappily, "I *know* you won't change. That's what makes it all so terrible. Must I sit here and call you names to convince you that it's hopeless?

Do I have to tell you that you're an ill-tempered, contriving Machiavellian, selfish pig of a man to live with? I used to think you were a sweet guy, Mitch. An idealist who cared for principles and ethics instead of money. I had every reason to think so. You told me so yourself, very convincingly. You were very plausible about my work too. You boned up on medicine, you came to watch me operate three times a week, you told all our friends while I was sitting right in the room listening to you how proud you were to be married to a surgeon. It took me three months to find out what you meant by that. Anybody could marry a girl who'd be a housewife. But it took a Mitchell Courtenay to marry a first-class rated surgeon and *make* her a housewife." Her voice was tremulous. "I couldn't take it, Mitch. I never will be able to. Not the arguments, the sulkiness, and the ever-and-ever fighting. I'm a doctor. Sometimes a life depends on me. If I'm all torn up inside from battling with my husband, that life isn't safe, Mitch. Can't you see that?"

Something that sounded like a sob.

I asked quietly: "Kathy, don't you still love me?"

She was absolutely quiet for a long moment. Then she laughed wildly and very briefly. "Here's the hospital, Mitch," she said. "It's midnight."

I threw back the top and we climbed out. "Wait," I said to the lead boy, and walked with her to the door. She wouldn't kiss me good night and she wouldn't make a date to see me again. I stood in the lobby for twenty minutes to make sure she was really staying there that night, and then got into the cab to go to the nearest shuttle station. I was in a vile mood. It wasn't helped any when the lead boy asked innocently after I had paid him off: "Say, mister, what does Mac—Machiavellian mean?"

"Spanish for 'mind your own God-damned business,'" I told him evenly. On the shuttle I wondered sourly how rich I'd have to be before I could buy privacy.

My temper was no better when I arrived at the office next morning. It took all Hester's tact to keep me from biting her head off in the first few minutes, and it was by the grace of God that there was not a Board meeting. After I'd got my mail and the overnight accumulation of interoffice memos, Hester intelligently disappeared for a while. When she came back she brought me a cup of coffee—authentic, plantation-grown coffee. "The matron in the ladies' room brews it on the sly," she explained. "Usually she won't let us take it out because she's afraid of the Coffiest team. But now that you're star class—"

I thanked her and gave her Jack O'Shea's tape to put through channels. Then I went to work.

First came the matter of the sampling area, and a headache with Matt Runstead. He's Market Research, and I had to work with and through him. But he didn't show any inclination to work with me. I put a map of southern California in the projector, while Matt and two of his faceless helpers boredly sprinkled cigarette ashes on my floor.

With the pointer I outlined the test areas and controls: "San Diego through Tijuana; half the communities around L.A. and the lower tip of Monterey. Those will be controls. The rest of Cal-Mexico from L.A. down we'll use for tests. You'll have to be on the scene, I guess, Matt; I'd recommend our Diego offices as headquarters. Turner's in charge there and he's a good man."

Runstead grunted. "Not a flake of snow from year's end to year's end. Couldn't sell an overcoat there if you threw in a slave girl as a premium. For God's sake, man, why don't you leave market research to somebody who knows something about it? Don't you see how climate nulls your sigma?"

The younger of his stamped-out-of-tin assistants started to back the boss up, but I cut him off. Runstead had to be consulted on test areas—it was his job. But Venus was my project and I was going to run it. I said, sounding just a little nasty: "Regional and world income, age, density of population, health, psyche-friction, age-group distribution and mortality causes and rates are seven-place sigmas, Matt. Cal-Mex was designed personally by God Himself as a perfect testing area. In a tiny universe of less than a hundred million it duplicates every important segment of North America. I will not change my project and we are going to stick to the area I indicated." I bore down on the word "my."

Matt said: "It won't work. The temperature is the major factor. Anybody should be able to see that."

"I'm not just anybody, Matt. I'm the guy in charge."

Matt Runstead stubbed out his cigarette and got up. "Let's go talk to Fowler," he said and walked out. There wasn't anything for me to do except follow him. As I left I heard the older of his helpers picking up the phone to notify Fowler Schocken's secretary that we were coming. He had a team all right, that Runstead. I spent a little time wondering how I could build a team like that myself before I got down to the business of planning how to put it to Fowler.

But Fowler Schocken has a sure-fire technique of handling inter-staff hassles. He worked it on us. When we came in he said exuberantly: "There you are! The two men I want to see! Matt, can you put out a fire for me? It's the A.I.G. people. They claim our handling of the PregNot account is hurting their trade. They're talking about going over to Taunton unless we drop PregNot. Their billing isn't much, but a birdie told me that Taunton put the idea into their heads." He went on to explain the intricacies of our relationship with the American Institute of Gynecologists. I listened only half-heartedly; our "Babies without Maybes" campaign on their sex-determination project had given them at least a 20 percent plus on the normal birthrate. They should be solidly ours after that. Runstead thought so too.

He said: "They don't have a case, Fowler. We sell liquor and hang-over remedies both. They've got no business bitching about any other account. Besides, what the hell does this have to do with Market Research?"

Fowler chuckled happily. "That's it!" he crowed. "We throw them a switch. They'll expect the account executives to give them the usual line—but instead we'll let you handle them yourself. Snow them under with a whole line of charts and statistics to prove that PregNot never *prevents* a couple from having a baby; it just permits them to *postpone* it until they can afford to do the job right. In other words, their unit of sale goes up and their volume stays the same. And—it'll be one in the eye for Taunton. And—lawyers get disbarred for representing conflicting interests. It's cost a lot of them a lot of money. We've got to make sure that any attempt to foist the same principle on our profession is nipped in the bud. Think you can handle it for the old man, Matt?"

"Oh, hell, sure," Runstead grumbled. "What about Venus?"

Fowler twinkled at me. "What about it? Can you spare Matt for a while?"

"Forever," I said. "In fact, that's what I came to see you about. Matt's scared of southern California."

Runstead dropped his cigarette and let it lay, crisping the nylon pile of Fowler's rug. "What the hell—" he started belligerently.

"Easy," said Fowler. "Let's hear the story, Matt."

Runstead glowered at me. "All I said was that southern California isn't the right test area. What's the big difference between Venus and here? Heat! We need a test area with continental-average climate. A New Englander might be attracted by the heat on Venus; a Tijuana man, never. It's too damn hot in Cal-Mex already."

"Um," said Fowler Schocken. "Tell you what, Matt. This needs going into, and you'll want to get busy on the A.I.G. thing. Pick out a good man to vice you on the Venus section while you're out, and we'll have it hashed over at the section meeting tomorrow afternoon. Meanwhile—" he glanced at his desk clock. "Senator Danton has been waiting for seven minutes. All right?"

It was clearly not all right with Matt, and I felt cheered for the rest of the day. Things went well enough. Development came in with a report on what they'd gleaned from O'Shea's tape and all the other available material. The prospects for manufacture were there. Quick, temporary ones like little souvenir globes of Venus manufactured from the organics floating around in what we laughingly call the "air" of Venus. Long-term ones—an assay had indicated pure iron: not nine-nines pure and not ninety-nine nines pure, but absolute iron that nobody would ever find or make on an oxygen planet like Earth. The labs would pay well for it. And Development had not developed but found a remarkable little thing called a high-speed Hilsch Tube. Using no power, it could refrigerate the pioneers' homes by using the hot tornadoes of Venus. It was a simple thing that had been lying around since 1943. Nobody until us had any use for it because nobody until us had that kind of wind to play with.

Tracy Collier, the Development liaison man with Venus Section, tried also to tell me about nitrogen-fixing catalysts. I nodded from time to time and gathered that sponge-platinum "sown" on Venus would, in conjunction with the continuous, terrific lightning, cause it to "snow" nitrates and "rain" hydrocarbons, purging the atmosphere of formaldehyde and ammonia.

"Kind of expensive?" I asked cautiously.

"Just as expensive as you want it to be," he said. "The platinum doesn't get used up, you know. Use one gram and take a million years or more. Use more platinum and take less time."

I didn't really understand, but obviously it was good news. I patted him and sent him on his way.

Industrial Anthropology gave me a setback. Ben Winston complained: "You *can't* make people want to live in a steam-heated sardine can. All our folkways are against it. Who's going to travel sixty million miles for a chance to spend the rest of his life cooped up in a tin shack—when he can stay right here on Earth and have corridors, elevators, streets, roofs, all the wide-open space a man could want? It's against human nature, Mitch!"

I reasoned with him. It didn't do much good. He went on telling me about the American way of life—walked to the window with me and pointed out at the hundreds of acres of rooftops where men and women could walk around in the open air, wearing simple soot-extractor nostril plugs instead of a bulky oxygen helmet.

Finally I got mad. I said: "*Somebody* must want to go to Venus. Otherwise why would they buy Jack O'Shea's book the way they do? Why would the voters stand still for a billion-and-up appropriation to build the rocket? God knows I shouldn't have to lead you by the nose this way, but here's what you are going to do: survey the bookbuyers, the repeat-viewers of O'Shea's TV shows, the ones who come early to his lectures and stand around talking in the lobby afterwards. O'Shea is on the payroll—pump him for everything you can get. Find out about the Moon colony—find out what types they have there. And then we'll know whom to aim our ads at. Any arguments, for God's sake?" There weren't.

Hester had done wonders of scheduling that first day, and I made progress with every section head involved. But she couldn't read my paperwork for me, and by quitting time I had six inches of it stacked by my right arm. Hester volunteered to stay with me, but there wasn't really anything for her to do. I let her bring me sandwiches and another cup of coffee, and chased her home.

It was after eleven by the time I was done. I stopped off in an all-night diner on the fifteenth floor before heading home, a windowless box of a place where the coffee smelled of the yeast it was made from and the ham in my sandwich bore the taint of soy. But it was only a minor annoyance and quickly out of my mind. For as I opened the door to my apartment there was a *snick* and an explosion, and something slammed into the doorframe by my head. I ducked and yelled. Outside the window a figure dangling from a rope ladder drifted away, a gun in its hand.

I was stupid enough to run over to the window and gawk out at the helicopter-borne figure. I would have been a perfect target if it had been steady enough to shoot at me again, but it wasn't.

Surprised at my calm, I called the Metropolitan Protection Corporation.

"Are you a subscriber, sir?" their operator asked.

"Yes, dammit. For six years. Get a man over here! Get a squad over here."

"One moment, Mr. Courtenay. . . . Mr. *Mitchell* Courtenay? Copysmith, star class?"

"No," I said bitterly. "Target is my profession. Will you kindly get a man over here before the character who just took a shot at me comes back?"

"Excuse me, Mr. Courtenay," said the sweet, unruffled voice. "Did you say you were *not* a copysmith, star class?"

I ground my teeth. "I'm star class," I admitted.

"Thank you, sir. I have your record before me, sir. I am sorry, sir, but your account is in arrears. We do not accept star-class accounts at the general rate because of the risk of industrial feuds, sir." She named a figure that made each separate hair on my head stand on end.

I didn't blow my top; she was just a tool. "Thanks," I said heavily, and rang off. I put the *Program-Printing to Quarry Machinery* reel of the Red Book into the reader and spun it to Protective Agencies. I got turndowns from three or four, but finally one sleepy-sounding private detective agreed to come on over for a stiff fee.

He showed up in half an hour and I paid him, and all he did was annoy me with unanswerable questions and look for nonexistent fingerprints. After a while he went away saying he'd work on it.

I went to bed and eventually to sleep with one of the unanswered questions chasing itself around and around in my head: who would want to shoot a simple, harmless advertising man like me?

four

· · ◆ · ·

I took my courage in my hands and walked briskly down the hall to Fowler Schocken's office. I needed an answer, and he might have it. He might also throw me out of the office for asking. But I needed an answer.

It didn't seem to be the best possible time to ask Fowler questions. Ahead of me, his door opened explosively and Tildy Mathis lurched out. Her face was working with emotion. She stared at me, but I'll take oath she didn't know my name. "Rewrites," she said wildly. "I slave my heart out for that white-haired old rat, and what does he give me? Rewrites. 'This is *good* copy, but I want better than good copy from *you*,' he says. 'Rewrite it,' he says. 'I want color,' he says, 'I want drive and beauty, and humble, human warmth, and ecstasy, and all the tender, sad emotion of your sweet womanly heart,' he says, 'and I want it in fifteen words.' I'll give him fifteen words," she sobbed, and pushed past me down the hall. "I'll give that sanctimonious, mellifluous, hyperbolic, paternalistic, star-making, genius-devouring Moloch of an old—"

The slam of Tildy's own door cut off the noun. I was sorry; it would have been a good noun.

I cleared my throat, knocked once, and walked into Fowler's office. There was no hint of his brush with Tildy in the smile he gave me. In fact, his pink, clear-eyed face belied my suspicions, but—I *had* been shot at.

"I'll only be a minute, Fowler," I said. "I want to know whether you've been playing rough with Taunton Associates."

"I always play rough," he twinkled. "Rough, but clean."

"I mean very, very rough and very, very dirty. Have you, by any chance, tried to have any of their people shot?"

"Mitch! *Really!*"

"I'm asking," I went on doggedly, "because last night a 'copter-borne marksman tried to plug me when I came home. I can't think of any angle except retaliation from Taunton."

"Scratch Taunton," he said positively.

I took a deep breath. "Fowler," I said, "man-to-man, you haven't been Notified? I may be out of line, but I've got to ask. It isn't just me. It's the Venus Project."

There were no apples in Fowler's cheeks at that moment, and I could see in his eyes that my job and my star-class rating hung in the balance.

He said: "Mitch, I made you star class because I thought you could handle the responsibilities that came with it. It isn't just the work. I know you can do that. I thought you could live up to the commercial code as well."

I hung on. "Yes, sir," I said.

He sat down and lit a Starr. After just exactly the right split second of hesitation, he pushed the pack to me. "Mitch, you're a youngster, only star class a short time. But you've got power. Five words from you, and in a matter of weeks or months half a million consumers will find their lives completely changed. That's power, Mitch, absolute power. And you know the old saying. Power ennobles. Absolute power ennobles absolutely."

"Yes, sir," I said. I knew all the old sayings. I also knew that he was going to answer my question eventually.

"Ah, Mitch," he said dreamily, waving his cigarette, "we have our prerogatives and our duties and our particular hazards. You can't have one without the others. If we didn't have feuds, the whole system of checks and balances would be thrown out of gear."

"Fowler," I said, greatly daring, "you know I have no complaints about the system. It works; that's all you have to say for it. I know we need feuds. And it stands to reason that if Taunton files a feud against us, you've got to live up to the code. You can't broadcast the information; every executive in the shop would be diving for cover instead of getting work done. But—Venus Project is in my head, Fowler. I can handle it better that way. If I write everything down, it slows things up."

"Of course," he said.

"Suppose you *were* Notified, and suppose I'm the first one Taunton knocks off—what happens to Venus Project?"

"You may have a point," he admitted. "I'll level with you, Mitch. There has been no Notification."

"Thanks, Fowler," I said sincerely. "I *did* get shot at. And that accident in Washington—maybe it wasn't an accident. You don't imagine Taunton would try anything without Notifying you, do you?"

"I haven't provoked them to that extent, and they'd never do a thing like that anyhow. They're cheap, they're crooked, but they know the rules of the game. Killing in an industrial feud is a misdemeanor. Killing *without* Notification is a *commercial offense.* You haven't been getting into any of the wrong beds, shall I say?"

"No," I said. "My life's been very dull. The whole thing's crazy. It must have been a mistake. But I'm glad that whoever-it-was couldn't shoot."

"So am I, Mitch, so am I! Enough of your personal life. We've got business. You saw O'Shea?" He had already dismissed the shooting from his mind.

"I did. He's coming up here today. He'll be working closely with me."

"Splendid! Some of that glory will rub off on Fowler Schocken Associates if we play our cards right. Dig into it, Mitch. I don't have to tell you how."

It was a dismissal.

O'Shea was waiting in the anteroom of my office. It wasn't an ordeal; most of the female personnel were clustered around him as he sat perched on a desk, talking gruffly and authoritatively. There was no mistaking the looks in their eyes. He was a thirty-five-inch midget, but he had money and fame, the two things we drill and drill into the population. O'Shea could have taken his pick of them. I wondered how many he had picked since his return to Earth in a blaze of glory.

We run a taut office, but the girls didn't scatter until I cleared my throat.

"Morning, Mitch," O'Shea said. "You over your shock?"

"Sure. And I ran right into another one. Somebody tried to shoot me." I told the story and he grunted thoughtfully.

"Have you considered getting a bodyguard?" he asked.

"Of course. But I won't. It must have been a mistake."

"Like that cargo nacelle?"

I paused. "Jack, can we *please* get off this subject? It gives me the horrors."

"Permission granted," he beamed. "Now, let's go to work—and on what?"

"First, words. We want words that are about Venus, words that'll tickle people. Make them sit up. Make them muse about change, and space, and other worlds. Words to make them a little discontented with what they are and a little hopeful about what they might be. Words to make them feel noble about feeling the way they do and make them happy about the existence of Indiastries and Starrzelius Verily and Fowler Schocken Associates. Words that will do all these things and also make them feel unhappy about the existence of Universal Products and Taunton Associates."

He was staring at me with his mouth open. "You aren't serious," he finally exclaimed.

"You're on the inside now," I said simply. "That's the way we work. That's the way we worked on you."

"What are you talking about?"

"You're wearing Starrzelius Verily clothes and shoes, Jack. It means we got you. Taunton and Universal worked on you, Starrzelius and Schocken worked on you—and you chose Starrzelius. We reached you. Smoothly, without your ever being aware that it was happening, you became persuaded that there was something rather nice about Starrzelius clothes and shoes and that there was something rather not-nice about Universal clothes and shoes."

"I never read the ads," he said defiantly.

I grinned. "Our ultimate triumph is wrapped up in that statement," I said.

"I solemnly promise," O'Shea said, "that as soon as I get back to my hotel room I'll send my clothes right down the incinerator chute—"

"Luggage too?" I asked. "Starrzelius luggage?"

He looked startled for a moment and then regained his calm. "Starrzelius luggage too," he said. "And then I'll pick up the phone and order a complete set of Universal luggage and apparel. And you can't stop me."

"I wouldn't dream of stopping you, Jack! It means more business for Starrzelius. Tell you what you're going to do: you'll get your complete set of Universal luggage and apparel. You'll use the luggage and wear the apparel for a while with a vague, submerged discontent. It's going to work on your libido, because our ads for Starrzelius—even though you say you don't read them—have convinced you that it isn't quite virile to trade with any other firm. Your self-esteem will suffer; deep down you'll *know* that you're not wearing the best. Your subconscious won't stand up under much of that. You'll find yourself 'losing' bits of Universal apparel. You'll find yourself 'accidentally' putting your foot through the cuff of your Universal pants. You'll find yourself overpacking the Universal luggage and damning it for not being roomier. You'll walk into stores and in a fit of momentary amnesia regarding this conversation you'll buy Starrzelius, bless you."

O'Shea laughed uncertainly. "And you did it with words?"

"Words and pictures. Sight and sound and smell and taste and touch. And the greatest of these is words. Do you read poetry?"

"My God, of course not! Who can?"

"I don't mean the contemporary stuff; you're quite right about that. I mean Keats, Swinburne, Wylie—the great lyricists."

"I used to," he cautiously admitted. "What about it?"

"I'm going to ask you to spend the morning and afternoon with one of the world's great lyric poets: a girl named Tildy Mathis. She doesn't know that she's a poet; she thinks she's a boss copywriter. Don't enlighten her. It might make her unhappy.

> 'Thou still unravish'd bride of quietness,
> Thou foster-child of Silence and slow Time—'

That's the sort of thing she would have written before the rise of advertising. The correlation is perfectly clear. Advertising up, lyric poetry down. There are only so many people capable of putting together words that stir and move and sing. When it became possible to earn a very good living in advertising by exercising this capability, lyric poetry was left to untalented screwballs who had to shriek for attention and compete by eccentricity."

"Why are you telling me all this?" he asked.

"I said you're on the inside, Jack. There's a responsibility that goes with the power. Here in this profession we reach into the souls of men and women. We do it by taking talent and—redirecting it. Nobody should play with lives the way we do unless he's motivated by the highest ideals."

"I get you," he said softly. "Don't worry about my motives. I'm not in this thing for money or fame. I'm in it so the human race can have some elbow room and dignity again."

"That's it," I said, putting on Expression Number One. But inwardly I was startled. The "highest ideal" I had been about to cite was Sales.

I buzzed for Tildy. "Talk to her," I said. "Answer her questions. Ask her some. Make it a long, friendly chat. Make her share your experiences. And, without knowing it, she'll write lyric fragments of your experiences that will go right to the hearts and souls of the readers. Don't hold out on her."

"Certainly not. Uh, Mitch, will she hold out on me?"

The expression on his face was from a Tanagra figurine of a hopeful young satyr.

"She won't," I promised solemnly. Everybody knew about Tildy.

That afternoon, for the first time in four months, Kathy called me.

"Is anything wrong?" I asked sharply. "Anything I can do?"

She giggled. "Nothing wrong, Mitch. I just wanted to say hello and tell you thanks for a lovely evening."

"How about another one?" I asked promptly.

"Dinner at my place tonight suit you?"

"It certainly does. It certainly, certainly does. What color dress will you be wearing? I'm going to buy you a real flower!"

"Oh, Mitch, you needn't be extravagant. We aren't courting and I already know you have more money than God. But there *is* something I wish you'd bring."

"Only name it."

"Jack O'Shea. Can you manage it? I saw by the 'cast that he came into town this morning and I suppose he's working with you."

Very dampened, I said: "Yes, he is. I'll check with him and call you back. You at the hospital?"

"Yes. And thanks so much for trying. I'd love to meet him."

I got in touch with O'Shea in Tildy's office. "You booked up for tonight?" I asked.

"Hmmm . . . I *could* be," he said. O'Shea was evidently learning about Tildy too.

"Here's my proposition. Quiet dinner at home with my wife and me. She happens to be beautiful and a good cook and a first-rate surgeon and excellent company."

"You're on."

So I called Kathy back and told her I'd bring the social lion about seven.

He stalked into my office at six, grumbling: "I'd better get a good meal out of this, Mitch. Your Miss Mathis appeals to me. What a dope! Does she have sense enough to come in out of the smog?"

"I don't believe so," I said. "But Keats was properly hooked by a designing wench, and Byron didn't have sense enough to stay out of the venereal ward. Swinburne made a tragic mess out of his life. Do I have to go on?"

"Please, no. What kind of marriage have you got?"

"Interlocutory," I said, a little painfully in spite of myself.

He raised his eyebrows a trifle. "Maybe it's just the way I was brought up, but there's something about those arrangements that sets my teeth on edge."

"Mine too," I said, "at least in my own case. In case Tildy missed telling you, my beautiful and talented wife doesn't want to finalize it, we don't live together, and unless I change her mind in four months we'll be washed up."

"Tildy did miss telling me," he said. "You're pretty sick about it, seems to me."

I almost gave in to self-pity. I almost invited his sympathy. I almost started to tell him how rough it was, how much I loved her, how she wasn't giving me an even break, how I'd tried everything I could think of and nothing would convince her. And then I realized that I'd be telling it to a sixty-pound midget who, if he married, might become at any moment his wife's helpless plaything or butt of ridicule.

"Middling sick," I said. "Let's go, Jack. Time for a drink and then the shuttle."

Kathy had never looked lovelier, and I wished I hadn't let her talk me out of shooting a couple of days' pay on a corsage at Cartier's.

She said hello to O'Shea and he announced loudly and immediately: "I like you. There's no gleam in your eye. No 'Isn't he cute?' gleam. No. 'My, he must be rich and frustrated!' gleam. No 'A girl's got a right to try anything once' gleam. In short, you like me and I like you."

As you may have gathered, he was a little drunk.

"You are going to have some coffee, Mr. O'Shea," she said. "I ruined myself to provide real pork sausages and real apple sauce, and you're going to taste them."

"Coffee?" he said. "Coffiest for me, ma'am. To drink coffee would be disloyal to the great firm of Fowler Schocken Associates with which I am associated. Isn't that right, Mitch?"

"I give absolution this once," I said. "Besides, Kathy doesn't believe the harmless alkaloid in Coffiest is harmless." Luckily she was in the kitchen corner with her back turned when I said that, and either missed it or could afford to pretend she did. We'd had a terrific four-hour battle over that very point, complete with epithets like "baby-poisoner" and "crackpot reformer" and a few others that were shorter and nastier.

The coffee was served and quenched O'Shea's mild glow. Dinner was marvelous. Afterward, we all felt more relaxed.

"You've been to the Moon, I suppose?" Kathy asked O'Shea.

"Not yet. One of these days."

"There's nothing there," I said. "It's a waste of time. One of our dullest, deadest accounts. I suppose we only kept it for the experience we'd get, looking ahead to Venus. A few thousand people mining—that's the *whole* story."

"Excuse me," O'Shea said, and retired.

I grabbed the chance. "Kathy, darling," I said, "it was very sweet of you to ask me over. Does it mean anything?"

She rubbed her right thumb and index finger together, and I knew that whatever she would say after that would be a lie. "It might, Mitch," she lied gently. "You'll have to give me time."

I threw away my secret weapon. "You're lying," I said disgustedly. "You always do this before you lie to me—I don't know about other people." I showed her, and she let out a short laugh.

"Fair's fair," she said with bitter amusement. "You always catch your breath and look right into my eyes when you lie to me—I don't know about your clients and fellow employees."

O'Shea returned and felt the tension at once. "I ought to be going," he said. "Mitch, do we leave together?"

Kathy nodded, and I said: "Yes."

There were the usual politenesses at the door, and Kathy kissed me good night. It was a long, warm, clinging kiss; altogether the kind of kiss that should start the evening rather than end it. It set her own pulse going—I felt that!—but she coolly closed the door on us.

"You thought about a bodyguard again?" O'Shea asked.

"It was a mistake," I said stubbornly.

"Let's stop by your place for a drink," he said ingenuously.

The situation was almost pathetic. Sixty-pound Jack O'Shea was bodyguarding me. "Sure," I said. We got on the shuttle.

He went into the room first and turned on the light, and nothing happened. While sipping a very weak whisky and soda, he drifted around the place checking window locks, hinges, and the like. "This chair would look better over there," he said. "Over there," of course, was out of the line of fire from the window. I moved it.

"Take care of yourself, Mitch," he said when he left. "That lovely wife and your friends would miss you if anything happened."

The only thing that happened was that I barked my shin setting up the bed, and that was happening all the time. Even Kathy, with a surgeon's neat, economical movements, bore the battle scars of life in a city apartment. You set up the bed at night, you took it down in the morning, you set up the table for breakfast, you took it down to get to the door. No wonder some shortsighted people sighed for the spacious old days, I thought, settling myself luxuriously for the night.

five

· · ◆ · ·

Things were rolling within a week. With Runstead out of my hair and at work on the PregNot–A.I.G. hassle, I could really grip the reins.

Tildy's girls and boys were putting out the copy—temperamental kids, sometimes doing a line a day with anguish; sometimes rolling out page after page effortlessly, with shining eyes, as though possessed. She directed and edited their stuff and passed the best of the best to me: nine-minute commercial scripts, pix cutlines, articles for planting, news stories, page ads, whispering campaign cuelines, endorsements, jokes-limericks-and-puns (clean and dirty) to float through the country.

Visual was hot. The airbrush and camera people were having fun sculpturing a planet. It was the ultimate in "Before and After" advertising, and they were caught by the sense of history.

Development kept pulling rabbits out of hats. Collier once explained to me when I hinted that he might be overoptimistic: "It's *energy*, Mr. Courtenay. Venus has got *energy*. It's closer to the sun. The sun pours all that energy into the planet in the form of heat and molecular bonds and fast particles. Here on Earth we don't have that level of tappable energy. We use windmills to tap the kinetic energy of the atmosphere. On Venus we'll use *turbines*. If we want electricity on Venus we'll just build an accumulator, put up a lightning rod and jump back. It's an entirely different *level*."

Market Research–Industrial Anthropology was at work in San Diego sampling the Cal-Mex area, trying Tildy's copy, Visual's layouts and films and extrapolating and interpolating. I had a direct wire to the desk of Ham Harris, Runstead's vice, in San Diego.

A typical day began with a Venus Section meeting: pep talk by me, reports of progress by all hands, critique and cross-department suggestions. Harris, on the wire, might advise Tildy that "serene atmosphere" wasn't going well as a cue phrase in his sampling and that she should submit a list of alternatives. Tildy might ask Collier whether it would be okay to say "topaz sands" in a planted article which would hint that Venus was crawling with uncut precious and semiprecious stones. Collier might tell Visual that they'd have to make the atmosphere redder in a "Before" panorama. And I might tell Collier to lay off because it was permissible license.

After adjournment everybody would go into production and I'd spend my day breaking ties, co-ordinating, and interpreting my directives from above down to the operational level. Before close of day we'd hold another meeting, which I would keep to some specific topic, such as: integration of Starrzelius products into the Venus economy, or income-level of prospective Venus colonists for optimum purchasing power twenty years after landing.

And then came the best part of the day. Kathy and I were going steady again. We were still under separate cover, but I was buoyantly certain that it wouldn't be long now. Sometimes she dated me, sometimes I dated her. We just went out and had fun eating well, drinking well, dressing well, and feeling that we were two good-looking people enjoying life. There wasn't much serious talk. She didn't encourage it and I didn't press it. I thought that time was on my side. Jack O'Shea made the rounds with us once before he had to leave for a lecture in Miami, and that made me feel good too. A couple of well-dressed, good-looking people who were so high-up they could entertain the world's number one celebrity. Life was good.

After a week of solid, satisfying progress on the job I told Kathy it was time for me to visit the outlying installations—the rocket site in Arizona and sampling headquarters in San Diego.

"Fine," she said. "Can I come along?"

I was silly-happy about it; it wouldn't be long now.

The rocket visit was routine. I had a couple of people there as liaison with Armed Forces, Republic Aviation, Bell Telephone Labs, and U.S. Steel. They showed Kathy and me through the monster, glib as tourist guides: ". . . vast steel shell . . . more cubage than the average New York office building . . . closed-cycle food and water and air regeneration . . . one-third drive, one-third freight,

one-third living space . . . heroic pioneers . . . insulation . . .
housekeeping power . . . sunside-darkside heat pumps . . . un-
precedented industrial effort . . . national sacrifice . . . national
security . . ."

Oddly, the most impressive thing about it to me was not the
rocket itself but the wide swathe around it. For a full mile the land
was cleared: no houses, no greenhouse decks, no food tanks, no sun
traps. Partly security, partly radiation. The gleaming sand cut by
irrigation pipes looked strange. There probably wasn't another
sight like it in North America. It troubled my eyes. Not for years had
I focused them more than a few yards.

"How strange," Kathy said at my side. "Could we walk out
there?"

"Sorry, Dr. Nevin," said one of the liaison men. "It's a deadline.
The tower guards are ordered to shoot anybody out there."

"Have contrary orders issued," I said. "Dr. Nevin and I want to
take a walk."

"Of course, Mr. Courtenay," the man said, very worried. "I'll do
my best, but it'll take a little time. I'll have to clear it with C.I.C.,
Naval Intelligence, C.I.A., F.B.I., A.E.C. Security and Intelligence—"

I looked at Kathy, and she shrugged with helpless amusement.
"Never mind," I said.

"Thank God!" breathed my liaison man. "Excuse me, Mr. Courtenay. It's never been done before so there aren't any channels to do
it through. You know what *that* means."

"I do indeed," I said, from the heart. "Tell me, has all the
security paid off?"

"It seems so, Mr. Courtenay. There's been no sabotage or espionage, foreign or Consie, that we know of." He rapped a knuckle of
his right hand solemnly on a handsome oak engagement ring he
wore on the third finger of his left hand. I made a mental note to
have his expense account checked up on. A man on his salary had no
business wearing that kind of jewelry.

"The Consies interested?" I asked.

"Who knows? C.I.C., C.I.A. and A.E.C. S.&I. say yes. Naval
Intelligence, F.B.I. and S.S. say no. Would you like to meet Com-
mander MacDonald? He's the O.N.I. chief here. A specialist in
Consies."

"Like to meet a Consie specialist, Kathy?" I asked.

"If we have time," she said.

"I'll have them hold the jet for you if necessary," the liaison man said eagerly, trying hard to undo his fiasco on the tower guards. He led us through the tangle of construction shacks and warehouses to the administration building and past seven security checkpoints to the office of the commander.

MacDonald was one of those career officers who make you feel good about being an American citizen—quiet, competent, strong. I could see from his insignia and shoulder flashes that he was a Contract Specialist, Intelligence, on his third five-year option from the Pinkerton Detective Agency. He was a regular; he wore the class ring of the Pinkerton Graduate School of Detection and Military Intelligence, Inc. It's pine with an open eye carved on it; no flashy inlay work. But it's like a brand name. It tells you that you're dealing with quality.

"You want to hear about Consies?" he asked quietly. "I'm your man. I've devoted my life to running them down."

"A personal grudge, Commander?" I asked, thinking I'd hear something melodramatic.

"No. Old-fashioned pride of workmanship if anything. I like the thrill of the chase, too, but there isn't much chasing. You get Consies by laying traps. Did you hear about the Topeka bombing? Of-course-I-shouldn't-knock-the-competition but those guards should have known it was a setup for a Consie demonstration."

"Why, exactly, Commander?" Kathy asked.

He smiled wisely. "Feel," he said. "The kind of thing it's hard to put over in words. The Consies don't like hydraulic mining—ever. Give them a chance to parade their dislike and they'll take it if they can."

"But *why* don't they like hydraulic mining?" she persisted. "We've got to have coal and iron, don't we?"

"Now," he said with pretended, humorous weariness, "you're asking me to probe the mind of a Consie. I've had them in the wrecking room for up to six hours at a stretch and never yet have they talked sense. If I caught the Topeka Consie, say, he'd talk willingly—but it would be gibberish. He'd tell me the hydraulic miner was destroying topsoil. I'd say yes, and what about it. He'd say, well can't you *see?* I'd say, see what? He'd say, the topsoil can never be replaced. I'd say, yes it can if it had to be and anyway tank farming's better. He'd say something like tank farming doesn't provide animal cover and so on. It always winds up with him telling me the world's going to hell in a hand-basket and people have got to be made to realize it—and me telling him we've always got along somehow and we'll keep going somehow."

Kathy laughed incredulously and the commander went on: "They're fools, but they're *tough*. They have discipline. A cell system. If you get one Consie you always get the two or three others in his cell, but you hardly ever get any more. There's no lateral contact between cells, and vertical contact with higher-ups is by rendezvous with middlemen. Yes, I think I know them and that's why I'm not especially worried about sabotage or a demonstration here. It doesn't have the right ring to it."

Kathy and I lolled back watching the commercials parade around the passenger compartment of the jet at eye level. There was the good old Kiddiebutt jingle I worked out many years ago when I was a trainee. I nudged Kathy and told her about it as it blinked and chimed Victor Herbert's *Toyland* theme at us.

All the commercials went blank and a utility announcement, without sound effects, came on.

> *In Compliance With Federal Law, Passengers Are Advised That They Are Now Passing Over The San Andreas Fault Into Earthquake Territory, And That Earthquake Loss And Damage Clauses In Any Insurance They May Carry Are Now Canceled And Will Remain Canceled Until Passengers Leave Earthquake Territory.*

Then the commercials resumed their parade.

"And," said Kathy, "I suppose it says in the small print that yak-bite insurance is good anywhere except in Tibet."

"Yak-bite insurance?" I asked, astonished. "What on earth do you carry that for?"

"A girl can never tell when she'll meet an unfriendly yak, can she?"

"I conclude that you're kidding," I said with dignity. "We ought to land in a few minutes. Personally, I'd like to pop in on Ham Harris unexpectedly. He's a good kid, but Runstead may have infected him with defeatism. There's nothing worse in our line."

"I'll come along with you if I may, Mitch."

We gawked through the windows like tourists as the jet slid into the traffic pattern over San Diego and circled monotonously waiting for its calldown from the tower. Kathy had never been there before. I had been there once, but there's always something new to see because buildings are always falling down and new ones being put up. And what buildings! They're more like plastic tents on plastic skeletons than anything else. That kind of construction means they give and sway when a quake jiggles southern California instead of snapping and crumbling. And if the quake is bad enough and the skeleton does snap, what have you lost? Just some plastic sheeting that broke along the standard snap grooves and some plastic structural members that may or may not be salvageable.

From a continental economic viewpoint, it's also a fine idea not to tie up too much fancy construction in southern California. Since the H-bomb tests did things to the San Andreas fault, there's been a pretty fair chance that the whole area would slide quietly into the Pacific some day—any day. But when we looked down out of the traffic pattern, it still was there and, like everybody else, we knew that it would probably stay there for the duration of our visit. Before my time there had been some panic when the quakes became daily, but I'd blame that on the old-style construction that fell hard and in jagged hunks. Eventually people got used to it and—as you'd expect in southern California—even proud of it. Natives could cite you reams of statistics to prove that you stand more chance of being struck by lightning or a meteorite than you do of getting killed in one of their quakes.

We got a speedy three-man limousine to whisk us to the local branch of Fowler Schocken Associates. My faint uneasiness about Market Research extended to the possibility that Ham Harris might have a tipster at the airport to give him time to tidy up for a full-dress inspection. And that kind of thing is worse than useless.

The receptionist gave me my first setback. She didn't recognize my face and she didn't recognize my name when I gave it to her. She said lazily: "I'll see if Mr. Harris is busy, Mr. Connelly."

"Mr. Courtenay, young lady. And I'm Mr. Harris's boss." Kathy and I walked in on a scene of idleness and slackness that curled my hair.

Harris, with his coat off, was playing cards with two young employees. Two more were gaping, glassy-eyed, before a hypnoteleset, obviously in trance state. Another man was lackadaisically punching a calculator, one-finger system.

"*Harris!*" I thundered.

Everybody except the two men in trance swiveled my way, open-mouthed. I walked to the hypnoteleset and snapped it off. They came to, groggily.

"Mum-mum-mum-mister Courtenay," Harris stuttered. "We didn't expect—"

"Obviously. The rest of you, carry on. Harris, let's go into your office." Unobtrusively, Kathy followed us.

"Harris," I said, "good work excuses a lot. We've been getting damn good work out of you on this project. I'm disturbed, gravely disturbed, by the slovenly atmosphere I see here. But that can be corrected—"

His phone rang, and I picked it up.

A voice said excitedly: "Ham? He's here. Make it snappy; he took a limousine."

"Thanks," I said and hung up. "Your tipster at the airport," I told Harris. He went white. "Show me your tally sheets," I said. "Your interview forms. Your punchcard codes. Your masters. Your sigma-progress charts. The works. Everything, in short, that you wouldn't expect me to ask to see. *Get them out.*"

He stood there a long, long time and finally said: "There aren't any."

"What have you got to show me?"

"Finalizations," he muttered. "Composites."

"Fakes, you mean? Fiction, like the stuff you've been feeding us over the wire?"

He nodded. His face was sick.

"How could you do it, Harris?" I demanded. *"How—could—you —do it?"*

He poured out a confused torrent of words. He hadn't meant to. It was his first independent job. Maybe he was just no damn good. He'd tried to keep the lower personnel up to snuff while he was dogging it himself but it couldn't be done; they sensed it and took liberties and you didn't dare check them up. His self-pitying note changed; he became weakly belligerent. What difference did it make anyway? It was just preliminary paperwork. One man's guess was as good as another's. And anyway the whole project might go down the drain. What if he had been taking it easy; he bet there were plenty of other people who took it easy and everything came out all right anyway.

"No," I said. "You're wrong and you ought to know you're wrong. Advertising's an art, but it depends on the sciences of sampling, area-testing, and customer research. You've knocked the props from under our program. We'll salvage what we can and start again."

He took a feeble stand: "You're wasting your time if you do that, Mr. Courtenay. I've been working closely with Mr. Runstead for a long time. I know what he thinks, and he's as big a shot as you are. He thinks this paperwork is just a lot of expensive nonsense."

I knew Matt Runstead better than that. I knew he was sound and so did everybody else. "What," I asked sharply, "have you got to back that statement up with? Letters? Memos? Taped calls?"

"I must have something like that," he said, and dived into his desk. He flipped through letters and memos, and played snatches of tape for minutes while the look of fear and frustration on his face deepened. At last he said in bewilderment: "I can't seem to find anything—but I'm *sure*—"

Sure he was sure. The highest form of our art is to convince the customer without letting him know he's being convinced. This weak sister had been indoctrinated by Runstead with the unrealistic approach and then sent in on my project, to do a good job of bitching it up.

"You're fired, Harris," I said. "Get out and don't come back. And I wouldn't advise you to try for a job in the advertising profession after this."

I went out into the office and announced: "You're through. All of you. Collect your personal stuff and leave the office. You'll get your checks by mail."

They gaped. Beside me, Kathy murmured: "Mitch, is that really necessary?"

"You're damned right it's necessary. Did one of them tip off the home office on what was going on? No; they just relaxed and drifted. I said it was an infection, didn't I? This is it." Ham Harris drifted past us toward the door, hurt bewilderment on his face. He had been *so* sure Runstead would back him up. He had his crammed briefcase in one hand and his raincoat in the other. He didn't look at me.

I went into his vacated office and picked up the direct wire to New York. "Hester? This is Mr. Courtenay. I've just fired the entire

San Diego branch. Notify Personnel and have them do whatever's necessary about their pay. And get me Mr. Runstead on the line."

I drummed my fingers impatiently for a long minute, and then Hester said: "Mr. Courtenay, I'm sorry to keep you waiting. Mr. Runstead's secretary says he's left for Little America on one of those tours. She says he cleaned up the A.I.G. thing and felt like a rest."

"Felt like a rest. Good God almighty. Hester, get me a New York to Little America reservation. I'm shooting right back on the next jet. I want to just barely touch ground before I zip off to the Pole. Got it?"

"Yes, Mr. Courtenay."

I hung up and found that Kathy was staring at me. "You know, Mitch," she said, "I've been uncharitable to you in my time. Kicking about your bad temper. I can see where you got it if this has been a typical operation."

"It's not typical," I said. "It's the worst case of flagrant obstructionism I've ever seen. But there's a lot of it. Everybody trying to make everybody else look bad. Darling, I've got to get to the field now and bull my way onto the next eastbound. Do you want to come too?"

She hesitated. "You won't mind if I stay and do a little tourist stuff by myself?"

"No, of course not. You have a good time and when you get back to New York I'll be there."

We kissed, and I raced out. The office was clear by then and I told the building manager to lock it until further notice when Kathy left.

I looked up from the street and she waved at me from the strange, flimsy building.

six

· · ◆ · ·

I swung off the ramp at New York, and Hester was right there. "Good girl," I told her. "When's the Pole rocket shoot off?"

"Twelve minutes, from Strip Six, Mr. Courtenay. Here are your ticket and the reservation. And some lunch in case—"

"Fine. I did miss a meal." We headed for Strip Six, with me chewing a regenerated cheese sandwich as I walked. "What's up at the office?" I asked indistinctly.

"Big excitement about you firing the San Diego people. Personnel sent up a complaint to Mr. Schocken and he upheld you—approximately Force Four."

That wasn't too good. Force Twelve—hurricane—would have been a blast from his office on the order of: "How dare you housekeepers question the decision of a Board man working on his own project? Never let me catch you—" and so on. Force Four—rising gale, small craft make for harbor—was something like: "Gentlemen, I'm sure Mr. Courtenay had perfectly good reasons for doing what he did. Often the Big Picture is lost to the purely routine workers in our organization—"

I asked Hester: "Is Runstead's secretary just a hired hand or one of his—" I was going to say "stooges" but smoothly reversed my field "—one of his confidants?"

"She's pretty close to him," Hester said cautiously.

"What was her reaction to the San Diego business?"

"Somebody told me she laughed her head off, Mr. Courtenay."

I didn't push it any harder. Finding out where I stood with respect to the big guns was legitimate. Asking about the help was asking her to rat on them. Not that there weren't girls who did. "I expect to be right back," I told her. "All I want to do is straighten something out with Runstead."

"Your wife won't be along?" she asked.

"No. She's a doctor. I'm going to tear Runstead into five or six pieces; if Dr. Nevin were along she might try to put them back together again."

Hester laughed politely and said: "Have a pleasant trip, Mr. Courtenay." We were at the ramp on Strip Six.

It wasn't a pleasant trip; it was a miserable trip on a miserable, undersized tourist rocket. We flew low, and there were prism windows at all seats, which never fail to make me airsick. You turn your head and look out and you're looking straight *down*. Worse, all the ads were Taunton Associates jobs. You look out the window and just as you convince your stomach that everything's all right and yourself that it's interesting country below, wham: a sleazy, over-sexed Taunton ad for some crummy product opaques the window and one of their nagging, stupid jingles drills into your ear.

Over the Amazon valley we were running into some very interesting stuff, and I was inspecting Electric Three, which happens to be the world's biggest power dam, when, wham:

> *BolsterBra, BolsterBra,*
> *Bolsters all the way;*
> *Don't you crumple, don't you slumple;*
> *Keep them up to stay!*

The accompanying before-and-after live pix were in the worst possible taste, and I found myself thanking God again that I worked for Fowler Schocken Associates.

It was the same off Tierra del Fuego. We went off the great circle course for a look at the whale fisheries, vast sea areas enclosed by booms that let the plankton in and didn't let the whales out. I was watching with fascination as a cow whale gave suck to her calf—it looked something like an aerial refueling operation—when the window opaqued again for another dose of Taunton shock treatment:

> *Sister, do you smell like this to your mister?*

The olfactory went on, and it was the very last straw. I had to use my carton while the ad chirped:

No wonder he's hard to get! Use Swett!

and one of those heavenly-harmony trios caroled in waltz time:

Perspire, perspire, perspire,
But don't—kill off his desire—

and then a gruff, prose, medical pitch:

DON'T TRY TO STOP PERSPIRATION.
IT'S SUICIDE. DOCTORS ADVISE
A DEODORANT AND NOT AN ASTRINGENT.

and then back to the first line and the olfactory. This time it made no difference; I had nothing more to give.

Taunton's was great on the gruff medical pitch; you'd think they invented it.

My seatmate, a nondescript customer in Universal apparel, watched with a little amusement as I retched. "Too much for you, friend?" he asked, showing the maddening superiority people who suffer from motion-sickness know too well.

"Uh," I said.

"Some of those ads are enough to make anybody sick," he said, greatly encouraged by my brilliant riposte.

Well, I couldn't let that get by. "Exactly what do you mean by that remark?" I asked evenly.

It frightened him. "I only meant that it smelled a little strong," he said hastily. "Just that particular ad. I didn't mean ads in general. There's nothing wrong with *me*, my friend!"

"Good for you," I said, and turned away.

He was still worried, and told me: "I'm perfectly sound, friend. I come from a good family, I went to a good school. I'm in the production end myself—die-maker in Philly—but I know the stuff's got to be sold. Channels of distribution. Building markets. Vertical integration. See? I'm perfectly sound!"

"Okay," I grunted. "Then watch your mouth."

He shriveled into his half of the seat. I hadn't enjoyed squelching him, but it was a matter of principle. He should have known better.

We were held up over Little America while a couple of other tourist craft touched down. One of them was Indian and I mellowed at the sight. That ship, from nose to tail, was Indiastry-built. The crewmen were Indiastry-trained and Indiastry-employed. The passengers, waking and sleeping, paid tribute minute by minute to Indiastry. And Indiastry paid tribute to Fowler Schocken Associates.

A tow truck hauled us into the great double-walled plastic doughnut that is Little America. There was only one check point. Little America is an invisible export—a dollar trap for the tourists of the world, with no military aspects. (There are Polar military bases, but they are small, scattered, and far under the ice.) A small thorium reactor heats and powers the place. Even if some nation desperate for fissionable material were to try and get it, they wouldn't have anything of military value. Windmills eke out the thorium reactor, and there's some "heat pump" arrangement that I don't understand which ekes out the windmills.

At the check point I asked about Runstead. The officer looked him up and said: "He's on the two-day tour out of New York. Thomas Cook and Son. His quarters are III–C–2205." He pulled out a map of the place and showed me that this meant third ring in, third floor up, fifth sector, twenty-second room. "You can't miss it. I can accommodate you with a nearby room, Mr. Courtenay—"

"Thanks. Later." I shoved off and elbowed my way through crowds chattering in a dozen languages to III–C–2205 and rang the bell. No answer.

A pleasant young man said to me: "I'm Mr. Cameron, the tour director. Can I help you?"

"Where's Mr. Runstead? I want to see him on business."

"Dear me. We try to get away from all that—I'll look in my register if you'll just wait a moment."

He took me to his office-bedroom-bath up the sector a way and pawed through a register. "The Starrzelius Glacier climb," he said. "Dear me. He went alone. Left at 0700, checked out in electric suit with R.D.F. and rations. He should be back in five hours or so. Have you arranged for quarters yet, Mr.—?"

"Not yet. I want to go after Runstead. It's urgent." And it was. I was going to burst a blood vessel if I didn't get my hands on him.

The slightly fluttery tour director spent about five minutes convincing me that the best thing for me to do was sign on for his tour and he'd arrange *everything*. Otherwise I'd be shifted from pillar to post buying and renting necessary equipment from concessionaires and then as like as not be turned back at checkout and not be able to find the concessionaires again while my vacation was ticking away. I signed on and he beamed. He gave me a room in the sector—plenty of luxury. It would have been twelve by eighteen if it hadn't been slightly wedge-shaped.

In five minutes he was dealing out equipment to me. "Power pack—strap it on *so*. That's the only thing that can go wrong; if you have a power failure take a sleepy pill and don't worry. You'll freeze, but we'll pick you up before there's tissue damage. Boots. Plug them in *so*. Gloves. Plug them in. Coveralls. Hood. Snowglasses. Radio direction finder. Just tell the checkout guard 'Starrzelius Glacier' and he'll set it. Two simple switches plainly labeled 'Out' and 'In.' Outward bound it goes 'beep-*beep*'—ascending. Inward bound it goes '*beep*-beep'—descending. Just remember, going *up* the glacier, the tone goes *up*. Going *down* the glacier, the tone goes *down*. Distress signal—a big red handle. You just pull and immediately you start broadcasting. The planes will be out in fifteen minutes. You have to pay expenses for the search and rescue, so I *wouldn't* yank the handle just for a ride back. It's always possible to rest, have a sip of Coffiest, and keep on going. Route-marked map. Snowshoes. Gyrocompass. And rations. Mr. Courteney, you are equipped. I'll lead you to checkout."

The outfit wasn't as bad as it sounded. I've been more heavily bundled up against the lakeside winds in a Chicago winter. The lumpy items, like the power pack, the R.D.F., and the rations, were well distributed. The snowshoes folded into a pair of staffs with steel points for ice climbing, and went into a quiver on my back.

Checkout was very thorough. They started with my heart and worked through my equipment, with particular emphasis on the power pack. I passed, and they set the R.D.F. for Starrzelius Glacier, with many more warnings not to overdo it.

It wasn't cold, not inside the suit. For a moment only I opened the face flap. *Wham!* I closed it again. Forty below, they had told me —a foolish-sounding figure until my nose felt it for a split second. I didn't need the snow shoes at the base of the towering plastic doughnut; it was crust ice that my spike-soled shoes bit into. I oriented the map with the little gyrocompass and trudged off into the vast whiteness along the proper bearing. From time to time I pressed my left sleeve, squeezing the molded R.D.F. switch, and heard inside my hood a cheerful, reassuring "Beep-*beep*. Beep-*beep*. Beep-*beep*."

There were some score people frolicking in one party I passed and waved cheerily at. They seemed to be Chinese or Indians. What an adventure it must be for them! But, like indifferent swimmers hugging a raft, they did their frolicking almost under the shadow of Little America. Farther out there were some people playing a game I didn't know. They had posts with bottomless baskets set up at either end of a marked-off rectangular field, and the object was to toss a large silicone ball through the baskets. Still farther out there was a large skiing class with instructors in red suits.

I looked back after trudging for what seemed only a few minutes and couldn't see the red suits any more. I couldn't see details of Little America—just a gray-white shadow. "Beep-*beep*," my R.D.F. said and I kept going. Runstead was going to hear from me. Soon.

The aloneness was eerie but not—not unpleasant. Little America was no longer visible behind me, not even as a gray-white blur. And I didn't care. Was this how Jack O'Shea felt? Was this why he fumbled for words to describe Venus and was never satisfied with the words he found?

My feet plunged into a drift, and I unshipped and opened the snowshoes. They snapped on, and after a little stumbling experiment, I fell into an easy, sliding shuffle that was a remarkably pleasant way of covering ground. It wasn't floating. But neither was it the solid jar of a shoe sole against a paved surface—all the walking I had known for thirty-odd years.

I marched the compass course by picking landmarks and going to them: an oddly-recurved ice hummock, a blue shadow on a swale of snow. The R.D.F. continued to confirm me. I was blown up with pride at my mastery of the wild, and after two hours I was wildly hungry all at once.

What I had to do was squat and open a silicone-tissue bell into which I fitted. Exposing my nose cautiously from time to time I judged the air warm enough in five minutes. I ravenously gulped self-heated stew and tea and tried to smoke a cigarette. On the second puff the little tent was thoroughly smoked and I was blinded with tears. Regretfully I put it out against my shoe, closed my face mask, stowed the tent, and stretched happily.

After another bearing I started off again. Hell, I told myself. This Runstead thing is just a difference of temperament. He can't see the wide-open spaces and you can. There's no malice involved. He just thinks it's a crackpot idea because he doesn't realize that there are people who go for it. All you've got to do is *explain* it—

That argument, born of well-being, crumbled at one touch of reason. Runstead was out on the glacier too. He most certainly could see the wide-open spaces if, of all the places on earth he could be, he chose the Starrzelius Glacier. Well, a showdown would shortly be forthcoming. "Beep-*beep*."

I sighted through the compass and picked a black object that was dead on my course. I couldn't quite make it out, but it was visible and it wasn't moving. I broke into a shuffling run that made me pant, and against my will I slowed down. It was a man.

When I was twenty yards away, the man looked impatiently at his watch, and I broke into the clumsy run again.

"Matt!" I said. "Matt Runstead!"

"That's right, Mitch," he said, as nasty as ever. "You're sharp today." I looked at him very slowly and very carefully, phrasing my opening remarks. He had folded skis thrust into the snow beside him.

"What's—what's—" I stammered.

"I have time to spare," he said, "but you've wasted enough of it. Good-by, Mitch." While I stood there dumbly he picked up his folded skis, swung them into the air, and poleaxed me. I fell backwards with pain, bewilderment, and shamed rage bursting my head. I felt him fumbling at my chest and then I didn't feel anything for a while.

I woke thinking I had kicked the covers off and that it was cold for early autumn. Then the ice-blue Antarctic sky knifed into my eyes, and I felt the crumbly snow beneath me. It had happened, then. My head ached horribly and I was cold. Too cold. I felt and found that the power pack was missing. No heat to the suit, gloves, and boots. No power to the R.D.F. coming or going. No use to pull the emergency signal.

I tottered to my feet and felt the cold grip me like a vise. There were footprints punched into the snow leading away—where? There was the trail of my snowshoes. Stiffly I took a step back along that trail, and then another, and then another.

The rations. I could thrust them into the suit, break the heat seals, and let them fill the suit with temporary warmth. Plodding step by step I debated: stop and rest while you drink the ration's heat or keep moving? You need a rest, I told myself. Something impossible happened, your head is aching. You'll feel better if you sit for a moment, open a ration or two, and then go on.

I didn't sit. I knew what that would mean. Painful step after painful step I fumbled a Coffiest can from its pocket with fingers that would barely obey me, and fumbled it into my suit. My thumb didn't seem strong enough to pop the seal and I told myself: sit down for a moment and gather your strength. You don't have to lie down, pleasant as that would be . . . my thumb drove through the seal and the tingling heat was painful.

It became a blur. I opened more cans, and then I couldn't work them out of their pockets any more. I sat down at least once and got up again. And then I sat down, feeling guilty and ashamed of the indulgence, telling myself I'd get up in one more second for Kathy, two more seconds for Kathy, three more seconds for Kathy.

But I didn't.

seven

• •◆• •

I fell asleep on a mountain of ice; I woke up in a throbbing, strumming inferno, complete with red fire and brutish-looking attendant devils. It was exactly what I would have consigned a Taunton copysmith to. I was confused to find myself there.

The confusion did not last long. One of the attendant devils shook my shoulder roughly and said: "Gimme a hand, sleepy. I gotta stow my hammock." My head cleared and it was very plain that he was simply a lower-class consumer—perhaps a hospital attendant?

"Where's this?" I asked him. "Are we back in Little America?"

"Jeez, you talk funny," he commented. "Gimme a hand, will ya?"

"Certainly not!" I told him. "I'm a star-class copysmith."

He looked at me pityingly, said "Punchy," and went away into the strumming, red-lit darkness.

I stood up, swaying on my feet, and grabbed an elbow hurrying past from darkness to darkness. "Excuse me," I said. "Where is this place? Is it a hospital?"

The man was another consumer, worse-tempered than the first. "Leggo my yarm!" he snarled. I did. "Ya want on sick call, ya wait until we land," he said.

"Land?"

"Yah, land. Listen, Punchy, don't ya know what ya signed up for?"

"Signed up? No; I don't. But you're being too familiar. I'm a star-class copysmith—"

His face changed. "Ahah," he said wisely. "I can fix ya up. Justa minnit, Punchy. I'll be right back wit' the stuff."

He was, too. "The stuff" was a little green capsule. "Only five hunnerd," he wheedled. "Maybe the last one on board. Ya wanta touch down wit' the shakes? Nah! This'll straighten ya out fer landing—"

"Landing *where?*" I yelled. "What's all this about? I don't know, and I don't want your dope. Just tell me where I am and what I'm supposed to have signed up for and I'll take it from there!"

He looked at me closely and said: "Ya got it bad. A hit in the head, maybe? Well, Punchy, yer in the Number Six Hold of the Labor Freighter *Thomas R. Malthus.* Wind and weather, immaterial. Course, 273 degrees. Speed 300, destination Costa Rica, cargo slobs like you and me for the Chlorella plantations." It was the rigmarole of a relieved watch officer, or a savage parody of it.

"You're—" I hesitated.

"Downgraded," he finished bitterly, and stared at the green capsule in the palm of his hand. Abruptly he gulped it and went on: "I'm gonna hit the comeback trail, though." A sparkle crept into his eyes. "I'm gonna introduce new and efficient methods in the plantations. I'll be a foreman in a week. I'll be works manager in a month. I'll be a director in a year. And then I'm gonna buy the Cunard Line and plate all their rockets with solid gold. Nothing but first-class accommodations. Nothing but the best for my passengers. I always kept her smooth on the Atlantic run. I'll build you a gold-plated imperial suite aboard my flag ship, Punchy. The best is none too good for my friend Punchy. If you don't like gold I'll get platinum. If you don't like—"

I inched away and he didn't notice. He kept babbling his hophead litany. It made me glad I'd never taken to the stuff. I came to a bulkhead and sat down hopelessly, leaning against it. Somebody sat down beside me and said "Hello there" in a cozy voice.

"Hello," I said. "Say, are we really headed for Costa? How can I get to see a ship's officer? This is all a mistake."

"Oh," said the man, "why worry about it? Live and let live. Eat, drink, and be merry is my motto."

"Take your God-damned hands off me!" I told him.

He became shrill and abusive, and I got up and walked on, stumbling over legs and torsos.

It occurred to me that I'd never really known any consumers except during the brief periods when they were serving me. I wanted very badly to get out of Number Six Hold. I wanted to get back to New York, find out what kind of stunt Runstead had pulled and why, get back to Kathy, and my friendship with Jack O'Shea, and my big job at Fowler Schocken. I had things to do.

One of the red lights said Crash Emergency Exit. I thought of the hundreds of people jammed in the hold trying to crowd out through the door, and shuddered.

"Excuse me, my friend," somebody said hoarsely to me. "You'd better move." He began to throw up, and apparently airsickness containers weren't issued aboard labor freighters. I rolled the emergency door open and slid through.

"Well?" growled a huge Detective Agency guard.

"I want to see a ship's officer," I said. "I'm here by some mistake. My name is Mitchell Courtenay. I'm a copysmith with the Fowler Schocken Associates."

"The number," he snapped.

"16–156–187," I told him, and I admit that there was a little pride in my voice. You can lose money and health and friendship, but they can't take a low Social Security number away from you . . .

He was rolling up my sleeve, not roughly. The next moment I went spinning against the bulkhead with my face burning from a ham-handed slap. "Get back between decks, Punchy!" the guard roared. "Yer not on an excursion and I don't like yer funny talk!"

I stared incredulously at the pit of my elbow. The tatto read: "1304–9974–1416–156–187723." My own number was buried in it, but the inks matched perfectly. The style of lettering was very slightly off—not enough for anybody to notice but me.

"Waddaya waitin' for?" the guard said. "You seen yer number before, ain't ya?"

"No," I said evenly, but my legs were quivering. I was scared—terribly scared. "I never saw this number before. It's been tattooed around my real number. I'm Courtenay, I tell you. I can prove it. I'll pay you—" I fumbled in my pockets and found no money. I abruptly realized that I was wearing a strange and shabby suit of Universal apparel, stained with food and worse.

"So pay," the guard said impassively.

"I'll pay you later," I told him. "Just get me to somebody responsible—"

A natty young flight lieutenant in Panagra uniform popped into the narrow corridor. "What's going on here?" he demanded of the guard. "The hatchway light's still on. Can't you keep order between decks? Your agency gets a fitness report from us, you know." He ignored me completely.

"I'm sorry, Mr. Kobler," the guard said, saluting and coming to a brace. "This man seems to be on the stuff. He came out and gave me an argument that he's a star-class copysmith on board by mistake—"

"Look at my number!" I yelled at the lieutenant.

His face wrinkled as I thrust my bared elbow under his nose. The guard grabbed me and snarled: "Don't you bother the—"

"Just a minute," said the Panagra officer. "I'll handle this. That's a high number, fellow. What do you expect to prove by showing me that?"

"It's been added to, fore and aft. My real number is 16–156–187. See? Before and after that there's a different lettering style! It's tampering!"

Holding his breath, the lieutenant looked very closely. He said: "Umm. Just barely possible . . . come with me." The guard hastened to open a corridor door for him and me. He looked scared.

The lieutenant took me through a roaring confusion of engine rooms to the purser's hatbox-sized office. The purser was a sharp-faced gnome who wore his Panagra uniform as though it were a sack. "Show him your number," the lieutenant directed me, and I did. To the purser he said: "What's the story on this man?"

The purser slipped a reel into the reader and cranked it. "1304–9974–1416–156–187723," he read at last. "Groby, William George; 26; bachelor; broken home (father's desertion) child; third of five sibs; H-H balance, male 1; health, 2.9; occupational class 2 for seven years; 1.5 for three months; education 9; signed labor contract B." He looked up at the flight officer. "A very dull profile, lieutenant. Is there any special reason why I should be interested in this man?"

The lieutenant said: "He claims he's a copysmith in here by mistake. He says somebody altered his number. And he speaks a little above his class."

"Tut," said the purser. "Don't let that worry you. A broken-home child, especially a middle sib from the lower levels, reads and views incessantly trying to better himself. But nevertheless you'll notice—"

"That's enough of that," I snarled at the little man, quite fed up. "I'm Mitchell Courtenay. I can buy you and sell you without straining my petty cash account. I'm in charge of the Fowler Schocken

Associates Venus Section. I want you to get New York on the line immediately and we'll wind up this farce. Now jump, damn you!"

The flight lieutenant looked alarmed and reached for the phone, but the purser smiled and moved it away from his hand. "Mitchell Courtenay, are you?" he asked kindly. He reached for another reel and put it in the viewer. "Here we are," he said, after a little cranking. The lieutenant and I looked.

It was the front page of the *New York Times*. The first column contained the obituary of Mitchell Courtenay, head of Fowler Schocken Associates Venus Section. I had been found frozen to death on Starrzelius Glacier near Little America. I had been tampering with my power pack, and it had failed. I read on long after the lieutenant had lost interest. Matt Runstead was taking over Venus Section. I was a loss to my profession. My wife, Dr. Nevin, had refused to be interviewed. Fowler Schocken was quoted in a ripe eulogy of me. I was a personal friend of Venus Pioneer Jack O'Shea, who had expressed shock and grief at the news.

The purser said: "I picked that up in Capetown. Lieutenant, get this silly son of a bitch back between decks, will you please?"

The guard had arrived. He slapped and kicked me all the way back to Number Six Hold.

I caromed off somebody as the guard shoved me through the door into the red darkness. After the relatively clear air of the outside, the stink was horrible.

"What did you do?" the human cushion asked amiably, picking himself up.

"I tried to tell them who I am . . ." That wasn't going to get me anywhere. "What happens next?" I asked.

"We land. We get quarters. We get to work. What contract are you on?"

"Labor contract B, they said."

He whistled. "I guess they really had you, huh?"

"What do you mean? What's it all about?"

"Oh—you were blind, were you? Too bad. B contract's five years. For refugees, morons, and anybody else they can swindle into signing up. There's a conduct clause. I got offered the B, but I told them if that was the best they could do I'd just go out and give myself up to the Brink's Express. I talked them into an F contract— they must have needed help real bad. It's one year and I can buy outside the company stores and things like that."

I held my head to keep it from exploding. "It can't be such a bad place to work," I said. "Country life—farming—fresh air and sunshine."

"Um," said the man in an embarrassed way. "It's better than chemicals, I guess. Maybe not so good as mining. You'll find out soon enough."

He moved away, and I fell into a light doze when I should have been making plans.

There wasn't any landing-ready signal. We just hit, and hit hard. A discharge port opened, letting in blinding tropical sunlight. It was agony after the murky hold. What swept in with it was not country air but a gush of disinfectant aerosol. I untangled myself from a knot of cursing laborers and flowed with the stream toward the port.

"Hold it, stupid!" said a hard-faced man wearing a plant-protection badge. He threw a number plaque on a cord around my neck. Everybody got one and lined up at a table outside the ship. It was in the shadow of the Chlorella plantation, a towering eighty-story structure, like office. "In-and-Out" baskets stacked up to the sky. There were mirrored louvers at each tier. Surrounding the big building were acres of eye-stabbing glare. I realized that this was more mirrored louvers to catch the sun, bounce it off more mirrors inside the tiers and onto the photosynthesis tanks. It was a spectacular, though not uncommon, sight from the air. On the ground it was plain hell. I should have been planning, planning. But the channels of my mind were choked by: "From the sun-drenched plantations of Costa Rica, tended by the deft hands of independent farmers with pride in their work, comes the juicyripe goodness of Chlorella Proteins . . ." Yes; I had written those words.

"Keep moving!" a plant-protection man bawled. "Keep it moving, you God-damned scum-skimmers! Keep it moving!" I shaded my eyes and shuffled ahead as the line moved past the table. A dark-glassed man at the table was asking me: "Name?"

"Mitchell Court—"

"That's the one I told you about," said the purser's voice.

"Okay; thanks." To me: "Groby, we've had men try to bug out of a B Contract before this, you know. They're always sorry they tried. Do you know what the annual budget of Costa Rica is, by any chance?"

"No," I mumbled.

"It's about a hundred and eighty-three billion dollars. And do you happen to know what the annual taxes of Chlorella Corporation are?"

"No. Damn it, man—"

He broke in: "About a hundred and eighty billion dollars. From that, a bright fellow like you will conclude that the government—*and courts*—of Costa Rica do just about what Chlorella wants done. If we want to make an example of a contract-breaker they'll do it for us. Bet your life. Now, what's your name, Groby?"

"Groby," I said hoarsely.

"First name? Educational level? H-H balance?"

"I don't remember. But if you'll give them to me on a piece of paper I'll memorize them."

I heard the purser laugh and say: "He'll do."

"All right, Groby," the man in dark glasses said genially. "No harm done. Here's your profile and assignment. We'll make a skimmer out of you yet. Move on."

I moved on. A plant protection man grabbed my assignment and bawled at me: "Skimmers that way."

"That way" was under the bottom tier of the building, into light even more blinding, down a corridor between evil-smelling, shallow tanks, and at last through a door into the central pylon of the structure. There was a well-lit room which seemed twilit after the triply reflected tropical sun outside.

"Skimmer?" said a man. I blinked and nodded at him. "I'm Mullane—shift assignment. I got a question to ask you, Groby." He peered at my profile card. "We need a skimmer on the sixty-seventh tier and we need a skimmer on the forty-first tier. Your bunk's going to be on the forty-third tier of the pylon. Frankly, which would you rather work on? I ought to mention that we don't have elevators for skimmers and the other Class 2 people."

"The forty-first-tier job," I told him, trying to make out his face.

"That's very sensible," he told me. "Very, very sensible." And then he just stood there, with seconds ticking away. At last he added: "I like to see a sensible man act sensible." There was another long pause.

"I haven't got any money on me," I told him.

"That's all right," he said. "I'll lend you some. Just sign this note and we can settle up on payday without any fuss. It's just a simple assignment of five dollars."

I read the note and signed it. I had to look at my profile card again; I had forgotten my first name. Mullane briskly scrawled "41" and his initials on my assignment, and hurried off without lending me five dollars. I didn't chase him.

"I'm Mrs. Horrocks, the housing officer," a woman said sweetly to me. "Welcome to the Chlorella family, Mr. Groby. I hope you'll spend many happy years with us. And now to work. Mr. Mullane told you this draft of crumbs—that is, the present group of contractees—will be housed on the forty-third tier, I think. It's my job to see that you're located with a congenial group of fellow-employees."

Her face reminded me faintly of a tarantula as she went on: "We have one vacant bunk in Dorm Seven. Lots of *nice, young* men in Dorm Seven. Perhaps you'd like it there. It means so much to be among one's *own kind* of people."

I got what she was driving at and told her I didn't want to be in Dorm Seven.

She went on brightly: "Then there's Dorm Twelve. It's a rather rough crowd, I'm afraid, but beggars can't be choosers, can they? They'd like to get a nice young man like you in Dorm Twelve. My, yes! But you could carry a knife or something. Shall I put you down for Dorm Twelve, Mr. Groby?"

"No," I said. "What else have you got? And by the way, I wonder if you could lend me five dollars until payday?"

"I'll put you down for Dorm Ten," she said, scribbling. "And of course I'll lend you some money. Ten dollars? Just sign and thumbprint this assignment, Mr. Groby. Thank you." She hurried off in search of the next sucker.

A red-faced fat man gripped my hand and said hoarsely: "Brother, I want to welcome you to the ranks of the United Slime-Mold Protein Workers of Panamerica, Unaffiliated, Chlorella Costa Rica Local. This pamphlet will explain how the U.S.M.P.W.P. protects workers in the field from the innumable petty rackets and abuses that useta plague the innustry. Yer inishiashun and dues are checked off automatically but this valuable pamphlet is an extra."

I asked him: "Brother, what's the worst that can happen to me if I don't buy it?"

"It's a long drop," he said simply.

He lent me five dollars to buy the pamphlet.

I didn't have to climb to Dorm Ten on the forty-third tier. There were no elevators for Class 2 people, but there was an endless cargo net we could grab hold of. It took a little daring to jump on and off, and clearance was negligible. If your rump stuck out you were likely to lose it.

The dorm was jammed with about sixty bunks, three high. Since production went on only during the daylight hours, the hotbed system wasn't in use. My bunk was all mine, twenty-four hours a day. Big deal.

A sour-faced old man was sweeping the central aisle lackadaisically when I came in. "You a new crumb?" he asked, and looked at my ticket. "There's your bunk. I'm Pine. Room orderly. You know how to skim?"

"No," I said. "Look, Mr. Pine, how do I make a phone call out of here?"

"Dayroom," he said, jerking his thumb. I went to the dayroom adjoining. There was a phone and a biggish hypnoteleset and readers and spools and magazines. I ground my teeth as the cover of *Taunton's Weekly* sparkled at me from the rack. The phone was a pay phone, of course.

I dashed back into the dorm. "Mr. Pine," I said, "can you lend me about twenty dollars in coin? I have to make a long-distance call."

"Twenty-five for twenty?" he asked shrewdly.

"Sure. Anything you say."

He slowly scrawled out an assignment slip and I signed and printed it. Then he carefully counted out the money from his baggy pockets.

I wanted to call Kathy, but didn't dare. She might be at her apartment, she might be at the hospital. I might miss her. I dialed the fifteen digits of the Fowler Schocken Associates number after I deposited a clanging stream of coins. I waited for the switchboard to say: "Fowler Schocken Associates; good afternoon; it's *always* a good afternoon for Fowler Schocken Associates and their clients. May I help you?"

But that isn't what I heard. The phone said: *"Su número de prioridad, por favor?"*

Priority number for long-distance calls. I didn't have one. A firm had to be rated a billion and fast pay before it could get a long-distance priority number in four figures. So jammed were the world's long lines that an individual priority in any number of figures was unthinkable. Naturally all that had never worried me when I made long-distance calls from Fowler Schocken, on the Fowler

Schocken priority number. A priority number was one of the little luxuries I'd have to learn to live without.

I hung up slowly. The coins were not returned.

I could write to everybody, I thought. Write to Kathy and Jack O'Shea and Fowler and Collier and Hester and Tildy. Leave no stone unturned. Dear Wife (or Boss): This is to advise you that your husband (or employee) who you know quite well is dead is not really dead but inexplicably a contract laborer for Costa Rican Chlorella and please drop everything and get him out. Signed, your loving husband (or employee), Mitchell Courtenay.

But there was the company censor to think of.

I wandered blankly back into the dorm. The rest of the Dorm Ten people were beginning to drift in.

"A crumb!" one of them yelled, sighting me.

"Court's called to order!" another one trumpeted.

I don't hold what followed against any of them. It was traditional, a break in the monotony, a chance to lord it over somebody more miserable than themselves, something they had all gone through too. I presume that in Dorm Seven it would have been a memorably nasty experience, and in Dorm Twelve I might not have lived through it. Dorm Ten was just high-spirited. I paid my "fine" —more pay vouchers—and took my lumps and recited the blasphemous oath and then I was a full-fledged member of the dorm.

I didn't troop with them to the mess hall for dinner. I just lay on my bunk and wished I were as dead as the rest of the world thought I was.

eight

· · ◆ · ·

Scum-skimming wasn't hard to learn. You got up at dawn. You gulped a breakfast sliced not long ago from Chicken Little and washed it down with Coffiest. You put on your coveralls and took the cargo net up to your tier. In blazing noon from sunrise to sunset you walked your acres of shallow tanks crusted with algae. If you walked slowly, every thirty seconds or so you spotted a patch at maturity, bursting with yummy carbohydrates. You skimmed the patch with your skimmer and slung it down the well, where it would be baled, or processed into glucose to feed Chicken Little, who would be sliced and packed to feed people from Baffinland to Little America. Every hour you could drink from your canteen and take a salt tablet. Every two hours you could take five minutes. At sunset you turned in your coveralls and went to dinner—more slices from Chicken Little —and then you were on your own. You could talk, you could read, you could go into a trance before the dayroom hypnoteleset, you could shop, you could pick fights, you could drive yourself crazy thinking of what might have been, you could go to sleep.

Mostly you went to sleep.

I wrote a lot of letters and tried to sleep a lot. Payday came as a surprise. I didn't know two weeks had slipped by. It left me owing Chlorella Proteins only eighty-odd dollars and a few cents. Besides the various assignments I had made, there were the Employee Welfare Fund (as closely as I could figure that one out, it meant that I was paying Chlorella's taxes); union dues and installment on the initiation fee; withholding tax (this time my own taxes); hospitalization (but try and get it, the older men said) and old age insurance.

One of the things I faintheartedly consoled myself with was the thought that when—*when*, I always said firmly—I got out I'd be closer to the consumers than any ad man in the profession. Of course at Fowler Schocken we'd had our boys up from the ranks: scholarship kids. I knew now that they had been too snobbish to give me the straight facts on consumers' lives and thoughts. Or they hadn't cared to admit even to themselves what they had been like.

I think I learned that ads work more strongly on the unconscious than even we in the profession had thought. I was shocked repeatedly to hear advertising referred to as "that crap." I was at first puzzled and then gratified to see it sink in and take effect anyway. The Venus-rocket response was, of course, my greatest interest. For one week I listened when I could to enthusiasm growing among these men who would never go to Venus, who knew nobody who would ever go to Venus. I heard the limericks we had launched from Fowler Schocken Associates chuckled over:

> *A midget space-jock named O'Shea*
> *Loved a girl who was built like a dray—*
> > Or:
> *A socially misfit machinist*
> *Asked his sweetheart: "Dear, what's come between us?"*

Or any of the others, with their engineered-in message: that Venus environment increased male potency. Ben Winston's subsection on Folkways, I had always said, was one of the most important talent groups in the whole Schocken enterprise. They were particularly fine on riddles: "Why do they call Venus the Mourning Star?" for instance. Well, it doesn't make sense in print; but the pun is basic humor, and the basic drive of the human race is sex. And what is, essentially, more important in life than to mold and channel the deepest torrential flow of human emotion into its proper directions? (I am not apologizing for those renegades who talk fancifully about some imagined "Death-Wish" to hook their sales appeals to. I leave that sort of thing to the Tauntons of our profession; it's dirty; it's immoral, I want nothing to do with it. Besides, it leads to fewer consumers in the long run, if they'd only think the thing through.)

For there is no doubt that linking a sales message to one of the great prime motivations of the human spirit does more than sell goods; it strengthens the motivation, helps it come to the surface, provides it with focus. And thus we are assured of the steady annual increment of consumers so essential to expansion.

Chlorella, I was pleased to learn, took extremely good care of its workers' welfare in that respect. There was an adequate hormone component in the diet, and a splendid thousand-bed Recreation Room on the 50th tier. The only stipulation the company made was that children born on the plantation were automatically indentured to Chlorella if either parent was still an employee on the child's tenth birthday.

But I had no time for the Recreation Room. I was learning the ropes, studying my milieu, waiting for opportunity to come. If opportunity didn't come soon I would make opportunity; but first I had to study and learn.

Meanwhile, I kept my ears open for the results of the Venus campaign. It went beautifully—for a while. The limericks, the planted magazine stories, the gay little songs had their effect.

Then something went sour.

There was a downtrend. It took me a day to notice it, and a week to believe it could be true. The word "Venus" drifted out of the small talk. When the space rocket was mentioned it was in connection with reference points like "radiation poisoning," "taxes," "sacrifice." There was a new, dangerous kind of Folkways material—"Didja hear the one about the punchy that got caught in his space suit?"

You might not have recognized what was going on, and Fowler Schocken, scanning his daily précis of the summary of the digests of the skeletonized reports of the abstracts of the charts of progress on Venus Project, would never have the chance to question or doubt what was told him. But I knew Venus Project. And I knew what was happening.

Matt Runstead had taken over.

The aristocrat of Dorm Ten was Herrera. After ten years with Chlorella he had worked his way up—topographically it was down—to Master Slicer. He worked in the great, cool vault underground, where Chicken Little grew and was cropped by him and other artisans. He swung a sort of two-handed sword that carved off great slabs of the tissue, leaving it to the lesser packers and trimmers and their faceless helpers to weigh it, shape it, freeze it, cook it, flavor it, package it, and ship it off to the area on quota for the day.

He had more than a production job. He was a safety valve. Chicken Little grew and grew, as she had been growing for decades. Since she had started as a lump of heart tissue, she didn't know any better than to grow up against a foreign body and surround it. She didn't know any better than to grow and fill her concrete vault and keep growing, compressing her cells and rupturing them. As long as she got nutrient, she grew. Herrera saw to it that she grew round and plump, that no tissue got old and tough before it was sliced, that one side was not neglected for the other.

With this responsibility went commensurate pay, and yet Herrera had not taken a wife or an apartment in one of the upper tiers of the pylon. He made trips that were the subject of bawdy debate while he was gone—and which were never referred to without careful politeness while he was present. He kept his two-handed slicer by him at all times, and often idly sleeked its edge with a hone. He was a man I had to know. He was a man with money—he *must* have money after ten years—and I needed it.

The pattern of the B labor contract had become quite clear. You never got out of debt. Easy credit was part of the system, and so were irritants that forced you to exercise it. If I fell behind ten dollars a week I would owe one thousand one hundred dollars to Chlorella at the end of my contract, and would have to work until the debt was wiped out. And while I worked, a new debt would accumulate.

I needed Herrera's money to buy my way out of Chlorella and back to New York: Kathy, my wife; Venus Section; my job. Runstead was doing things I didn't like to Venus Section. And God alone knew what Kathy was doing, under the impression that she was a widow. I tried not to think of one particular thing: Jack O'Shea and Kathy. The little man had been getting back at womankind for their years of contempt. Until the age of twenty-five he had been a laughable sixty-pound midget, with a touch of grotesquerie in the fact that he had doggedly made himself a test pilot. At the age of twenty-six he found himself the world's number one celebrity, the first man to land a ship on Venus, an immortal barely out of his teens. He had a lot of loving to catch up on. The story was that he'd been setting records on his lecture tours. I didn't like the story. I didn't like the way he liked Kathy or the way Kathy liked him.

And so I went through another day, up at dawn, breakfast, coveralls and goggles, cargo net, skimming and slinging for blazing hour after hour, dinner and the dayroom and, if I could manage it, a chat with Herrera.

"Fine edge on that slicer, Gus. There's only two kinds of people in the world: the ones who don't take care of their tools and the smart ones."

Suspicious look from under his Aztec brows. "Pays to do things right. You're the crumb, ain't you?"

"Yeah. First time here. Think I ought to stay?"

He didn't get it. "You *gotta* stay. Contract." And he went to the magazine rack.

Tomorrow's another day.

"Hello, Gus. Tired?"

"Hi, George. Yeah, a little. Ten hours swinging the slicer. It gets you in the arms."

"I can imagine. Skimming's easy, but you don't need brains for it."

"Well, maybe some day you get upgraded. I think I'll trance."

And another:

"Hi, George. How's it going?"

"Can't complain, Gus. At least I'm getting a sun-tan."

"You sure are. Soon you be dark like me. Haw-haw! How'd you like that?"

"Porqué no, amigo?"

"Hey, tu hablas español! Cuando aprendiste la lengua?"

"Not so fast, Gus! Just a few words here and there. I wish I knew more. Some day when I get a few bucks ahead I'm going to town and see the girls."

"Oh, they all speak English, kind of. If you get a nice steady li'l girl it would be nice to speak a li'l Spanish. She would appreciate it. But most of them know 'Gimmy-gimmy' and the li'l English poem about what you get for one buck. Haw-haw!"

And another day—an astonishing day.

I'd been paid again, and my debt had increased by eight dollars. I'd tormented myself by wondering where the money went, but I knew. I came off shift dehydrated, as they wanted me to be. I got a squirt of Popsie from the fountain by punching my combination—twenty-five cents checked off my payroll. The squirt wasn't quite enough so I had another—fifty cents. Dinner was drab as usual; I couldn't face more than a bite or two of Chicken Little. Later I was hungry and there was the canteen where I got Crunchies on easy credit. The Crunchies kicked off withdrawal symptoms that could be quelled only by another two squirts of Popsie from the fountain. And Popsie kicked off withdrawal symptoms that could only be quelled by smoking Starr cigarettes, which made you hungry for Crunchies . . . Had Fowler Schocken thought of it in these terms when he organized Starrzelius Verily, the first spherical trust? Popsie to Crunchies to Starrs to Popsie?

And you paid 6 percent interest on the money advanced you.

It had to be soon. If I didn't get out soon I never would. I could feel my initiative, the thing that made me *me*, dying, cell by cell, within me. The minute dosages of alkaloid were sapping my will, but most of all it was a hopeless, trapped feeling that things were this way, that they always would be this way, that it wasn't too bad, that you could always go into trance or get really lit on Popsie or maybe try one of the green capsules that floated around from hand to hand at varying quotations; the boys would be glad to wait for the money.

It had to be soon.

"Como 'stá, Gustavo?"

He sat down and gave me his Aztec grin. *"Como 'stá, amigo Jorge? Se fuma?"* He extended a pack of cigarettes.

They were Greentips. I said automatically: "No thanks. I smoke Starrs; they're tastier." And automatically I lit one, of course. I was becoming the kind of consumer we used to love. Think about smoking, think about Starrs, light a Starr. Light a Starr, think about Popsie, get a squirt. Get a squirt, think about Crunchies, buy a box. Buy a box, think about smoking, light a Starr. And at every step roll out the words of praise that had been dinned into you through your eyes and ears and pores.

"I smoke Starrs; they're tastier. I drink Popsie; it's zippy. I eat Crunchies; they tang your tongue. I smoke—"

Gus said to me: "You don't look so happy, Jorge."

"I don't feel so happy, amigo." This was it. "I'm in a very strange situation." Wait for him, now.

"I figured there was something wrong. An intelligent fellow like you, a fellow who's been around. Maybe you can use some help?"

Wonderful; wonderful. "You won't lose by it, Gus. You're taking a chance, but you won't lose by it. Here's the story—"

"Sst! Not here!" he shushed me. In a lower voice he went on: "It's always a risk. It's always worth it when I see a smart young fellow wise up and begin to *do* things. Some day I make a mistake, *seguro.* Then they get me, maybe they brainburn me. What the hell, I can laugh at them. I done my part. Here. I don't have to tell you to be careful where you open this." He shook my hand and I felt a wad of something adhere to my palm. Then he strolled across the dayroom to the hypnoteleset, punched his clock number for a half-hour of trance and slid under, with the rest of the viewers.

I went to the washroom and punched my combination for a ten-minute occupancy of a booth—bang went another nickel off my pay —and went in. The adhesive wad on my palm opened up into a single sheet of tissue paper which said:

A Life Is in Your Hands

This is Contact Sheet One of the World Conservationist Association, popularly known as "The Consies." It has been passed to you by a member of the W.C.A. who judged that you are (a) intelligent; (b) disturbed by the present state of the world; (c) a potentially valuable addition to our ranks. His life is now in your hands. We ask you to read on before you take any action.

Facts About the W.C.A.

The Facts: The W.C.A. is a secret organization perse-cuted by all the governments of the world. It believes that reckless exploitation of natural resources has created need-less poverty and needless human misery. It believes that continued exploitation will mean the end of human life on Earth. It believes that this trend may be reversed if the people of the Earth can be educated to the point where they will demand planning of population, reforestation, soil-building, deurbanization, and an end to the wasteful pro-duction of gadgets and proprietary foods for which there is no natural demand. This educational program is being car-ried on by propaganda—like this—demonstrations of force, and sabotage of factories which produce trivia.

Falsehoods About the W.C.A.

You have probably heard that "the Consies" are mur-derers, psychotics, and incompetent people who kill and destroy for irrational ends or out of envy. None of this is true. W.C.A. members are humane, balanced persons, many of them successful in the eyes of the world. Stories to the contrary are zealously encouraged by people who profit from the exploitation which we hope to correct. There are irrational, unbalanced and criminal persons who do commit outrages in the name of conservation, either idealistically or as a shield for looting. The W.C.A. dissociates itself from such people and regards their activities with repugnance.

What Will You Do Next?

That is up to you. You can (a) denounce the person who passed you this contact sheet; (b) destroy this sheet and forget about it; (c) go to the person who passed you the sheet and seek further information. We ask you to think before you act.

I thought—hard. I thought the broadside was (a) the dullest, lousiest piece of copysmithing I had ever seen in my life; (b) a wildly distorted version of reality; (c) a possible escape route for me out of Chlorella and back to Kathy.

So these were the dreaded Consies! Of all the self-contradictory gibberish—but it had a certain appeal. The ad was crafted—unconsciously, I was sure—the way we'd do a pharmaceutical-house booklet for doctors only. Calm, learned, we're all men of sound judgment and deep scholarship here; we can talk frankly about bedrock issues. Does your patient suffer from hyperspasm, Doctor?

It was an appeal to reason, and they're always dangerous. You can't trust reason. We threw it out of the ad profession long ago and have never missed it.

Well, there were obviously two ways to do it. I could go to the front office and put the finger on Herrera. I'd get a little publicity maybe; they'd listen to me, maybe; they *might* believe enough of what I told them to check. I seemed to recall that denouncers of Consies were sometimes brainburned on the sensible grounds that they had been exposed to the virus and that it might work out later, after the first healthy reaction. That wasn't good. Riskier but more heroic: I could bore from within, playing along with the Consies. If they were the world-wide net they claimed to be, there was no reason why I shouldn't wind up in New York, ready and able to blow the lid off them.

Not for a moment did I have any doubts about being able to get ahead. My fingers itched for a pencil to mark up that contact sheet, sharpening the phrases, cutting out the dullness, inserting see-hear-taste-feel words with real shock. It could use it.

The door of the booth sprang open; my ten minutes were up. I hastily flushed the contact sheet down the drain and went out into the day room. Herrera was still in the trance before the set.

I waited some twenty minutes. Finally he shook himself, blinked, and looked around. He saw me, and his face was immobile granite. I smiled and nodded, and he came over. "All right, *compañero?*" he asked quietly.

"All right," I said. "Any time you say, Gus."

"It will be soon," he said. "Always after a thing like that I plug in for some trance. I cannot stand the suspense of waiting to find out. Some day I come up out of trance and find the bulls are beating hell out of me, eh?" He began to sleek the edge of his slicer with the pocket hone.

I looked at it with new understanding. "For the bulls?" I asked.

His face was shocked. "No," he said. "You have the wrong idea a little, Jorge. For me. So I have no chance to rat."

His words were noble, even in such a cause. I hated the twisted minds who had done such a thing to a fine consumer like Gus. It was something like murder. He could have played his part in the world, buying and using and making work and profits for his brothers all around the globe, ever increasing his wants and needs, ever increasing everybody's work and profits in the circle of consumption, raising children to be consumers in turn. It hurt to see him perverted into a sterile zealot.

I resolved to do what I could for him when I blew off the lid. The fault did not lie with him. It was the people who had soured him on the world who should pay. Surely there must be some sort of remedial treatment for Consies like Gus who were only dupes. I would ask—no; it would be better not to ask. People would jump to conclusions. I could hear them now: "I don't say Mitch isn't sound, but it was a pretty farfetched idea." "Yeah. Once a Consie, always a Consie." "Everybody knows that. I don't say Mitch isn't sound, mind you, but—"

The hell with Herrera. He could take his chances like everybody else. Anybody who sets out to turn the world upside down has no right to complain if he gets caught in its gears.

nine

· · ◆ · ·

Days went by like weeks. Herrera talked little to me, until one evening in the dayroom he suddenly asked: "You ever see *Gallina?*" That was Chicken Little. I said no. "Come on down, then, I can get you in. She's a sight."

We walked through corridors and leaped for the descending cargo net. I resolutely shut my eyes. You look straight down that thing and you get the high-shy horrors. Forty, Thirty, Twenty, Ten, Zero, Minus Ten—

"Jump off, Jorge," Herrera said. "Below Minus Ten is the machinery." I jumped.

Minus Ten was gloomy and sweated water from its concrete walls. The roof was supported by immense beams. A tangle of pipes jammed the corridor where we got off. "Nutrient fluid," Herrera said.

I asked about the apparently immense weight of the ceiling. "Concrete and lead. It shields cosmic rays. Sometimes a *Gallina* goes cancer." He spat. "No good to eat for people. You got to burn it all if you don't catch it real fast and—" He swung his glittering slicer in a screaming arc to show me what he meat by "catch."

He swung open a door. "This is her nest," he said proudly. I looked and gulped.

It was a great concrete dome, concrete-floored. Chicken Little filled most of it. She was a gray-brown, rubbery hemisphere some fifteen yards in diameter. Dozens of pipes ran into her pulsating flesh. You could see that she was alive.

Herrera said to me: "All day I walk around her. I see a part growing fast, it looks good and tender, I slice." His two-handed blade screamed again. This time it shaved off an inch-thick Chicken Little steak. "Crumbs behind me hook it away and cut it up and put it on the conveyor." There were tunnel openings spotted around the circumference of the dome, with idle conveyor belts visible in them.

"Doesn't she grow at night?"

"No. They turn down the nutrient just enough; they let the waste accumulate in her just right. Each night she almost dies. Each morning she comes to life like San Lázaro. But nobody ever pray before *pobrecita Gallina,* hey?" He whacked the rubbery thing affectionately with the flat of his slicer.

"You like her," I said inanely.

"Sure, Jorge. She does tricks for me." He looked around and then marched the circuit of the nest, peering into each of the tunnel mouths. Then he took a short beam from one of them and casually braced it against the door to the nest. It fitted against a cross-bar on the door and against a seemingly-random groove in the concrete floor. It would do very well as a lock.

"I'll show you the trick," he said, with an Aztec grin. With a magician's elaborate gesture he took from his pocket a sort of whistle. It didn't have a mouthpiece. It had an air tank fed by a small hand pump. "I didn't make this," he hastened to assure me. "They call it Galton's whistle, but who this Galton is I don't know. Watch—and listen."

He began working the pump, pointing the whistle purposefully at Chicken Little. I heard no sound, but I shuddered as the rubbery protoplasm bulged in away from the pipe in the hemispherical depression.

"Don't be scared, *compañero,*" he told me. "Just follow." He pumped harder and passed me a flashlight which I stupidly turned on. Herrera played the soundless blast of the whistle against Chicken Little like a hose. She reacted with a bigger and bigger cavity that finally became an archway whose floor was the concrete floor of the nest.

Herrera walked into the archway, saying: "Follow." I did, my heart pounding frightfully. He inched forward, pumping the whistle, and the archway became a dome. The entrance into Chicken Little behind us became smaller . . . smaller . . . smaller . . .

We were quite inside, in a hemispherical bubble moving slowly through a hundred-ton lump of gray-brown, rubbery flesh. "Light on the floor, *compañero,"* he said, and I flashed it on the floor. The concrete was marked with lines that looked accidental, but which guided Herrera's feet. We inched forward, and I wondered vividly what would happen if the Galton whistle sprang a leak . . .

After about two thousand years of inch-by-inch progress my light flashed on a crescent of metal. Herrera piped the bubble over it, and it became a disk. Still pumping, he stamped three times on it. It flipped open like a manhole. "You first," he said, and I dived into it, not knowing or caring whether the landing would be hard or soft. It was soft, and I lay there, shuddering. A moment later Herrera landed beside me and the manhole above clapped shut. He stood up, massaging his arm. "Hard work," he said. "I pump and pump that thing and I don't hear it. Some day it's going to stop working and I won't know the difference until—" He grinned again.

"George Groby," Herrera introduced me. "This is Ronnie Bowen." He was a short, phlegmatic consumer in a front-office suit. "And this is Arturo Denzer." Denzer was very young and nervous.

The place was a well-lighted little office, all concrete, with air regenerators. There were desks and communication equipment. It was hard to believe that the only way to get in was barred by that mountain of protoplasm above. It was harder to believe that the squeak of inaudibly high-frequency sound waves could goad that insensate hulk into moving aside.

Bowen took over. "Pleased to have you with us, Groby," he said. "Herrera says you have brains. We don't go in a great deal for red tape, but I want your profile."

I gave him Groby's profile and he took it down. His mouth tightened with suspicion as I told him the low educational level. "I'll be frank," he said. "You don't talk like an uneducated man."

"You know how some kids are," I said. "I spent my time reading and viewing. It's tough being right in the middle of a family of five. You aren't old enough to be respected and you aren't young enough to be the pet. I felt kind of lost and I kept trying to better myself."

He accepted it. "Fair enough. Now, what can you do?"

"Well . . . I think I can write a better contact sheet than you use."

"Indeed. What else?"

"Well, propaganda generally. You could start stories going

around and people wouldn't know they were from the Co—from us. Things to make them feel discontented and wake them up."

"That's a very interesting idea. Give me an example."

My brain was chugging nicely. "Start a rumor going around the mess hall that they've got a way of making new protein. Say it tastes exactly like roast beef and you'll be able to buy it at a dollar a pound. Say it's going to be announced in three days. Then when the three days are up and there's no announcement start a wisecrack going. Like: 'What's the difference between roast beef and Chicken Little?' Answer, 'A hundred and fifty years of progress.' Something like that catches on and it'll make them think about the old days favorably."

It was easy. It wasn't the first time I'd turned my talent to backing a product I didn't care for personally.

Bowen was taking it down on a silenced typewriter. "Good," he said. "Very ingenious, Groby. We'll try that. Why do you say 'three days'?"

I couldn't very well tell him that three days was the optimum priming period for a closed social circuit to be triggered with a catalytic cue-phrase, which was the book answer. I said instead, with embarrassment: "It just seemed about right to me."

"Well, we'll try it at that. Now, Groby, you're going to have a study period. We've got the classic conservationist texts, and you should read them. We've got special publications of interest to us which you should follow: *Statistical Abstracts, Journal of Space Flight, Biometrika, Agricultural Bulletin,* and lots more. If you run into tough going, and I expect you will, ask for help. Eventually you should pick a subject to which you're attracted and specialize in it, with an eye to research. An informed conservationist is an effective conservationist."

"Why the *Journal of Space Flight?*" I asked, with a growing excitement. Suddenly there seemed to be an answer: Runstead's sabotage, my kidnaping, the infinite delays and breakdowns in the project. Were they Consie plots? Could the Consies, in their depraved, illogical minds, have decided that space travel was antisurvival, or whatever you call it?

"Very important," said Bowen. "You need to know all you can about it."

I probed. "You mean so we can louse it up?"

"Of course not!" Bowen exploded. "Good God, Groby, think what Venus means to us—an unspoiled planet, all the wealth the race needs, all the fields and food and raw materials. Use your head, man!"

"Oh," I said. The Gordian knot remained unslashed.

I curled up with the reels of *Biometrika* and every once in a while asked for an explanation which I didn't need. *Biometrika* was one of the everyday tools of a copysmith. It told the story of population changes, IQ changes, death rate and causes of death, and all the rest of it. Almost every issue had good news in it for us—the same news that these Consies tut-tutted over. Increase of population was always good news to us. More people, more sales. Decrease of IQ was always good news to us. Less brains, more sales. But these eccentrically oriented fanatics couldn't see it that way, and I had to pretend to go along with them.

I switched to the *Journal of Space Flight* after a while. There the news was bad—*all* bad. There was public apathy; there was sullen resistance to the shortages that the Venus rocket construction entailed; there was defeatism about planting a Venus colony at all; there was doubt that the colony could do anything if it ever did get planted.

That damned Runstead!

But the worst news of all was on the cover of the latest issue. The cutline said: "Jack O'Shea Grins As Pretty Friend Congratulates With Kiss After President Awards Medal Of Honor." The pretty friend was my wife Kathy. She never looked lovelier.

I got behind the Consie cell and pushed. In three days there was a kind of bubbling discontent about the mess hall chow. In a week the consumers were saying things like: "I wish to hell I was born a hundred years ago . . . I wish to hell this dorm wasn't so God-damned crowded . . . I wish to hell I could get out on a piece of land somewheres and work for myself."

The minute cell was elated. Apparently I had done more in a week than they had done in a year. Bowen—he was in Personnel—told me: "We need a head like yours, Groby. You're not going to sweat your life away as a scum-skimmer. One of these days the assignment boss will ask you if you know nutrient chemistry. Tell him yes. I'll give you a quickie course in everything you need to know. We'll get you out of the hot sun yet."

It happened in another week, when everybody was saying things like: "Be nice to walk in a forest some day. Can y'imagine all those trees they useta have?" and: "God-damn salt-water soap!" when it had never before occurred to them to think of it as "salt-water soap." The assignment boss came up to me and duly said: "Groby! You know any nutrient chemistry?"

"Funny you should ask," I told him. "I've studied it quite a bit. I know the sulfur-phosphorus-carbon-oxygen-hydrogen-nitrogen ratios for chlorella, I know the optimum temperatures and stuff like that."

Obviously this little was much more than he knew. He grunted, "Yeah?" and went away, impressed.

A week later everybody was telling a dirty joke about the Starrzelius Verily trust and I was transferred to an eight-hour job inside the pylon, reading gauges and twisting valves that controlled the nutrient flow to the tanks of chlorella. It was lighter and easier work. I spent my time under Chicken Little—I could pass through her with a Galton whistle almost without cringing—rewriting the Consies' fantastically inept Contact Sheet One:

CAN YOU QUALIFY FOR *TOP-LEVEL* PROMOTION?

You and *only you* can answer these important questions:

Are you an intelligent, forward-looking man or woman between the ages of 14 and 50—Do you have the drive and ambition needed to handle the really BIG JOBS tomorrow will bring—Can you be trusted—*absolutely trusted*—with the biggest, hopefulest news of our time? If you can't stand up and shout YES! to *every one* of these questions, please read no further!

But if you *can*, then you and your friends or family can get in on the *ground floor* of. . . .

And so on. Bowen was staggered. "You don't think that appeal to upper-level IQs limits it too much, do you?" he asked anxiously. I didn't tell him that the only difference between that and the standard come-on for Class 12 laborers was that the Class 12s got it aurally—they couldn't read. I said I didn't think so. He nodded. "You're a natural-born copysmith, Groby," he told me solemnly. "In a Conservationist America, you'd be star class." I was properly modest. He went on, "I can't hog you; I've got to pass you on to a higher echelon. It isn't right to waste your talents in a cell. I've forwarded a report on you—" he gestured at the communicator, "and I expect you'll be requisitioned. It's only right. But I hate to see you go. However, I'm pulling the strings already. Here's the Chlorella Purchasers' Handbook . . ."

My heart bounded. I knew that Chlorella contracted for raw materials with a number of outlets in New York City.

"Thanks," I mumbled. "I want to serve wherever I best can."

"I know you do, Groby," he soothed. "Uh—say, one thing before you go. This isn't official, George, but—well, I do a little writing too. I've got some of my things here—sketches, I guess you'd call them—and I'd appreciate it a lot if you'd take them along and . . ."

I finally got out with the handbook, and only fourteen of Bowen's "sketches." They were churlish little scraps of writing, with no sell in them at all that I could see. Bowen assured me he had lots more that he and I could work on.

I hit that handbook hard.

Twisting valves left me feeling more alive at the end of a day than scum-skimming, and Bowen made sure my Consie labors were as light as possible—to free me for work on his "sketches." The result was that, for the first time, I had leisure to explore my milieu. Herrera took me into town with him once, and I discovered what he did with those unmentioned weekends. The knowledge shocked, but did not disgust me. If anything, it reminded me that the gap between executive and consumer could not be bridged by anything as abstract and unreal as "friendship."

Stepping out of the old-fashioned pneumatic tube into a misty Costa Rican drizzle, we stopped first at a third-rate restaurant for a meal. Herrera insisted on getting us each a potato, and insisted on being allowed to pay for it—"No, Jorge, you call it a celebration. You let me go on living after I gave you the contact sheet, no? So we celebrate." Herrera was brilliant through the meal, a fountain of conversation and bilingual badinage with me and the waiters. The sparkle in his eye, the rapid, compulsive flow of speech, the easy, unnecessary laughter were like nothing so much as the gaiety of a young man on a date.

A young man on a date. I remembered my first meeting with Kathy, that long afternoon at Central Park, strolling hand in hand down the dim-lit corridors, the dance hall, the eternal hour we stood outside her door. . . .

Herrera reached over and pounded me on the shoulder, and I

saw that he and the waiter were laughing. I laughed too, defensively, and their laughter doubled; evidently the joke had been on me. "Never mind, Jorge," said Herrera, sobering, "we go now. You will like what I have for us to do next, I think." He paid the check, and the waiter raised an eyebrow.

"In back?"

"In back," said Herrera. "Come, Jorge."

We threaded our way between the counters, the waiter leading the way. He opened a door and hissed something rapid and Spanish to Herrera. "Oh, don't worry," Herrera told him. "We will not be long."

"In back," turned out to be—a library.

I was conscious of Herrera's eyes on me, and I don't think I showed any of what I felt. I even stayed with him for an hour or so, while he devoured a wormy copy of something called *Moby Dick* and I glanced through half a dozen ancient magazines. Some of those remembered classics went a long way toward easing my conscience —there was actually an early "Do You Make These Common Mistakes in English?" and a very fine "Not a Cough in a Carload" that would have looked well on the wall of my office, back in Schocken Tower. But I could not relax in the presence of so many books without a word of advertising in any of them. I am not a prude about solitary pleasures when they serve a useful purpose. But my tolerance has limits.

Herrera knew, I think, that I lied when I told him I had a headache. When, much later, he came stumbling into the dorm I turned my head away. We scarcely spoke after that.

A week later, after a near-riot in the mess hall—sparked by a rumor that the yeast fritters were adulterated with sawdust—I was summoned to the front office.

A veep for Personnel saw me after I had waited an hour. "Groby?"

"Yes, Mr. Milo."

"Remarkable record you've made. Quite remarkable. I see your efficiency rating is straight fours."

That was Bowen's work. He kept records. He had taken five years to worm himself into that very spot. "Thank you, Mr. Milo."

"Welcome, I'm sure. We, uh, happen to have a vacancy approaching. One of our people up North. I see his work is falling off badly."

Not his work—the ghost of his work; the shadow on paper of his work; the shadow carefully outlined and filled in by Bowen. I began to appreciate the disproportionate power that Consies could wield.

"Do you happen to have any interest in purchasing, Groby?"

"It's odd that you should ask, Mr. Milo," I said evenly. "I've always had a feel for it. I think I'd make good in purchasing."

He looked at me skeptically; it was a pretty standard answer. He began firing questions and I respectfully regurgitated answers from the Chlorella manual. He had memorized it twenty-odd years ago, and I had memorized it only a week ago. He was no match for me. After an hour he was convinced that George Groby was the only hope of Chlorella Protein, and that I should be hurled into the breach forthwith.

That night I told the cell about it.

"It means New York," Bowen said positively. "It means New York." I couldn't keep back a great sigh. Kathy, I thought. He went on, heedlessly: "I've got to tell you some special things now. To begin with—the recognition signals."

I learned the recognition signals. There was a hand sign for short range. There was a grand hailing sign of distress for medium range. For long range there was a newspaper-ad code; quite a good one. He made me practice the signs and memorize the code cold. It took us into the small hours of the morning. When we left through Chicken Little I realized that I hadn't seen Herrera all day. I asked as we emerged what had happened.

"He broke," Bowen said simply.

I didn't say anything. It was a kind of shorthand talk among Consies. "Soandso broke." That meant: "Soandso toiled for years and years in the cause of the W.C.A. He gave up his nickels and dimes and the few pleasures they could buy him. He didn't marry and he didn't sleep with women because it would have imperiled security. He became possessed by doubts so secret that he didn't admit them to himself or us. The doubts and fears mounted. He was torn too many ways and he turned on himself and died."

"Herrera broke," I said stupidly.

"Don't brood about it," Bowen said sharply. "You're going North. You've got a job to do."

Indeed I had.

ten

· ·◆· ·

I went to New York City almost respectably, in a cheap front-office suit, aboard a tourist rocket, steerage class. Above me the respectable Costa Rican consumers oohed and ahed at the view from the prism windows or anxiously counted their pennies, wondering how far they'd take them in the pleasures for sale by the colossus of the North.

Below decks we were a shabbier, tougher gang, but it was no labor freighter. We had no windows, but we had lights and vending machines and buckets. A plant protection man had made a little speech to us before we loaded: "You crumbs are going North, out of Costa Rican jurisdiction. You're going to better jobs. But don't forget that they are *jobs.* I want each and every one of you to remember that you're in hock to Chlorella and that Chlorella's claim on you is a prior lien. If any of you think you can break your contract, you're going to find out just how fast and slick extradition for a commercial offense can be. And if any of you think you can just disappear, try it. Chlorella pays Burns Detective Agency seven billion a year, and Burns delivers the goods. So if you crumbs want to give us a little easy exercise, go ahead; we'll be waiting for you. Is everything clear?" Everything was clear. "All right, crumbs. Get aboard and good luck. You have your assignment tickets. Give my regards to Broadway."

We slid into a landing at Montauk without incident. Down below, we sat and waited while the consumers on tourist deck filed out, carrying their baggage kits. Then we sat and waited while Food Customs inspectors, wearing the red-and-white A&P arm bands, argued vociferously with our stewards over the surplus rations—

four of us had died on the trip, and the stewards, of course, had held out their Chicken Little cutlets to sell in the black market. Then we sat and waited.

Finally the order came to fall out in fifties. We lined up and had our wrists stamped with our entry permits; marched by squads to the subway; and entrained for the city. I had a bit of luck. My group drew a freight compartment.

At the Labor Exchange we were sorted out and tagged for our respective assignments. There was a bit of a scare when it came out that Chlorella had sold the contracts on twenty of us to I. G. Farben —nobody wants to work in the uranium mines—but I wasn't worried. The man next to me stared moodily as the guards cut out the unlucky twenty and herded them off. "Treat us like slaves," he said bitterly, plucking at my sleeve. "It's a crime. Don't you think so, Mac? It violates the essential dignity of labor."

I gave him an angry glare. The man was a Consie, pure and simple. Then I remembered that I was a Consie too, for the time being. I considered the use of the handclasp, and decided against it. He would be worth remembering if I needed help; but if I revealed myself prematurely he might call on *me*.

We moved on to the Chlorella depot in the Nyack suburbs.

Waste not, want not. Under New York, as under every city in the world, the sewage drains led to a series of settling basins and traps. I knew, as any citizen knows, how the organic waste of twenty-three million persons came water-borne through the venous tracery of the city's drains; how the salts were neutralized through ion-exchange, the residual liquid piped to the kelp farms in Long Island Sound, the sludge that remained pumped into tank barges for shipment to Chlorella. I knew about it, but I had never seen it.

My title was Procurement Expeditor, Class 9. My job was coupling the flexible hoses that handled the sludge. After the first day, I shot a week's pay on soot-extractor plugs for my nostrils; they didn't filter out all the odor, but they made it possible to live in it.

On the third day I came off shift and hit the showers. I had figured it out in advance: after six hours at the tanks, where no vending machines were for the simple reason that no one could conceivably eat, drink, or smoke *anything* in the atmosphere, the pent-up cravings of the crew kept them on the Popsie-Crunchie-Starrs cycle for half an hour before the first man even thought of a shower. By sternly repressing the craving, weaker in me than in most because it had had less time to become established, I managed to have the showers almost alone. When the mob arrived, I hit the vending machines. It was a simple application of intelligence, and if that doesn't bear out the essential difference between consumer and copysmith mentality, what does? Of course, as I say, the habits weren't as strong in me.

There was one other man in the shower, but, with only two of us, we hardly touched. He handed me the soap as I came in; I lathered and let the water roar down over me under the full pressure of the recirculators. I was hardly aware he was there. But, as I passed the soap back to him, I felt his third finger touch my wrist, the index finger circle around the base of my thumb.

"Oh," I said stupidly, and returned the handclasp. "Are you my con—"

"Ssh!" he hissed. He gestured irritatedly to the Muzak spymike dangling from the ceiling. He turned his back on me and meticulously soaped himself again.

When he returned the soap a scrap of paper clung to it. In the locker room I squeezed it dry and spread it out. It read: "Tonight is pass night. Go to the Metropolitan Museum of Art, Classics Room. Be in front of the Maidenform exhibit at exactly five minutes before closing time."

I joined the queue at the supervisor's desk as soon as I was dressed. In less than half an hour I had a stamped pass authorizing me to skip bedcheck for the night. I returned to my bunk to pick up my belongings, warned the new occupant of the bed about the sleep-talking of the man in the tier above, turned in my bag to the supply room, and caught the shuttle down to Bronxville. I transferred to a north-bound local, rode one station, switched to the south-bound side, and got out at Schocken Tower. No one appeared to be following me. I hadn't expected anyone to, but it never pays to take chances.

My Consie rendezvous at the Met was almost four hours off. I stood around in the lobby until a cop, contemptuously eyeing my cheap clothing, moved toward me. I had hoped Hester or perhaps even Fowler Schocken himself might come through; no such luck. I saw a good many faces I recognized, of course, but none I was sure I could trust. And, until I found out what lay behind the double cross on Starrzelius Glacier, I had no intention of telling just anybody that I was still alive.

The Pinkerton boomed, "You want to give the Schocken people your business, crumb? You got a big account for them, maybe?"

"Sorry," I said, and headed for the street door. It didn't figure that he would bother to follow me through the crowd in the lobby; he didn't. I dodged around the recreation room, where a group of consumers were watching a PregNot light love story on the screen and getting their samples of Coffiest, and ducked into the service elevators. "Eightieth," I said to the operator, and at once realized I had blundered. The operator's voice said sharply through the speaker grille:

"Service elevators go only to the seventieth floor, you in Car Five. What do you want?"

"Messenger," I lied miserably. "I got to make a pickup from Mr. Schocken's office. I *told* them I wouldn't be let in to Mr. Schocken's office, a fellow like me. I told them, 'Look, he's probably got twenty-five seckataries I got to go through before they let me see him,' I said—"

"The mail room is on forty-five," the operator said, a shade less sharply. "Stand in front of the door so I can see you."

I moved into range of the ike. I didn't want to, but I couldn't see any way out. I thought I heard a sound from the grille, but there was no way of being sure. I had never been in the elevator operators' room, a thousand feet below me, where they pushed the buttons that sent the cars up and down the toothed shafts; I would have given a year's pay to have been able to look into it then.

I stood there for half a minute. Then the operator's voice said noncommittally. "All right, you. Back in the car. Forty-fifth floor, first slide to the left."

The others in the car stared at me through an incurious haze of Coffiest's alkaloids until I got out. I stepped on the leftbound slidewalk and went past the door marked "Mail Room," to the corridor juncture where my slidewalk dipped down around its roller. It took me a little while to find the stairway, but that was all right. I needed the time to catch up on my swearing. I didn't dare use the elevators again.

Have you ever climbed thirty-five flights of stairs?

Toward the end the going got pretty bad. It wasn't just that I was aching from toe to navel, or that I was wasting time, of which I had none too much anyway. It was getting on toward ten o'clock, and the consumers whose living quarters were on the stairs were beginning to drift there for the night. I was as careful as I could be, but it nearly came to a fist fight on the seventy-fourth, where the man on the third step had longer legs than I thought.

Fortunately, there were no sleepers above the seventy-eighth; I was in executive country.

I skulked along the corridors, very conscious of the fact that the first person who paid any attention to me would either recognize me or throw me out. Only clerks were in the corridors, and none I'd known at all well; my luck was running strong.

But not strong enough. Fowler Schocken's office was locked.

I ducked into the office of his secretary[3], which was deserted, and thought things over. Fowler usually played a few holes of golf at the country club after work. It was pretty late for him still to be there, but I thought I might as well take the chance—it was only four more flights to the club.

I made it standing up. The country club is a handsome layout, which is only fair because the dues are handsome too. Besides the golf links, the tennis court and the other sports facilities, the whole north end of the room is woods—more than a dozen beautifully simulated trees—and there are at least twenty recreation booths for reading, watching movies, or any other spectator pleasure.

A mixed foursome was playing golf. I moved close to their seats as unobtrusively as possible. They were intent on their dials and buttons, guiding their players along the twelfth hole fairway. I read their scores from the telltale with a sinking heart; all were in the high nineties. Duffers. Fowler Schocken averaged under eighty for the course. He couldn't be in a group like that, and as I came close I saw that both the men were strangers to me.

I hesitated before retreating, trying to decide what to do next. Schocken wasn't in sight anywhere in the club. Conceivably he was in one of the recreation booths, but I could scarcely open the doors of all of them to see; I'd be thrown out the first time I blundered into an occupied one, unless God smiled and the occupant was Fowler.

A babble of conversation from the golfers caught my ear. One of the girls had just sunk a four-inch putt to finish the hole; smiling happily as the others complimented her, she leaned forward to pull the lever that brought the puppet players back to the tee and changed the layout to the dogleg of the thirteenth hole, and I caught a glimpse of her face. It was Hester, my secretary.

That made it simple. I couldn't quite guess how Hester came to be in the country club, but I knew everything else there was to know about Hester. I retreated to an alcove near the entrance to the ladies' room; it was only about a ten-minute wait before she showed up.

She fainted, of course. I swore and carried her into the alcove. There was a couch; I put her on it. There was a door; I closed it.

She blinked up at me as consciousness came back. "Mitch," she said, in a tone between a whisper and a shriek.

"I am not dead," I told her. "Somebody else died, and they switched bodies. I don't know who 'they' are; but I'm not dead. Yes, it's really me. Mitch Courtenay, your boss. I can prove it. For instance, remember last year's Christmas party, when you were so worried about—"

"Never mind," she said hastily. "My God, Mitch—I mean, Mr. Courtenay—"

"Mitch is good enough," I said. I dropped the hand I had been massaging, and she pushed herself up to get a better look at me. "Listen," I said, "I'm alive, all right, but I'm in a kind of peculiar foul-up. I've got to get in touch with Fowler Schocken. Can you fix it —right away?"

"Uh." She swallowed and reached for a cigarette, recovering. I automatically took out a Starr. "Uh, no, Mitch. Mr. Schocken's on the Moon. It's a big secret, but I guess I can tell *you* about it. It's something to do with the Venus project. After you got killed—well, you know what I mean—after that, when he put Mr. Runstead on the project and it began to slip so, he decided to take matters into his own hands. I gave him all your notes. One of them said something about the Moon, I guess; anyway, he took off a couple of days ago."

"Hell," I said. "Well, who'd he leave in charge here? Harvey Bruner? Can you reach—"

Hester was shaking her head. "No, not Mr. Bruner, Mitch. Mr. Runstead's in charge. Mr. Schocken switched in such a hurry, there wasn't anyone to spare to take over *his* job except Mr. Runstead. But I can call him right away."

"*No,*" I said. I looked at my watch, and groaned. I would have just about time to make it to the Met. "Look," I said. "I've got to leave. Don't say anything to *anybody*, will you? I'll figure something out, and I'll call you. Let's see, when I call I'll say I'm—what's the name of that doctor of your mother's?—Dr. Gallant. And I'll arrange to meet you and tell you what we're going to do. I can count on you, Hester, can't I?"

"Sure, Mitch," she said breathlessly.

"Fine," I said. "Now you'll have to convoy me down in the elevator. I haven't got time to walk, and there'll be trouble if a guy like me gets caught on the club floor." I stopped and looked her over. "Speaking of which," I said, "what in the world are you doing here?"

Hester blushed. "Oh, you know how it is," she said unhappily. "After you were gone there weren't any other secretarial jobs; the rest of the executives had their girls, and I just couldn't be a consumer again, Mitch, not with the bills and all. And—well, there was this opening up here, you see. . . ."

"Oh," I said. I hope nothing showed on my face; God knows I tried. Damn you to hell, Runstead, I said to myself, thinking of Hester's mother and Hester's young man that she'd maybe been going to marry some day, and the absolute stinking injustice of a man like Runstead taking the law into his own hands and wrecking executive lives—mine—and staff lives—Hester's—and dragging them down to the level of consumers.

"Don't worry, Hester," I said gently. "I'll owe you something for this. And believe me, you won't have to remind me. I'll make everything up to you." And I knew how to do it, too. Quite a lot of the girls on the ZZ contract manage to avoid the automatic renewal and downgrading. It would cost a lot for me to buy out her contract before the year was up, so that was out of the question; but some of the girls do pretty well with single executives after their first year. And I was important enough so that if I made a suggestion to some branch head or bureau chief, he would not be likely to ignore it, or even to treat her badly.

I don't approve of sentiment in business matters, but as you see I'm an absolute sucker for it in any personal relationship.

Hester insisted on lending me some money, so I made it to the Met with time to spare by taking a cab. Even though I had paid the driver in advance, he could not refrain from making a nasty comment about high-living consumers as I got out; if I hadn't had more important things on my mind I would have taught him a lesson then and there.

I have always had a fondness for the Met. I don't go much for religion—partly, I suppose, because it's a Taunton account—but there is a grave, ennobling air about the grand old masterpieces in the Met that gives me a feeling of peace and reverence. I mentioned that I was a little ahead of time. I spent those minutes standing silently before the bust of G. Washington Hill, and I felt more relaxed than I had since that first afternoon at the South Pole.

At precisely five minutes before midnight I was standing before the big, late-period Maidenform—number thirty-five in the catalogue: "I Dreamed I Was Ice-Fishing in My Maidenform Bra"—when I became conscious of someone whistling in the corridor behind me. The notes were irrelevant; the cadence formed one of the recognition signals I'd learned in the hidey-hole under Chicken Little.

One of the guards was strolling away. She looked over her shoulder at me and smiled.

To all external appearances, it was a casual pickup. We linked arms, and I felt the coded pressure of her fingers on my wrist: "D-O-N-T T-A-L-K W-H-E-N I L-E-A-V-E Y-O-U G-O T-O T-H-E B-A-C-K O-F T-H-E R-O-O-M S-I-T D-O-W-N A-N-D W-A-I-T."

I nodded. She took me to a plastic-finished door, pushed it open, pointed inside. I went in alone.

There were ten or fifteen consumers sitting in straight-back chairs, facing an elderly consumer with a lectorial goatee. I found a seat in the back of the room and sat in it. No one paid any particular attention to me.

The lecturer was covering the high spots of some particularly boring precommercial period. I listened with half my mind, trying to catch some point of similarity in the varying types around me. All were Consies, I was reasonably sure—else why would I be here? But the basic stigmata, the surface mark of the lurking fanatic inside, that should have been apparent, escaped me. They were all consumers, with the pinched look that soyaburgers and Yeasties inevitably give; but I could have passed any of them in the street without a second glance. Yet—this was New York, and Bowen had spoken of it as though the Consies I'd meet here were pretty high up in the scale, the Trotskys and Tom Paines of the movement.

And that was a consideration too. When I got out of this mess—

when I got through to Fowler Schocken and cleared up my status—I might be in a position to break up this whole filthy conspiracy, if I played my cards right. I looked over the persons in the room a little more attentively, memorizing their features. I didn't want to fail to recognize them, next time we came in contact.

There must have been some sort of signal, but I missed it. The lecturer stopped almost in midsentence, and a plump little man with a goatee stood up from the first row. "All right," he said in an ordinary tone, "we're all here and there's no sense wasting any more time. We're against waste; that's why we're here." He stepped on the little titter. "No noise," he warned, "and no names. For the purpose of this meeting we'll use numbers; you can call me 'One,' you 'Two'—" he pointed to the man in the next seat, "and so on by rows to the back of the room. All clear? Okay, now listen closely. We've got you together because you're all new here. You're in the big leagues now. This is world operational headquarters, right here in New York; you can't go any higher. Each of you was picked for some special quality—you know what they are. You'll all get assignments right here, tonight. But before you do, I want to point out one thing. You don't know me and I don't know you; every one of you got a big buildup from your last cells, but sometimes the men in the field get a little too enthusiastic. If they were wrong about you . . . Well, you understand these things, eh?"

There was a general nod. I nodded too, but I paid particular attention to memorizing that plump little goatee. One by one numbers were called, and one by one the new-johns got up, conferred briefly with the goatee, and left, in couples and threes, for unannounced destinations. I was almost the last to be called; besides me, only a very young girl with orange hair and a cast in her eye was still in the room.

"Okay, you two," said the man with the goatee. "You two are going to be a team, so you might as well know names. Groby, meet Corwin. Groby's a kind of copysmith. Celia's an artist."

"Okay," she said, lighting a Starr from the butt of another in a flare of phosphorus. A perfect consumer type if only she hadn't been corrupted by these zealots; I noticed her jaws working on gum even while she chain-smoked.

"We'll get along fine," I said approvingly.

"You sure will," said the man in the goatee. "You have to. You understand these things, Groby. In order to give you a chance to show your stuff, we'll have to let you know a lot of stuff that we don't want to read in the morning paper. If you don't work out for us, Groby," he said pleasantly, "you see the fix we're in; we'll have to make some other arrangements for you." He tapped a little bottle of colorless fluid on the desk top. The tinny rattle of the aluminum top was no tinnier than my voice as I said, "Yes, sir," because I knew what little bottles of colorless fluid could reasonably be assumed to contain.

It turned out, though, that it wasn't much of a problem. I spent three difficult hours in that little room, then I pointed out that if I didn't get back to barracks I would miss the morning work call and there would be hell to pay. So they excused me.

But I missed work call anyhow. I came out of the Museum into a perfect spring dawn, feeling, all in all, pretty content with life. A figure loomed out of the smog and peered into my face. I recognized the sneering face of the taxi-runner who had brought me to the Museum. He said briskly, "Hel-lo, Mr. Courtenay," and then the obelisk from behind the Museum, or something very much like it, smacked me across the back of the neck.

eleven

· · ◆ · ·

"—Awake in a few minutes," I heard somebody say.

"Is he ready for Hedy?"

"Good God, no!"

"I was only asking."

"You ought to know better. First you give them amphetamine, plasma, maybe a niacin megaunit. *Then* they're ready for Hedy. She doesn't like it if they keep blacking out. She sulks."

Nervous laugh with a chill in it.

I opened my eyes and said: "Thank God!" For what I could see was a cerebral-gray ceiling, the shade you find only in the brain room of an advertising agency. I was safe in the arms of Fowler Schocken Associates—or was I? I didn't recognize the face that leaned over me.

"Why so pleased, Courtenay?" the face inquired. "Don't you know where you are?"

After that it was easy to guess. "Taunton's," I croaked.

"That is correct."

I tried my arms and legs and found they didn't respond. I couldn't tell whether it was drugs or a plasticocoon. "Look," I said steadily. "I don't know what you people think you're doing, but I advise you to stop it. Apparently this is a kidnaping for business purposes. You people are either going to let me go or kill me. If you kill me without a Notification you'll get the *cerebrin,* so of course you won't kill me. You're going to let me go eventually, so I suggest that you do it now."

"Kill you, Courtenay?" asked the face with mocking wonder.

"How would we do that? You're dead already. Everybody knows that. You died on Starrzelius Glacier; don't you remember?"

I struggled again, without results. "They'll brainburn you," I said. "Are you people crazy? Who wants to be brainburned?"

The face said nonchalantly: "You'd be surprised." And in an aside to somebody else: "Tell Hedy he'll be ready soon." Hands did something, there was a click, and I was helped to sit up. The skin-tight pulling at my joints told me it was a plasticocoon and that I might as well save my strength. There was no point to struggling.

A buzzer buzzed and I was told sharply: "Keep a respectful tongue in your head, Courtenay. Mr. Taunton's coming in."

B. J. Taunton lurched in, drunk. He looked just the way I had always seen him from afar at the speakers' table in hundreds of banquets: florid, gross, overdressed—and drunk.

He surveyed me, feet planted wide apart, hands on his hips, and swaying just a little. "Courtenay," he said. "Too bad. You might have turned out to be something if you hadn't cast your lot with that swindling son of a bitch Schocken. Too bad."

He was drunk, he was a disgrace to the profession, and he was responsible for crime after crime, but I couldn't keep my respect for an entrepreneur out of my voice. "Sir," I said evenly, "there must be some misunderstanding. There's been no provocation of Taunton Associates to commercial murder—has there?"

"Nope," he said, tight-lipped and swaying slightly. "Not as the law considers it provocation. All that bastard Schocken did was steal my groundwork, take over my Senators, suborn my committee witnesses, and *steal Venus from me!*" His voice had risen to an abrupt shriek. In a normal voice he continued: "No; no provocation. He's carefully refrained from killing any of my people. Shrewd Schocken; ethical Schocken; damned-fool Schocken!" he crooned.

His glassy eyes glared at me: "You bastard!" he said. "Of all the low-down, lousy, unethical, cheap-jack stunts ever pulled on me, yours was the rottenest. *I—*"he thumped his chest, briefly threatening his balance. "*I* figured out a way to commit a safe commercial murder, and you played possum like a scared yellow rat. You ran like a rabbit, you dog."

"Sir," I said desperately, "I'm sure I don't know what you're driving at." His years of boozing, I thought briefly, had finally caught up with him. The words he was uttering could only come from a wet brain.

He sat down unconcernedly; one of his men darted in and there was a chair seat to meet his broad rump in the nick of time. With an expansive gesture B. J. Taunton said to me: "Courtenay, I am essentially an artist."

The words popped out of me automatically: "Of course, Mr.—" I almost said "Schocken." It was a well-conditioned reflex. "Of course, Mr. Taunton," I said.

"Essentially," he brooded, "essentially an artist. A dreamer of dreams; a weaver of visions." It gave me an uncanny sense of double vision. I seemed to see Fowler Schocken sitting there instead of his rival, the man who stood against everything that Fowler Schocken stood for. "I wanted Venus, Courtenay, and I shall have it. Schocken stole it from me, and I am going to repossess it. Fowler Schocken's management of the Venus project will stink to high heaven. No rocket under Schocken's management is ever going to get off the ground, if I have to corrupt every one of his underlings and kill every one of his section heads. For I am essentially an artist."

"Mr. Taunton," I said steadily, "you can't kill section heads as casually as all that. You'll be brainburned. They'll give you *cerebrin*. You can't find anybody who'll take the risk for you. Nobody wants twenty years in hell."

He said dreamily: "I got a mechanic to drop that 'copter pod on you, didn't I? I got an unemployable bum to plug at you through your apartment window, didn't I? Unfortunately both missed. And then you crossed us up with that cowardly run-out on the glacier."

I didn't say anything. The run-out on the glacier had been no idea of mine. God only knew whose idea it had been to have Runstead club me, shanghai me, and leave a substitute corpse in my place.

"You almost escaped," Taunton mused. "If it hadn't been for a few humble, loyal servants—a taxi-runner, a few others—we never would have had you back. But I have my tools, Courtenay.

"They might be better, they might be worse, but it's my destiny to dream dreams and weave visions. The greatness of an artist is in his simplicity, Courtenay. You say to me: 'Nobody wants to be brainburned.' That is because you are mediocre. *I* say: '*Find* somebody who wants to be brainburned and *use* him.' That is because I am great."

"Wants to be brainburned," I repeated stupidly. "Wants to be brainburned."

"Explain," said Taunton to one aide. "I want him thoroughly convinced that we are in earnest."

One of his men told me dryly: "It's a matter of population, Courtenay. Have you ever heard of Albert Fish?"

"No."

"He was a phenomenon of the dawn; the earliest days of the Age of Reason—1920 or thereabouts. Albert Fish stuck needles into himself, burned himself with alcohol-saturated wads of cotton, flogged himself—he *liked* it. He would have liked brainburning, I'll wager. It would have been twenty delightful subjective years of being flayed, suffocated, choked, and nauseated. It would have been Albert Fish's dream come true.

"There was only one Albert Fish in his day. Pressures and strains of a very high order are required to produce an Albert Fish. It would be unreasonable to expect more than one to be produced out of the small and scattered population of the period—less than three billion. With our vastly larger current population there are many Albert Fishes wandering around. You only have to find them. Our matchless research facilities here at Taunton have unearthed several. They turn up at hospitals, sometimes in very grotesque shape. They are eager would-be killers; they want the delights of punishment. A man like you says we can't hire killers because they'd be afraid of being punished. But Mr. Taunton, now, says we *can* hire a killer if we find one who *likes* being punished. And the best part of it all is, the ones who like to get hurt are the ones who just love hurting others. Hurting, for instance—you."

It had a bloodcurdlingly truthful ring to it. Our generation must be inured to wonder. The chronicles of fantastic heroism and abysmal wickedness that crowd our newscasts—I knew from research that they didn't have such courage or such depravity in the old days. The fact had puzzled me. We have such people as Malone, who quietly dug his tunnels for six years and then one Sunday morning blew up Red Bank, New Jersey. A Brink's traffic cop had got him sore. Conversely we have James Revere, hero of the *White Cloud* disaster. A shy, frail tourist-class steward, he had rescued on his own shoulders seventy-six passengers, returning again and again into the flames with his flesh charring from his bones, blind, groping his way along red-hot bulkheads with his hand-stumps. It was true. When there are *enough* people, you will always find somebody who can and will be any given thing. Taunton *was* an artist. He had grasped this broad and simple truth and used it. It meant that I was as good as dead. *Kathy,* I thought. *My Kathy.*

Taunton's thick voice broke in on my reflections. "You grasp the pattern?" he asked. "The big picture? The theme, the message, what I might call the essential juice of it is that I'm going to repossess Venus. Now, beginning at the beginning, tell us about the Schocken Agency. All its little secrets, its little weaknesses, its ins and outs, its corruptible employees, its appropriations, its Washington contacts—*you* know."

I was a dead man with nothing to lose—I thought. "No," I said.

One of Taunton's men said abruptly: "He's ready for Hedy," got up and went out.

Taunton said: "You've studied prehistory, Courtenay. You may recognize the name of Gilles de Rais." I did, and felt a tightness over my scalp, like a steel helmet slowly shrinking. "All the generations of prehistory added up to an estimated five billion population," Taunton rambled. "All the generations of prehistory produced only one Gilles de Rais, whom you perhaps think of as Bluebeard. Nowadays we have our pick of several. Out of all the people I might have picked to handle special work like that for me I picked Hedy. You'll see why."

The door opened and a pale, adenoidal girl with lank blond hair was standing in it. She had a silly grin on her face; her lips were thin and bloodless. In one hand she held a six-inch needle set in a plastic handle.

I looked into her eyes and began screaming. I couldn't stop screaming until they led her away and closed the door again. I was broken.

"Taunton," I whispered at last. "Please . . ."

He leaned back comfortably and said: "Give."

I tried, but I couldn't. My voice wouldn't work right and neither would my memory. I couldn't remember whether my firm was Fowler Schocken or Schocken Fowler, for instance.

Taunton got up at last and said: "We'll put you on ice for a while, Courtenay, so you can pull yourself together. I need a drink myself." He shuddered involuntarily, and then beamed again. "Sleep on it," he said, and left unsteadily.

Two of his men carted me from the brain room, down a corridor and into a bare cubbyhole with a very solid door. It seemed to be night in executives' country. Nothing was going on in any of the offices we passed, lights were low, and a single corridor guard was yawning at his desk.

I asked unsteadily: "Will you take the cocoon off me? I'm going to be a filthy mess if I don't get out of it."

"No orders about it," one of them said briefly, and they slammed the solid door and locked it. I flopped around the small floor trying to find something sharp enough to break the film and give me an even chance of bursting the plastic, but there was nothing. After incredible contortions and a dozen jarring falls I found that I could never get to my feet. The doorknob had offered a very, very faint ghost of hope, but it might as well have been a million miles away.

Mitchell Courtenay, copysmith. Mitchell Courtenay, key man of the Venus section. Mitchell Courtenay, destroyer-to-be of the Consies. Mitchell Courtenay flopping on the floor of a cell in the offices of the sleaziest, crookedest agency that ever blemished the profession, without any prospect except betrayal and—with luck—a merciful death. Kathy at least would never know. She would think I had died like a fool on the glacier, meddling with the power pack when I had no business to . . .

The lock of the door rattled and rattled. They were coming for me.

But when the door opened I saw from the floor not a forest of trousered legs but a single pair of matchstick ankles, nylon-clad.

"I love you," said the strange, dead voice of a woman. "They said I would have to wait, but I couldn't wait." It was Hedy. She had her needle.

I tried to cry for help, but my chest seemed paralyzed as she knelt beside me with shining eyes. The temperature of the room seemed to drop ten degrees. She clamped her bloodless lips on mine; they were like heated iron. And then I thought the left side of my face and head were being torn off. It lasted for seconds and blended into a red haze and unconsciousness.

"Wake up," the dead voice was saying. "I want you. Wake up." Lightning smashed at my right elbow, and I cried out and jerked my arm. My arm moved—

It moved.

The bloodless lips descended on mine again, and again her needle ran into my jaw, probing exactly for the great lump of the trigeminal facial nerve, and finding it. I fought the red haze that was trying to swallow me up. My arm had moved. She had perforated the membrane of the cocoon, and it could be burst. The needle searched again and somehow the pain was channeled to my right arm. In one convulsive jerk it was free.

I think I took the back of her neck in my hand and squeezed. I am not sure. I do not want to be sure. But after five minutes she and her love did not matter. I ripped and stripped the plastic from me and got to my feet an inch at a time, moaning from stiffness.

The corridor guard could not matter any more. If he had not come at my cries he would never come. I walked from the room and saw the guard apparently sleeping face-down on his desk. As I stood over him I saw a very little blood and serum puddled and coagulating in the small valley between the two cords of his shrunken old neck. One thrust transfixing the medulla had been enough for Hedy. I could testify that her knowledge of the nervous system's topography was complete.

The guard wore a gun that I hesitated over for a moment and then rejected. In his pockets were a few dollars that would be more useful. I hurried on to the ladders. His desk clock said 0605.

I knew already about climbing up stairs. I learned then about climbing down stairs. If your heart's in good shape there's little to choose between them. It took me an estimated thirty minutes in my condition to get down the ladders of executives' country and onto the populated stairs below. The first sullen stirrings of the workbound consumers were well under way. I passed half a dozen bitter fist fights and one cutting scrape. The Taunton Building nightdwellers were a low, dirty lot who would never have been allowed stairspace in the Schocken Tower, but it was all to the good. I attracted no attention whatsoever in my filthy clothes and sporting a fresh stab wound in my face. Some of the bachelor girls even whistled, but that was all. The kind of people you have in the ancient, run-down slum buildings like R.C.A. and Empire State would have pulled me down if I'd taken their eye.

My timing was good. I left the building lobby in the very core of a cheek-by-jowl mob boiling out the door to the shuttle which would take them to their wretched jobs. I thought I saw hardguys in plain clothes searching the mob from second-floor windows, but I didn't look up and I got into the shuttle station.

At the change booth I broke all my bills and went in the washroom. "Split a shower, bud?" somebody asked me. I wanted a shower terribly, and by myself, but I didn't dare betray any white-collar traits. She and I pooled our coins for a five-minute salt, thirty-second fresh, with soap. I found that I was scrubbing my right hand over and over again. I found that when the cold water hit the left side of my face the pain was dizzying.

After the shower I wedged myself into the shuttle and spent two hours zigzagging under the city. My last stop was Times Square, in the heart of the market district. It was mostly a freight station. While cursing consumers hurled crates of protein ticketed for various parts of town onto the belts I tried to phone Kathy again. Again there was nobody home.

I got Hester at the Schocken Tower. I told her: "I want you to raise every cent you can, borrow, clean our your savings, buy a Starrzelius apparel outfit for me, and meet me with it soonest at the place where your mother broke her leg two years ago. The exact place, remember?"

"Mitch," she said. "Yes, I remember. But my contract—"

"Don't make me beg you, Hester," I pleaded. "Trust me. I'll see you through. For God's sake, hurry. And—if you get here and I'm in the hands of the guards, don't recognize me. Now, into action."

I hung up and slumped in the phone booth until the next party hammered indignantly on the door. I walked slowly around the station, had Coffiest and a cheese sandwich, and rented a morning paper at the newsstand. The story about me was a bored little item on page three out of a possible four: SOUGHT FOR CB & FEMICIDE. It said George Groby had failed to return from a pass to his job with Chlorella and had used his free time to burglarize executives' country in the Taunton Building. He had killed a secretary who stumbled on him and made his escape.

Hester met me half an hour later by the loading chute from which a crate had once whizzed to break her mother's leg. She looked frantically worried; technically she was as guilty of contract breach as "George Groby."

I took the garment box from her and asked: "Do you have fifteen hundred dollars left?"

"Just about. My mother was frantic—"

"Get us reservations on the next Moon ship; today if possible. Meet me back here; I'll be wearing the new clothes."

"Us? The Moon?" she squeaked.

"Yes; us. I've got to get off the Earth before I'm killed. And this time it'll be for keeps."

twelve

· · ◆ · ·

My little Hester squared her shoulders and proceeded to work miracles.

In ten hours we were grunting side by side under the take-off acceleration of the Moon ship *David Ricardo*. She had cold-bloodedly passed herself off as a Schocken employee on special detail to the Moon and me as Groby, a sales analyst 6. Naturally the dragnet for Groby, expediter 9, had not included the Astoria spaceport. Sewage workers on the lam from CB and femicide wouldn't have the money to hop a rocket, of course.

We rated a compartment and the max ration. The *David Ricardo* was so constructed that most passengers rated compartments and max rations. It wasn't a trip for the idly curious or the submerged fifteen sixteenths of the population. The Moon was strictly business —mining business—and some sight-seeing. Our fellow-passengers, what we saw of them at the ramp, were preoccupied engineers, a few laborers in the minute steerage, and silly-rich men and women who wanted to say they'd been there.

After take-off, Hester was hysterically gay for a while, and then snapped. She sobbed on my shoulder, frightened at the enormity of what she'd done. She'd been brought up in a deeply moral, sales-fearing home, and you couldn't expect her to commit the high commercial crime of breaking a labor contract without there being a terrific emotional lashback.

She wailed: "Mr. Courtenay—Mitch—if only I could be *sure* it was all right! I know you've always been good to me and I know you wouldn't do anything wrong, but I'm so scared and miserable!"

I dried her eyes and made a decision.

"I'll tell you what it's all about, Hester," I said. "You be the judge. Taunton has discovered something very terrible. He's found out that there are people who are not deterred by the threat of *cerebrin* as the punishment for an unprovoked commercial murder. He thinks Mr. Schocken grabbed the Venus project from him unethically, and he'll stop at nothing to get it back. He's tried twice at least to kill me. I thought Mr. Runstead was one of his agents, assigned to bitch up Schocken's handling of the Venus account. Now, I don't know. Mr. Runstead clubbed me when I went after him at the South Pole, spirited me away to a labor freighter under a faked identity, and left a substitute body for mine. And," I said cautiously, "there are Consies in it."

She uttered a small shriek.

"I don't know how they dovetail," I said. "But I was in a Consie cell—"

"Mis-ter *Courtenay!*"

"Strictly as a blind," I hastily explained. "I was stuck in Chlorella Costa Rica and the only way north seemed to be through the Consie network. They had a cell in the factory, I joined up, turned on the talent, and got transferred to New York. The rest you know."

She paused for a long time and asked: "Are you sure it's all right?"

Wishing desperately that it were, I firmly said: "Of course, Hester."

She gave me a game smile. "I'll get our rations," she said, unsnapping herself. "You'd better stay here."

Forty hours out I said to Hester: "The blasted blackmarketing steward is going too far! Look at this!" I held up my bulb of water and my ration box. The seal had clearly been tampered with on both containers, and visibly there was water missing. "Max rations," I went on oratorically, "are supposed to be tamper-proof, but this is plain burglary. How do yours look?"

"Same thing," she said listlessly. "You can't do anything about it. Let's not eat just yet, Mr. Courtenay." She made a marked effort to be vivacious. "Tennis, anyone?"

"All right," I grumbled, and set up the field, borrowed from the ship recreation closet. She was better at tennis than I, but I took her in straight sets. Her co-ordination was 'way off. She'd stab for a right forecourt deep cross-court return and like as not miss the button entirely—if she didn't send the ball into the net by failing to surge power with her left hand on the rheostat. A half hour of the exercise seemed to do both of us good. She cheered up and ate her rations and I had mine.

The tennis match before meals became a tradition. There was little enough to do in our cramped quarters. Every eight hours she would go for our tagged rations, I would grumble about the shortage and tampering, we'd have some tennis, and then eat. The rest of the time passed somehow, watching the ads come and go—all Schocken—on the walls. Well enough, I thought. Schocken's on the Moon and I won't be kept from him there. Things weren't so crowded. Moon to Schocken to Kathy—a twinge of feeling. I could have asked casually what Hester had heard about Jack O'Shea, but I didn't. I was afraid I might not like what she might have heard about the midget hero and his triumphal procession from city to city and woman to woman.

A drab service announcement at last interrupted the parade of ads: COOKS TO THE GALLEY (the *David Ricardo* was a British ship) FOR FINAL LIQUID FEEDING. THIS IS H-8 AND NO FURTHER SOLID OR LIQUID FOOD SHOULD BE CONSUMED UNTIL TOUCHDOWN.

Hester smiled and went out with our tray.

As usual it was ten minutes before she returned. We were getting some minor course corrections, enough to unsettle my stomach. I burped miserably while waiting.

She came back with two Coffiest bulbs and reproached me gaily: "Why, Mitch, you haven't set up the tennis court!"

"Didn't feel like it. Let's eat." I put out my hand for my bulb. She didn't give it to me. "Well?"

"Just one set?" she coaxed.

"Hell, girl, you heard me," I snapped. "Let's not forget who's who around here." I wouldn't have said it if it hadn't been Coffiest, I suppose. The Starrzelius-red bulb kicked things off in me—nagging ghosts of withdrawal symptoms. I'd been off the stuff for a long time, but you never kick Coffiest.

She stiffened. "I'm sorry, Mr. Courtenay." And then she clutched violently at her middle, her face distorted. Astounded, I grabbed her. She was deathly pale and limp; she moaned with pain.

"Hester," I said, "what is it? What—?"

"Don't drink it," she croaked, her hand kneading her belly. "The

Coffiest. Poison. Your rations. I've been tasting them." Her nails tore first the nylon of her midriff and then her skin as she clawed at the pain.

"Send a doctor!" I was yelling into the compartment mike. "Woman's dying here!"

The chief steward's voice answered me: "Right away, sir. Ship's doctor'll be there right away."

Hester's contorted face began to relax, frightening me terribly. She said softly: "Bitch Kathy. Running out on you. Mitch and bitch. Funny. You're too good for her. *She* wouldn't have. My life. Yours." There was another spasm across her face. "Wife versus secretary. A laugh. It always was a laugh. You never even kissed me—"

I didn't get a chance to. She was gone, and the ship's doctor was hauling himself briskly in along the handline. His face fell. We towed her to the lazarette and he put her in a cardiac-node exciter that started her heart going again. Her chest began to rise and fall and she opened her eyes.

"Where—are—you?" asked the doctor, loudly and clearly. She moved her head slightly, and a pulse of hope shot through me.

"Response?" I whispered to the doctor.

"Random," he said with professional coldness. He was right. There were more slight head movements and a nervous flutter of the eyelids, which were working independently. He kept trying with questions. "Who—are—you?" brought a wrinkle between her eyes, and a tremor of the lip, but no more. Except for a minute, ambiguous residue, she was gone.

Gently enough, the doctor began to explain to me: "I'm going to turn it off. You mustn't think there's any hope left. Evidently irreversible clinical death has occurred. It's often hard for a person with emotional ties to believe—"

I watched her eyelids flutter, one with a two-four beat, the other with a three-four beat. "Turn it off," I said hoarsely. By "it" I meant Hester and not the machine. He cut the current and withdrew the needle.

"There was nausea?" he asked. I nodded. "Her first space flight?" I nodded. "Abdominal pain?" I nodded. "No previous distress?" I shook my head. "History of vertigo?" I nodded, though I didn't know. He was driving at something. He kept asking, and the answers he wanted were as obvious as a magician's forced card. Allergies, easy bleeding, headaches, painful menses, afternoon fatigue—at last he said decisively: "I believe it's Fleischman's Disease. We don't know much about it. It stems from some derangement of function in the adrenocorticotropic bodies under free flight, we think. It kicks off a chain reaction of tissue-incompatibilities which affects the cerebrospinal fluid—"

He looked at me and his tone changed. "I have some alcohol in the locker," he said. "Would you like—"

I reached for the bulb and then remembered. "Have one with me," I said.

He nodded and, with no stalling, drank from one of the nipples of a twin-valve social flask. I saw his Adam's apple work. "Not too much," he cautioned me. "Touchdown's soon."

I stalled with conversation for a few minutes, watching him, and then swallowed half a pint of hundred proof. I could hardly tow myself back to the compartment.

Hangover, grief, fear, and the maddening red tape of Moon debarkation. I must have acted pretty stupidly. A couple of times I heard crewmen say to port officials something like: "Take it easy on the guy. He lost his girl in flight."

The line I took in the cramped receiving room of the endless questionnaires was that I didn't know anything about the mission. I was Groby, a 6, and the best thing to do would be to send me to Fowler Schocken. I understood that we had been supposed to report to him. They pooh-poohed that possibility and set me to wait on a bench while queries were sent to the Schocken branch in Luna City.

I waited and watched and tried to think. It wasn't easy. The busy crowds in Receiving were made up of people going from one place to another place to do specified things. I didn't fit in the pattern; I was a sore thumb. They were going to get me . . .

A tube popped and blinked at the desk yards away. I read between half-closed eyes: S-C-H-O-C-K-E-N T-O R-E-C-E-I-V-I-N-G R-E Q-U-E-R-Y N-O M-I-S-S-I-O-N D-U-E T-H-I-S F-L-I-G-H-T N-O G-R-O-B-Y E-M-P-L-O-Y-E-D B-Y U-S F-O-W-L-E-R S-C-H-O-C-K-E-N U-N-Q-U-E-R-I-E-D B-U-T I-M-P-O-S-S-I-B-L-E A-N-Y U-N-D-E-R S-T-A-R-C-L-A-S-S P-E-R-S-O-N-N-E-L A-S-S-I-G-N-E-D R-E-P-O-R-T H-I-M A-C-T D-I-S-C-R-E-T-I-O-N O-B-V-I-O-U-S-L-Y N-O-T O-U-R B-A-B-Y E-N-D.

End indeed. They were glancing at me from the desk, and talking in low tones. In only a moment they would be beckoning the Burns Detective guards standing here and there.

I got up from the bench and sauntered into the crowd, with only one alternative left and that a frightening one. I made the casual gestures that, by their order and timing, constitute the Grand Hailing Sign of Distress of the Consies.

A Burns guard shouldered his way through the crowd and put the arm on me. "Are you going to make trouble?" he demanded.

"No," I said thickly. "Lead the way."

He waved confidently at the desk and they waved back, with grins. He marched me, with his nightstick in the small of my back, through the startled crowd. Numbly I let him take me from the receiving dome down a tunnel-like shopping street.

SOUVENIRS OF LUNA

CHEAPEST IN TOWN

YE TAYSTEE GOODIE SHOPPE ON YE MOONE

YOUR HOMETOWN PAPER

MOONSUITS RENTED

"50 YEARS WITHOUT A BLOWOUT"

RELIABLE MOONSUIT RENTAL CO.

"73 YEARS WITHOUT A BLOWOUT"

MOONMAID FASHIONS

STUNNING CONVERSATION PIECES

PROVE YOU WERE HERE

Warren Astron, D.P.S.

Readings by Appointment Only

blinked and twinkled at me from the shopfronts as new arrivals sauntered up and down, gaping.

"Hold it," growled the guard. We stopped in front of the *Warren Astron* sign. He muttered: "Twist the nightstick away from me. Hit me a good lick over the head with it. Fire one charge at the streetlight. Duck into Astron's and give him the grip. Good luck—and try not to break my skull."

"You're—you're—" I stammered.

"Yeah," he said wryly. "I wish I hadn't seen the hailing sign. This is going to cost me two stripes and a raise. Get moving."

I did. He surrendered the nightstick, and I tried not to make it too easy or too hard when I clouted him. The buckshot charge boomed out of the stick's muzzle, shattered the light overhead, and brought forth shrieks of dismay from the strollers. It was thunderous in the vaulted street. I darted through the chaste white Adam door of Astron's in the sudden darkness and blinked at a tall, thin man with a goatee.

"What's the meaning of this?" he demanded. "I read by appointment—" I took his arm in the grip. "Refuge?" he asked, abruptly shedding a fussy professional manner.

"Yes. Fast."

He led me through his parlor into a small, high observatory with a transparent dome, a refracting telescope, Hindu star maps, clocks and desks. One of these desks he heaved on mightily, and it turned back on hinges. There was a pit and handholds. "Down you go," he said.

Down I went, into darkness.

It was some six feet deep and six by four in area. It had a rough, unfinished feel to it. There was a pick and shovel leaning against one wall, and a couple of buckets filled with moonrock. Obviously a work in progress.

I inverted one of the buckets and sat on it in the dark. After five hundred and seventy-six counted pulse-beats I sat on the floor and stopped counting. After that got too rugged I tried to brush moonrock out of the way and lie down. After going through this cycle five times I heard voices directly overhead. One was the fussy, professional voice of Astron. The other was the globby, petulant voice of a fat woman. They seemed to be seated at the desk which sealed my hidey-hole.

"—really seems excessive, my dear doctor."

"As Madam wishes. If you will excuse me, I shall return to my ephemeris—"

"But Dr. Astron, I wasn't implying—"

"Madam will forgive me for jumping to the conclusion that she was unwilling to grant me my customary honorarium . . . that is correct. Now, please, the birth date and hour?"

She mumbled them, and I wondered briefly about the problem Astron must have with women who shaded their years.

"So . . . Venus in the house of Mars . . . Mercury ascendant in the trine . . ."

"What's that?" she asked with shrill suspicion. "I know quite a bit about the Great Art and I never heard that before."

Blandly: "Madam must realize that a Moon observatory makes possible many things of which she has never heard before. It is possible by lunar observation to refine the Great Art to a point unattainable in the days when observations were made perforce through the thick and muddled air of Earth."

"Oh—oh, of course. I've heard that, of course. Please go on, Dr. Astron. Will I be able to look through your telescope and see my planets?"

"Later, madam. So . . . Mercury ascendant in the trine, the planet of strife and chicanery, yet quartered with Jupiter, the giver of fortune, so . . ."

The "reading" lasted perhaps half an hour, and there were two more like it that followed, and then there was silence. I actually dozed off until a voice called me. The desk had been heaved back again and Astron's head was silhouetted against the rectangular opening. "Come on out," he said. "It's safe for twelve hours."

I climbed out stiffly and noted that the observatory dome had been opaqued.

"You're Groby," he stated.

"Yes," I said, dead-pan.

"We got a report on you by courier aboard the *Ricardo*. God knows what you're up to; it's too much for me." I noticed that his hand was in his pocket. "You turn up in Chlorella, you're a natural-born copysmith, you're transferred to New York, you get kidnaped in front of the Met—in earnest or by prearrangement—you kill a girl and disappear—and now you're on the Moon. God knows what you're up to. It's too much for me. A Central Committee member will be here shortly to try and figure you out. Is there anything you'd care to say? Like confessing that you're an *agent provocateur*? Or subject to manic-depressive psychosis?"

I said nothing.

"Very well," he said. Somewhere a door opened and closed. "That will be she," he told me.

And my wife Kathy walked into the observatory.

thirteen

· · ◆ · ·

"Mitch," she said dazedly. "My God, Mitch." She laughed, with a note of hysteria. "You wouldn't wait, would you? You wouldn't stay on ice."

The astrologer took the gun out of his pocket and asked her: "Is there—?"

"No, Warren. It's all right. I know him. You can leave us alone. Please."

He left us alone. Kathy dropped into a chair, trembling. I couldn't move. My wife was a kingpin Consie. I had thought I'd known her, and I'd been wrong. She had lied to me continuously and I had never known it.

"Aren't you going to say anything?" I asked flatly.

She visibly took hold of herself. "Shocked?" she asked. "You, a star-class copysmith consorting with a Consie? Afraid it'll get out and do you no good businesswise?" She forced a mocking smile that broke down as I looked at her. "Damn it," she flared, "all I ever asked from you after I came to my senses was for you to get out of my life and stay out. The biggest mistake I ever made was keeping Taunton from killing you."

"You had Runstead shanghai me?"

"Like a fool. What in God's name are you doing here? What are these wild-man stunts of yours? Why can't you leave me alone?" She was screaming by then.

Kathy a Consie. Runstead a Consie. Deciding what was best for poor Mitch and doing it. Taunton deciding what was best for poor Mitch and doing it. Moving me this way and that across the chessboard.

"Pawn queens," I said, and picked her up and slapped her. The staring intensity left her eyes and she looked merely surprised. "Get what's-his-name in here," I said.

"Mitch, what are you up to?" She sounded like herself.

"Get him in here."

"You can't order me—"

"You!" I yelled. "The witch-doctor!"

He came running, right into my fist. Kathy was on my back, a clawing wildcat, as I went through his pockets. I found the gun—a wicked .25 UHV machine pistol—and shoved her to the floor. She looked up at me in astonishment, mechanically rubbing a bruised hip. "You're a mean son of a bitch," she said wonderingly.

"All of a sudden," I agreed. "Does Fowler Schocken know you're on the Moon?"

"No," she said, rubbing her thumb and forefinger together.

"You're lying."

"My little lie-detector," she crooned jeeringly. "My little fire-eating copysmith—"

"Level with me," I said, "or you get this thing across the face."

"Good God," she said. "You mean it." She put her hand to her face slowly, looking at the gun.

"I'm glad that's settled. Does Fowler Schocken know you're on the Moon?"

"Not exactly," she said, still watching the gun. "He did advise me to make the trip—to help me get over my bereavement."

"Call him. Get him here."

She didn't say anything or move to the phone.

"Listen," I said. "This is Groby talking. Groby's been slugged, knifed, robbed, and kidnaped. He saw the only friend he had in the world poisoned a few hours ago. He's been played with by a lady sadist who knew her anatomy lessons. He killed her for it and he was glad of it. He's so deep in hock to Chlorella that he'll never get out. He's wanted for femicide and CB. The woman he thought he was in love with turned out to be a lying fanatic and a bitch. Groby has nothing to lose. I can put a burst through the dome up there and we'll all suck space. I can walk out into the street, give myself up, and tell exactly what I know. They won't believe me but they'll investigate to make sure, and sooner or later they'll get corroboration—after I've been brainburned, but that doesn't matter. I've nothing to lose."

"And," she asked flatly, "what have you got to gain?"

"Stop stalling. Call Schocken."

"Not without one more try, Mitch. One word hurt specially—
'fanatic.' There were two reasons why I begged Runstead to shanghai you. I wanted you out of the way of Taunton's killers. And I
wanted you to get a taste of the consumer's life. I thought—I don't
know. I thought you'd see how fouled-up things have become. It's
hard to see when you're star class. From the bottom it's easier to see.
I thought I'd be able to talk sense to you after we brought you back
to life, and we'd be able to work together on the only job worth
doing. So it didn't work. That damned brain of yours—so good and
so warped. All you want is to be star class again and eat and drink
and sleep a little better than anybody else. It's too bad you're not a
fanatic too. Same old Mitch. Well, I tried.

"Go ahead and do whatever you think you have to do. Don't fret
about it hurting me. It's not going to hurt worse than the nights we
used to spend screaming at each other. Or the times I was out on
Consie business and couldn't tell you and had to watch you being
jealous. Or shipping you to Chlorella to try and make you a whole
sane man in spite of what copysmithing's done to you. Or never
being able to love you all the way, never being able to give myself to
you entirely, mind or body, because there was this secret. I've been
hurt. Pistol-whipping's a joke compared to the way I've been hurt."

There was a pause that seemed to go on forever.

"Call Schocken," I said unsteadily. "Tell him to come here.
Then get out and take the stargazer with you. I—I don't know what
I'm going to tell him. But I'm going to give you and your friends a
couple of days' grace. Time to change headquarters and hailing
signs and the rest of your insane rigmarole. Call Schocken and get
out of here. I don't ever want to see you again."

I couldn't read the look on her face as she picked up the phone
and punched a number.

"Mr. Schocken's sec³, please," she said. "This is Dr. Nevin—
widow of Mr. Courtenay. You'll find me on the through list, I believe
. . . thank you. Mr. Schocken's sec², please. This is Dr. Nevin, Mr.
Courtenay's widow. May I speak to Mr. Schocken's secretary? I'm
listed . . . thank you . . . Hello, Miss Grice; this is Dr. Nevin. May
I speak to Mr. Schocken? . . . Certainly . . . thank you . . ." She
turned to me and said: "I'll have to wait a few moments." They
passed in silence, and then she said: "Hello, Mr. Schocken . . .

Well, thank you. I wonder if you could come and see me about a matter of importance . . . business *and* personal . . . the sooner the better, I'm afraid . . . Shopping One, off Receiving—Dr. Astron's . . . no, nothing like that. It's just a convenient meeting place. Thank you very much, Mr. Schocken."

I wrenched the phone from her and heard Fowler Schocken's voice say: "Quite all right, my dear. The mystery is intriguing. Good-by." *Click.* She was quite clever enough to have faked a one-sided conversation, but had not. The voice was unmistakable. The memories it brought back of Board mornings with their brilliance of dialectic interplay, hard and satisfying hours of work climaxed with a "Well done!" and shrewd guidance through the intricacies of the calling overwhelmed me with nostalgia. I was almost home.

Silently and efficiently Kathy was shouldering the stargazer's limp body. Without a word she walked from the observatory. A door opened and closed.

The hell with her. . . .

It was minutes before there was a jovial halloo in the voice of Fowler Schocken: "Kathy! Anybody home?"

"In here," I called.

Two of our Brink's men and Fowler Schocken came in. His face went mottled purple. "Where's—" he began. And then: "You look like—*you are! Mitch!*" He grabbed me and waltzed me hilariously around the circular room while the guards dropped their jaws. "What kind of a trick was that to play on an old man? What's the story, boy? Where's Kathy?" He stopped, puffing even under moon-weight.

"I've been doing some undercover work," I said. "I'm afraid I've got myself into some trouble. Would you call for more guards? We may have to stand off Luna City Inc.'s Burns men." Our Brink's men, who took an artisan's pride in their work, grinned happily at the thought.

"Sure, Mitch. Get it done," he said sidewise to the sergeant, who went happily to the phone. "Now what's all this about?"

"For the present," I said, "let's say it's been a field trip that went sour. Let's say I downgraded myself temporarily and voluntarily to assess Venus Section sentiment among the consumers—and I got stuck. Fowler, please let me beg off any more details. I'm in a bad way. Hungry, tired, scared, dirty."

"All right, Mitch. You know my policy. Find a good horse, give

him his head, and back him to the limit. You've never let me down—
and God knows I'm glad to see you around again. Venus Section can
use you. Nothing's going right. The indices are down to 3.77 com-
posite for North America when they should be 4.0 and rising. And
turnover? God! I'm here recruiting, you know: a little raid on Luna
City Inc., Moonmines, and the other outfits for some space-sea-
soned executives."

It was good to be home. "Who's heading it up?" I asked.

"I am. We rotated a few Board men through the spot and there
wasn't any pickup. In spite of my other jobs I had to take over Venus
Section direct. *Am* I glad to see you!"

"Runstead?"

"He's vice-ing for me, poor man. What's this jam you're in with
the guards? Where's Kathy?"

"Please, later . . . I'm wanted for femicide and CB on Earth.
Here I'm a suspicious character without clearance. Also I resisted
arrest, clouted a guard, and damaged Luna City property."

He looked grave. "You know, I don't like the sound of CB," he
said. "I assume there was a flaw in the contract?"

"Several," I assured him.

He brightened. "Then we'll pay off the fines on the rest of the
stuff and fight the CB clear up to the Chamber of Commerce if we
have to. What firm?"

"Chlorella Costa Rica."

"Hmmm. Middling-sized, but solid. Excellent people, all of
them. A pleasure to do business with."

Not from the bottom up, I thought, and said nothing.

"I'm sure they'll be reasonable. And if they aren't, I have a
majority of the C of C in my pocket anyway. I ought to get something for my retainers, eh?" He dug me slyly in the ribs. His relief at
getting Venus Section off his neck was overwhelming.

A dozen of our Brink's boys churned in. "That should do it,"
Fowler Schocken beamed. "Lieutenant, the Luna City Inc. Burns
people may try to take Mr. Courtenay here away from us. We don't
want that to happen, do we?"

"No, sir," said the lieutenant, dead-pan.

"Then let's go."

We strolled down Shopping One, amazing a few night-owl tourists. Shopping One gave way to Residential One, Two, and Three,
and then to Commercial One.

"Hey, you!" a stray Burns patrolman called. We were in somewhat open order. Evidently he didn't realize that the Brink's men were my escort.

"Go play with your marbles, Punchy," a sergeant told him.

He went pale, but beeped his alarm, and went down in a tangle of fists and boots.

Burns patrolmen came bounding along the tunnel-like street in grotesque strides. Faces appeared in doorways. Our detail's weapons-squad leader said: "*Hup!*" and his boys began to produce barrels, legs, belts of ammo, and actions from their uniforms. Snap-snap-snap-snap, and there were two machine guns mounted on the right tripod ready to rake both ends of the street. The Burns men braked grotesquely yards from us and stood unhappily, swinging their nightsticks.

Our lieutenant called out: "What seems to be the trouble, gentlemen?"

A Burns man called back: "Is that man George Groby?"

"Are you George Groby?" the lieutenant asked me.

"No. I'm Mitchell Courtenay."

"You hear him," the lieutenant called. The weapons men full-cocked their guns at a signal from the squad leader. The two clicks echoed from the vaulting, and the few last-ditch rubber-necks hanging from the doors vanished.

"Oh," said the Burns man weakly. "That's all right then. You can go ahead." He turned on the rest of the patrolmen. "Well? What are you dummies waiting for? Didn't you hear me?" They beat it, and we moved on down Commercial One, with the weapons men cradling their guns. The Fowler Schocken Associates Luna City Branch was 75 Commercial One, and we went in whistling. The weapons men mounted their guns in the lobby.

It was a fantastic performance. I had never seen its like. Fowler Schocken explained it as he led me down into the heart of the agency. "It's frontier stuff, Mitch. Something you've got to get into your copy. 'The Equalizer' is what they call it. A man's rank doesn't mean much up here. A well-drilled weapons squad is the law topside of the stratosphere. It's getting back to the elemental things of life, where a man's a man no matter how high his Social Security number."

We passed a door. "O'Shea's room," he said. "He isn't in yet, of course. The little man's out gathering rosebuds while he may—and the time isn't going to be long. The only Venus roundtripper. We'll lick that, won't we, Mitch?"

He showed me into a cubicle and lowered the bed with his own hands. "Cork off with these," he said, producing a sheaf of notes from his breast pocket. "Just some rough jottings for you to go over. I'll send in something to eat and then Coffiest. A good hour or two of work on them, and then the sound sleep of the just, eh?"

"Yes, Mr. Schocken."

He beamed at me and left, drawing the curtain. I stared glazedly at the rough jottings. "Six-color doubletrux. Downhold unsuccessful previous flights. Cite Learoyd '29, Holden '38, McGill '46 et al heroic pioneers supreme sacrifice etc etc. *No* mention Myers-White flopperoo '51 acct visibly exploded bfr passng moon orbit. Try get M-W taken out of newssheet files & history bks? Get cost estimate. Search archives for pix LH & McG. Shd be blond brunet & redhead. Ships in backgrnd. Looming. Panting woman but heroic pioneers dedicated look in eye not interested. Piquant bcs unavlbl . . ."

Thoughtfully, there was a pencil and copypaper in the cubicle. I began to write painfully: "We were ordinary guys. We liked the earth and the good things it gave us. The morning tang of Coffiest . . . the first drag on a Starr . . . the good feel of a sharp new Verily pinstripe suit . . . a warm smile from a girl in a bright spring dress —but they weren't enough. There were far places we had to see, things we had to know. The little guy's Learoyd. I'm Holden. The redhead with the shoulders is McGill. Yes; we're dead. But we saw the far places and we learned what we had to learn before we died. Don't pity us; we did it for you. The long-hair astronomers could only guess about Venus. Poison gas, they said. Winds so hot they'd set your hair on fire and so strong they'd pick you up and throw you away. But they weren't sure. What do you do when you aren't sure? You go and see."

A guard came in with sandwiches and Coffiest. I munched and gulped with one hand and wrote with the other.

"We had good ships for those days. They packed us and enough fuel to get us there. What they didn't have was enough fuel to get us back. But don't pity us; we had to know. There was always the chance that the long-hairs were wrong, that we'd be able to get out, breathe clean air, swim in cool water—and then make fuel for the return trip with the good news. No; it didn't work out that way. It worked out that the long-hairs knew their stuff. Learoyd didn't wait to starve in his crate; he opened the hatch and breathed methane after writing up his log. My crate was lighter. The wind picked it up and broke it—and me with it. McGill had extra rations and a heavier ship. He sat and wrote for a week and then—well; it was pretty certain after two no-returns. He'd taken cyanide with him. But don't pity us. We went there and we saw it and in a way we sent back the news by not coming back ourselves. Now you folks know what to do and how to do it. You know the long-hairs weren't guessing. Venus is a mean lady and you've got to have the stuff and the know-how to tame her. She'll treat you right when you do. When you find us and our crates don't pity us. We did it for you. We knew you wouldn't let us down."

I was home again.

fourteen

· · ◆ · ·

"Please, Fowler," I said. "Tomorrow. Not today."

He gave me a steady look. "I'll go along, Mitch," he said. "I've never been a back-seat driver yet." He displayed one of the abilities that made him boss-man. He wiped clean out of his mind the burning curiosity about where I had been and what I had been doing. "That's good copy," he said, slapping my work of the previous night on his desk. "Clear it with O'Shea, won't you? He can give it some extra see-taste-smell-hear-feel if anybody can. And pack for return aboard the *Vilfredo Pareto*—I forgot. You haven't got anything to pack. Here's some scratch, and shop when you get a chance. Take a few of the boys with you, of course. The Equalizer—remember?" He twinkled at me.

I went to find O'Shea curled up like a cat in the middle of his full-sized bunk in the cubicle next to mine. The little man looked ravaged when he rolled over and stared blearily at me. "Mitch," he said thickly. " 'Nother goddam nightmare."

"Jack," I said persuasively. "Wake up, Jack."

He jerked bolt upright and glared at me. "What's the idea—? Hello, Mitch. I remember. Somebody said something when I got in 'smorning." He held his small head. "I'm dying," he said faintly. "Get me something, will you? My deathbed advice is this: don't ever be a hero. You're too nice a guy . . ."

The midget lapsed into torpor, swaying a little with each pulse-beat. I went to the kitchen and punched Coffiest, Thiamax, and a slice of Bredd. Halfway out, I returned, went to the bar, and punched two ounces of bourbon.

O'Shea looked at the tray and hiccuped. "What the hell's that stuff?" he said faintly, referring to the Coffiest, Thiamax, and Bredd. He shot down the bourbon and shuddered.

"Long time no see, Jack," I said.

"Ooh," he groaned. "Just what I needed. Why do clichés add that extra something to a hangover?" He tried to stand up to his full height of thirty-five inches and collapsed back onto the cot, his legs dangling. "My aching back," he said. "I think I'm going to enter a monastery. I'm living up to my reputation, and it's killing me by inches. Ooh, that tourist gal from Nova Scotia! It's springtime, isn't it? Do you think that explains anything? Maybe she has Eskimo blood."

"It's late fall," I said.

"Urp. Maybe she doesn't have a calendar . . . pass me that Coffiest." No "please." And no "thank you." Just a cool, take-it-for-granted that the world was his for the asking. He had changed.

"Think you can do some work this morning?" I asked, a little stiffly.

"I might," he said indifferently. "This is Schocken's party after all. Say, what the hell ever became of you?"

"I've been investigating," I said.

"Seen Kathy?" he asked. "That's a wonderful girl you have there, Mitch." His smile might have been reminiscent. All I was sure of was that I didn't like it—not at all.

"Glad you enjoyed her," I said flatly. "Drop in any time." He sputtered into his Coffiest and said, carefully setting it down: "What's that work you mentioned?"

I showed him my copy. He gulped the Thiamax and began to steady on his course as he read.

"You got it all fouled up," he said at last, scornfully. "I don't know Learoyd, Holden, and McGill from so many holes in the ground, but like hell they were selfless explorers. You don't get *pulled* to Venus. You get *pushed.*" He sat brooding, cross-legged.

"We're assuming they got pulled," I said. "If you like, we're trying to convince people that they got pulled. What we want from you is sense-impressions to sprinkle the copy with. Just talking off the front of your face, how do you resonate to it?"

"With nausea," he said, bored. "Would you reserve me a shower, Mitch? Ten minutes fresh, one hundred degrees. Damn the cost. You too can be a celebrity. All you have to do is be lucky like me." He swung his short legs over the edge of the cot and contemplated his toes, six inches clear of the floor. "Well," he sighed, "I'm getting it while the getting's good."

"What about my copy?" I asked.

"See my reports," he said. "What about my shower?"

"See your valet," I said, and went out, boiling. In my own cubicle I sweated sense-impressions into the copy for a couple of hours and then picked up a guard squad to go shopping. There were no brushes with the patrolmen. I noticed that Warren Astron's shop-front now sported a chaste sign:

> *Dr. Astron Regrets That*
> *Urgent Business*
> *Has Recalled Him to Earth on*
> *Short Notice*

I asked one of our boys: "Has the *Ricardo* left?"

"Couple hours ago, Mr. Courtenay. Next departure's the *Pareto*, tomorrow."

So I could talk.

So I told Fowler Schocken the whole story.

And Fowler Schocken didn't believe a goddamned word of it.

He was nice enough and he tried not to hurt my feelings. "Nobody's blaming you, Mitch," he said kindly. "You've been through a great strain. It happens to us all, this struggle with reality. Don't feel you're alone, my boy. We'll see this thing through. There are times in life when anybody needs—help. My analyst—"

I'm afraid I yelled at him.

"Now, now," he said, still kind and understanding. "Just to pass the time—laymen shouldn't dabble in these things, but I think I know a thing or two about it and can discuss it objectively—let me try to explain—"

"Explain *this!*" I shouted at him, thrusting my altered Social Security tattoo under his nose.

"If you wish," he said calmly. "It's part of the whole pattern of your brief—call it a holiday from reality. You've been on a psychological bender. You got away from yourself. You assumed a new identity, and you chose one as far-removed from your normal, hard-working, immensely able self as possible. You chose the lazy, easy-going life of a scum-skimmer, drowsing in the tropic sun—"

I knew then who was out of touch with reality.

"Your horrible slanders against Taunton are crystal-clear to, ah, a person with some grasp of our unconscious drives. I was pleased to hear you voice them. They meant that you're halfway back to your real self. What is our central problem—the central problem of the real Mitchell Courtenay, copysmith? Lick the opposition! Crush the competing firms! Destroy them! Your fantasy about Taunton indicates to, ah, an informed person that you're struggling back to the real Mitchell Courtenay, copysmith. Veiled in symbols, obscured by ambivalent attitudes, the Taunton-fantasy is nevertheless clear. Your imagined encounter with the girl 'Hedy' might be a textbook example!"

"God damn it," I yelled, "look at my jaw! See that hole? It still hurts!"

He just smiled and said: "Let's be glad you did nothing worse to yourself, Mitch. The id, you see—"

"What about Kathy?" I asked hoarsely. "What about the complete data on the Consies I gave you? Grips, hailing signs, passwords, meeting places?"

"Mitch," he said earnestly, "as I say, I shouldn't be meddling, but they aren't real. Sexual hostility unleashed by the dissociation of your personality into 'Groby'-Courtenay identified your wife with a hate-and-fear object, the Consies. And 'Groby' carefully arranged things so that your Consie data is uncheckable and therefore unassailable. 'Groby' arranged for you—the *real* you—to withhold the imaginary 'data' until the Consies would have had a chance to change all that. 'Groby' was acting in self-defense. Courtenay was coming back and he knew it; 'Groby' felt himself being 'squeezed out.' Very well; he can bide his time. He arranged things so that he can make a comeback—"

"I'm not insane!"

"My analyst—!"

"You've got to believe me!"

"These unconscious conflicts—"

"I tell you Taunton has killers!"

"Do you know what convinced me, Mitch?"

"What?" I asked bitterly.

"The fantasy of a Consie cell embedded in Chicken Little. The symbolism—" he flushed a little, "well, it's quite unmistakable."

I gave up except on one point: "Do people still humor the insane, Mr. Schocken?"

"You're *not* insane at all, my boy. You need—help, like a lot of—"

"I'll be specific. Will you humor me in one respect?"

"Of course," he grinned, humoring me.

"Guard yourself and me too. Taunton has killers—all right; I think, or Groby thinks, or some damn body thinks that Taunton has killers. If you humor me to the extent of guarding yourself and me, I promise not to start swinging from the ceiling and gibbering. I'll even go to your analyst."

"All right," he smiled, humoring me.

Poor old Fowler. Who could blame him? His own dreamworld was under attack by every word I had to say. My story was blasphemy against the god of Sales. He couldn't believe it, and he couldn't believe that I—the real I—believed it. How could Mitchell Courtenay, copysmith, be sitting there and telling him such frightful things as:

The interests of producers and consumers are not identical;

Most of the world is unhappy;

Workmen don't automatically find the job they do best;

Entrepreneurs don't play a hard, fair game by the rules;

The Consies are sane, intelligent, and well organized.

They were hammer-blows at him, but Fowler Schocken was nothing if not resilient. The hammer bounced right off and the dents it made were ephemeral. There was an explanation for everything and Sales could do no wrong. Therefore, Mitchell Courtenay, copysmith, was not sitting there telling him these things. It was Mitchell Courtenay's wicked, untamed id or the diabolic 'George Groby' or somebody—anybody but Courtenay.

In a dissociated fashion that would have delighted Fowler Schocken and his analyst I said to myself: "You know, Mitch, you're talking like a Consie."

I answered: "Why, so I am. That's terrible."

"Well," I replied, "I don't know about that. Maybe . . ."

"Yeah," I said thoughtfully. "Maybe . . ."

It's an axiom of my trade that things are invisible except against a contrasting background. Like, for instance, the opinions and attitudes of Fowler Schocken.

Humor me, Fowler, I thought. *Keep me guarded. I don't want to run into an ambivalent fantasy like Hedy again, ever. The symbolism may have been obvious, but she hurt me bad with her symbolic little needle.*

fifteen

· · ◆ · ·

Runstead wasn't there when our little procession arrived in executives' country of the Schocken Tower. There were Fowler, me, Jack O'Shea, secretaries—and the weapons squads I had demanded.

Runstead's secretary said he was down the hall, and we waited . . . and waited . . . and waited. After an hour I suggested that he wasn't coming back. After another hour word got to us that a body had been found smashed flat on the first setback of the Tower, hundreds of feet below. It was very, very difficult to identify.

The secretary wept hysterically and opened Runstead's desk and safe. Eventually we found a diary covering the past few months of Runstead's life. Interspersed with details of his work, his amours, memos for future campaigns, notes on good out-of-the-way restaurants, and the like were entries that said: "He was here again last night. He told me to hit harder on the shock-appeal. He scares me . . . He says the Starrzelius campaign needed guts. He scares *hell* out of me. Understand he used to scare everybody in the old days when he was alive . . . GWH again last night . . . *Saw him by daylight* first time. Jumped and yelled but nobody noticed. Wish he'd go away . . . GWH teeth seem bigger, pointier today. I ought to get help . . . He said I'm no good, disgrace to profession . . ."

After a while we realized that "he" was the ghost of George Washington Hill, father of our profession, founder of the singing commercial, shock-value, and God knows what else.

"Poor fellow," said Schocken, white-faced. "Poor, poor fellow. If only I'd known. If only he'd come to me in time."

The last entry said raggedly: "Told me I'm no good. I know I'm no good. Unworthy of the profession. They all know it. Can see it in their faces. Everybody knows it. He told them. Damn him. Damn him and his teeth. Damn—"

"Poor, poor fellow," said Schocken, almost sobbing. He turned to me and said: "You see? The overwhelming strains of our profession . . ."

Sure I saw. A prefabricated diary and an unidentifiable splash of protoplasm. It might have been 180 pounds of Chicken Little down there on the first setback. But I would have been wasting my breath. I nodded soberly, humoring him.

I was restored to my job at the top of Venus Section. I saw Fowler's analyst daily. And I kept my armed guard. In tearful sessions the old man would say: "You must relinquish this symbol. It's all that stands between you and reality now, Mitch. Dr. Lawler tells me—"

Dr. Lawler told Fowler Schocken what I told Dr. Lawler. And that was the slow progress of my "integration." I hired a medical student to work out traumas for me backwards from the assumption that my time as a consumer had been a psychotic fugue, and he came up with some honeys. A few I had to veto as not quite consistent with my dignity, but there were enough left to make Dr. Lawler drop his pencil every once in a while. One by one we dug them up, and I have never been so bored in my life.

But one thing I would not surrender, and that was my insistence that my life and Fowler Schocken's life were in danger.

Fowler and I got closer and closer—a thing I've seen before. He thought he had made a convert. I was ashamed to string him along. He was being very good to me. But it was a matter of life or death. The rest was side show.

The day came when Fowler Schocken said gently: "Mitch, I'm afraid heroic measures are in order. I don't ask you to dispense with this fence of yours against reality. But *I* am going to dismiss *my* guards."

"They'll kill you, Fowler!" burst from me.

He shook his head gently. "You'll see. I'm not afraid." Argument was quite useless. After a bit of it, acting on sound psychological principles, he told the lieutenant of his office squad: "I won't be needing you any more. Please report with your men to Plant Security Pool for reassignment. Thank you very much for your loyalty and attention to detail during these weeks."

The lieutenant saluted, but he and his men looked sick. They were going from an easy job in executives' country to lobby patrol or night detail or mail guard or messenger service at ungodly hours. They filed out, and I knew Fowler Schocken's hours were numbered.

That night he was garroted on his way home by somebody who had slugged his chauffeur and substituted himself at the pedals of the Fowler Schocken Cadillac. The killer, apparently a near-moron, resisted arrest and was clubbed to death, giggling. His tattoo had been torn off; he was quite unidentifiable.

You can easily imagine how much work was done in the office the next day. There was a memorial Board meeting held and resolutions passed saying it was a dirty shame and a great profession never would forget and so on. Messages of condolence were sent by the other agencies, including Taunton's. I got some odd looks when I crumpled the Taunton message in my fist and used some very bad language. Commercial rivalry, after all, goes just so far. We're all gentlemen here, of course. A hard, clean fight and may the best agency win.

But no Board member paid it much mind. They all were thinking of just one thing: the Schocken block of voting shares.

Fowler Schocken Associates was capitalized at 7×10^{13} shares. Of these, $3.5 \times 10^{13} + 1$ shares were purchasable only by employees holding AAAA labor contracts or better—roughly speaking, star class. The remaining shares by SEC order had been sold on the open market in order to clothe Fowler Schocken Associates with public interest. As customary, Fowler Schocken himself had through dummies snapped these up at the obscure stock exchanges where they had been put on sale.

In his own name he held a modest $.75 \times 10^{13}$ shares and distributed the rest with a lavish hand. I myself, relatively junior in spite of holding perhaps the number two job in the organization, had accumulated via bonuses and incentive pay only about $.857 \times 10^{12}$ shares. Top man around the Board table probably was Harvey Bruner. He was Schocken's oldest associate and had corralled $.83 \times 10^{13}$ shares over the years. (Nominally this gave him the bulge on Fowler—but he knew, of course, that in a challenge those other

$3.5 \times 10^{13} + 1$ shares would come rolling in on carloads of proxies, all backing Fowler with a mysterious unanimity. Besides, he was loyal.) He seemed to think he was heir-apparent, and some of the more naive Research and Development people were already sucking up to him, more fools they. He was an utterly uncreative, utterly honest wheel horse. Under his heavy hand the delicate thing that was Fowler Schocken Associates would disintegrate in a year.

If I were gambling, I would have given odds on Sillery, the Media chief, for copping the Schocken bloc and on down in descending order to myself, on whom I would have taken odds—long, long odds. That obviously was the way most of them felt, except the infatuated Bruner and a few dopes. You could tell. Sillery was surrounded by a respectful little court that doubtless remembered such remarks from Fowler as: "Media, gentlemen, is basic-basic!" and: "Media for brains, copysmiths for talent!" I was practically a leper at the end of the table, with my guards silently eyeing the goings-on. Sillery glanced at them once, and I could read him like a book: *"That's* been going on long enough; we'll knock off that eccentric first thing."

What we had been waiting for came about at last. "The gentlemen from the American Arbitration Association, Probate Section, are here, gentlemen."

They were of the funereal type, according to tradition. Through case-hardening or deficient senses of humor they refrained from giggling while Sillery gave them a measured little speech of welcome about their sad duty and how we wished we could meet them under happier circumstances and so on.

They read the will in a rapid mumble and passed copies around. The part I read first said: "To my dear friend and associate Mitchell Courtenay I bequeath and devise my ivory-inlaid oak finger-ring (inventory number 56,987) and my seventy-five shares of Sponsors' Stock in the Institute for the Diffusion of Psychoanalytic Knowledge, a New York Non-Profit Corporation, with the injunction that he devote his leisure hours to active participation in this organization and the furtherance of its noble aim." Well, Mitch, I told myself, you're through. I tossed the copy on the table and leaned back to take a swift rough inventory of my liquid assets.

"Hard lines, Mr. Courtenay," a brave and sympathetic research man I hardly knew told me. "Mr. Sillery seems pleased with himself."

I glanced at the bequest to Sillery—paragraph one. Sure enough, he got Fowler's personal shares and huge chunks of stock in Managerial Investment Syndicate, Underwriters Holding Corporation and a couple of others.

The research man studied my copy of the will. "If you don't mind my saying so, Mr. Courtenay," he told me, "the old man could have treated you better. I never heard of this outfit and I'm pretty familiar with the psychoanalytic field."

I seemed to hear Fowler chuckling nearby, and sat bolt upright. "Why the old so-and-so!" I gasped. It fitted like lock and key, with his bizarre sense of humor to oil the movement.

Sillery was clearing his throat and an instant silence descended on the Board room.

The great man spoke. "It's a trifle crowded here, gentlemen. I wish somebody would move that all persons other than Board members be asked to leave—"

I got up and said: "I'll save you the trouble, Sillery. Come on, boys. Sillery, I may be back." I and my guard left.

The Institute for the Diffusion of Psychoanalytic Knowledge, a New York Non-Profit Corporation, turned out to be a shabby three-room suite downtown in Yonkers. There was a weird old gal in the outer office pecking away at a typewriter. It was like something out of Dickens. A sagging rack held printed pamphlets with flyspecks on them.

"I'm from Fowler Schocken Associates," I told her.

She jumped. "Excuse me, sir! I didn't notice you. How is Mr. Schocken?"

I told her how he was, and she began to blubber. He was such a *good* man, giving so *generously* for the Cause. What on Earth would she and her poor brother ever do now? Poor Mr. Schocken! Poor her! Poor brother!

"All may not be lost," I told her. "Who's in charge here?" She sniffled that her brother was in the inner office. "Please break it to him gently, Mr. Courtenay. He's so delicate and sensitive—"

I said I would, and walked in. Brother was snoring-drunk, flopped over his desk. I joggled him awake, and he looked at me with a bleary and cynical eye. "Washawan?"

"I'm from Fowler Schocken Associates. I want to look at your books."

He shook his head emphatically. "Nossir. Only the old man himself gets to see the books."

"He's dead," I told him. "Here's the will." I showed him the paragraph and my identification.

"Well," he said. "The joy-ride's over. Or do you keep us going? You see what it says there, Mr. Courtenay? He enjoins you to participate—"

"I see it," I told him. "The books, please."

He got them out of a surprising vault behind a plain door.

A mere three hours of backbreaking labor over them showed me that the Institute was in existence solely for holding and voting 56 per cent of the stock of an outfit called General Phosphate Reduction Corporation of Newark according to the whims of Fowler Schocken.

I went out into the corridor and said to my guards: "Come on, boys. Newark next."

I won't bore you with the details. It was single-tracked for three stages and then it split. One of the tracks ended two stages later in the Frankfort Used Machine Tool Brokerage Company, which voted 32 per cent of the Fowler Schocken Associates "public sale" stock. The other track forked again one stage later and wound up eventually in United Concessions Corp. and Waukegan College of Dentistry and Orthodontia, which voted the remainder.

Two weeks later on Board morning I walked into the Board room with my guards.

Sillery was presiding. He looked haggard and worn, as though he'd been up all night every night for the past couple of weeks looking for something.

"Courtenay!" he snarled. "I thought you understood that you were to leave your regiment outside!"

I nodded to honest, dumb old Harvey Bruner, whom I'd let in on it. Loyal to Schocken, loyal to me, he bleated: "Mr. Chairman, I move that members be permitted to admit company plant-protection personnel assigned to them in such number as they think necessary for their bodily protection."

"Second the motion, Mr. Chairman," I said. "Bring them in, boys, will you?" My guards, grinning, began to lug in transfer cases full of proxies to me.

Eyes popped and jaws dropped as the pile mounted. It took a long time for them to be counted and authenticated. The final vote stood: For, 5.73×10^{13}; against, 1.27×10^{13}. All the Against votes were Sillery's and Sillery's alone. There were no abstentions. The others jumped to my side like cats on a griddle.

Loyal old Harve moved that chairmanship of the meeting be transferred to me, and it was carried unanimously. He then moved that Sillery be pensioned off, his shares of voting stock to be purchased at par by the firm and deposited in the bonus fund. Carried unanimously. Then—a slash of the whip just to remind them—he moved that one Thomas Heatherby, a junior Art man who had sucked up outrageously to Sillery, be downgraded from Board level and deprived without compensation of his minute block of voting shares. Carried unanimously. Heatherby didn't even dare scream about it. Half a loaf is better than none, he may have said to himself, choking down his anger.

It was done. I was master of Fowler Schocken Associates. And I had learned to despise everything for which it stood.

sixteen

· · ◆ · ·

"Flash-flash, Mr. Courtenay," said my secretary's voice. I hit the GA button.

"Consie arrested Albany on neighbor's denunciation. Shall I line it up?"

"God-damn it!" I exploded. "How many times do I have to give you standing orders? Of course you line it up. Why the hell not?"

She quavered: "I'm sorry, Mr. Courtenay—I thought it was kind of far out—"

"Stop thinking, then. Arrange the transportation." Maybe I shouldn't have been so rough on her—but I wanted to find Kathy, if I had to turn every Consie cell in the country upside down to do it. I had driven Kathy into hiding—out of fear that I would turn her in—now I wanted to get her back.

An hour later I was in the Upstate Mutual Protective Association's HQ. They were a local outfit that had a lot of contracts in the area, including Albany. Their board chairman himself met me and my guards at the elevator. "An honor," he burbled. "A great, great honor, Mr. Courtenay, and what may I do for you?"

"My secretary asked you not to get to work on your Consie suspect until I arrived. Did you?"

"Of course not, Mr. Courtenay! Some of the employees may have roughed him up a little, informally, but he's in quite good shape."

"I want to see him."

He led the way anxiously. He was hoping to get in a word that might grow into a cliency with Fowler Schocken Associates, but he was afraid to speak up.

The suspect was sitting on a stool under the usual dazzler. He was a white-collar consumer of thirty or so. He had a couple of bruises on his face.

"Turn that thing off," I said.

A square-faced foreman said: "But we always—" One of my guards, without wasting words, shoved him aside and switched off the dazzler.

"It's all right, Lombardo," the board chairman said hastily. "You're to co-operate with these gentlemen."

"Chair," I said, and sat down facing the suspect. I told him: "My name's Courtenay. What's yours?"

He looked at me with pupils that were beginning to expand again. "Fillmore," he said, precisely. "August Fillmore. Can you tell me what all this is about?"

"You're suspected of being a Consie."

There was a gasp from all the UMPA people in the room. I was violating the most elementary principle of jurisprudence by informing the accused of the nature of his crime. I knew all about that, and didn't give a damn.

"Completely ridiculous," Fillmore spat. "I'm a respectable married man with eight children and another coming along. Who on earth told you people such nonsense?"

"Tell him who," I said to the board chairman.

He stared at me, goggle-eyed, unable to believe what he had heard. "Mr. Courtenay," he said at last, "with all respect, I can't take the responsibility for such a thing! It's quite unheard of. The entire body of law respecting the rights of informers—"

"I'll take the responsibility. Do you want me to put it in writing?"

"No, no, no, no, no! Nothing like that! Please, Mr. Courtenay—suppose I tell the informer's name to you, understanding that you know the law and are a responsible person—and then I leave the room?"

"Any way you want to do it is all right with me."

He grinned placatingly, and whispered in my ear: "A Mrs. Worley. The two families share a room. Please be careful, Mr. Courtenay—"

"Thanks," I said. He gathered eyes like a hostess and nervously retreated with his employees.

"Well, Fillmore," I told the suspect, "he says it's Mrs. Worley."

He began to swear, and I cut him off. "I'm a busy man," I said.

"You know your goose is cooked, of course. You know what Vogt says on the subject of conservation?"

The name apparently meant nothing to him. "Who's that?" he asked distractedly.

"Never mind. Let's change subjects. I have a lot of money. I can set up a generous pension for your family while you're away if you co-operate and admit you're a Consie."

He thought hard for a few moments and then said: "Sure I'm a Consie. What of it? Guilty or innocent, I'm sunk so why not say so?"

"If you're a red-hot Consie, suppose you quote me some passages from Osborne?"

He had never heard of Osborne, and slowly began to fake: "Well, there's the one that starts: 'A Consie's first duty, uh, is to, to prepare for a general uprising—' I don't remember the rest, but that's how it starts."

"Pretty close," I told him. "Now how about your cell meetings? Who-all's there?"

"I don't know them by name," he said more glibly. "We go by numbers. There's a heavyset dark-haired fellow, he's the boss, and, uh—"

It was a remarkable performance. It certainly, however, had nothing to do with the semi-mythical Conservationist heroes, Vogt and Osborne, whose books were required reading in all cells—when copies could be found.

We left.

I told the board chairman, hovering anxiously outside in the corridor: "I don't think he's a Consie."

I was president of Fowler Schocken Associates and he was only the board chairman of a jerkwater local police outfit, but *that* was too much. He drew himself up and said with dignity: "We administer justice, Mr. Courtenay. And an ancient, basic tenet of justice is: 'Better that one thousand innocents suffer unjustly than one guilty person be permitted to escape.' "

"I am aware of the maxim," I said. "Good day."

My instrument corporal went *boing* as the crash-crash priority signal sounded in his ear and handed me the phone. It was my secretary back in Schocken Tower, reporting another arrest, this one in Pile City Three, off Cape Cod.

We flew out to Pile City Three, which was rippling that day over a long, swelling sea. I hate the Pile Cities—as I've said, I suffer from motion sickness.

This Consie suspect turned out to be a professional criminal. He had tried a smash-and-grab raid on a jewelry store, intending to snatch a trayful of oak and mahogany pins, leaving behind a lurid note all about Consie vengeance and beware of the coming storm when the Consies take over and kill all the rich guys. It was intended to throw off suspicion.

He was very stupid.

It was a Burns-protected city, and I had a careful chat with their resident manager. He admitted first that most of their Consie arrests during the past month or so had been like that, and then admitted that *all* their Consie arrests for the past month or so had been like that. Formerly they had broken up authentic Consie cells at the rate of maybe one a week. He thought maybe it was a seasonal phenomenon.

From there we went back to New York, where another Consie had been picked up. I saw him and listened to him rant for a few minutes. He was posted on Consie theory and could quote you Vogt and Osborne by the page. He also asserted that God had chosen him to wipe the wastrels from the face of Mother Earth. He said of course he was in the regular Consie organization, but he would die before he gave up any of its secrets. And I knew he certainly would, because he didn't know any. The Consies wouldn't have accepted anybody that unstable if they were down to three members with one sinking fast.

We went back to Schocken Tower at sunset, and my guard changed. It had been a lousy day. It had been, as far as results were concerned, a carbon copy of all the days I had spent since I inherited the agency.

There was a meeting scheduled. I didn't want to go, but my conscience troubled me when I thought of the pride and confidence Fowler Schocken must have felt in me when he made me his heir. Before I dragged myself to the Board room I checked with a special detail I had set up in the Business Espionage section.

"Nothing, sir," my man said. "No leads whatsoever on your—on Dr. Nevin. The tracer we had on the Chlorella personnel man petered out. Uh, shall we keep trying—?"

"Keep trying," I said. "If you need a bigger appropriation or more investigators, don't hesitate. Do me a real job."

He swore loyalty and hung up, probably thinking that the boss was an old fool, mooning over a wife—not even permanently married to him—who had decided to slip out of the picture. What he made out of the others I had asked him to trace, I didn't know. All I knew was that they had vanished, all my few contacts with the Consies picked up in Costa Rica, the sewers of New York, and on the Moon. Kathy had never come back to her apartment or the hospital, Warren Astron had never returned to his sucker-trap on Shopping One, my Chlorella cellmates had vanished into the jungle—and so it went, all down the line.

Board meeting.

"Sorry to be late, gentlemen. I'll dispense with opening remarks. Charlie, how's Research and Development doing on the Venus question?"

He got up. "Mr. Courtenay, gentlemen, in my humble way I think I can say, informally, that R. and D. is in there punching and that my boys are a credit to Fowler Schocken Associates. Specifically, we've tested out the Hilsch tube in a nine-hundred-degree wind tunnel and got *eleven hundred degrees separation.* The experiment confirmed the predictions of our physics and thermodynamics sections based on theory and math. What that means is that, at ambient wind velocities on any of a hundred mountain ranges on Venus, we can put these scaled-up Hilsch tubes at the top of a hill and let the wind blow through them, and out of the low-temperature valve we can get *liquid nitrogen.* Of course, we don't want liquid nitrogen. But we can adjust the apertures and get volumes of gas at that temperature or any higher one we want, with increasing volumes available as the temperature rises. The Hilsch tube, as you know, relies on the vortex generated within the tube by the passage of air to separate the hot from the cold air molecules, in the manner of the so-called Maxwell's demon—"

I said, "Charlie. Are you saying you can get enough cooling to make a dwelling on Venus habitable?"

"Absolutely, Mr. Courtenay! That's exactly what I'm saying! And you can take power off the hot end to make electricity!"

"How certain?"

"Quite certain, Mr. Courtenay," he said, hardly able to suppress the you-couldn't-be-expected-to-understand smile that technical people give you. "The O'Shea reports corroborate satellite, lander and telemetry data, and Gibbs phase-rule analysis clearly shows—"

I interrupted again. "Would you go to Venus on the strength of that certainty, other things being equal?"

"Certainly," he said, a little offended. "Shall I go into the technical details?"

"No. Just run the whole test again with a different crew of experts for confirmation."

"Right, Mr. Courtenay," Charlie said, scribbling busily.

"Right. Does anybody else have anything special on the Venus program before we go on?"

Bernhard, our comptroller, stuck his hand up, and I nodded.

"Question about Mr. O'Shea," he rumbled. "We're carrying him as a consultant at a very healthy figure. I've been asking around—and I hope I haven't been going offside, Mr. Courtenay, but it's my job—I've been asking around and I find that we've been getting damn-all consultation from him. Also, I should mention that he's drawn heavily in recent weeks on retainers not yet due. If we canned—if we severed our connection with him at this time, he'd be owing us money. Also—well, this is trivial, but it gives you an idea. The girls in my department are complaining about his annoying them."

My eyebrows went up. "I think we should hang onto him for whatever prestige rubs off, Ben, though his vogue does seem to be passing. Give him an argument about further advances. And as for the girls—well, I'm surprised. I thought they didn't complain when he made passes at them."

"Seen him lately?" grunted Bernhard.

No; I realized I hadn't.

The rest of the meeting went fast.

Back in my office I asked my night-shift secretary whether O'Shea was in the building, and if so to send for him.

He came in smelling of liquor and complaining loudly. "Damn it, Mitch, enough is enough! I just stepped in to pick up one of the babes for the night and you grab me. Aren't you taking this consultation thing too seriously? You've got my name to use; what more do you want?"

He looked like hell. He looked like a miniature of the fat, petulant, shabby Napoleon I at Elba. But a moment after he had come in I suddenly couldn't think of anything but Kathy. It took me a moment to figure out.

"Well?" he demanded. "What are you staring at? Isn't my lipstick on straight?"

The liquor covered it up some, but a little came through: *Ménage à Deux,* the perfume I'd had created for Kathy and Kathy alone when we were in Paris, the stuff she loved and sometimes used too much of. I could hear her saying: "I can't help it, darling; it's *so* much nicer than formalin, and that's what I usually smell of after a day at the hospital . . ."

"Sorry, Jack," I said evenly. "I didn't know it was your howling-night. It'll keep. Have fun."

He grimaced and left, almost waddling on his short legs.

I grabbed my phone and slammed a connection through to my special detail in Business Espionage. "Put tails on Jack O'Shea," I snapped. "He's leaving the building soon. Tail him and tail everybody he contacts. Night and day. If I hit paydirt on this you and your men get upgraded and bonused. But God help you if you pull a butch."

seventeen

· · ◆ · ·

I got so nobody dared to come near me. I couldn't help myself. I was living for one thing only: the daily reports from the tails on O'Shea. Anything else I tried to handle bored and irritated me to distraction.

After a week there were twenty-four tails working at a time on O'Shea and people with whom he had talked. They were headwaiters, his lecture agent, girls, an old test-pilot friend of his stationed at Astoria, a cop he got into a drunken argument with one night—but was he really drunk and was it really an argument?—and other unsurprising folk.

One night, quietly added to the list was: "Consumer, female, about 30, 5'4", 120 lbs., redhead, eyes not seen, cheaply dressed. Subject entered Hash Heaven (restaurant) 1837 after waiting 14 minutes outside and went immediately to table waited on by new contact, which table just vacated by party. Conjecture: subject primarily interested in waitress. Ordered hash, ate very lightly, exchanged few words with contact. Papers may have been passed but impossible to observe at tailing distance. Female operative has picked up contact."

About thirty, five-four, one-twenty. It could be. I phoned to say: "Bear down on that one. Rush me everything new that you get. How about finding out more from the restaurant?"

Business Espionage began to explain, with embarrassment, that they'd do it if I insisted, but that it wasn't good technique. Usually the news got to the person being tailed and—

"Okay," I said. "Do it your way."

"Hold it a minute, Mr. Courtenay, please. Our girl just checked in—the new contact went home to the Taunton Building. She has Stairs 17 to 18 on the thirty-fifth floor."

"What's the thirty-fifth?" I asked, heavy-hearted.

"For couples."

"Is she—?"

"She's unattached, Mr. Courtenay. Our girl pretended to apply for the vacancy. They told her Mrs. 17 is holding 18 for the arrival of her husband. He's upstate harvesting."

"What time do the stairs close at Taunton's?" I demanded.

"2200, Mr. Courtenay."

I glanced at my desk clock. "Call your tail off her," I said. "That's all for now."

I got up and told my guards: "I'm going out without you, gentlemen. Please wait here. Lieutenant, can I borrow your gun?"

"Of course, Mr. Courtenay." He passed over a .25 UHV. I checked the magazine and went out on foot, alone.

As I left the lobby of Schocken Tower a shadowy young man detached himself from the wall and drifted after me. I crossed him up by walking in the deserted street, a dark, narrow slit between the mighty midtown buildings. Monoxide and smog hung heavily in the unconditioned air, but I had antisoot plugs. He did not. I heard him wheeze at a respectable distance behind me. An occasional closed cab whizzed past us, the driver puffing and drawn as he pumped the pedals.

Without looking back I turned the corner of Schocken Tower and instantly flattened against the wall. My shadow drifted past and stopped in consternation, peering into the gloom.

I slammed the long barrel of the pistol against the back of his neck in a murderous rabbit punch and walked on. He was probably one of my own men; but I didn't want anybody's men along.

I got to the Taunton Building's night-dweller entrance at 2159. Behind me the timelock slammed the door. There was an undersized pay elevator. I dropped in a quarter, punched 35, and read notices while it creaked upward. "NIGHT-DWELLERS ARE RESPONSIBLE FOR THEIR OWN POLICING. MANAGEMENT ASSUMES NO RESPONSIBILITY FOR THEFTS, ASSAULTS, OR RAPES." "NIGHT-DWELLERS WILL NOTE THAT BARRIERS ARE UPPED AT 2210 NIGHTLY AND ARRANGE THEIR CALLS OF NATURE ACCORDINGLY." "RENT IS DUE AND PAYABLE NIGHTLY IN ADVANCE AT THE AUTOCLERK." "MANAGEMENT RESERVES THE RIGHT TO REFUSE RENTAL TO PATRONS OF STARRZELIUS PRODUCTS."

The door opened on the stairwell of the thirty-fifth floor. It was like looking into a maggoty cheese. People, men and women, squirming uneasily, trying to find some comfort before the barriers upped. I looked at my watch and saw: 2208.

I picked my way carefully and very, very slowly in the dim light over and around limbs and torsos, with many apologies, counting . . . at the seventeenth step I stepped over a huddled figure as my watch said: 2210.

With a rusty clank, the barriers upped, cutting off steps seventeen and eighteen, containing me and—

She sat up, looking scared and angry, with a small pistol in her hand.

"Kathy," I said.

She dropped the pistol. "Mitch. You fool." Her voice was low and urgent. "What are you doing here? They haven't given up, they're still out to murder you—"

"I know all that," I said. "I'm grandstanding, Kathy. I'm putting my head into the lion's mouth to show you I mean it when I say that you're right and I was wrong."

"How did you find me?" she asked suspiciously.

"Some of your perfume came off on O'Shea. *Ménage à Deux.*"

She looked around at the cramped quarters and giggled. "It certainly is, isn't it?"

"The heat's off, Kathy," I told her. "I'm not just here to paw you, with or without your consent. I'm here to tell you that I'm on your side. Name it and you can have it."

She looked at me narrowly and asked: "Venus?"

"It's yours."

"Mitch," she said, "if you're lying—if you're lying—"

"You'll know by tomorrow if we get out of here alive. Until then there's nothing more to be said about it, is there? We're in for the night."

"Yes," she said. "We're in for the night." And then, suddenly, passionately: "God, how I've missed you!"

Wake-up whistles screamed at 0600. They were loaded with skull-rattling subsonics, just to make sure that no slugabeds would impede the morning evacuation.

Kathy began briskly to stow away the bedding in the stairs. "Barriers down in five minutes," she snapped. She lifted Stair seventeen's lid and fished around in it for a flat box that opened into a makeup kit. "Hold still."

I yelped as a razor raked across the top of my right eyebrow. "Hold—*still!*" R-R-R-R-ip! It cut a swathe across my left eyebrow. Briskly she touched my face here and there with mysterious brushes.

"Flup!" I said as she turned up my upper lip and tucked a pledget of plastic under it. Two gummy wads pasted my ears against my head and she said: "There," and showed me the mirror.

"Good," I told her. "I got out of here once in the morning rush. I think we can do it again."

"There go the barriers," she said tensely, hearing some preliminary noise that was lost on my inexperienced ear.

The barriers clanged down. We were the only night-dwellers left on the thirty-fifth floor. But we were not alone. B. J. Taunton and two of his boys stood there. Taunton was swaying a little on his feet, red-faced and grinning. Each of his boys had a machine pistol trained on me.

Taunton hiccuped and said: "This was a hell of an unfortunate place for you to go chippy-chasing, Courtenay, ol' man. We have a photo-register for gate-crashers like you. Girlie, if you will kindly step aside—"

She didn't step aside. She stepped right into Taunton's arms, jammed her gun against his navel. His red face went the color of putty. "You know what to do," she said grimly.

"Boys," he said faintly, "drop the guns. For God's sake, drop them!"

They exchanged looks. *"Drop them!"* he begged.

They took an eternity to lay down their machine pistols, but they did. Taunton began to sob.

"Turn your backs," I told them, "and lie down." I had my borrowed UHV out. It felt wonderful.

The elevator could too easily have been flooded with gas. We walked down the stairs. It was a long, slow, careful business, though all night-dwellers had been cleared hours ago for B. J.'s coup. He sobbed and babbled all the way. At the tenth-floor landing he wailed: "I've got to have a drink, Courtenay. I'm really dying. There's a bar right here, you can keep that gun on me—"

Kathy laughed humorlessly at the idea, and we continued our slow step-by-step progress.

At the night-dweller exit I draped my coat over Kathy's gun hand in spite of the winter outside. "It's all right!" B. J. called quaveringly to an astounded lobby guard who started our way. "These people are friends of mine. It's quite all right!"

We walked with him to the shuttlemouth and dived in, leaving him, gray-faced and sweating, in the street. It was safety in numbers. The only way he could get at us was by blowing up the entire shuttle, and he wasn't equipped for it. We zigzagged for an hour, and I called my office from a station phone. A plant protection detail rendezvoused with us at another station, and we were in the Schocken Tower fifteen minutes later.

A morning paper gave us our only laugh so far that day. It said, among other things, that a coolant leak had been detected at 0300 today in the stairwell of the Taunton Building. B. J. Taunton himself, at the risk of his life, had supervised the evacuation of the Taunton Building night-dwellers in record time and without casualties.

Over a tray breakfast on my desk I told Kathy: "Your hair looks like hell. Does that stuff wash out?"

"Enough of this lovemaking," she said. "You told me I could have Venus. Mitch, I meant it. And Venus by-God belongs to us. We're the only people who know what to do with it and also we landed the first man there. O'Shea is one of us, Mitch."

"Since when?"

"Since his mother and father found he wasn't growing, that's since when. They knew the W.C.A. was going to need spacepilots soon—and the smaller the better. Earth didn't discover Venus. The W.C.A. did. And we demand the right to settle it. Can you deliver?"

"Sure," I said. "God, it's going to be a headache. We have our rosters filled now—eager suckers itching to get to Venus and be exploited by and for the Earth and Fowler Schocken. Well, I'll backtrack."

I thought for a minute and then said to Kathy: "Can you bring Runstead back to life for me? I don't know where the W.C.A. has been holding him, but we need him here. This is going to be a job. A copysmith's highest art is to convince people without letting them know that they're being convinced. What I've got to do is make my copysmiths unconvince people without letting either the copysmiths or the people know what I'm doing to them. I can use some highgrade help that I can talk freely to."

"It can be arranged," she said, kissing me lightly. "That's for saying 'We.'"

"Huh?" I said. "Did I say 'we'?" Then I understood. "Oh. Look, darling, I've got a dandy executive's living suite, twelve by twelve, upstairs. You had a hard night. Suppose you head upstairs and cork off for a while. I've got a lot of work to do."

She kissed me again and said: "Don't work too hard, Mitch. I'll see you tonight."

eighteen

· ·◆· ·

I couldn't have done it without Runstead—not in time. He came whistling back from Chi, where he'd been holed up since he pretended suicide, in response to an underground message from Kathy. He arrived in the middle of a Board meeting; we shook hands and the Board cheerfully swallowed the story that he'd dropped out of sight to do some secret work. After all, they'd swallowed it once before. He knew what the job was; he sank his teeth in it.

Consie or no Consie, I still thought Runstead was a rat.

But I had to admit things were leaping.

On the surface level, Fowler Schocken Associates had launched a giant all-client slogan contest, with fifteen hundred first prizes—all of them a berth on the Venus rocket. There were eight hundred thousand prizes in all, but the others didn't matter. Judging was turned over to an impartial firm of contest analyzers, which turned out to be headed by the brother-in-law of a friend of Runstead's. Only fourteen hundred of the prize winners, Matt told me, were actually members of the Consie underground. The other hundred were dummy names entirely, to take care of last minute emergencies.

I took Kathy with me to Washington to spark the final clearance of the rocket for flight, while Runstead minded the baby back in New York. I'd been in Washington often enough for a luncheon or an afternoon, but this was going to be a two-day job; I looked forward to it like a kid. I parked Kathy at the hotel and made her promise not to do any solo sight-seeing, then caught a cab to the State Department. A morose little man in a bowler hat was waiting in the anteroom; when he heard my name he got up hastily and offered me his seat. Quite a change from the Chlorella days, Mitch, old boy, I told myself. Our attaché came flustering out to greet me; I calmed him and explained what I wanted.

"Easiest thing in the world, Mr. Courtenay," he promised. "I'll get the enabling bill put through committee this afternoon, and with any luck at all it'll clear both houses tonight."

I said expansively, "Fine. Need any backing?"

"Oh, I don't think so, Mr. Courtenay. Might be nice for you to address the House in the morning, if you can find the time. They'd love to hear from you, and it would smooth things over a little for a quick passage."

"Glad to," I said, reaching down for my bag. The man in the bowler hat beat me to it and handed it to me with a little bow. "Just set your time, Abels," I told the legate. "I'll be there."

"Thank you very *much*, Mr. Courtenay!" He opened the door for me. The little man said tentatively:

"Mr. Abels?"

The legate shook his head. "You can see how busy I am," he said, not unkindly. "Come back tomorrow."

The little man smiled gratefully and followed me out the door. We both hailed a cab and he opened the door for me. You know what cabs are like in Washington. "Can I drop you anywhere?" I asked.

"It's very good of you," he said, and followed me in. The driver leaned back on his pedals and looked in at us.

I told him: "The Park Starr for me. But drop the other gentleman off first."

"Sure." The driver nodded. "White House, Mr. President?"

"Yes, please," said the little man. "I can't tell you how pleased I am to meet you, Mr. Courtenay," he went on. "I overheard your conversation with Mr. Abels, you know. It was very interesting to hear that the Venus rocket is so near completion. Congress has pretty well got out of the habit of keeping me posted on what's going on. Of course, I know they're busy with their investigations and all. But—" He smiled. Mischievously, he said: "I entered your contest, Mr. Courtenay. My slogan was, 'I'm starry-eyed over Starrs, verily I am.' I don't suppose I could have gone along though, even if I'd won."

I said very sincerely: "I can't see how it would have been possible." And, a little less sincerely, "Besides, they must keep you pretty busy right here."

"Oh, not particularly. January's heavy; I convene Congress, you see, and they read me the State of the Union message. But the rest of the year passes slowly. Will you really address Congress tomorrow, Mr. Courtenay? It would mean a joint session, and they usually let me come for that."

"Be delighted to have you," I said cordially.

The little man had a warm smile, glinting through his glasses. The cab stopped and the President shook my hand warmly and got out. He poked his head in the door. "Uh," he said, looking apprehensively at the driver, "you've been swell. I may be stepping out of line in saying this, but if I might make a suggestion—I understand something about astronomy, it's a kind of hobby, and I hope you won't delay the ship's take-off past the present conjunction."

I stared. Venus was within ten degrees of opposition and was getting farther away—not that it mattered, since most of the trip would be coasting anyhow.

He held a finger to his lips. "Good-bye, sir," he said. I spent the rest of the trip staring at the backs of the driver's hairy ears, and wondering what the little man had been driving at.

We took the evening off, Kathy and I, to see the sights. I wasn't too much impressed. The famous cherry blossoms were beautiful, all right, but, with my new-found Conservationist sentiments, I found them objectionably ostentatious. "A dozen would have been plenty," I objected. "Scattering them around in vase after vase this way is a plain waste of the taxpayer's money. You know what they'd cost in Tiffany's?"

Kathy giggled. "Mitch, Mitch," she said. "Wait till we take over Venus. Did you ever think of what it's going to be like to have a whole *planet* to grow things in? Acres and acres of flowers—trees—everything?"

A plump schoolteacher-type leaning on the railing beside us straightened up, glared, sniffed, and walked away. "You're giving us a bad name," I told Kathy. "Before you get us in trouble, let's go to —let's go back to the hotel."

I woke up to an excited squeal from Kathy. "Mitch," she was saying from the bathroom, two round eyes peering wonderingly over the towel that was draped around her, "they've got a *tub* here! I opened the door to the shower stall, and it wasn't a stall at all! Can I, Mitch? Please?"

There are times when even an honest conservationist finds pleasure in being the acting head of Fowler Schocken Associates. I yawned and blew her a kiss and said, "Sure. And—make it all fresh water, hear?"

Kathy pretended to faint, but I noticed that she wasted no time calling room service. While the tub was filling I dressed. We breakfasted comfortably and strolled to the Capitol hand in hand.

I found Kathy a seat in the pressbox and headed for the floor of the House. Our Washington lobby chief pushed through the crowd to me. He handed me a strip of facsimile paper. "It's all here, Mr. Courtenay," he said. "Uh—is everything all right?"

"Everything's just fine," I told him. I waved him off and looked at the facsimile. It was from Dicken, on the scene at the rocket:

> Passengers and crew alerted and on standby. First movement into ships begins at 1145 EST, loading completed by 1645 EST. Ship fully fueled, supplied, and provisioned since 0915. Security invoked but MIA, CIC, and Time-Life known to have filed coded dispatches through dummies. Chartroom asks please remind you: Take-off possible only in A.M. hours.

I rubbed the tape between my palms; it disintegrated into ash. As I climbed to the podium, someone tugged at my elbow. It was the President, leaning out of his ceremonial box. "Mr. Courtenay," he whispered, his smile masklike on his face, "I guess you understood what I was trying to tell you yesterday in the cab. I'm glad the rocket's ready. And—" he widened his grin and bobbed his head in the precise manner of a statesman exchanging inconsequentialities with a distinguished visitor, "you probably know this, but—he's here."

I had no chance to find out who "he" was. As the Speaker of the House came toward me hand outstretched and the applause started from the floor, I forced a smile to my face. But it was a trick of the rictus muscles entirely. I had little to smile about, if the news about the Venus rocket had trickled down to the President.

Fowler Schocken was a pious old hypocrite and Fowler Schocken was a grinning fraud, but if it hadn't been for Fowler Schocken I could never have got through that speech. I could hear his voice in my ears: "Sell 'em, Mitch; you can sell them if you'll keep in mind that they *want* to buy." And I sold the assembled legislators precisely what they wanted to own. I touched briefly on American enterprise and the home; I offered them a world to loot and a whole plunderable universe beyond it, once Fowler Schocken's brave pioneers had opened the way for it; I gave them a picture of assembly-line planets owned and operated by our very selves, the enterprising American businessmen who had made civilization great. They loved it. The applause was fantastic.

As the first waves died down, there were a dozen standing figures in the hall, clapping their hands and begging the chair for recognition. I hardly noticed; astonishingly, Kathy was gone from the press-box. The Speaker selected white-haired old Colbee, lean and dignified with his four decades of service.

"The chair recognizes the gentleman from Yummy-Cola."

"Thank you very much, Mr. Speakuh." Colbee's face wore a courtly smile; but his eyes seemed to me the eyes of a snake. Yummy-Cola was nominally one of the few big independents; but I remembered that Fowler had commented once on their captive agency's surprising closeness to Taunton. "If I may ventuah to speak for the Upper Chamber, I should like to thank ouah distinguished guest for his very well-chosen remarks heah. I am certain that we all have enjoyed listening to a man of his calibeh and standing." Go back to the Berlitz school, you Westchester phony, I thought bitterly. I could feel the wienie coming as Colbee rumbled on. "With the permission of the chair, I should like to ask ouah guest a number of questions involving the legislation we have been asked to consider heah today." *Consider* indeed, you bastard, I thought. By now even the galleries had caught on to what was happening. I hardly needed to hear the rest:

"It may have escaped youah attention, but we are fortunate in having with us another guest. I refer of course to Mr. Taunton." He waved gracefully to the visitor's gallery, where B. J.'s red face appeared between two solid figures that I should have recognized at the first moment as his bodyguards. "In a brief discussion before ouah meeting heah, Mr. Taunton was good enough to give me some information which I would like Mr. Co'tenay to comment upon. First—" the snake eyes were steel now, "I would ask Mr. Co'tenay if the name of George Groby, wanted for Contract Breach and Femicide, is familiar to him. Second, I would like to ask if Mr. Co'tenay *is* Mr. Groby. Third, I would like to ask Mr. Co'tenay if there is any truth to the repo't, given me in confidence by someone in whom Mr. Taunton assures me I can repose absolute trust, that Mr. Co'tenay is a membeh in good standing of the World Conservation Association, known to most of us who are loyal Amurricans as—"

Even Colbee himself could not have heard the last words of his sentence. The uproar was like a physical blast.

nineteen

· · ◆ · ·

Seen in retrospect, everything that happened in the next wild quarter of an hour blurs and disappears like the shapes in a spinning kaleidoscope. But I remember tableaux, frozen moments of time that seem almost to have no relation to each other:

The waves of contempt and hatred that flowed around me, the contorted face of the President below me, screaming something unheard to the sound engineer in his cubicle, the wrathful eyes of the Speaker as he reached out for me.

Then the wild motion halted as the President's voice roared through the chamber at maximum amplification: "I declare this meeting adjourned!"—and the stunned expressions of the legislators at his unbelievable temerity. There was greatness in that little man. Before anyone could move or think he clapped his hands—the magnified report was like atomic fission—and a smartly uniformed squad moved in on us. "Take him away," the President declaimed, with a magnificent gesture, and at double-time the squad surrounded me and hustled me off the podium. The President convoyed us as far as the door while the assembly gathered its wits. His face was white with fear, but he whispered: "I can't make it stick, but it'll take them all afternoon to get a ruling from the C of C. God bless you, Mr. Courtenay."

And he turned back to face them. I do not think Caligula's Christians walked more courageously into the arena.

The guards were the President's own, honor men from Brink's leadership academy. The lieutenant said never a word to me, but I could read the controlled disgust on his face as he read the slip of paper the President had handed him. I knew he didn't like what he was ordered to do, and I knew he would do it.

They got me to Anacostia and put me on the President's own transport; they stayed with me and fed me, and one of them played cards with me, as the jets flared outside the ports and we covered territory. All they would not do was talk to me.

It was a long flight in that clumsy old luxury liner that "tradition" gave the President. Time had been wasted at the airport, and below us I could see the fuzzy band of the terminator creeping past. As we came down for a landing, it was full dark. And the waiting was not yet over, nor the wondering if Kathy had got out all right too and when I would see her again. The lieutenant left the ship alone; he was gone for a long, long time.

I spent the time kicking questions around in my mind—questions that had occurred to me before, but which I had dismissed. Now, with all the time in the world, and a future full of ifs, I took them out and looked them over.

For instance:

Kathy and Matt Runstead and Jack O'Shea had plotted together to put me on ice literally. All right, that accounted for most of the things that puzzled me. But it didn't account for Hester. And, when you stopped to think of it, it didn't account for all of Runstead's work, either.

The Consies were in favor of space travel. But Runstead had sabotaged the Venus test in Cal-Mex. There was no doubt of that; I had as good as a confession from his fall-guy. Could it have been a double cross? Runstead posing as a Consie who was posing as a copysmith, and in reality what?

I began wishing for Kathy for a completely new reason.

When the lieutenant came back it was midnight. "All right," he said to me. "A cab's waiting for you outside. The runner knows where to go."

I climbed out and stretched. "Thanks," I said awkwardly.

The lieutenant spat neatly on the ground between my feet. The door slammed, and I scrambled out of the way of the take-off.

The cab-runner was Mexican. I tried him on a question; no English. I tried again in my Chlorella U. Spanish; he gaped at me. There were fifty good reasons why I didn't want to go along with him without a much better idea of what was up. But when I stopped to think of it, I had damnall choice. The lieutenant had followed his orders. Now the orders were complied with, and I could see his active little military mind framing the report that would tip someone off to where they could find the notorious Consie, Mitchell Courtenay.

I would be a sitting duck; it would depend on whether Taunton or the police got to me first. It was not a choice worth spending much time over.

I got in the cab.

You'd think the fact that the runner was a Mexican would have tipped me off. It didn't, though. It was not until I saw the glimmer of starlight on the massive projectile before me that I knew I was in Arizona, and knew what the President had done for me.

A mixed squad of Pinkertons and our own plant protection men closed in on me and hustled me past the sentry-boxes, across the cleared land, up to the rocket itself. The OIC showed me the crescent he could make with thumb and forefinger and said: "You're safe now, Mr. Courtenay."

"But I don't *want* to go to Venus!" I said.

He laughed out loud.

Hurry up and wait; hurry up and wait. The long, dreary flight had been a stasis; everything at both ends of it had been too frantic with motion over which I had no control to permit thought. They gave me no chance to think here, either; I felt someone grabbing the seat of my pants, and I was hoisted inside. There I was dragged more than led to an acceleration hammock, strapped in and left.

The hammock swung and jolted, and twelve titans brooded on my chest. Good-by, Kathy; good-by, Schocken Tower. Like it or not, I was on my way to Venus.

But it wasn't good-by to Kathy.

It was she herself who came to unstrap me when the first blast was over.

I got out of the hammock and tottered weightlessly, rubbing my back. I opened my mouth to make a casual greeting. What came out was a squeaky, "Kathy!"

It wasn't a brilliant speech, but I didn't have time for a brilliant speech. Kathy's lips and my lips were occupied.

When we stopped for breath I said, "What alkaloids do *you* put into the product?" but it was wasted. She wanted to be kissed again. I kissed her.

It was hard work, standing up. Every time she moved we lurched against the rail or drifted off the floor entirely; only a standby jet was operating and we were otherwise beyond any consideration.

We sat down.

After a while, we talked.

I stretched and looked around me. "Lovely place you have here," I said. "Now that that's taken care of, I have something else on my mind. Questions: two of them." I told her what the questions were.

I explained about Runstead's lousing up San Diego and Venus Project. And about Hester's murder.

"Oh, Mitch," she said. "Where do I begin? How'd you ever get to be star class?"

"Went to night school," I said. "I'm still listening."

"Well, you should be able to figure it out. Sure, we Consies wanted space travel. The human race needs Venus. It needs an unspoiled, unwrecked, unexploited, unlooted, un—"

"Oh," I said.

"—unpirated, undevastated—well, you see. Sure we wanted a ship to go to Venus. But we didn't want Fowler Schocken on Venus. Or Mitchell Courtenay, either. Not as long as Mitchell Courtenay was the kind of guy who would gut Venus for an extra megabuck's billing. There aren't too many planets around that the race can expand into, Mitch. We couldn't have Fowler Schocken's Venus Project succeed."

"Um," I said, digesting. "And Hester?"

Kathy shook her head. "You figure that one out," she said.

"You don't know the answer?"

"I do know the answer. It isn't hard."

I coaxed, but she wouldn't play. So I kissed her for a while again, until some interfering character with a ship's-officer rosette on his shoulder came grinning in. "Care to look at the stars, folks?" he asked, in a tourist-guide way that I detested. It didn't pay to pull rank on him, of course; ships' officers always act a cut above their class, and it would have been ungraceful, at least, to brace him for it. Besides—

Besides.

The thought stopped me for a moment: I was used to being star class by now. It wasn't going to be fun, being one of the boys. I gave my Consie theory a quick mental runthrough. No, there was nothing in it that indicated I would have a show-dog's chance of being sirred and catered to any more.

Hello, Kathy. Good-by, Schocken Tower.

Anyway, we went up to the forward observation port. All the faces were strange to me.

There isn't a window to be found on the Moon ships; radar-eyed, GCA-tentacled, they sacrifice the esthetic but useless spectacle of the stars for the greater strength of steel. I had never seen the stars in space before.

Outside the port was white night. Brilliant stars shining against a background of star particles scattered over a dust of stars. There wasn't a breadth of space the size of my thumbnail where there was blackness; it was all light, all fiery pastels. A rim of fire around the side of the port showed the direction of the sun.

We turned away from the port. "Where's Matt Runstead?" I asked.

Kathy giggled. "Back in Schocken Tower, living on wake-up pills, trying to untangle the mess. *Somebody* had to stay behind, Mitch. Fortunately, Matt can vote your proxies. We didn't have much time to talk in Washington; he's going to have a lot of questions to ask, and nobody around with the answers."

I stared. "What in the world was Runstead doing in Washington?"

"Getting you off the spot, Mitch! After poor little Jack O'Shea broke—"

"After *what?*"

"Oh, good Lord. Look, let's take it in order. O'Shea broke. He got drunk one night too often, and he couldn't find a clear spot in his arm for the needle, and he picked out the wrong girl to break apart in front of. They had him sewed up tight. All about you, and all about me, and the rocket, and everything."

"Who did?"

"Your great and good friend, B. J. Taunton." Kathy struck a match for her cigarette viciously. I could read her mind a little, too. Little Jack O'Shea, sixty pounds of jellied porcelain and melted wax, thirty-five inches of twisted guts and blubber. There had been times in the past weeks when I had not liked Jack. I canceled them all, paid in full, when I thought of that destructible tiny man in the hands of Taunton's anthropoids. "Taunton got it all, Mitch," Kathy said. "All that mattered, anyhow. If Runstead hadn't had a tap on Taunton's interrogation room we would have been had, right then. But Matt had time to get down to Washington and warn me and the President —oh, he's no Consie, the President, but he's a good man. He can't help being born into office. And—here we are."

The captain interrupted us. "Five minutes till we correct," he said. "Better get started back to your hammocks. The correction blasts may not be much—but you never know."

Kathy nodded and led me away. I plucked the cigarette from her lips, took a puff—and gave it back. "Why, Mitch!" she said.

"I'm reformed," I told her. "Uh—Kathy. One more question. It isn't a nice question."

She sighed. "The same as between you and Hester," she said.

I asked, "What was between Jack—uh?"

"You heard me. What was between Jack and me was the same as between you and Hester. All one way. Jack was in love with me, maybe. Something like that. I—wasn't." And torrentially: "Because I was too damn crazy mad in love with you!"

"Uh," I said. It seemed like the moment to reach out and kiss her again, but it must not have been because she pushed me away. I cracked my head against the corridor wall. "Ouch," I said.

"That's what you're so stupid about, curse you!" she was saying. "Jack wanted me, but I didn't want anyone but you, not ever. And you never troubled to figure it out—never knew how much I cared about you any more than you knew how much Hester cared about you. Poor Hester—who knew she could never have you. Good lord, Mitch, how blind can you be?"

"Hester in love with me?"

"Yes, damn it! Why else would she have committed suicide?" Kathy actually stamped her foot, and rose an inch above the floor as a result.

I rubbed my head. "Well," I said dazedly.

The sixty-second beeper went off. "Hammocks," said Kathy, and the tears in her eyes flooded out. I put my arm around her.

"This is a stinking undignified business," she said. "I have exactly one minute to kiss and make up, let you get over your question-and-answer period, intimate that I have a private cabin and there's two hammocks in it, and get us both fastened in."

I straightened up fast. "A minute is a long time, dear," I told her.

It didn't take that long.

THE
MERCHANTS'
WAR

For
John and David
and for
Ann, Karen, Fred the Fourth and Kathy
with abiding love

Why do I write satire?
Ask, instead, how can I help it?
—Juvenal

Tennison Tarb

· · ◆ · ·

I

The woman was a wimp. Pathetically she had tried to make herself pretty for the interview. It was a waste of time. She was a sallow, sickly-looking little creature, and she licked her lips as she stared around my office. It is not an accident that the walls of the interview office are covered with full-D, full-movement advertising posters for brand-name goods. "Gee," she sighed, "I'd do just about anything for a slug of good old Coffiest!"

I gave her my most dishonest look of honest bewilderment. I touched her dossier display. "That's funny. It says here that you warned Venusians that Coffiest was addictive and health threatening."

"Mr. Tarb, I can explain!"

"And then there's what it says on your visa application." I shook my head. "Can this be right? 'The planet Earth is rotten to the core, raped by vicious advertising campaigns, the citizens mere animals and the property of the rapacious advertising Agencies'?"

She gasped, "How did you get that? They said the visa documents were secret!" I shrugged noncommittally. "But I had to say that. They make you abjure advertising or they won't let you in," she wailed.

I maintained my bland expression—seventy-five per cent "I'd like to help you," twenty-five per cent "But you really are *disgusting*." The whole performance was old stuff by now. I'd been seeing this wimp's kind at least once a week for the four years of my tour on

Venus, and habit didn't make them any more attractive. "I know I made a bad mistake, Mr. Tarb," she whimpered, voice full of sincerity, eyes big and staring out of an emaciated face. Well, the sincerity was fake, although well enough done. But the eyes were terrified. The terror was real, because she surely didn't want to stay on Venus any more. You could always tell the desperate cases. The emaciation was the tip-off. The medics call it "anorexia ignatua." It's what happens when a decent, well-brought-up Terrestrial consumer finds himself in a Veenie store, day after day, and can't ever figure out what to buy for dinner because he hasn't had the wise and useful counseling of brand-name advertising to guide him. "So please, I beg you—can't I have a return visa?" she finished, with what I suppose she thought was a prettily pleading smile.

I winked up at the hologram of Fowler Schocken on the wall. Normally I would have left the creature to stew in the room with the commercials for ten minutes or so while I went off on some pretended errand. But my instincts told me she didn't need any more softening up—and besides, a little tingle in my glands reminded me that I was not talking only to the wimp.

I let down the hammer; nice-guy time was over. "Elsa Dyckman Hoeniger," I barked, reading her name off the visa application, "you are a traitor!" The bony jaw dropped in shock. The big eyes started to fill with tears. "According to your dossier you came of good consumer stock. Member of the Junior Copysmiths as a child. A fine education at G. Washington Hill University in New Haven. A responsible job in Customer Relations with one of the largest credit jewelry chains—and, I see, with a lifetime refund ratio of less than one tenth of one per cent, a record that got you a 'Superior' rating in your personnel file! And yet you turned your back on all of it. You denounced the system that gave you birth and defected to this sales-forsaken wasteland!"

"I was misled," she whimpered, the tears spilling down.

"Of course you were misled," I snarled, "but you should have had enough common decency to keep that from happening!"

"Oh, please! I'll—I'll do anything! Just let me come back home!"

It was the moment of truth. I pursed my lips in silence for a moment. Then, "Anything," I repeated, as though I had never heard such a word from a chickened-out turncoat before. I let her sob herself dry, peering into my face with fear and despair. When the first touch of hope began to show through, I made my pitch.

"There *might* be a way," I said. And stopped there.

"Yes, yes! Please!"

I made a production of studying her dossier all over again. "Not right away," I cautioned at last.

"That's all right," she cried eagerly. "I'll wait—weeks, if I have to!"

I laughed scornfully. "Weeks, eh?" I shook my head. "Elsa," I said, "I don't think you're serious. What you did can't be paid for in a couple of lousy weeks—or months, either. You've got the wrong attitude. Forget what I said. Application denied." And I stamped her form and handed it back to her with a big red legend that glittered *Refused.*

I leaned back and waited for the rest of the performance. It came just the way it always did. First there was shock. Then a searing glare of rage. Then, slowly, she got up and blindly pushed her way out of my office. The scenario never changed, and I was really good at my part.

As soon as the door was closed, I grinned up at Fowler Schocken's picture and said, "How'd it go?" The picture disappeared. Mitzi Ku grinned back at me.

"First-rate, Tenny," she called. "Come on down and celebrate." It was the right answer, and I paused only long enough to stop by the commissary and pick up something to celebrate with.

When they built the Earth Embassy in Courtenay Center—it would be more accurate to say when they dug it—they had to use native labor. It was a treaty rule. On the other hand, the crumbly, fried Venusian rock is easy to dig. So when the first lot of dips moved in, their Marine guard was given double duty for a year. Four hours in smart uniform, standing outside the Embassy lock; another four hours down in the depths of the Embassy, quarrying out extra space and lining it for our War Room. The Veenies never guessed we had it, in spite of the fact that half the Embassy was swarming with Veenie workers during business hours—they weren't allowed into the dips' lavatories, and through the end cubicle in each toilet was the secret entrance to what was, primarily, the place where Cultural Attaché Mitsui Ku kept her noncultural records.

When I got there, breathless and balancing the bottle of genuine Earthside drinking whiskey and ice on a tray, Mitzi was patterning data on the wimp into her file. She rasied a hand to keep me from interrupting and pointed to a chair, so I mixed a couple of drinks and waited, feeling good.

Mitzi Ku is a brassy lady—starting with her skin color, which is that creamy Oriental tone; and she talks brassy and acts brassy. Just the type I like. She has that startlingly black Oriental hair, but her eyes are blue. She's as tall as I am, though a lot better built. Take her all in all—as I was always anxious to do—and she was about the best-looking agent-runner we'd ever had in the Embassy. "I wish I weren't going home," I offered, as she came to what seemed to be a pause.

"Yeah, Tenny," she said absently, reaching out for her drink. "Real damn shame."

"You could rotate, too," I suggested—not for the first time—and she didn't even answer. I hadn't expected her to. She wasn't going to do that, and I knew why. Mitzi had only eighteen months on Venus, and you don't get Brownie points from your Agency for anything less than three years hard duty. Quick-trick people don't really pay their travel expense. I tried a different tack: "Think you can turn her?"

"Her? The wimp? God, yes," said Mitzi contemptuously. "I watched her leave the Embassy on the closed-circuit. She was breathing flame and fury. She'll be telling all her friends that Earth's even rottener than she thought when she defected. Then it'll begin to hit her. I'll give her another couple days, then call her in for—let's see—yeah, to straighten out some credit charge from back on Earth. Then I'll give her the pitch. She'll turn."

I leaned back and enjoyed my drink. "You could say a little more," I encouraged.

Those blue eyes narrowed alarmingly, but obediently she said, "You did a good job on her, Tenny."

"More than that even, maybe," I persisted. "Like, 'You did a good job on the wimp, Tenny dear, and why don't we get back together again?' "

The narrowed eyes became a genuine frown—a serious one. "Hell, Tenny! It was great, you and me, but it's over. I'm reupping and you're going back, and that's the end of it."

I didn't have the sense to give up. "I'm here for another week," I pointed out, and she really flared.

"Cut it out, damn it!"

So I cut it out. And I damned it. Especially I damned Hay Lopez

—Jesus Maria Lopez on the books—who was not as handsome as I, or (I hoped) as good in bed as I, but had one big advantage over me. Hay Lopez was staying and I was going home, and so Mitzi was taking thought for the morrow.

"You can be a real pain, Tenny," she complained. The frown was solid. When Mitzi frowned you knew she was frowning. Even before she frowned, while the tempest was still gathering on the horizon, you could see the clouds, two narrow vertical lines above her nose, between her pencil-thin brows. They meant, *Beware! Storm coming!* And then the blue eyes would freeze, and the lightning would flash—

Or not. This time it was not. "Tenny," she said, relaxing a bit, "I've got an idea about the wimp. Do you suppose we could work her into the Veenie spy system?"

"Why bother?" I grunted. The Veenies just didn't have the brains to be good spies. They were dregs. Half the crazy Conservationists that emigrated to Venus were going to wish they'd never come within the first six months, and half of those were going to beg to be let back on Earth. I was the one in charge of telling them they didn't have a prayer—my main title at the Embassy was Deputy Chief of Consular Services. Mitzi was the one who picked them up a little later and turned them into her agents. Her title was Associate Manager of Cultural Relationships, but the main Cultural Relationship she had with the Veenies was a bomb in an airport locker or a fire in a warehouse. Sooner or later the Veenies would wake up to the fact that they couldn't beat a planet of forty billion people, even if it was a long way off in space. Then they'd be down on their knees begging to be let back into the fellowship of prosperous, civilized humanity. Meanwhile, it was Mitzi's job to keep them from getting comfortable out in the cold. Or, more accurately—considering what sort of a hellhole their planet was—out in the hot. Spies? We didn't have to worry about Veenie spies! "—What?" I said, suddenly aware she was still talking.

"They're up to something, Tenny," she said. "Last time I went to Port Kathy my hotel room was searched."

"Forget it," I said positively. "Listen. What shall we do with the time I've got left?"

The twin creases above her nose flickered for a moment, then waned again. "Well," she said, "what've you got in mind?"

"A little trip," I offered. "The shuttle's at the PPC now, so I'll have to go up there for the prisoner bargaining—I thought you might want to come along—"

"Aw, Tenny," she said earnestly, "you have the *worst* ideas! Why would I want to go there?" It was true that the Polar Penal Colony wasn't high on Venus's list of tourist attractions—not that there was anything else on the list to speak of, either, Venus being what it is. "Anyway the shuttle's coming here next, and I'll be up to my ears. Thanks. But no." She hesitated. "Still, it's a pity you didn't see the real Venus."

"The real Venus?" It was my turn to scoff. The heat of real Venus would melt the fillings in your teeth if you ever exposed yourself to it—even around the cities, where there's been substantial climate modification, the temperature is still awful and the air is poison gas outside the enclosures. You want to know what the "real" Venus was like? Look in an old-fashioned coal furnace after the fire's gone out but it's still too hot to touch.

"I don't mean the badlands," she said quickly. "What about Russian Hills, though? You've never been to see the Venera spacecraft, and it's only an hour away—I mean, if we wanted to spend a day together."

"Fine!" I could think of better things to do on a day together, but was willing to settle for any offer. "Today?"

"Hell, no, Tenny, where's your mind? It's their Day of Planetary Mourning. All recreational things will be shut down."

"When, then?" I pressed, but she only shrugged. I didn't want the frown lines to set in again, so I changed the subject. "What are you going to offer her?"

She looked startled. "Who? Oh, you mean the renegade. The usual thing, I guess. I'll get five years as an agent out of her, then we'll repatriate her—though only if she's done a good job."

I said, "Maybe you don't have to go that high. I was watching her closely, and she's prime. How about if you just give her PX privileges once a month? Once she gets in the store and gets some of those good old Earth brand names she'll do anything you want."

Mitzi finished her drink and put the glass back on the tray, looking at me in a peculiar way. "Tenny," she said, half-laughing, half-shaking her head, "I'm going to miss you when you rotate. You know what I think sometimes, like when I can't get to sleep right away? I think maybe, looked at in a certain way, it's not such a morally good thing I do, turning ordinary citizens into spies and saboteurs—"

"Now, wait a minute!" I snapped. There are some things you don't say even as a joke. But she held up her hand.

"And then I look at you," she said, "and I see that, viewed in a certain way, compared to you I'm practically a saint. Now get out of here and let me get back to work, will you?"

So I got, wondering whether I'd gained or lost by that little discussion. But at least we had a sort of date, and I had an idea for improving on it.

The Day of Planetary Mourning was one of the nastiest of the Venusian holidays. It was the anniversary of the death of that old bastard Mitchell Courtenay. So naturally the Veenie clerical help and porters took the day off, and I had to get my own coffee-sub to take to the second-floor lounge. From there I had a good look at the "celebrations" outside the Embassy.

Your basic Veenie is a troglodyte, which is to say a cave dweller, which is to say that, Hilsch tubes or none, they're a long way from blowing off all the nasty gases that stink up their air. I admit they've made progress. You can go outdoors in a thermal suit and air-pack if you want to, at least in the suburbs around the cities—personally, I seldom wanted to. But even there the air is still poison. So the Veenies picked out the steepest, deepest valleys on the planet's cracked and craggy surface and roofed them over. Long and narrow and winding, your typical Veenie city is what Mitzi calls an "eel's lair". But your typical Veenie city isn't anywhere near being a real city, of course. The biggest of them is maybe a pitiful hundred thousand people, and that's only when pumped full of tourists on one of their disgusting national holidays. Imagine celebrating the traitor Mitch Courtenay! Of course, the Veenies don't know the inside story of Mitch Courtenay the way I do. My grandmom's dad was Hamilton Harns, a senior vice-president at Fowler Schocken Associates, the very Agency that Courtenay had betrayed and disgraced. When I was little, Grandmom used to tell how her father had spotted Courtenay for a troublemaker at once—Courtenay had even fired him, and a bunch of other loyal, sales-fearing executives in the San Diego branch, to cover up his wickedness. Of course, the Veenies are so crazy they'd call that a victory for right and justice.

The Embassy is located on the city's main drag. O'Shea Boulevard, and of course on a day like this the Veenies were busy at their favorite sport—demonstrations. There were signs saying *No advertising!* and signs saying *Earthmen go home!* The usual stuff. I was amused to see the morning's wimp appear, wrench a banner from a tall man with red hair and green eyes and go marching and shouting slogans back and forth in front of the Embassy. Right on schedule. The fever in the wimp was rising, and when it fell she would be weak and unresisting.

The lounge began to fill with senior staff for the eleven o'clock briefing session, and one of the first to arrive was my roommate and rival, Hay Lopez. I jumped up and got his coffee-sub for him, and he looked at me with suspicion. Hay and I were not friends. We shared a duplex suite: I had the top berth. There were real good reasons for us not to like each other. I could imagine how he had felt, all those months, listening to Mitzi and me in the bunk above. I didn't have to imagine, really, since I had come to know what it was like to hear sounds from below.

But there was a way of dealing with Hay Lopez, because he had a black mark on his record. He had fouled up somehow when he was a Junior Media Director at his Agency. So naturally they furloughed him to the military for nearly a year, on reservation duty, trying to bring the Port Barrow Eskimos up to civilized standards. I didn't know exactly what he'd done. But Hay didn't know I didn't know, and so a couple of judicious hints had kept him worried. He ran scared anyway, trying to erase that old blot, working harder than anybody else in the Embassy. What he didn't want was another tour of duty north of the Arctic Circle; after the sea-ice and the tundra, he was the only one among us who never complained about the Venusian climate. So, "Hay," I said, "I'm going to miss the old place when I get back to the Agency."

That doubled the suspicion in his eyes, because he knew that was a lie. What he didn't know was why I was telling it. "We'll miss you, too, Tenny," he lied back. "Got any idea what you'll be assigned to?"

That was the opening I wanted. "I'm thinking of putting in for Personnel," I lied. "I think it's a natural, don't you? Because the first thing they'll want is updates on performance here—say," I said, as though suddenly remembering, "we're from the same Agency! You and me and Mitzi. Well, I'll have a lot to say about you two! Real star-class performers, both of you." Of course, if Lopez thought it over he'd realize the last thing I'd put in for—or get—would be Personnel, because my whole training was Copy and Production. But I only said Hay was hard-working, I never said he was smart; and before he knew what was happening I'd got his promise to take over my Polar Penal Colony trip for me—"to break in in case he got the assignment when I left." I left him puzzling it out and went over to join a conversation about the kinds of cars we'd owned back on Earth.

The Embassy had a hundred and eight on the duty roster—the Veenies were always after us to cut the number in half, but the Ambassador fought them off. He knew what those extra sixty people were there for—of course, so did the Veenies. I was maybe tenth or eleventh in the hierarchy, both because of my consular duties and my side assignment as Morale Officer. This meant that I was the one who selected commercials for the in-house TV circuits and—well— kept an eye on the other hundred and seven for Conservationist leanings. That didn't take much of my time, though. We were a hand-picked crew. More than half of us were former Agency personnel, and even the consumers were a respectable bunch, for consumers. If anything, some of the young ones were *too* loyal. There'd been incidents. A couple of the Marine guards, just weeks before, had got a little too much popskull into them and flashed eye-resonating commercials at three of the natives with their hand weapons. The Veenies were not amused, and we'd had to put the Marines under house arrest for deportation. They weren't present now, of course; the eleven o'clock briefing was only for us twenty-five or so seniors. I made sure there was a place next to me when Mitzi came in, late as usual; she glanced at Hay Lopez, sulking by the window, then shrugged and sat down to join the conversation.

"Morning, Mitzi," grunted the Protocol Chief, just in front of us, and went right on: "I used to have a Puff Adder, too, but pumping with your hands that way you can't get the acceleration—"

"You can if you put the muscle in it, Roger," I told him. "And, see, half the time you're stuck in traffic anyway, right? So one hand's plenty for propulsion. You've got the other free for, well, signaling or something."

"Signaling," he said, staring at me. "How long have you been driving, Tenny?" And the Chief Code Clerk leaned past Mitzi to put in:

"You ought to try a Viper, with that lightweight direct drive. No pedals, just put your foot down on the roadway and push. Talk about get-up-and-go!"

Roger looked at her scornfully. "Yeah, and what about braking? You can fracture your leg in an emergency stop. No, I say the foot pedal and chain drive is the only way to go—" His expression changed. "Here they come," he grunted, and turned around to face front as the heavyweights came in.

The Ambassador is a really imposing man, Media back on Earth, with that pepper-and-salt curly hair and that solid, humorous, dark-complected face. He wasn't from our Agency, as it happened—the big ones took turns naming the top people, and it hadn't been our turn—but I could respect him as a craftsman. And he knew how to run a meeting. First order of business was the Political Officer, fluttering anxiously over one more of the crises that plagued his days. "We've had another note from the Veenies," he said, wringing his hands. "It's about Hyperion. They claim we're violating basic human rights by not allowing the gas miners freedom to choose their own communications media—you know what that means."

We did, and there were instant mutters of "What nerve!" "Typical Veenie arrogance!" The helium-3 miners on the moon Hyperion only amounted to about five thousand people, and as a market they'd never be missed. But it was a matter of principle to keep them well supplied with advertising—one Venus in the Solar System was enough.

The Ambassador was having none of it. "Reject the note," he rapped frostily. "It's none of their damned business, and you shouldn't have let them hand it to you in the first place, Howard."

"But how could I know until I read it?" wailed the Political Officer, and the Ambassador gave him the I'll-see-you-later look before relaxing into a smile.

"As you all know," he said, "the Earth ship has been orbiting for ten days now, should be sending the shuttle down here any time. I've been in touch with the captain, and there's good news and bad. The good news is they've got some fine stuff for us—a troop of ethnic dancers, disco and Black Bottom, as cultural exchange, Mitzi, you'll be in charge of them, of course. They've also got ten metric tons of supplies—Coffiest, ReelMeet, tapes of the latest commercials, all the goodies you've all been waiting for!" General expressions of joy and satisfaction. I took the opportunity to reach out for

Mitzi's hand, and she didn't withdraw it. The Ambassador went on: "That's the good news. The bad news is, as you all know, when the shuttle takes off she'll be taking with her one of our favorite members of our happy family here. We'll say good-by to him in a better way the night before he leaves—but meanwhile, Tennison Tarb, would you like to stand up so we can show you how much we're going to miss you?"

Well, I hadn't expected it. It was one of the great moments of my life. There is no applause like the plaudits of your peers, and they gave it unstintingly—even Hay Lopez, though he was frowning as he clapped.

I don't know what I said, but when it was over and I was back in my chair I was surprised to find I didn't have to reach out for Mitzi's hand again. She had taken mine.

In the afterglow I leaned over to whisper in her ear, meaning to tell her that I'd fobbed the Polar Penal Colony trip off on Hay, and so we could have the whole suite to ourselves that night. It didn't get said. She shook her head, smiling, because the Ambassador had sneaked the new commercial tapes down early in the diplomatic pouch, and of course we all wanted to be quiet while we watched them.

It never did get said. I sat there, dumb and happy, with my arm over Mitzi's shoulder, and it didn't even strike me as worrisome when I noticed Hay's eye on us, glum and resentful—not until he edged his way over to the Ambassador and began whispering in his ear as soon as the films were over. And then it was too late. The son of a gun had thought it through. As soon as the lights went up he came grinning and nodding toward us, all cheer and good-fellowship, and I knew what he was going to say: "Hell, Tenny boy! The damnedest thing! I can't take that PPC sortie for you. Big huddle with the Ambassador tomorrow—know you'll understand how it is —hell of a thing to make you do in your last days here—"

I didn't listen to the rest of it. He was right. It was a hell of a thing to make me do, and I did understand. I understood real well that night, fretfully trying to pillow my head on the uncomfortable seatback of the supersonic flight to the Polar Penal Colony. It would have been a lot easier to get my head comfortable if I hadn't been so dismally sure that I knew exactly where Hay Lopez was pillowing his.

ll

At eight o'clock the next morning I was sitting in the conference room of the prison, across from the Veenie Immigration and Passport Control bureaucrat. "Nice to see you again, Tarb," he said, unsmiling.

"Always a pleasure to meet with you, Harriman," I answered. Neither of us meant it. We'd sat opposite each other every few months, every time a prison ship came in from Earth, for four years, and we knew there was nothing nice or pleasurable to be expected.

The Polar Penal Colony wasn't really "polar" exactly, because it was up in the Akna Montes, about where the Arctic Circle would have been if Venus had had one. Naturally it wasn't arctic. It wasn't even appreciably less hot than the rest of the planet, but I guess the first Agency survey ships thought it would be. Otherwise why would they claim some of the least desirable real estate on Venus? It was Earth property, precariously established before the Veenie colonists were strong enough to do anything about it, and retained out of habit, like the foreign compounds in Shanghai before the Boxer Rebellion. At the moment we were on Veenie territory, in one of the few aboveground buildings at the perimeter of the PPC itself. The Veenies had rigid roofs over valleys. The prisoners—*greks,* we called them—had caves. The whole Polar Prison Colony was right outside our window, but you couldn't see it. Here, too, since the kiln-dried Venusian rock was easy to dig, the prison had been dug.

"I ought to tell you, Tarb," he said smiling, but the tone was ominous, "that I've had some criticisms aimed at me since our last meeting. They say I've been too flexible. I don't think I can be as accommodating this time."

I responded to the ploy instantly: "Funny you should say that, Harriman, because I've had the same thing. The Ambassador was furious over my letting you take those two credit delinquents." Actually the Ambassador hadn't said a word, but then neither had Harriman's bosses. He nodded, acknowledging the end of the first round with no decision either way and began to roll the dossiers.

Harriman was a hardball bargainer, and sneaky. So was I. We both knew the other fellow was out to gain victories, straight mano-a-mano, the only difference being that the best victories were when the other fellow never found out what he had lost. Earth had emptied its jails and dumped the worst of the scum here. Murderers, rapists, credit-card frauds, arsonists were the least of them. Or the worst, depending on your point of view. We didn't want the occasional mugger, for instance—didn't want the expense of feeding him, didn't want the task of keeping him in line. Neither did the Veenies. What the Veenies wanted out of each prisoner contingent was the vilest of the traitors. Conservationists. Contract Breach felons. Antiadvertising zealots, the kinds that deface billboards and short-circuit holograms. They wanted to make them full Venusian citizens. We didn't want to give them up. They were the kind we used to brainburn, sometimes still do, and if they were lucky enough to get away with five or ten PPC years from some soft-hearted judge we felt they should serve them out in full. Those people *earned* their sentences! Letting them go free into the Venusian population was no punishment at all. In practice, it came down to a horse trade. Both of us gave a little, took a little; the art of the bargaining was to reluctantly "give" what you were really anxious to have the other guy take.

I plinked the display key and cursored the top six names. "Moskowicz, McCastry, Bliven, the Farnell family—I suppose you want those, but you can't have them until they've served at least six months hard."

"Three months," he bargained. They were all down as CCs—criminal Conservationists—just the kind of misfits the Veenies welcomed into their population.

I said positively, "*Six* months, and I ought to hold out for a year. On Earth they're the worst kind of criminals, and they need to be taught a lesson."

He shrugged, disliking me. "What about this next prisoner, Hamid?"

"Worst of the lot," I declared. "You can't have him. He's convicted of credit-card larceny, and he's a Consie to boot."

He tensed at the epithet but inspected the printout. "Hamid wasn't convicted of, ah, Conservationism," he pointed out.

"Well, no. We couldn't get a confession." I smiled confidentially, one law-enforcement officer to another. "We didn't have any first-hand witnesses, either, because, as I understand it, his whole cell was picked up and liquidated some time ago, and he was never able to make contact again. Oh, and there's some evidence 'Hamid' isn't his real name—the technicians think his Social Security tattoo's been altered."

"You didn't prosecute him for that," said Harriman thoughtfully.

"Didn't need to. Didn't need to press the Conservationist count, either—we had him fair and square on credit-card. Now," I said, rushing him on, "what about these three? They're all Medicare malingerers, not a very serious offense—I could commute them right away if you want to take them in—"

If there's one thing Veenies hate, it's being put in a position where their "ideals" tell them one thing and their common sense something else. He flushed and stammered. Theoretically the Medicare frauds were perfect candidates for Venusian citizenship. They were also *old*, and therefore liabilities in what is still, after all, a pretty rugged frontier society. It took his mind right off Hamid, as I had wanted it to do.

Four hours later we were at the bottom of the list. I'd given him fourteen greks, six right away, the others over a matter of months. He'd refused two, and I'd held onto another twenty or so. We still hadn't settled Hamid. He glanced at his notes. "I am instructed," he said, "to inform you that my government is not satisfied with your compliance with the Protocol of '53. Under it we have the right to inspect this prison at yearly intervals."

"Reciprocally," I corrected him. I knew the Protocol by heart; each power had agreed, fulsomely and generously, to let the other inspect all penal, corrective or rehabilitative institutions to assure compliance with humanitarian standards. Fat chance! Their Xeng Wangbo "retraining center" was in the middle of the Equatorial Anti-Oasis, and no dip had ever been allowed near it. Of course, what we did inside the PPC was none of their business, either. Veenie law insisted that every grek get his own bunk with a minimum of twenty-four cubic feet of space. That was no punishment at all! There were plenty of sales-revering consumers back home that never saw that much space. There was no use arguing about it, though. The Veenie building inspectors had insisted we build in that much space, but as soon as the prison was finished the warden just closed off a couple of bays and doubled everybody up.

"It's a matter of basic human standards," he snapped. I didn't bother to answer, only laughed at him silently—I didn't have to mention Xeng Wangbo. "All right," he grumped, "then what about commercials? Several parolees have testified that you're in violation there!"

I sighed. Same old argument, every time. I said, "According to section 6-C of the Protocol a commercial is defined as 'a persuasive offering of goods or services.' There's no offer, is there? I mean, the things can't be *offered* when they're not available, and the greks can't ever have such things. It's part of their punishment." The rest of their punishment, to be sure, was that they were continually bombarded with advertising for the things they couldn't have. But that, too, was none of his business.

The quick gleam in Harriman's eye warned me I had fallen into a trap. "Of course," I backtracked swiftly, "there are exceptions to the general rule, so trivial in nature that one need not even mention them—"

"Exceptions," he said gleefully. "Yes, Tarb, there are exceptions, all right. We have affidavits from no fewer than eight parolees stating that prisoners have been driven by the commercials to write their families and friends back on Earth for some of the advertised goods! In particular, we have evidence that Coffiest, Mokie-Koke and Starrzelius brand Nick-O-Teen Chewies have been included in prisoners' Red Cross packages for that reason. . . ."

We were off. I abandoned all hope of catching the return flight that night, because I knew we would be haggling now well past midnight.

So we were, with much consultation of "clarificatory notes" and "position statements" and "emendations without prejudice." I knew he wasn't serious. He was just trying to establish a bargaining position for what he really wanted. But he argued tenaciously, until I offered to cancel all Red Cross packages completely for the greks if that would make him happy. Well, obviously he didn't want that, so he offered a deal. He dropped the question of commercials in return for early commutation for some of his pet greks.

So I gave him slap-on-the-wrist, token ten-day sentences for Moskowicz, McCastry, Bliven, the Farnell family . . . and Hamid. As I had planned to all along.

Harriman was all smiles and hospitality once I'd given him what he wanted—or thought he wanted. He insisted I spend the night in his pied-à-terre in the Polar town. I slept badly, having refused his offer of a nightcap or several—I didn't intend to take chances on spilling information I didn't want him to have. Also, all night long I kept waking up with that panicky agoraphobic feeling you get when you're in a place that's *too large*. Crazy Veenies! They have to fight for every cubic foot of living space, and yet Harriman had *three whole rooms!* And in an apartment he didn't use more than ten nights a year! So I got up early the next morning and by six A.M. I was standing in line at the airport check-in counter. Ahead of me was a teenage Veenie with one of those "patriotic" tee shirts that say *Hucks Go Home* on the front and *No *DV*RT*S*NG* on the back—as though "advertising" were a dirty word! I wouldn't give him the satisfaction of looking at him, so I turned away. Behind me was a short, slim black woman who looked vaguely familiar. "Hello, Mr. Tarb," she said, amiably enough, and it turned out she was familiar enough—a local fire inspector or something back at the port. She'd toured the Embassy a few times, checking for violations.

She turned out to be my seatmate on the flight, as well. I had automatically assumed she was a Veenie spy—all the natives who got into the Embassy for any reason at all, we knew, were likely to file reports on what they'd seen. But she was surprisingly open and friendly. Not your typical Veenie crackpot at all. She didn't talk politics. What she talked about was a lot more interesting to me: Mitzi. She'd seen the two of us together in the Embassy and guessed we were lovers—true enough then!—and she said all the right things about Mitzi. Beautiful. Intelligent. Energetic.

What I had intended to do on the return flight was sleep, but the conversation was so congenial that I spent the whole time chatting. By the time we touched down I was babbling about all my hopes and dreams. How I had to return to Earth myself. How I wished Mitzi would rotate with me, but how determined she was to stay on. How I dreamed of a longtime relationship—maybe even marriage. A home in Greater New York, maybe out toward the Forest Preserve Acre at Milford . . . maybe a kid or two. . . . It was funny. The more I said, the sadder and more thoughtful it seemed to make her.

But I was sad enough myself, because I couldn't believe that any of that was going to happen.

III

But things began to brighten astonishingly when I got back to the Embassy. First I encountered Hay Lopez, coming out of the men's room—coming out of Mitzi's hideaway, I was pretty sure. But he didn't say anything, just growled as we passed. The expression on his face, glum and irritated, was exactly what I might have hoped to see.

And when I flushed my way through the private door into the War Room, the look on Mitzi's face was just as good. She was grimly punching data into her files, flustered and annoyed. Whatever had gone on those two nights I had been away, it was no idyll. "I got Hamid in," I reported proudly, and leaned over to kiss her. No problem! No enthusiasm, either, but she did kiss me back, tepidly.

"I was sure you would, Tenny," she sighed, and the frown lines began to dwindle; they hadn't been aimed at me. "When can he report for duty?"

"Well, I didn't actually talk to him, of course. But he's got a ten-day parole. I'd say two weeks at the outside."

She looked really pleased. She made a note to herself, then pushed back her chair and gazed into space. "Two weeks," she said thoughtfully. "Wish we'd had him here for the Day of Planetary Mourning—he could have heard all kinds of things in that crowd. Still, there's other stuff coming up—they're going to have one of their elections next month, so there'll be all sorts of political meetings—"

I put my finger on her mouth. "What's coming up," I said, "and that tomorrow night, is my farewell party. Would you be my date for the party?"

She gave me an actual smile. "On your big night? Of course I will."

"And maybe take the day off tomorrow so we can do something together?"

Faint shadow of the frown lines coming back. "Well, I'm really awfully busy right now, Tenn—"

I took a chance. "But not with Hay Lopez, right?"

Frown lines deep and blazing. "No chance!" she hissed dangerously. *"Nobody* can treat me the way he wants to—thinks he owns me!"

I kept my face bland and sympathetic, but inside I was grinning the top of my head off. "So about tomorrow?"

"Well, why not? Maybe we'll—I don't know—go out to Russian Hills maybe. Something, anyway." She leaned forward and pecked my cheek. "If I'm going to take tomorrow off I've got a heavy day today, Tenny—so clear out, will you?" But she said it fondly.

To my surprise, she was serious about making us visit the old Russian Venera rocket. I humored her. I suppose, in a way, it would have been missing something for me to leave Venus without taking a look at one of its most famous artifacts. We ducked out of the Embassy early and took an electrohack to the tram station before the streets were really crowded.

Around the major cities the Veenies have managed to grow some grass and weeds and even a few spindly things they call trees—of course, they're specially engineered genetically, somehow or other, but they do show some green now and then. Russian Hills, though, hasn't been changed at all. On purpose.

Do you want to know what kind of crackpots the Venusians are? All right, let me tell you one simple anecdote. You see, they've got that huge planet—five times as much land area as the whole planet Earth, you know, because there aren't any oceans yet. In order to make it into something decent, they've been busting their backs for forty years and more trying to make green things grow. But that's hellishly difficult, because of the kind of planet Venus is. Plants have a tough time. One, there's not really enough light; two, there's damn near no water at all; three, it's way too hot. So to make anything grow at all takes all kinds of technological wizardry and enormous effort. First they had to nuke some tectonic faults to set off volcanos—that's to bring whatever water vapor there is up out of the core (that's the way the Earth got its water billions of years ago, they say). Second, they had to cap the volcanos to catch the water vapor. Third, they had to provide something cold enough to condense the vapor to a liquid; that's the cold end of the Hilsch tubes—you see them on mountaintops all over Venus, big things like one-hole piccolos, with the hot end blasting gases out through the atmosphere to get lost in space and the cold end providing cooling for the cities—and generating a little electricity while they do it. Fourth, they have to pipe that trickle of water to where things are planted, and they have to do it underground so it won't boil away in the first ten feet. Fifth, they have to have special, genetically tailored plants that can whisk that water up through their stems and leaves before letting it boil away—it's a miracle they got any of this done, especially considering they don't have much work force to spare for big projects. There are only about eight hundred thousand Veenies all in all.

And yet—here's the funny thing—if you take the tram out to Russian Hills, the first thing you see in the park itself is a six-man crew working all around the clock, climbing those ugly sharp rocks with hundred-pound backpacks of plant killer, zapping every green thing they see!

Crazy? Of course it's crazy. It's the insanity of Conservationism carried to its lunatic conclusion: the Conservationists want to keep the Venera setting just the way it was when the probe landed. But the lunacy isn't really surprising. "If Veenies weren't crazy they would have stayed on the Earth in the first place," I told Mitzi as we rattled along the tramline. "Look at the dumps they live in!" We were passing through roofed-over suburbs. They were supposed to be high-class residential areas, and yet they were filled with scraggly weeds and pressed-plastic tenements; they didn't even have Astro-Turf!

It occurred to me that I might be talking a little too loudly. The other passengers, all Veenies, were turning around to look at me. That was no big treat. Veenies are almost all grossly tall—even taller than Mitzi, usually—and they seem to take pride in their fishbelly-white skins. Of course, they never get any sun. But they could use UV lamps like we do—all of us—even Mitzi, who doesn't need tanning to have that nice velvet-brass skin.

"Watch your mouth," Mitzi whispered nervously. The Veenie family just in front of us—Daddy, Mommy and four (yes, I said *four!*) kids—were half-turning their heads to get a look at us, and their expressions weren't friendly. Veenies don't like us much. They think we're city slickers trying to gobble them up. That's a laugh, because what have they got worth gobbling? And if we're taking an interest in their affairs, obviously it's for their own good—they're just not intelligent enough to realize it.

Fortunately we had entered the tunnel that goes through the ring of peaks around Russian Hills. Everybody began getting ready to get out. As I started to rise, Mitzi nudged me, and I saw a grossly tall he-Veenie, green eyes and red hair with that ugly dead-white skin, giving me a bad look. I took Mitzi's hint. I gave the Veenie my sweetest forgive-me-for-my-blunders smile and slipped past him out the door. While I stopped to buy a souvenir booklet, Mitzi was standing behind me, gazing after the man with the traffic-light head. "Look at this," I said, opening the guide book, but Mitzi wasn't listening.

"Do you know," she said, "I think I've seen him before. Day before yesterday. When they were demonstrating."

"Come on, Mitz! There were five hundred Veenies out there!" And so there had been—maybe more—at the time, I could have sworn half of Venus was silently parading around our Embassy with their stupid signs—"No Advertising!" and "Take Your Filth Back Where It Belongs!" I didn't mind the picketing so much—but, oh, the pathetic amateurishness of their slogan writers! "They're crazy," I said—a complicated shorthand that didn't mean "crazy" for thinking we would use advertising techniques on them, but "crazy" because they were getting upset about it—as though there were any possibility that, given a chance, we wouldn't.

I also meant crazy in the specific context of incompetent copy-smithing, and that was what I wanted to show Mitzi. I glanced around the noisy car barn—another was just rattling up toward the switching point for the return trip to Port Kathy. No Veenies were within earshot. "Look here," I said, opening to the page marked *Facilities—Food and Drink*. It said:

> If for any reason you do not want to bring your own refreshments while visiting Russian Hills, some items like hamburgers, hot dogs and soy sandwiches are available in the Venera Lounge. They're inspected by the Planetary Health Service, but the quality is mediocre. Beer and other drinks can also be purchased, at about twice the cost of the same things in town.

"Pathetic?" I groaned.

She said absently, "Well, they're honest."

I raised my eyebrows. What did honesty have to do with moving product? And this place was a copysmith's dream! They had a captive clientele, one. They had a theme to hang the copy on, two. And they had customers who were in a holiday mood, ready to buy anything that was for sale, three, and most important of all! All they had to do was call their hot dogs "Genuine Odessa Wurst" and the hamburgers "Komsomol Burgers" to give the consumers an excuse to buy—but instead they talked them right out of it! Consumers didn't expect to *get* what advertising promised. They just wanted that one tiny moment of hope before the "Sleep-Tite Super-Soft" mattress stuck a spring into their bottoms and the "Nature-Fresh Golden-Tropical-Fruit Elixir" turned out to taste of tar. "Well," I said, "we've come this far. Let's go look at their damn space probe."

Venus was a garbage planet to start out. The air was poison, and too much of it, so the pressure was appalling. The heat boiled everything boilable away. There was nothing growing that was worth talking about when the first Earth ship landed, and fifty years of human colonization hadn't made it good: just microscopically less awful. The Veenies' attempts to turn the atmosphere into something a human being could stand weren't finished, but they'd gone far enough that in some places you could get around without a pressure suit nowadays . . . though you needed to carry a breathing tank on your back, because there was precious little oxygen.

This part they called the "Venera–Russian Hills Planetary Park" —so the sign at the tram stop said—wasn't really much worse than the rest of it, no matter how much the Veenie Conservationists patted themselves on the back for retaining its "unspoiled wilderness quality." I gazed at it through the window, and felt no impulse to get closer.

"Let's go, Tenn," Mitzi urged.

"Are you sure you want to do this?" It was nasty enough in the tram station, with the noise of the cars and the Veenies with their giggling brats. Going out of doors meant a whole higher order of nastiness. We'd have to put on the air tanks and sip air from tubes in our mouths, and it would mean even more heat than the interior ovens the Veenies seemed to thrive on. "Maybe we should eat first," I offered, eyeing the refreshment stand. Under the painted legend "Chef's Recommendation for Today" someone had chalked, "Stay away from the scrambled eggs."

"Oh, come on, Tenn! You're always telling me how much you hate Veenie food. I'll go get us a couple of breathers."

When you don't have any choice, go along—that's the motto of the Tarbs. It has served our family well, for we've been members of the advertising profession since the old days of Madison Avenue and the Pepsi-Cola jingle. So I strapped the damn tank on my back and put the damn tube in my mouth and, whispering around the mouthpiece, said, "Into the valley of death, march on!"

Mitzi didn't laugh. She was in a sort of down mood that whole day, I know—I assumed because I was leaving. So I clapped her on the back and we stumbled down the path to the Venera.

The Venera space probe is a hunk of dead metal, about the size of a pedicab, with spiky rods and dishes sticking out of it. It is not in good shape. Time was when it perched on top of a rocket in snowy Tyuratam and blasted its way across a hundred million miles of space to come blazing down through Venus's blistering air. It must have made quite a sight, but of course there wasn't anybody there to see it. After all that trouble and expense it had a working life of a couple of hours. It was long enough for it to radio back some pressure and temperature readings, and transmit a few out-of-focus distorted pictures of the rocks it was sitting on. That was its whole career. Then the poison gases seeped in, and all the circuits and gadgets and gizmos died. I suppose, really, that you'd have to say that the Venera was quite an accomplishment for those old pretechnological days. Those foggy gray camera eyes produced the first look at the surface of Venus that any human being ever had, and when the Veenies stumbled across it, in their first months of colonizing the planet, you would have expected them to want to celebrate it as a triumph, right? Oh, hell, no. The reason the Veenies made such a fuss about this hunk of junk was just more of their weirdness. See, back in those days the Russians were what they called Soviets. I'm not real sure what Soviets were—I always get them mixed up with the Scientologists and the Ghibellines—but I do know that they didn't believe in—wait for it!—in *profit!* That's right. Profit. They didn't believe in people making money out of things. And as for profit's major handmaiden, advertising, well, they just didn't have any! I know that sounds strange, and when we were taking History I back in college I couldn't believe it, so I checked it out. It's true enough. Bar some piddly little things like electric signs boasting about steel production and TV commercials begging the factory hands not to get drunk in working hours, advertising just didn't exist. But it was almost the same now, with the Veenies, and that's why they made a shrine out of two tons of scrap metal. The big difference between the Veenies and the Russians is that after a while the Russians smartened up and joined the free confraternity of profit-loving people, while the Veenies tried their best to go the other way.

After half an hour of climbing around the Venera I'd had about enough. The place was full of Veenie tourists, and I can get real tired of drinking my air out of a soda straw. So while Mitzi was bent over, her lips moving as she tried to make out the Cyrillic script on the nameplate, I reached behind me to the relief valve on my oxygen tank and gave it a little twist. It made a shrill squeal as the gas poured out, but I took a fit of coughing at that moment, and, anyway, the scream of the Hilsch tubes on the hills all around us drowned out most minor sounds. Then I nudged her.

"Oh, damn it all to hell, look at this!" I cried, and showed her my oxygen gauge. It was way down into the yellow, almost touching the red danger zone—I'd cut it a little finer than I intended. "Damn Veenies sold me a half-empty tank! Well," I said, tone reeking with resignation, "I'm sorry about this, but I'm going to have to get back inside the station. Then maybe we should think about heading home."

Mitzi gave me a funny look. She didn't say anything, just turned and started back up the slope. I had no doubt that she had checked the tank gauge when she paid for it, but it wasn't likely she would be *sure* she had. To take the sting out of it, while we were trudging back I caught up with her, took the tube out of my mouth and suggested, "How about a drink in the lounge before we catch the tram?" It's true that I can't stand Veenie food—it's the CO_2 in the air, it makes things grow real fast, and besides the Veenies eat everything fresh, so you never get that good flash-frozen tang. But liquor is liquor, anywhere in the solar system! And besides, eighteen months of dating Mitzi had taught me that she was always a lot more fun with a couple of drinks in her. She brightened right away, and as soon as we'd ditched the tanks—I persuaded her not to make a fuss about the light load in mine—we headed for the stairs to the lounge.

The tram station was typical Veenie construction—it wouldn't have passed muster for a Consumer-level comfort station back home. No vending machines, no games, no educational displays of new products and services. It was hollowed out of the solid rock, and about all they'd done to beautify it was to slap some paint on the walls and plant some flowers and things. The tramline came in through a tunnel at one end. They'd blasted and dug a space for the tram platforms and a waiting room and things like that. They hadn't wanted to spoil the capital-N-Natural capital-B-Beauty of the park, see, so they hid the station inside the hill.

The worst thing about it, I thought at first, was the noise. When a tram barreled into that hard-surfaced echo chamber it was like demolition day in a scrap-iron plant. I almost changed my mind about the drink, but I didn't want to disappoint Mitzi. Then, when we got settled in at a table in the upper-deck lounge, I found out what was even worse. "Look at this," I said in disgust, turning the menu card so we could both read it. It was more of that sickening Veenie "candor," of course:

All cocktails are canned premixes, and they taste like it.

The red wine is corky and not a good year. The white is a little better.

If you want anything to eat you'd do better to go downstairs and bring it up for yourself—otherwise there's a $2 service charge.

Mitzi shrugged. "It's their planet," she said, determined to have a good time, and craned her neck to peer out the window. And that was another thing. So as not to spoil the looks from outside they had artfully hidden the windows in clefts in the rock. From outside it was maybe a good idea; but from inside you couldn't see out without straining, and what's the use of an observation window you can't see out of?

Grin and bear it! I was on my way out of this hellhole anyway. We ordered the white wine, obediently, and Mitzi commented, "Look, there's an ambulance chopper by the path. I wonder if somebody got hurt."

"They probably keep it there for the people they swindle on the oxygen," I joked, bending to look out. The chopper had been there a while, because the rotors were still. Two men were having some kind of an argument beside it. I was mildly surprised to see that one of them was the man with the traffic-light head from the tram. That wasn't so surprising, because there are just so many Veenies and you can't help running into the same ones over and over. But I was beginning to get a little tired of this particular one. "Drink up," I said, dismissing him and paying the waiter at the same time. "A toast! To our good times together—past, present and future!"

"Ah, Tenn," said Mitzi, raising her glass, "I wish. But I'm still going to reup."

The wine was good and cold—well, no; it wasn't all that good, but at least it was cold. Thinking about Mitzi wasting herself for another year and a half, at least, on this smelly cinder of a planet spoiled it for me. "They say if you spend too much time with the Veenies you'll turn into one." I was half-joking—half at the most. And immediately she got her defensive look.

"My Agency has no reason for dissatisfaction with my work," she said stiffly. "The Veenies aren't so bad! A little misguided."

"A little." I gazed around the lounge. The tables were bare plastic. There was no Muzak, no friendly advertising posters decorating the walls.

"It's just a different life-style," she insisted. "Of course, compared to what we have on Earth it's *pathetic*. But all they want from us, really, is just to be left alone."

The conversation was not going at all the way I wanted it to. Sometimes, when I was talking to Mitzi when she was off-duty and off-guard, I wondered if the old saying wasn't true for her. She had been on Venus for eighteen months. She had covered the whole planet, just about, and she had dealt with its seamiest citizens, the turncoats. If there was anybody in the Embassy who should have been sick and disgusted with this primitive place it was Mitzi Ku. But she wasn't. She was going to sign up for another hitch in the oven. She even, sometimes, acted as though she *liked* it here! There were even stories that sometimes she went shopping in the Veenie stores instead of the PX. I didn't believe them, of course. But sometimes I wondered. . . . And yet what she said was true. Her Agency, which was the same as my own, could certainly find nothing wrong with her record on Venus. Her official designation at the Embassy was "visa clerk," but her real work was running a network of spies and saboteurs that stretched from Port Kathy to the Polar Penal Colony. She did it superbly. The computer analyses said the Veenie Gross Planetary Product was off a good 3 per cent just because of Mitzi's work.

And yet she said such strange things! Like, "Oh, Tenn, give them credit. They took a planet that an Arizona rattlesnake couldn't stay alive on, and in less than thirty years they've made it livable—"

"Livable!" I sneered, gazing meaningfully out the window.

"Sure it's livable! At least where they've covered it over. Naturally it's not a South Seas paradise, but they've done a pretty good job, considering what they had to work with." She glanced irritably across the room, where a Veenie family was trying to quiet a screaming child. Then she shrugged. "Oh, they're annoying," she admitted. "But they're not such bad people. Consider what they started from—half of them came here because they were misfits on the Earth and the other half got exiled as criminals."

"Misfits and criminals, right! The dregs of society! And they haven't got much better here!"

But there was no sense spending our last day together arguing politics. I swallowed and changed direction. "Some of them aren't so bad," I conceded. "Especially the kids." That was safe enough, everybody's in favor of kids, and the poor little tyke hadn't stopped screaming. "I wish I could cheer him up," I offered tentatively, "but I think I'd scare him out of his mind—some big huck coming at him that way—"

"Let him yell," said Mitzi, gazing out the window.

I sighed—but silently. There were times when I wondered whether it was worthwhile trying to keep up with Mitzi's moods and peculiarities. But it was. The important thing about Mitzi Ku was that she was a gorgeous woman. She had that perfect silky-brassy honey-almond skin and, for a person of Oriental ancestry, quite a womanly figure. Her eyes weren't that Oriental shoe-button black, either; they were light blue—some fooling around among the progenitors, no doubt. And she had perfect teeth and knew just when to, very delicately, use them. Take her all in all, she was well worth the taking.

So I tried again. I reached out for her hand and said sentimentally, "There's something about that little boy, honey. I look at him and I wish you and I could some day have—"

She flared, "Knock it off, Tarb!"

"I only meant—"

"I know what you meant! Let me tell you the facts. One, I don't like kids. Two, I don't have to like kids, because I don't have to have any—there are plenty of consumers to keep the population up. Three, you're not interested in a kid anyway, you're only interested in what you do to get one started, and the answer is *no*."

I let it drop. It wasn't true, though. Not much more than half-true, anyway.

But then things began to get a little better. I had a powerful ally in the Veenie wine; however it tasted, it had a handsome kick. And the other ally I had was Mitzi herself because the logic of the situation convinced her the way it had convinced me: there was no sense getting into a spat when we had so little time left.

By the time we finished the capsule I had moved over next to her. When I slid my hand around her waist it was just like old times, and, like old times, she leaned into my arm. With my free hand I lifted my glass, with the last quarter-inch of wine in it, and offered a toast: "Here's to us, Mits, and to our last time together." Funny, I thought, peering past her—that bus-person clearing off the tables at the far end of the room: she looked a lot like the woman I'd sat next to on the flight from the Pole.

But I thought no more of it, because Mitzi raised her own glass, smiling at me over the brim, and gave back the toast: "To our last day together, Tenn, and our last night."

That was as clear an exit line as I'd ever heard. We got up and headed for the stairs to the tram station, arms around each other. We were definitely fuzzy from the wine, but even so I nudged Mitzi as we passed the table by the door. Half the Veenies I had ever met seemed to be in this place today; this one was old red-hair green-eyes again. Evidently he'd settled his argument out at the ambulance chopper because he was sitting alone, pretending to be reading the menu—as if that could take more than ten seconds! He glanced up just as we passed. What the hell. I wouldn't have to be seeing any of their bleached dumb faces any more after the shuttle took off, so I gave him a smile. He didn't smile back.

I didn't expect him to, after all. So I just led Mitzi out the door and down the stairs, and forgot the whole incident—for a while.

Hand in hand we strolled to the nearest platform where a tram was waiting. I had thought I had seen people boarding it, but as we were about to get on a Veenie guard hurried up. "Sorry, folks," he panted, out of breath, "but this one's out of service. It's got, uh, a mechanical defect. The next one out—" he pointed—"will be right over there on Platform Three."

There was no tram at Platform Three, but I could see that there was one at the junction point, its nose just poking out from the tunnel, waiting for the signal lights to clear so it could enter the platform.

For some reason I was feeling a little dizzy and generally vague. The wine, I assumed. It kept me from wanting to argue. We turned to start back down the platform but the guard waved us across the tracks. "Save time if you just cut through here," he said helpfully.

Mitzi seemed a little blurry, too, but she asked, "Isn't that dangerous?" And the guard gave us an indulgent let's-not-hit-the-booze-so-hard-next-time chuckle and guided us to the track. No, he didn't guide us. He *shoved* us . . . just as there was a clatter from the end of the platform.

Out of the corner of one eye I saw the tram galumphing down on us. We were right bull's-eye in its path.

"Jump!" I yelled, and, "Jump, Tenny!" yelled Mitzi at the same moment, and jump we both did. I grabbed for Mitzi, and she grabbed for me, and it would have worked out really well if we had jumped in the same direction. But we didn't. We bumped each other. If Mitzi had been smaller, instead of taller, than me, I might have tossed her or tugged her clear; as it was she went one way and I went another, but not quite in time. The tram slammed me out onto the platform, with yells and cursing and screeching of brakes. Flames of pain ran up my legs as I slid across rough concrete on my knees. Somewhere along the line I hit my head a good one—or the tram did.

The next thing I knew my knee and my head were competing to see which one could hurt me the most, and I was hearing yelling voices—

"—couple of hucks tried to cross the track—"

"—one dead and one pretty bad—"

"Get that medic in here!"

And somebody out of the tram was leaning over me, ruddy whiskered face pop-eyed with surprise, and to my astonishment it was Marty MacLeod, the Deputy Station Chief.

I don't remember much of the next little while. There are only flashes: Marty demanding I be taken at once to the Embassy, the medic obstinate that ambulance patients went to the hospital and nowhere else, someone peering over Marty's shoulder and blurting, "Jeez! It's the male huck, and he's alive!" The someone was the traffic-light Veenie.

Then I remember the cement-mixer bumps and jolts of the

ambulance chopper as it leaped the hills around the park, and I went
quietly to sleep. Thinking about Mitzi. Thinking about how I felt.
Thinking that it wouldn't be right to say that I loved her, exactly,
and certainly nothing she ever said to me, in bed or out, sounded
like she felt anything like that . . . but thinking mostly that it was
really sad that she was dead.

But she wasn't.

They kept me an hour in the emergency room—a couple of
Band-Aids and an X-ray series—and when they released me into
Marty's custody they told me Mitzi had nine fractures counted and
at least six internal ruptures that showed on the tomography. She
was in intensive care, and they'd keep us posted.

Good news! But it didn't make my heart sing. Because by then I
was getting my head straight, and the straighter it got the more
certain it became in my mind that the accident had been no accident.

I will say for Marty that when we got inside the bug-proof Embassy
compound she listened seriously while I told her what I thought.
"We'll check," she promised grimly. "Can't do anything till we see
what Mitzi has to say, though—and for now, you're going to sleep."
It wasn't a suggestion. It wasn't even an order. It was a fact, because
they'd slipped me a shot when I wasn't looking, and it was bye-bye
time.

When I woke up I had barely time to dress and get down to the
farewell party in my honor.

Now, really, that's kind of a joke. The Veenies don't have many
public holidays, but the ones they have they celebrate with a lot of
enthusiasm. That's embarrassing for us dips. We need to be part of
the festivities, because that's what diplomacy is all about, but we
certainly can't admit to celebrating most of their holidays—they
have names like "Freedom from Advertising Day" and "Anti-Christ-
mas." Still, we have to do something, so for every holiday we cook
up an excuse to hold a party—for a totally different reason, of
course—at that time. There's always some excuse. Sometimes the
excuses are arranged before the dip gets assigned here. There's old
Jim Holder, for instance, from Codes & Ciphers; they say he was
sent here because he happened to be born on the same date as the
renegade Mitchell Courtenay.

So tonight's party was—nominally—a send-off for me. All the
people I ran into congratulated me on shaking this place loose at

last—and, a couple of steps down on the priority list, oh, yes, your lucky escape from the tram, too, Tenny. That is, the Earth people did that; the Veenies were as always a whole other thing.

Let's be fair to the Veenies. They don't like these ceremonial parties any more than we do, I guess. If they're high enough on the totem pole they get invited. If they get invited they come. Nobody says they have to enjoy themselves. They're polite about it—reasonably polite—if they're female they dance two dances with two separate male Earth dips. I think they like that part, at least, because they're almost always taller than their partners. The conversation is almost always about the same—

"Hot today."

"Was it? I didn't notice."

"The new Hilsch plant's coming along nicely."

"Thank you."

—then the second obligatory dance with a different partner and then, if you happen to look around for them—though why you would do that I can't guess—they're gone. The male Veenies do about the same, except that it's two drinks at the bar instead of two dances, and the conversation isn't about the weather, it's about Port Kathy's chances against North Star in the rolley-hockey league. It's just as bad when we have to go to one of their formal parties. We don't linger, either. Mitzi says that her spies tell her the Veenies' parties usually get to be real hell-roaring balls after we leave, but none of us are ever urged to stay. Dips' parties are meant to be diplomatic: nothing heavy discussed, and certainly not much fun.

But sometimes it doesn't go like that. My first duty dance was with a slim young thing from the Veenie Department of Extraplanetary Affairs—fishbelly skin, of course, but it went well enough with her almost platinum hair. If I hadn't been so sore about Mitzi I might have enjoyed dancing with her, but she would have spoiled it anyway. "Mr. Tarb," she said right off, "do you think it's fair to make the Hyperion miners listen to your advertising slop?"

Well, she was *very* junior. Her bosses wouldn't have said anything like that. The trouble was, it was my bosses who were nearby, and the conversation got worse: Why were armed Earth spacecraft orbiting Venus every now and then without explaining their errands? And why had we refused permission for the Veenies to send a "scientific" mission to Mars? And—and everything else was pretty much the same. I made all the right defensive replies, but she'd been speaking pretty loudly and people were looking at us. Hay Lopez was one of them; he was standing with the Chief of Station, and they exchanged glances in a way I didn't much like. When the dance was at last over I was glad to head for the bar. The only open space was next to Pavel Borkmann, head of some section of the Veenie Department of Heavy Industry. I'd met him before and intended ten minutes of nonthreatening chat about how their new Hilsch barrage in the Anti-Oasis was going, or whether they were satisfied with the new rocket plant. That didn't work out either, because he too had heard snatches of my little dialogue with the Extraplanetary Affair. "You ought not to get into fights where you're overmatched," he grinned, referring both to my late dance partner and to the obvious scars I had collected from the tram. If I'd had any sense I would have chosen the meaning that was least chancy and told him all about the tram accident. My feelings were ruffled; I took the other course, "She was way out of line," I complained, signaling for a drink I certainly didn't need.

But Borkmann had had a drink more than he needed too, it seemed, because he too took the path with the beartraps in it. "Oh, I don't know," he said. "You have to understand that we Free Venusians have moral objections to forcing people to buy things—especially at the point of a gun."

"There aren't any guns pointed at Hyperion, Borkmann! You know that."

"Not yet," he admitted, "but haven't there been such cases right on your home planet?"

I laughed, pitying him. "You're talking about the abos, I suppose."

"I'm talking about the pitiful few corners of the Earth that haven't yet been corrupted by advertising, yes."

Well, by then I was getting irritated. "Borkmann," I said, "you know better than that. We do maintain a peacekeeping body, of course. I suppose some few of them have guns, but they're only for protection. I did my own reserve training in college; I know what I'm talking about. They are *never* used offensively, only to preserve order. You must realize that even among the worst of the aboriginals there are plenty of people who want to have the benefits of the market society. Naturally, the old fuddy-duddies resist. But when the better elements ask for help, why, of course we give it."

"You send in the troops," he nodded.

"We send in advertising teams," I corrected him. "There is no *compulsion*. There is no *force*."

"And," he mimicked, "there is no *escape*—they found that out in New Guinea."

"It's true that things got out of hand in New Guinea," I admitted. "But really—"

"Really," he said, slamming down his glass, "I have to be going now, Tarb. Nice talking to you." And he left me fuming. Why, there was really nothing wrong in New Guinea! There had been less than a thousand deaths all told. And now the island was firmly a part of the modern world—we even had a branch of the Agency in Papua! I swallowed my drink in one gulp and turned away . . . and almost bumped into Hay Lopez, grinning at me. Walking away, glancing back at me over her shoulder, was the Chief of Station. I saw her join the Ambassador and whisper in his ear, still looking at me, and realized this was turning out to be a pretty bad day. Since I was on my way home anyway there was little the Embassy people could do to me, but still I resolved to behave like a proper dip for the rest of the evening.

That didn't work out, either. Through the luck of the draw, the second partner I drew was Dirty Berthie, the Turncoat Earthie. I should've been faster on my feet; I guess I was still a little groggy. I turned around, and there she was, boozy breath, sloppy-fat face and hair piled up on her head to make her look taller. "My dance, I believe, Tenny?" she giggled.

So gallantly I lied, "I've been looking forward to it!" What you can say for Dirty Berthie is that even in those spike heels and hay-stack hairdo, she doesn't tower over you the way the natives do. That's about all you can say for her. Converts are always the worst, and Bertha, who is now Deputy Curator for the entire planet-wide Venus library system, was once a Senior Research Vice-President for the Taunton, Gatchweiler and Schocken Agency! She gave all that up to migrate to Venus, and now she has to prove with every word she says that she's more Veenie than the Venusians. "Well, Mr. Tennison Tarb," she said, leaning back against my arm to study my shiner, "looks like somebody's husband came back when he wasn't supposed to."

Just a harmless jocularity, right? Wrong. Dirty Berthie's little jokes are always nasty. It's "How's organized lying today?" for a hello, and, "Well, I mustn't keep you from peddling some more poison baby food," when she says good-by. *We* aren't allowed to do that kind of thing. To be fair, most of the native Veenies don't, either, but Bertha is the worst of both worlds. Our official policy on Bertha is smile and say nothing. That's what I had done for all those long years, but enough was enough. I said—

Well, I can't defend what I said. To understand it you have to know that Bertha's husband, the one she gave up her star class job on Earth for, was a pilot on the Kathy-to-Discovery airline, who lost part of his right leg and an unspecified selection of adjacent parts in a crash the year after they were married. It's the one thing she's sensitive about. So I gave her a sweet, sweet smile and said, "I was just trying to do Carlos's work as a favor to him, but I got the wrong house."

My joke wasn't very funny. Bertha didn't even try for one in response. She gasped. She pushed free of my arms, stood stockstill in the middle of the dance floor and cried, loud and clear, "You bastard!" There were actual tears in her eyes—rage, I guess.

I did not have a chance to study her reaction. A beartrap grip closed on my shoulder and the Chief of Station herself said politely, "If I can borrow Tenny a moment, Bertha, there are some last-minute things we have to settle. . . ." Out in the corridor she squared off, head to head. "You *ass*," she hissed. Sprinkles of saliva like snake venom ate pits in my cheeks.

I tried to defend myself. "She started it! She said—"

"I heard what she said, and the whole damned room heard what *you* said! Jesus, Tarb!" She had let go of my shoulder, and now she looked as though she wanted to take me by the throat instead.

I backed away. "Pam, I know I was out of line, but I'm a little shook up. Don't forget somebody nearly murdered me today!"

"It was an *accident*. The Embassy has officially listed it as an *accident*. Try to remember that. It doesn't make sense any other way. Why would anybody bother to murder you when you're on your way home?"

"Not me. Mitzi. Maybe there's a double agent among the spies she's recruited, and they know what she's doing."

"*Tarb*." There was no snake venom this time and no hiss, not even anger. This was just an icy warning. She looked quickly around to make sure no one was nearby. Well, of course I shouldn't have said anything like that while there were Veenies in the building— that was Rule Number One. I started to say something, and she raised her hand. "Mitsui Ku is not dead," she said. "They've operated on her. I saw her myself in the hospital, an hour and a half ago. She hadn't regained consciousness, but the prognosis is good. If they wanted her dead, they could have done it in the operating room and we never would have known it. They didn't."

"All the same—"

"Go back to bed, Tarb. Your injuries are more severe than we realized." She didn't let me interrupt, but pointed toward the private rooms. "*Now*. And I've got to get back to my guests—after I stop in my office to add some remarks to an efficiency report. Yours." She stood there and watched me out of sight.

And that was the last I saw of the Chief of Station, and almost the last I saw of anything at all for quite a while—two years and a bit—because the next morning I was hustled out of bed by two Embassy guards, bundled into a station car, hurried to the port, packed into a shuttle. In three hours I was in orbit. In three hours and a half I was lying in a freezer cocoon, waiting for the sleepy drug to put me out and the chill-down to start. The space liner was not due to start its main engines for another nine orbits—more than half a day—but the Ambassador had given orders to get me put away. And get me put away they did.

The next thing I knew I was being eaten alive by fire ants, that unbearable arm's-asleep feeling you get when you're first thawed. I was still in the cocoon but I was wearing an electrically warmed skinsuit with only my eyes exposed, and bending over me was somebody I knew. "Hello there, Tenn," said Mitzi Ku. "Surprised to see me?"

I was. I said I was, but I doubt that I managed to express just how surprised I was, because the last thought I remembered, just before the whirly-down sleepiness took over, was rueful regret that I hadn't had that last farewell appearance in Mitzi's bed, and was not likely ever to get a chance to make it up.

I was startled at her appearance. Half her face was bandaged, only the mouth and chin exposed, with two little slits in the dressing for eyes. Of course, that was natural enough. Healing doesn't take place when you're frozen. Effectively Mitzi was only a few days out of surgery. "Are you all right?" I asked.

She said sharply, "Sure I am. I'm fine! I mean," she qualified, "I probably won't be *all* fine for weeks yet, but I'm ambulatory. As you see," she grinned. I *think* she was grinning. "When the doctors said I could leave the hospital I made up my mind that Venus had seen the last of me. So I tore up my reenlistment papers and they got me on the last shuttle. I stayed unfrozen for a while, until they could get the stitches out—and here I am!"

The itching had dwindled to the almost bearable range. The world suddenly looked brighter, and I started to peel off the hotsuit. Mitzi nodded. "That's the spirit, Tenn! We touch down on the Moon in ninety minutes—better get your pants on!"

Tarb's Homecoming

· · ◆ · ·

I

To my surprise, the two deported Marines were on the same ship. That was a good thing. Without them helping me limp off I doubt I would have made it. Mitzi, all bandaged and broken, was fine. I was not. I was sick, and by that I mean, man, *sick*. I've always been susceptible to motion sickness, but it had never occurred to me that it was just as bad to be on the Moon.

Venus is terrible, sure, but at least on Venus you weigh what you expect to weigh. The Moon isn't that friendly. They say after the first six weeks you stop throwing your coffee across the room when you only want to put it to your lips but I'll never know that for myself —I don't like the place. If we'd come on a regular Earth rocket we'd have shuttled down to the surface right away, but it was a Veenie vessel and had to stop at quarantine.

And that, really, was a farce! I'm not saying anything against the Agencies. They run the Earth very well. But the whole idea of quarantine is to keep Veenie diseases out, right? That includes the worst Veenie disease, the political pestilence of Conservationism. So you'd expect that on the Moon they'd give the Veenies a hard time in Customs and Immigration. In fact Immigration waved them past with no more than a cursory look at their passports. I don't mean just the crew, who weren't going anywhere but the nearest flopjoint anyway. Even the handful of Veenie business people and dips, transshipping to the Earth, got greased through in no time.

But us Terrestrials—wow! They sat Mitzi and me down and

magnetic-checked our papers and pried through our bags, and then the questions began. It was report all contact with Venusian nationals in line of duty for past eighteen months; give purpose of contact and nature of information communicated. Report all such contacts *not* in line of duty—purpose and information included. We were three hours in that sealed cubicle, filling out forms and answering questions, and then the interrogator got serious. "It has been ascertained," he said—grammatically speaking the voice was passive, but the actual voice rang with loathing and contempt, "that certain Earth nationals, to secure easy admission to Venus, have performed ritual acts of desecration."

Well, that was true enough. It was just another typical lousy Veenie trick, like the Japanese making Europeans trample on Bibles centuries ago. When you got to the Veenie Immigration checkpoints you had a choice. You could go through four or five hours of close questioning, with all your belongings opened and most likely a body search. Or you could take an oath renouncing "advertising, publicity, media persuasion or any other form of manipulation of public opinion"; toss off a few slanders of your Agency; and then, depending on how good an actor you were, breeze right through. It was a big joke, of course. I chuckled and started to explain it to him, but Mitzi cut in ahead of me. "Oh, yes," she said, nodding earnestly, her expression as disapproving as his own, "we've heard that, too." She gave me a warning look. "Do you happen to know if it's true?"

The Immigration man put down his stylus to study her face. "You mean you don't know whether that happens or not?"

She said carelessly, "One hears stories, sure. But when you try to put your finger on it, you just can't find a single concrete bit of evidence. It's always, no, it didn't happen to me, but I heard from this person that he had a friend who—Anyway, I can't really believe a decent Terrestrial would do such a thing. *I* certainly wouldn't, and neither would Tennison. Apart from the plain immorality of it, we know we'd have to face the consequences when we came back!"

So grudgingly the man passed us, and as soon as we were outside I whispered to Mitzi, "You saved my tail—thanks!"

"They just started doing that a couple years ago," she said. "If we'd admitted taking a false oath it would go on our records—then we'd be in the stuff."

"Funny you heard that that was happening and I didn't."

"I'm glad you can see the humor of it," she said bitingly, and for some reason, I perceived, she was furious. Then she said, "Sorry. I'm in a bad mood. I think I'll try to get a few more of these bandages off—then it'll be time for the shuttle!"

Earth! The birthplace of homo sapiens. The homeland of true humanity. The flowering of civilization. When we came to the shuttle in its lock and I caught a glimpse of its graffiti I knew I was home. "Everett Loves Alice." "Tiny Miljiewicz has herpes in his ears." "Rams all the way!" There's nothing on Venus like our native Terrestrial folk art!

So we came down from the sky, jolting and slamming; I worried about Mitzi's healing scars, but she only mumbled and turned over to sleep. Out over the wide ocean, greeny gray with slime—clear across the wide, welcoming North American continent, with its patchwork carpet of cities glowing welcomingly up through the smog—then the sun we had left behind rising again before us as we skidded out over the Atlantic, made our U-turn to spill out the last of our altitude and speed, and touched down finally on the broad runways of New York Shuttleport. Little old New York! The hub the universe spins on! I felt my heart throbbing with pride, and with joy at homecoming . . . and Mitzi, strapped in beside me, had slept through the whole thing.

She sat up drowsily while we were waiting for the tractor to hook on and tow us to the terminal. She made a face. "Isn't it great to be back?" I demanded, grinning at her.

She leaned over me to stare out the window. "Sure is," she said, but her tone was a long way from enthusiastic. "I wish—"

But I never found out what she wished, because she broke out in a fit of furious coughing. "My God!" she gasped. "What's that stuff?"

"That's good old New York City air you're breathing!" I told her. "You've been away too long—you've forgotten what it's like!"

"At least they could filter it," she complained. Well, of course it was filtered, but I didn't bother to correct her. I was too busy getting our stuff out of the overhead racks and lining up to disembark.

It was seven A.M., local time. There weren't too many people in the terminal yet, which was a plus, but the minus that balanced that in the equation was the lack of baggage handlers. Mitzi trailed sulkily after me to the baggage claim, and there I got a surprise. The surprise's name was Valentine Dambois, Senior Vice-President and

Associate General Manager, pink cheeks, twinkly blue eyes, plump figure jiggling as he hurried across to greet us.

I told myself that I shouldn't have been surprised—I'd done a good job on Venus, and I'd never doubted that the Agency would treat me kindly when I got back. But not *this* kindly! You didn't get a star-class executive to welcome you home at that hour of the morning unless you were really *special*. So, full of cheer and great hopes, I stuck out my hand to him. "Great to see you, Val," I began—

And he went right past me. Right to Mitzi.

Val Dambois was a tubby little man, and the fattest thing about him was his face; when he smiled he looked like a Halloween pumpkin. The smile he gave Mitzi was like a pumpkin on the verge of splitting in two. "Mitzi-wits!" he yelled, though he was only two feet away from her and closing fast. "Missed you, sweety-bumps!" He flung his arms around her and stood on tiptoe to give her a big kiss.

She didn't kiss back. She pulled her head back so the kiss only got as far as her chin. "Hello," she said—"Val."

His face fell. For a minute I thought Mitzi had blown every chance of promotion she ever had, but Dambois did a great reconstruction job on his smile. By the time he put it back on his face it was as good as new, and he patted her rump affectionately—but hastily. He stepped back, chuckling. "You sure made yourself a killing," he said warmly. "I take my hat off to you, Mits!"

I didn't know what he was talking about, of course. For a minute I didn't think Mitzi did, either, because a swift shadow clouded her eyes and her jaw tensed, but Dambois was already looking at me. "Missed the boat, I guess," he said good-naturedly—rueful good nature, that was, with just a slight shading of contempt.

Now, I wasn't too surprised by the way Dambois greeted Mitzi. There were little bits of gossip here and there about Mitzi and one or two star-level agency executives, Val Dambois included. It meant nothing to me. Hell, it's a rough course you have to run if you want to get ahead in the advertising business. If you can help yourself along by giving a little joy to the right parties, why not? But she hadn't said anything to me about a killing. "What are you talking about, Val?" I demanded.

"She didn't tell you?" He pursed his plump little lips, grinning. "Her damage suit against the tram company. They settled out of court—six megabucks and change—it's all waiting for her right now in the Agency bank!"

I had to try twice to say it. "Six—Six mill—"

"Six million dollars tax-free and spendable, right on!" he gloated. The man was as pleased as though the money had been his own—maybe he had some idea of making it so. I cleared my throat.

"About this damage suit—" I began, but Mitzi leaned past me to point.

"There, that one's mine," she said as the bags began to come off the conveyor. Val leaped forward and, puffing, swung it off and set it beside her.

"What I mean—" I began. Nobody was listening.

Dambois said jovially, slipping a pudgy arm around Mitzi's waist —as far around as it would go: "Well, that's the first bag. Probably not more than another twenty or so, eh?"

"No, that's the only one. I like to travel light," she said, and moved away from his arm.

Dambois looked up at her reproachfully. "You've changed a lot," he complained. "I think you even got taller."

"Comes from being on a lighter planet." That was a joke, of course. Venus is only minutely smaller than the Earth. But I didn't laugh, because I was puzzling over why it was that Mitzi had got herself a whopping chunk of change and I hadn't—then that was driven out of my mind as I saw what was coming down the conveyor.

"Aw, *shit,*" I cried. It was the bag I had marked Delicate Handling —the steamer trunk, with sturdy sides and a double lock. They hadn't been enough to save it. The trunk looked as if somebody had run one of the spacecraft tractors over a corner of it. One side was squashed like a fallen soufflé, and it was leaking an aromatic slop of liquor, colognes, toothpaste and god-knows-what. Naturally I had put all the breakables in it.

"What a mess," Dambois complained. He tsked impatiently a couple of times and glanced at his watch. "I was going to offer you a lift," he said, "but really—that stuff in my car would smell it up for weeks—and I suppose you've got other bags—"

I knew my lines. "Go ahead," I said glumly. "I'll take a taxi." I watched them go, wondering a lot about why I hadn't been allowed to get in on the damage suit, but actually wondering even more just then whether I should hightail it for the baggage claim office or wait for the rest of my stuff.

I made the wrong decision. I decided to wait. After the last visible bag had long since been removed and the conveyor had stopped running I realized I had a problem.

When I reported the problem the superintendent in charge of denying all responsibility for anything, ever, told me that he'd check out the missing pieces, if I wanted him to, while I filled out the claim forms, if I thought that was worthwhile—although it looked a lot to him, he said, as though the damage to my case was old stuff.

He had plenty of time to check, because there was plenty to fill out. When I turned in the claims he kept me waiting only another half-hour or so. I called the Agency to say I'd be delayed. It didn't seem to worry them. They gave me the address of the housing they'd lined up for me, told me to settle in and said I wasn't expected until tomorrow morning anyway. It is nice to be missed. Then the claims superintendent reported that the rest of my bags seemed to have gone either to Paris or Rio de Janeiro, and in neither case was I likely to see them for a while.

So, bagless, I joined the glum queue waiting for the next city subline.

Half an hour later, finally at the head of the line, I realized I hadn't changed any Veenie currency and so I didn't have enough cash for the fare—found a cash machine, punched in my I.D., got a bodiless voice cooing, "I am deeply sorry, sir or madam, but this Kwik-Check One-Stop Anytime cash dispenser terminal is temporarily out of service. Please consult map for nearest alternate location." But when I looked around the booth there wasn't any map. Welcome home, Tenn!

II

New York, New York. What a wonderful town! All my fretful annoyances were submerged, even the one about why Mitzi cut me out of the gravy train. Six years didn't seem to have changed the tall buildings that disappeared into the gray, flaky air. The *cold*, gray, flaky air. It had gone winter again; there were patches of dirty snow in corners, and an occasional consumer furtively scooping them up to take home to avoid the freshwater tax. After Venus, it was heaven! I gawked like a Wichita tourist at the Big Apple. I walked liked one, too, bumping into scurrying pedestrians, and things worse than pedestrians. My traffic skills were gone. After the years on Venus I just wasn't used to civilized ways. There was a twelve-pusher pedibus here, three cabs competing for one gap in the flow there, pedestrians leaping desperately between the vehicles all over—the streets were jammed, the sidewalks were packed, every building pumped a few hundred more people in and out as I passed—oh, it was marvelous! For me, I mean. For the people I was bumping into or tripped or made dodge around me, it might not have been so delightful, I suppose. I didn't care! They yelled after me, and I don't doubt what they yelled were insults, but I was floating in sooty, choky, chilly bliss. Advertising slogans flickered in liquid-crystal display on every wall, the newest ones bright as sunrise, the older ones muddied and finally buried by graffiti. Samplers stood along the curbs to pass out free hits of Glee-Smoke and Coffiest, and discount coupons for a thousand products. There were hologram images in the smoggy air of miraculous kitchen appliances and fantastically exotic three-day tours, and sales jingles ringing from everywhere—I was *home*. I loved it! But it was, admittedly, a little difficult to make my way through the streets, and when I saw a miraculously clear stretch of sidewalk I took it.

I wondered at the time why the elderly man I pushed aside getting to the sidewalk gave me such a strange look. "Watch it, buster!" he called. He was waving at a signpost, but of course it was graffiti-covered. I wasn't in a mood to worry about some minor civil ordinance. I walked past—

And WOWP a blast of sound shook my skull and FLOOP a great supernova flare of light burned my eyes, and I went staggering and reeling as tiny, tiny elf voices shouted like needles in my ears *Mokie-Koke, Mokie-Koke, MokieMokieMokie-Koke!* And went on doing it, with variations, for what seemed like a hundred years or more. Stenches smote my nose. Subsonic shivers shook my body. And—a couple of centuries later—while my ears were still ringing and my eyes still stinging with that awful blast of sound and light, I picked myself up from where I lay sprawled on the ground.

"I warned ya," yelled the little old man from a safe distance. It hadn't been centuries at all. He was still standing there, still with the same peculiar expression—half-eagerness, half-pity. "I warned ya! Ya wooden listen, but I warned ya!"

He was still waving at the signpost, so I staggered closer and blearily managed to decipher the legend under the graffiti:

Warning!
COMMERCIAL ZONE
Enter at Own Risk

Evidently there had been some changes while I was away, after all. The man reached cautiously past the sign and tugged me away. He wasn't all that old, I realized; mostly he was *used*. "What's a 'Mokie-Koke'?" I asked.

He said promptly, "Mokie-Koke is a refreshing, taste-tingling blend of the finest chocolate-type flavoring, synthetic coffee extract and selected cocaine analogues. You want some?" I did. "You got money on you?" I had—a little, anyway—the change left over from the cash dispenser I'd finally located. "Would you tip me one if I showed you where to score some?" he wheedled.

Well, who needed him for that? But I couldn't help feeling sorry for the woebegone little guy, so I let him lead me around the corner. There was a vending machine, just like all the other Mokie-Koke machines I'd been seeing all along, on the Moon, in the spaceport, along the city streets. "Don't fool with the singles," he advised anxiously. "Go for the six-pack, okay?" And when I gave him the first bottle out of the batch he pulled the tab and raised it to his lips and swigged it down where he stood. Then he exhaled loudly. "Name's Ernie, mister," he said. "Welcome to the club!"

I had been drinking my own Mokie-Koke curiously. It seemed pleasant enough, but nothing special, so that I wondered what the fuss was all about. "What club are you talking about?" I asked, opening another bottle out of curiosity.

"You been campbelled. You shoulda listened," he said virtu- ously, "but, say, long as you didn't, you mind if I walk along with you wherever you're going?"

Poor old guy! I felt so sorry for him that I split the six-pack as we headed for the address the Agency had given me. Three shots apiece. He thanked me with tears in his eyes but, all the same, out of the second six-pack I only gave him one.

The Agency had done well by me. When we got to my new home I shook Ernie off and hurried in. It was a new sea-condo just towed in from the Persian Gulf—former oil tanker—nearly a hundred square feet of floor space with kitchen privileges just for me, and it was about as convenient to the Agency building as you could hope, moored right off Kip's Bay, only three ships out into the river.

Of course, the bad side was what it cost. All the savings I'd accumulated on Venus went to the down payment, and I had to sign a mortgage for three years' pay. But that wasn't so bad. I'd served the Agency well on Venus. There was little doubt in my mind that I was due for a raise—not only a raise, but a promotion—not only a promotion, but maybe a corner office! Altogether I was well satisfied with the world (not counting a couple little questions that nagged at my mind, like that damned lawsuit I hadn't been invited to join) as I relished a Mokie-Koke and gazed around my new domain.

But to work! There was so much to do! Until they located my bags, if that ever happened, I needed clothes and food and all the other necessities of life. So I spent the rest of the day shopping and lugging packages back to the sea-condo, and by dinner time I was just about settled in. Picture of G. Washington Hill over the foldaway bed. Picture of Fowler Schocken on the hideaway bureau. Clothes in one place, toilet stuff in my personal locked cabinet in the bath—it took all day, and it was tiring, too, because the heat was on full blast in my room and there didn't seem to be any way to turn it off. I had a Moke and sat down to think it over, enjoying the spaciousness and the quiet luxury. There was a special condo-only band on the vid, and I watched it reel off the many attractions available to us lucky tenants. The condo had its own pool, with seating for six at a time, and a driving range. I made a note to sign up for that as soon as I got my own cue. The future looked bright. I dialed back to the pool—gallons and gallons of sparkling pure water, nearly armpit deep—and sentimental thoughts began to steal into my mind: me and Mitzi side by side in the pool . . . me and Mitzi sharing the big foldout bed . . . me and Mitzi—But even if Mitzi decided after all to share my life, with six megabucks of her own to throw around she'd probably want to share it in some fancier place than even the sea-condo. . . .

Well, rework that daydream. Leave Mitzi out for a minute: the future was still bright. Even though I'd signed up for heavy money to get the condo, I should still have spare purchasing power. A new car? Why not? And which kind of car—a direct-drive model where you kneel one leg on the seat and push with the other, or some fancy geared-up make-out wagon?

It was getting very hot. I tried again to turn off the heat, and failed again.

I found myself drinking Mokes one after another. And, actually, for a moment I thought seriously about pulling out the bed and getting a good night's sleep.

Tired or not, I couldn't spend my first night home that way! It called for a celebration.

A celebration called for somebody to celebrate with. Mitzi? But when I called Agency personnel they didn't have a home number for her yet, and she had already left the office. And all the other dates I could think of were either years stale, or millions of miles away. I didn't even know which were the in places to celebrate in any more!

That part, anyway, could be handled. I had a neat Omni-V console that came along with the apartment, two hundred and forty channels. I ran through the selector—housewares commercials, florists' commercials, outerwear commercials (male), outerwear commercials (female), news, restaurant commercials—yes, that was the channel I wanted. I picked a nice place only two blocks from the seacondo, and it was all that I'd wanted. Because I had made a reservation I was only kept an hour or so in the bar, drinking gin-and-Mokes and chatting up my neighbors; the dinner was the best of brand-name soya cutlets and reconstituted mashed veggies; there was brandy with the coffee, and two waiters dancing attendance to unwrap my portions and pull the tabs on my drinks. There was one little funny thing. When the check came I looked at it quickly, then more slowly, then called the waiter over again. "What's this?" I said, pointing at the column of printouts that said,

Mokie-Koke, $2.75
Mokie-Koke, $2.75
Mokie-Koke, $2.75
Mokie-Koke, $2.75

"They're Mokie-Kokes, sir," he explained, "a refreshing, taste-tingling blend of the finest chocolate-type—"

"I know what a Mokie-Koke is," I interrupted. "I just don't remember ordering any."

"I'm sorry, sir," he said, all deference. "Actually you did. I'll play back the voice tape if you like."

"Never mind the voice tape," I said. "I don't want them now. I'll just go."

He looked shocked. "But, sir—you've already drunk them!"

Nine A.M. Bright and early. I paid off my pedicab, pulled the soot-extractor plugs out of my nostrils and strutted into the main lobby of the huge Taunton, Gatchweiler and Schocken Agency Tower.

We get older and we get cynical, but after the years of absence there was almost an epiphany of feeling that shook me as I entered. Imagine two thousand years ago entering the court of Augustus Caesar, and knowing that here, in this place, the affairs of the entire world had their control center and inspiration. With the Agency, the same. True, there were other agencies—but it was a bigger world, too! Here was where Power was. The whole vast building was dedicated to one sublime mission: the betterment of mankind through the inspiration to buy. More than eighteen thousand people worked in that building. Copysmiths and apprentice word-jugglers; media specialists who could sound a commercial out of the ambient air or print a message on your eyeball; product researchers dreaming up, every day, new and more sellable drinks, foods, gadgets, vices, possessions of all sorts; artists; musicians; actors; directors; space buyers and time buyers—the list went on indefinitely—and above them all, on the fortieth floor and higher, there was Executive Country where the geniuses who directed it all brooded and conceived their godlike plans. Oh, sure. I joked about the civilizing mission of us who dedicated our lives to advertising—but under the joking was the same real reverence and commitment that I'd felt as a cub scout in the Junior Copywriters, going after my first merit badges and just then beginning to perceive where my life could lead. . . .

Well. Anyway. There I was, in the heart of the universe. There was one funny thing. I had remembered it as vast and vaulted. Vaulted it was—but vast? Actually it seemed tinier, and more crowded, than the Russian Hills tram station; so those years on Venus had corrupted my sensibilities. The people even looked shabbier, and the guard at the weapons detector gave me a surly and suspicious look as I approached.

No problem there. I simply put my wrist into the scanner, and the data store recognized my Social Security number at once, even though it had been six years since its last use. "Oh," said the guard, studying my stats as the recognition light flashed green, "you're Mr.

Tarb. Nice to see you back!" There was a false implication there, of course. From the look of her she'd still been in high school last time I entered the Agency building, but her heart was in the right place. I gave her bottom a friendly pat and swaggered toward the lift. And the first person I saw on forty-five as I let go of the handbar was Mitzi Ku.

I'd had twenty-four hours to get over resentment at that lawsuit deal. It hadn't been enough, really, but at least the sharp edges of jealousy had blunted a bit, and she really looked good. Not perfect. Although she was out of her bandages, that funny blurring around the eyes and mouth told you she was wearing plastiflesh where healing had not quite finished. But she was smiling at me tentatively as she said hello. "Mitzi," I said, the words popping out of my mouth unexpectedly—I had not known I had been thinking them— "shouldn't I sue the tram people, too?"

She looked embarrassed. What she would have said I don't know, because from behind her Val Dambois popped out. "Too late, Tarb," he said. I didn't mind the words. I minded the contemptuous tone, and the grin. "Statute of limitations, you know? Like I told you, you missed the boat. Come on, Mitzi, we can't keep the Old Man waiting—"

The morning was one shock after another; the Old Man was who I was going to see. Mitzi allowed Dambois to take her arm, but she hung back to peer at me. "Are you all right, Tenny?" she asked.

"I'm fine—" Well, I was, mostly, not counting a slightly frayed ego. "I'm a little thirsty, maybe, because it's so hot in here. Do you happen to know if there's a Mokie-Koke vending machine on this floor?"

Dambois gave me a poisonous look. "Some jokes," he gritted, "are in lousy taste."

I watched him flounce off, dragging Mitzi after him into the Old Man's sanctum. I sat down to wait, trying to look as though I had simply decided to rest my feet there for a moment.

The moment turned out to be well past an hour.

Of course, nobody thought anything of that. Over in her own corner of the cell the Old Man's sec[3] kept busy with her communicator and her data screen, glancing up to smile at me now and then the way she was paid to do. People who wait only an hour to see the Old Man generally gave thanks for their blessings, since most people never got to see him at all. Old Man Gatchweiler was a legend in his own time, poor boy, consumer stock, who rose out of obscure origins to pull off so grand a scam that it was still whispered about in the Executive Country bars. Two of the grandest old-line Agencies had wrecked themselves in flaming scandals, old B. J. Taunton nailed for Contract Breach, Fowler Schocken dead and his Agency in ruins. Their Agencies carried on a spectral existence as shells, written off forever by the wiseacres. Then Horatio Gatchweiler appeared out of nowhere to swallow the wreckage and turn it into T., G. & S. No one wrote Taunton, Gatchweiler and Schocken off! We were tops in Sales and Service. Our clients led the charts in Sales, and as to Service, well, no thousand-dollar-a-hit stallion ever serviced his mares as thoroughly as we serviced the consumers. A name to conjure with, Horatio Gatchweiler! It was almost literally a name to conjure with, for it was like the unspeakable name of God. No one ever spoke it. Behind his back he was the "Old Man," to his face nothing but "sir."

So sitting in his tiny sec³'s anteroom while I pretended to study the *Advertising Age* hourlies in the tabletop screen was nothing new for me. It was even an honor. At least, it would have been except for the sulky, nagging annoyance at the fact that he had given Mitzi and Val Dambois precedence.

When at last the Old Man's sec³ turned me over to the sec², who led me to the secretary, who admitted me to his own private office, he did try to make me welcome. He didn't stand up or anything, but, "Come right in, Farb!" he boomed jovially from his chair. "Good to see you back, boy!"

I had almost forgotten how magnificent his place was—two windows! Of course, both had the shades drawn; you can't take chances on somebody bouncing a pencil-beam off the glass to pick up the vibrations of secret talks inside. "That's Tarb, sir," I offered.

"Of course it is! And you're back from a tour on Venus—good work. Of course," he added, peering up at me slyly, "it wasn't *all* good, was it? There's a little note on your personnel file that you probably didn't bribe anybody to put there—"

"I can explain about that Agency party, sir—"

"Of course you can! And it won't stand in your way. You young people who volunteer for a tour on Venus deserve well of us— nobody expects you to stand that kind of life without a little, uh, strain." He leaned back dreamily. "I don't know if you know this,

Farb," he said to the ceiling, "but I was on Venus myself once, long ago. Didn't stay there. I won their lottery, you know."

I was startled. "Lottery? I had no idea the Veenies ever ran a lottery. It seems so out of character for them."

"Never did again," he guffawed, "since a huck won the first one! They gave up the idea right after that—besides declaring me persona non grata, so I got hustled right back here!" He chuckled for several seconds at the fecklessness of the Veenies. "Of course," he said, sobering, "I kept my skills up while I was on Venus." From the way he peered at me I knew it was a question.

I had the right answer, too. "So did I, sir," I said eagerly. "Every chance I got! All the time! For instance—well, I don't know if you've ever seen the inside of what the Veenies call a grocery store—"

"Seen a hundred of them, boy," he boomed jovially.

"Well, then you know how incompetent they are. Signs like, 'These tomatoes are all right if you're going to eat them today, otherwise they'll spoil,' and 'Prepared mixes cost twice what making the dish from basic ingredients would'—things like that."

He laughed out loud, and wiped his eyes. "Haven't changed a bit, I guess," he said.

"No, sir. Well, I'd go through the store and then come back to the Embassy and write *real* copy for them. You know? Like for the tomatoes, 'Luscious ripe flavor-full at the peak of perfection' or 'Save! Save! Save precious time with these chef-prepared ready-to-cook masterpieces!' That sort of thing. And then I'd review all the latest Earth commercials for the staff—at least two hour-long pep meetings every week—and we'd have contests to see who could come up with better original variations on the basic sales themes—"

He looked at me with real affection. "You know, Tarb," he said, with kindness verging on sentimentality, "you remind me of myself when I was your age. A little. Well, listen, let's get ourselves comfortable while we decide what you'd like to do for us now that you're back. What'll you have to drink?"

"Oh, I think a Mokie-Koke, sir," I said absently.

The climate in the room took a swift change for the worse. The Old Man's finger stopped over the call button that would have summoned his sec[2], in charge of bringing in coffee and refreshments. "What did you say, Farb?" he gritted.

I opened my mouth, but it was too late. He didn't let me speak. "A *Moke*? Here in my office?" The expression went clear across the scale, from benevolence through shock to wrath. Livid, he stabbed down on a completely different button. "Emergency services!" he roared. "Get a medic in here right away—I've got a Moke-head in my office!"

They got me out of the Old Man's office fast as any leper ousted from the sight of Louis XIV. Treated me that way, too. While I was waiting for the results of my tests I sat in the common-clinic waiting room in Subbasement Three, but, although it was crowded, there were empty seats on both sides of me.

At last, "Mr. Tennison Tarb," crackled the voice from the over-head speaker. I got up and stumbled through the underbrush of hastily moved legs and pulled-aside ankles to the consultation room. It was like walking the Last Mile in those old prison movies, except that there were no mumbled words of encouragement from my fellow cons. There was the same expression on every face, and it said, *Thank God it's you, not me!*

I expected that past the sliding door would be the doctor who would prescribe my fate. Surprisingly there were two people there; one the doctor—you could tell by her ritual stethoscope around the neck—and the other, of all people, little Dan Dixmeister, grown all lank and gloomy. "Hey, there, Danny!" I greeted him, sticking out my hand for old time's sake.

And for the same sake, I guess—his version of it—he studied my hand for a moment before reluctantly putting out his own. It wasn't a shake. It was more like his offering his hand for me to kiss—no grip, just a limp touch and withdrawal.

Now, Danny Dixmeister had been my copy cub trainee half a dozen years earlier. I went to Venus. He stayed behind. Clearly he hadn't wasted his time. He wore Deputy Department Head epau-lettes and, on his sleeve, fifty-thousand-a-year stripes, and he looked at me as though I were the new apprentice and he the exec. "You really screwed up, Tarb," he rasped joylessly. "Dr. Mosskristal will review your medical problem for you." And the tone said *bad news*.

Bad news it was. "What you've got," said the doctor, "is a Campbellian addiction." Her tone was neither kind nor unkind. It was the tone in which a doctor announces a white-blood-corpuscle count in a laboratory animal, and the look she turned on me was exactly the same look as Mitzi used to give a would-be returnee who might be recruited for her spy chains. "I suppose you could be reprogrammed," she said, studying the results on the display before her. "Hardly worth the effort, I'd say. A very uninteresting chart."

I swallowed. It was hard for me to take in that it was my *life* they were talking about. "Tell me what I'm up against," I begged. "Maybe if I understood what was wrong I could fix it."

"Fix it? *Fix* it? You mean overcome the programming by yourself? Oh-ho-ho-ho," she laughed, glancing at Dixmeister and shaking her head humorously. "What strange notions you laymen have."

"But you said there was a cure—"

"You mean reprogramming and detoxing," she corrected. "I don't think you want to go through *that*. Maybe ten years from now it might be worth a try, although there's about a forty per cent mortality rate. But in the early stages, right after exposure—uh-uh." She leaned back, pressing her fingertips together, and I got ready for the lecture. "What you have," she explained, "is a Campbellian reflex. Named after Dr. H. J. Campbell. Famous pioneering psychologist in the old days, inventor of limbic-pleasure therapy."

"I never heard of limbic-pleasure therapy," I said.

"No," she admitted, "the secret was lost for many years." She leaned forward, depressed an intercom button and called, "Maggie, bring in the Campbell. According to Dr. Campbell," she resumed to me, *"pleasure* is the name we give to the feeling we experience when the limbic areas of our brain are electrically active. He was first led to this research, I believe, when he discovered that many of his students were deriving great pleasure from what was called rock music. Saturating the senses in this way stimulated the limbic area— thus pleasure—thus, he discovered a cheap and easy way of conditioning subjects in desirable ways. Ah, here we are." The sec[2] had brought in a transparent plastic box containing—of all things!—a *book*. Faded, tattered, hidden inside its plastic case, it was still about the best example I had ever seen of that quaint old art form. Instinctively I reached out for it, and Dr. Mosskristal snatched it away. "Don't be silly," she rapped.

But I could read the title: *The Pleasure Areas*, by H. J. Campbell. "If I could just borrow it," I pleaded. "I'll bring it back within the week—"

"You will, *hell*. You'll read it here, if you read it at all, with my sec[3] watching you and making sure you pump the nitrogen back in when you put it back in the box. But I'm not sure it's a good idea. Laymen shouldn't try to understand medical problems, they're simply not equipped. Let's just say that you've had your limbic areas stimulated; under the influence of that great upwelling of pleasure you've become conditioned to associate Mokie-Koke with joy, and there's nothing to be done about it." She glanced at her watch and stood up. "Now I've got a patient to visit," she announced. "Dixmeister, you can use this room for your interview with the patient if you like —just so you're out of here in twenty minutes." And she flounced away, clutching her book.

And leaving me with Danny Dixmeister. "Pity," he said, shaking his head at the screen, which still displayed my test results. "You probably had a reasonably good future ahead of you at one time, Tarb, if you hadn't got yourself hooked."

"But it's not fair, Danny! I didn't know—"

He looked honestly perplexed. "Fair? True, campbelling is something new—I don't suppose you were watchful enough. But the areas for limbic commercials are clearly marked."

"Clearly!" I sneered. "It's a dirty, vicious trick and you know it! Certainly our own Agency would never do such a thing to move goods!"

Dixmeister pursed his lips. "The question," he said, "hasn't come up, since the competition owns the patents. Now. Let's talk about you. You realize, Tarb, that any kind of high-level position is out of the question for you now."

"Now hold on, Danny! I don't see that at all. I just put in a lot of lousy years on Venus for this Agency!

"It's a simple matter of security," he explained. "You're a Mokehead. You'd do anything for a Mokie-Koke, including betraying your grandmother—or even the Agency. So we just can't take the chance of letting you work on any high-security area—not to mention," he added bitchily, "that you've shown a certain lack of moral fiber in letting yourself get hooked in the first place."

"But I have seniority! Tenure! A record of—"

He shook his head impatiently. "Oh, we'll find something for you, of course. But not creative. How are your typing skills, Tarb? No? That's a pity—well, that's a problem for Personnel, after all."

I leveled a look at him for a moment. "Danny," I said, "I must have given you a harder time than I realized when you were my stooge."

He didn't answer. He only gave me a look that was both cryptic and long. I was out of that room, up the elevator to *Personnel*—

General Service on the fifth floor, waiting my turn with the fresh, young college kids and the middle-aged semi-employables before I quite deciphered that look. It wasn't dislike, or even triumph. It was pity.

What Dr. Mosskristal didn't tell me about was one of the side effects of campbellization. Depression. She didn't warn me, and when it happened I didn't recognize it for what it was. I guess that's what depression is. When you're having it, it just seems like the way the world is. You never think of it as a problem, only a state of being.

I had a lot to be depressed about. They found work for me, all right. Delivering art, carrying flowers to the stars of our commercials, dashing out into the street to flag and hold a pedicab for somebody from Executive Country, fetching soyaburgers and Coffiest for the secretaries—oh, I had a million things to do! I worked harder as a General Services dogsbody than I ever had as a star-class copysmith, but of course for that kind of work they don't pay star-class money. I had to give up the sea-condo. I didn't mind. What did I need such luxury for except to entertain, and who was there to entertain? Mitzi had moved herself up to a loftier sphere. All my old girl friends were transferred or married or promoted, and the new crop didn't seem to want to get involved with somebody in the deep freeze.

Speaking of deep freeze, the thing I had mostly forgotten about home was what it was like to be cold. I mean capital-K-*cold.* Cold to where the pedicab-pullers' breath steamed out around their faces, and they'd slip and stumble on the icy streets. Cold to where I could almost wish to change places with them for the exercise instead of sitting in the hard, bare seat with my teeth hurting from the wintry New York air—well, I said "almost." Even being a messenger boy was better than pulling a cab.

Especially now that it was getting cold. Those six years on Venus had thinned my blood. Even if I could have afforded to go out very often, the desire wasn't there. So I spent my days in the messenger pool, and my evenings at home, watching commercials on the Omni-V, talking with my new roommates when they were around— sitting. Mostly just sitting. And it was quite a surprise when the buzzer sounded, and I had a visitor, and the visitor was Mitzi.

If she had come to be nice to me, she had a funny idea about how to do it. She looked around with her nose wrinkled and her lips clamped shut, as though the place smelled of decay. She seemed to wear the twin frown lines between her brows all the time now. "Tenn," she said sternly, "you've got to pull yourself out of this! Look at you! Look at this dump! Look at what a shambles you've made of your life!"

I looked around the room, trying to see what she meant. Of course, when I couldn't afford the sea-condo payments any more I had to make other arrangements. It wasn't easy. Getting out of the contract cost me most of my saved-up pay, and this shared-time condo was about all I could afford. It was true that my roommates were pretty sloppy. One was into junk food, the other had gotten himself into one of those interminable collections of Nearly Silver Miniature Presidential Busts from the San Jacinto Mint. But still! "It's not so bad," I said defensively.

"It's *filthy*. Don't you ever throw out those old Moke bottles? Tenn, I know it's hard, but there are people who successfully take the cold turkey cure every year—"

I laughed. I was actually sorry for her, because she simply didn't understand how it was, having never been hooked. "Mitzi," I said, "is that why you came here, to tell me what a shambles I'm making of my life?"

She looked at me silently for a moment. "Well, I suppose the cure's pretty dangerous," she admitted, looking around for a place to sit. I cleared some of Nelson Rockwell's Hittite Emperors and a few of Charlie Bergholm's taco wrappers off the second chair. "I'm not really sure just why I did come here," she said, inspecting the seat carefully before sitting down.

I said bitterly, "If it was for a roll in the hay, forget it." I pointed to the closed bed box, where Rockwell, my two-to-ten roomie, was taking his share of sack time.

She—I was about to say flushed, but I guess darkened is a better word. "I guess in some way I feel a little responsible," she said.

"For not telling me about the damage suit? For letting me go broke while you collect millions? For some little things like that?"

She shrugged. "Something of the sort, maybe. Tenny? All right, I accept that you can't rise very high in the Agency again while you're a Moke-head, but there are plenty of other things you can do! Why not go back to school? Learn a new skill, start over in some other profession, I don't know, doctor, lawyer—"

I looked at her in amazement. "And give up *advertising?*"

"Oh, God! What's so holy about advertising?"

Well, that one took me back. All I could find to say was, "You've sure changed a lot, Mitzi." And I meant it as a reproof.

She said morosely, "Maybe I made a mistake coming here." Then her face brightened. "I know! What would you say to Intangibles? I think I could get you in there—not right away, of course, but when there's a vacancy—"

"Intangibles!" I sneered. "Mitzi, I'm a *product* person. I sell *goods*. Intangibles is for the has-beens and the never-wases—and, anyway, what makes you think you could do it?"

She hesitated, then said, "Oh, I just think I could. I mean—well, you might as well know, although it's a company secret for a while. I've taken my damage money and they've let me buy into the Agency."

"Buy in! You mean a stockholder?"

"Sure, a stockholder." She seemed apologetic about it—as though there were any reason for that! To be a stockholder in the Agency was about the next thing to being God. It had simply never occurred to me that anybody I knew would ever have the capital to do something like that.

But I shook my head. "I'm Product," I said proudly.

"Really," she flashed, "do you have any better offers?"

And of course I hadn't.

I surrendered. "Have a Mokie-Koke," I said, "and let's talk it over.

So I went to bed that night, even if alone, nevertheless with something I hadn't had before: hope. As I drifted off to sleep I was thinking impossible dreams: back to school, get that Master of Advertising Philosophy degree I'd planned for when I was a kid, learn some additional skills, do some research into Intangibles . . . kick the Moke habit.

They all seemed like good ideas. Whether anything would have been left of them in the cold light of dawn I do not know, but I had a powerful reinforcement. I woke up with a banging on the bed lid and the growly, grumbly voice of Nelson Rockwell, my two-to-ten roomie, telling me that he switched turns with Bergholm and it was time for his turn.

Sleepy as I was, I saw at once that he was looking really bad, bruise like a crushed grape stain over his right cheekbone, limping as he backed away to let me get out of the bed box. "What *happened,* Nelson?"

He looked as though I'd accused him of a crime. "Little misunderstanding," he muttered.

"It looks like a damn *big* misunderstanding to me. You've been beaten up, man!"

He shrugged, and winced as his muscles objected to the movement. "I got a little behind in my payments, so San Jacinto sent a couple of collectors around to the grommet works. Say, Tenn, you couldn't let me have fifty till payday, could you? Because they said next time it's my kneecaps."

"I don't have fifty," I said—nearly true, too. "Why don't you sell some of your figurines?"

"Sell them? Sell some of my stuff? Why, Tenn," he cried, "that's the stupidest thing I ever heard of! These here are investment-grade collectibles! All I have to do is hold onto them for market appreciation—and then, boy, wait'll you see! They're all limited editions! Twenty years from now I'll have my place in the Everglades, taking it easy, and they're what's going to pay for it . . . only," he added sadly, "if I don't get caught up on the payments they're gonna repossess. *And* kneecap me."

I fled down the hall to the bathroom because I couldn't stand hearing any more of that. Limited-edition collectibles! Good lord, that was one of the first accounts I ever worked on—limited edition to as many copies as we could sell, fifty thousand anyway; collectible meaning that once you had them there was nothing you could do with them *but* collect them.

So I cleaned up quick and got out of the room fast, and by seven A.M. I was up on the campus of Columbia A&P University, poring through the catalog readout and signing up for courses. There were plenty of electives that would count for credit toward the master's; I picked a sampling of the most interesting. History. Mathematics—that's sampling techniques, mostly. Even creative writing. I figured that that might be an easy credit, mostly, but I also had it in the back of my mind that if the copy job in Intangibles didn't come through there might be some use to it. If I weren't going to be allowed to write anything real, at least I could bang out a few novels. Admittedly, there's no big bucks there. But there's always a market, because there's always a few misfits in the world who can't get it together enough to watch sports or follow the stories on Omni-V, so they can't think of anything better to do than *read.* I'd tried it myself, a time or two, calling up some of the old classics on the tube. It's a little flaky, but the market is there and it's no disgrace to pick up some loose change catering to it.

That's the other funny thing about depression. When you're sunk in the middle of it everything looks so hard and there are so many things to worry about that it's pretty nearly impossible to make a move. But as soon as you take the first step, the second gets easier, and the third—in fact, that very day I decided I would have to do something about the Mokes I was swigging. Not quit cold turkey. Not even cut down right away. The first thing to do was to analyze the problem. So I began noting the time of every Moke. I kept it up for a week and, my God, do you know, I was averaging *forty* of the damn things a day! And not enjoying them all that much, either.

I decided to deal with it. I didn't want to kick the habit, because actually each Mokie-Koke in itself was a pretty good thing. They're actually rather a taste-tingling blend of really good chocolate-type flavoring, along with synthetic coffee extract and some of those cocaine analogues to give it zip. Makes a nice drink. The thing was not to *stop,* but only to *cut down.* Put that way, it was a simple problem in schedule making and logistics, like when you schedule an optimal mix of consumer impacts for your advertising spots. Forty Mokes a day was ridiculous. About eight, I reckoned, would be just enough. I'd keep that little lift you get every time, but I wouldn't jade my taste buds.

A Moke every two hours, I calculated, would do it just right. So I drew up a little chart:

6:00 A.M.
8:00 A.M.
10:00 A.M.

—and so on through the day until ten at night, when I could turn Nelson Rockwell out of our bed box, take the last one for a nightcap and so off to sleep.

When I counted them up, it turned out that a Moke every two hours for the sixteen waking hours of every day added up to nine instead of eight—unless I wanted to give up either the one to wake up or the one to go to sleep. I didn't want to do that. Anyway, what the hell, nine wasn't too many. I was very pleased about my little chart. It was such a powerful and effective scheme that I couldn't understand why no one seemed to have thought of it before me.

And, by gosh, I stuck to it. For very nearly a whole day.

It took a little willpower to wait out that first two hours until eight A.M., but I dawdled over breakfast and hung in the shower until the other tenants began banging on the door. Then ten A.M. was a long way off, but I took my time walking to the Agency building, and then I worked out a little supplementary scheme. They sent me out on deliveries right away. I didn't even look at my watch while I was pedaling from one place to another—well, mostly I didn't—what I did was wait till I got to a stop, then look at the watch and calculate how many more stops it would be before the next Moke was due. So I'd say to myself, "Not at the graphics studio, not at the bank, not at the box office for Audrey Wixon's tickets— when I get to the restaurant to pick up Mr. Xen's glasses that he forgot there last night, that's about when the next one will be due." It worked all right. Well—pretty nearly all right. There was a little mishap right after lunch, when I read my watch wrong and had the two o'clock Mokie-Koke at one by mistake. That wasn't really seri- ous. I just decided to stick to the odd hours instead of the even for the rest of that day. It was bad for a while in the afternoon, when they kept me waiting around the reception desk until 3:14 for a package that was slow in coming, but I got through the day all right.

The night, not so all right. The Moke at five was to celebrate the end of the working day; that was fine. Seven was harder to wait for, but I dragged out eating dinner as long as I could. And then back to the room, and then, dear heaven, nine o'clock was such a long time coming! About a quarter past eight I took a Moke out of the six-pack and held it in my hands. I had the Omni-V on, and it was showing one of those grand old historical epics about the early days of mail- order advertising, but I wasn't really following it very well. The place my eyes clung to was the clock. Eight eighteen. Eight twenty. Eight twenty-two . . . by eight fifty my eyes were glazing over, but I made it all the way to the tick of nine before I popped the tab.

I drank it down, enjoying it, and proud of the fact that I'd held out.

And then I faced the fact that it would be six A.M.—nine long hours!—before I could have another.

It was more than I could handle. By the time Charlie Bergholm scratched and yawned his way out of the bed box to make room for me I had killed a whole new six-pack.

Courses began. I made attempts now and then to cut down on the Mokes, but I decided that the important thing was to deal with the rest of my life. And one part of my life was taking on more importance than I had anticipated.

It's funny. It's as though a person has just so much love and tenderness to spend. I told myself that the Moke addiction wasn't that bad, really; didn't interfere with my work really; certainly didn't make me worth, really, any less. . . . I didn't believe it. The lower I fell in my own eyes, the more esteem I had left over, without a good place to invest it. Any more.

The life of a diplomat is full of complicated taboos and vacancies. There we were on Venus, surrounded by eight hundred thousand irreconcilable enemies. There were only a hundred and eight of us diplomats. In such circumstances, what do you do for friendship? More than that, what do you do about—well—love? You have a universe of perhaps fifty opposite-gender candidates to choose from. Probably a dozen are married—I mean faithfully married—and a dozen or more are too old, and about the same are too young. If you're lucky there may be as many as ten really eligible lovers in the pool, and what are the odds that even one of those will turn you on, and be turned on in return? Not good. Dips are as inbred as the *Bounty* survivors on Pitcairn Island. When Mitzi Ku came along I lucked in. We liked each other. We had the same feelings about sex. She was an immense convenience for me and I for her—not just for the physical act of sex, but for all the pair-bonding things that go along with it, like pillow gossip and remembering each other's birthdays. It was nice having Mitzi there for such things. She was maybe the most valued accessory the Embassy furnished me. I appreciated the convenience. We were most candid and outspoken with each other, but there was a four-letter word neither of us ever spoke to the other. The word was "love."

And now there wasn't any good way for me to say it to her. Mitzi had risen as fast as I had fallen. I didn't even see her from one week to another, except fleeting glimpses. I hadn't forgotten that she promised to get me on as a copy trainee in Intangibles. But I thought she had—until I brought Val Dambois's lunch up to him and discovered Mitzi in his office. Not just there. Head to head with him; and when I opened the door they sprang apart. "Damn it, Tarb," yelled Dambois, "don't you know enough to knock?"

"Sorry," I shrugged. I dropped his soyaburger on the desk and turned to go. I had no desire to break up their little cozy time . . . or, if I did, I certainly didn't want to show it. Mitzi put out a hand to stop me. She looked at me with that special, birdlike interest in her bright eyes, and then nodded.

"Val," she said, "we can finish this up later. Tenny? I think they might be ready to do something for you in Intangibles. Come on, I'll go down there with you and see what we can get going."

It was lunchtime and so we had to wait for the elevator. I was feeling nervous—wondering, not very happily, why she hadn't called me if the job had opened up; whether she ever would have remembered it again if I hadn't turned up just then. They were not ego-inflating thoughts. I tried to make conversation. "So what were you two conspiring about?" I asked jokingly. The way she looked at me made me think my tone had been a touch too sharp. I tried to smooth it over: "I guess I'm a little strung out," I apologized, assuming she would take that as natural from a Mokie-head. But it wasn't that at all. It might even have been jealousy. "It seems a long time since you were running your spy ring on Venus," I said wistfully. What I meant by that was that my perceptions of Mitzi had changed a lot since then. She seemed—I don't know. Soberer? Kinder? Of course, it couldn't be that *she* had changed. What was different was that, having lost her, I valued her more highly.

And, having lost her, I stood open-mouthed, gaping at her when, having stepped off the descending elevator and waiting for me, she called up, "If you're not busy tonight, Tenny, how about dinner at my place?"

I don't know what expression was on my face, but whatever it was it made her laugh. "I'll pick you up after work," she said. "Now, the man I want you to meet is Desmond Haseldyne, and that's his office right down there. Come along!"

If Mitzi had surprised me with unexpected warmth, Haseldyne was a shock in the other direction. While Mitzi was introducing us he was glaring at me, and the only reading I could give his expression was loathing.

Why? I couldn't guess. I'd seen the man around the Agency from time to time, of course. But I certainly couldn't think of anything I'd done to offend him. And Desmond Haseldyne was not a man you would specially wish to have dislike you. He was *huge*. He was six feet six inches at least, shoulders like a stallion, fists that swallowed my hand up without a trace when he deigned to shake it. Haseldyne was one of those freaky talents that Advertising fits into odd places in its great machine—a mathematician, they said; also a poet; also he had, curiously, had a very successful career in the import-export business before giving it up to turn to advertising. I got my first glimpse of a reason for his expression when he growled, "Hell, Mitzi! He's the geek that's always looking at his watch!"

"He's also my friend," she said firmly, "and a star-class copy-smith who suffered from an accident that was not his fault. I want you to give him a chance. You can't blame a person for being a victim of unethical advertising, can you?"

He relented. "I guess not," he admitted—and didn't even cover himself by adding, *and thank heaven we at this Agency don't stoop to such practices*, as anyone else would have had the sense to do. You never know who's bugging you. He stood up and lumbered around the desk to get a better look at me. "I guess," he conceded, "that we can give him a try. You can run along, Mitzi. See you tonight?"

"No, I've got a date. Another time, Des," she said, and winked at me as she closed the door.

Haseldyne sighed and passed a hand over his face. Then he returned to his chair. "Sit down, Tarb," he boomed. "You know why you're here?"

"I think so—Mr. Ha—Des," I said firmly. I'd made up my mind that I was going to be treated like what I was, not just another trainee. It caused him to look at me sharply, but all he said was:

"This is the Department of Intangible Accounts. We've got about thirty main areas of exploitation, but there are two lines that far outweigh all the others. One is politics. The other is religion. Do you know anything about either one of them?"

I shrugged. "What I studied in college," I said. "Personally, I was always a commodity man. I sold *goods*, not airy-fairy *ideas*."

He looked at me in a way that made me think it wouldn't be so bad, really, to go back to delivering packages, but he had made up his mind to give me a job, and give me a job he would. "If you don't care which," he said, "I guess the place we need help right now is religion. Maybe you don't realize what a valuable account religion is?" Well, I didn't, but I didn't say anything. "You talk about com-

modities. Goods. All right, Tarb, figure it out. If you sell somebody
a jar of Coffiest they pay maybe a dollar for it. Forty cents of that
goes to the retailer and the jobber. The label and the jar cost a
nickel, and you have to spend maybe three cents for the contents."

"Nice margin of profit," I said approvingly.

"That's where you're wrong! Add it up. Nearly half your money
goes to the damn *product*. It's the same with appliances, the same
with clothes, the same with all those tangible things. But religion!
Ah, *religion,* " he said softly, his face beaming with a reverential glow.
"In religion the product doesn't cost a damn *cent*. Maybe we spend a
few bucks on land and construction—it looks really good if you can
show some cathedral or temple or something, though mostly we just
use miniatures and process shots. Maybe we print a few pamphlets.
Sometimes a couple of books. But you just look at the P&L statements, Tenny, and you'll see that the bottom line is *sixty per cent*
profit! And most of the rest is promotion cost which, don't forget, is
our money too."

I shook my head wonderingly. "I had no idea," I said.

"Of course you had no idea! You product people are all the
same. And that's just religion. Politics, the same—even a bigger cash
spin-off because we don't have to build any churches. . . . Although," he said, his expression suddenly wistful, "it's hard to get
people to take an interest in politics these days. I used to think that
could be the biggest of all, but—" He shook his head. "Well," he
said, "that's the picture. Want to give it a try?"

Well, you bet I did. I charged into the copy console room with my
adrenalin flowing, ready to meet the challenge—I'd forgotten that I
was still a trainee. That meant that when they needed me to deliver a
package they could still draft me, and Mr. Dambois's suits needed to
be picked up at the cleaners, and there was a sample of a new
package for Kelpos, the Krispy Snack, that had to get to Production
. . . it was closing time when I got back to my console. And I didn't
get to see Mitzi that night after all. Instead of my date there was a
message on my machine: *Something came up. Sorry. Reschedule tomorrow?*

It was a jolt. I'd been prepping myself for a happy evening, and
now it was taken away from me.

On the way home I hit the Mokes pretty hard, and when I finally
got my turn in the bed box and fell asleep my thoughts were not

cheerful, in spite of the new job. Things had changed a lot! Back on Venus, Mitzi Ku had been happy enough to date a section head. Even flattered! Now the world for the two of us had turned upside down. I could whistle, but unless she happened to feel like it she wouldn't come. Worse than that, somebody else might have a louder and more compelling whistle. The hardest thing for me to reconcile myself to was that there were two other toms preening their plumage in her direction. Evidently what I was supposed to do was take a number and wait until called. And I didn't care much for the contest. Competition from Val Dambois I could understand—I didn't say *like*. Haseldyne was another matter. Who was this sumo blimp with all the muscles who had suddenly turned up in Mitzi's life?

On the other hand, other things had changed a lot, too. When I finally got to work the next morning—after only an hour of coffee/doughnut runs for the secretaries and the model pool—I realized that the state of the art I had left behind when I boarded the shuttle for Venus was like flintlocks and mainframe computers compared to what was going on now. That was demonstrated to me the first time I sat down at my copy console and reached to turn on the grid-resolution interlock. There wasn't any.

It took me all the rest of the morning to learn how to operate the console, and at that I had to get help from the office girl.

But you don't get to be a star-class copysmith for nothing, and I hadn't lost all my skills while I was on Venus. I made a quick search of the files and discovered, as I thought, that there were areas the Department of Intangibles hadn't explored. I couldn't compete right away in the latest technology. What I could do was go back to some tried and true procedures of the past—always good, sometimes overlooked by the new people—and by four that afternoon I had completed my rough. I pulled the spool out of the console and charged into Haseldyne's office. "Take a look, Des," I ordered, plugging it into his reader. "Of course this is only preliminary. It isn't fully interactive yet, so don't ask it any hard questions, and maybe the model I used isn't the best for the purpose—"

"Tarb," he rumbled dangerously, "what the hell are you talking about?"

"Door to door!" I cried. "The oldest advertising technique there is! A whole new campaign, based on the soundest, best-tested procedures there are!"

I hit the switch, and immediately the three-dimensional image sprang up, a grave, gaunt figure in a cowl, face shadowed but benign, gazing directly into Haseldyne's eyes. Unfortunately it was only about two feet tall, and there was a halo of blue sparks around its edges.

"I guess I didn't get the size match right," I apologized, "and there's interference to be cleaned up—"

"Tarb," he growled, "shut up, will you?" But he was interested as the figure advanced toward him and began to speak:

"Religion, sir! Yes, that's what I have to offer! Salvation! Peace of mind! The washing away of sins, or simply the acceptance of the will of a Supreme Being. I carry a complete line, Roman Catholic, C. of E., twenty-two kinds of Baptist, Unification, Scientology, Methodist—"

"Everybody has those already," snapped Haseldyne, glancing irritably at me. I gloated; it was the reaction I had programmed for. The little image glanced over its shoulder as though making sure no one could hear, and then leaned forward confidentially.

"Right you are, sir! I should have seen you weren't the kind of person to adopt what everybody else has. So how about a genuine antique? I'm not talking your Buddha or your Confucius. I'm talking Zoroaster! Ahura Mazda and Ahriman! The forces of light and darkness! Why, half the religions you get these days are just sleazy plagiarisms of Zoroaster—and, listen, there's no fasting, there's no dietary laws, no don't-do-this or don't-do-that. Zoroaster is a religion for persons of *quality*. And—you won't believe this—I can let you have the whole thing, conversion included, for less than the price of an ordinary retreat or bar mitzvah. . . ."

I could see that he was really hooked. He watched the figure run through to the close. As it faded away in another shower of those blue sparks—these automatic grid-resolution devices weren't all they were cracked up to be—he nodded slowly. "Might work," he said.

"It's bound to work, Haseldyne! I admit it's still rough. I need to talk to Legal about the contract signing at the close, of course, and I'm not sure about the cowl—maybe a sort of Indian dancing-girl outfit with a female vendor instead?"

"Tarb," he said heavily, "don't knock your own work. It's good. Clean up the size and the interference, and tomorrow we'll call a staff meeting and get it started." And I took the spool out of his machine and left him staring into space. It struck me as funny that he didn't seem pleased—after all, he'd admitted it was good! But when I got back to my console there was a message on it that drove such worries out of my mind:

I've been called out of the office, so why don't you come right to my place? Expect you about eight.

When I went back to my place to clean up, Nelson Rockwell was waiting for me. "Tenny," he coaxed, "if you could just let me have a few bucks till payday—"

"No way, Nelson! You're just going to have to work it out one way or another with the San Jacinto Mint."

"Mint? Who said anything about the mint?" he demanded. "This is something brand new—take a look!" And he pulled out of his pocket a little scrap of a picture in a cheap plastic frame. "It's the Frameable Treasury Secretary Lithographed Portrait Series on Banknote-Quality Paper!" he declared proudly. "They're pure gold, and all I need's a hundred to get my subscription started. Make it two hundred and I can get in on the charter subscriptions for Cabinet-Sized All-Metal Renderings of Famous American Suspension Bridges—" I left him still talking while I headed for the bathroom to spruce up. Tikli-Talc on my chin, LuvMe in my armpits—it had been a long time between dates. I figured I ought to bring something, so on the way I stopped to pick up a couple of six-packs of Moke. Naturally the supermarket was crowded. Naturally the checkout lines were interminable. I took the shortest one I could find, but it just didn't move. I craned past the stout lady with the full cart in front of me and saw that the checkout person was deeply involved in endless computations of discount coupons, special offers, rainchecks, scratch-a-line lottery tickets and the like, and, worse than that, the matron before me had at least twice as many clutched in her plump little fist. I groaned, and she turned to me with sympathy. "Don't you just *hate* standing in these lines? Gosh, me too! That's why I never go to Ultimaximarts any more." She waved proudly at the holosigns: *Speedy Service! Ultrafast Checkouts! We do everything to make shopping with us a joy!*

"The thing is," I said, "I've got a date."

"Aw," she said sympathetically, "so you're in a hurry, of course. Tell you what. You help me sort out these coupons, and it'll go a lot faster when I get to the desk. The thing is, see, I've got this thirty cents off on Kelpy Krisps, but the coupon's only valid if I buy a ten-

ounce tube of Glow-Tooth Double-Duty Dentifricial Analgesics, but
they only had the fourteen-ounce size. Do you think they'll accept
that?" They wouldn't, of course. That was a T., G. & S. promotion,
and I knew we would never have issued those coupons except when
the ten-ounce size was being discontinued. I was spared having to
tell her that, though. A red light flashed, a klaxon sounded to chase
her out of the way, the barrier slammed shut in her face and a
display lit up to say:

> We regret this Speedy Service Ultrafast Checkout Line is
> now closed. Please take your purchases to another of our
> counters for prompt attention from our friendly cashiers.

"Oh, *hell*," I groaned, staring unbelievingly at the sign. That was
a mistake. It wrecked my timing.

One of the slogans I'd come across on the Religion account was
"the last shall be first." In this case, my hesitation made it true
enough. The whole long line behind me broke and scattered and I
was caught staring. That's when the finely honed consuming skills
that you've developed over a lifetime meet their test. The split-
second decisions come on you without warning: which line to jump
to? You've got a dozen independent variables to weigh, and not just
the obvious ones. There are things like the number of persons in
line, the number of items for each, the factor for number of coupons
per item—that's what you learn while you're still hanging on the end
of Mom's cart with your thumb in your mouth and the can of
Sweetees you've bawled your lungs out for clutched in your grubby
little fist. Then you've got to learn to read the individual consumer.
You look for the nervous twitching of the fingers that suggests this
one may be close to a credit overdraft, so the whole line will crash
shut while the Wackerhuts come to take him away. Or that other one
sneaked a magnetic pen through the detectors to try to change a
bonus offer. You've got to assign a value to each and integrate them,
and then there's the physical stuff you've practiced, feinting to the
wrong line, pretending not to notice a shopping cart left to save a
place, use of elbows—all that is standard survival stuff, but my skills
were rusty from the years on Venus. I wound up at the tail end of a
line longer than ever, and even Miss Fourteen-Ounce had squeezed
in ahead of me.

Something had to be done.

I peered over her shoulder to study the baskets in the line ahead and worked out my tactics. "Oh, *darn*," I said as though to myself— but loud enough for all to hear, "I forgot the Vita-Smax." Nobody had any. They couldn't have. The line had been discontinued even before I left for Venus—some trouble about heavy-metal poisoning. Three steps ahead of me, an old man with a full double-decker cart glanced at me, nibbling at the bait.

I grinned at him and called, "Remember those grand old Vita-Smax commercials? 'The All-American Cheese, Bran and Honey Breakfast Treat'?"

Miss Fourteen-Ounce looked up from her frantic inventorying of coupons. " 'Keeps You Regular—Tantalizes Your Tongue—Builds Health, Health, Health in Every Bite!' " she quoted. "Gee! I haven't had Vita-Smax in a long time! We used to call it the milk and honey cereal." Besides the heavy metals, the simulated milk solids had caused liver damage and the synthetic sucrose syrup rotted the teeth, but naturally no one would remember a thing like that.

"Mom used to make them every morning," said another woman dreamily.

I had them on the tip. I chuckled ruefully. "Mine too. I could kick myself for not picking up a box or two from the stack in Gourmet Foods."

Heads turned. "I didn't see any Vita-Smax there," the old man argued querulously.

"Really? The big stack under the sign that said, 'Buy 1 Get 1 Free'?" The line quivered. "With the special double-allowance coupon reintroductory offer?" I added, and that was what did it. They broke. Every one of them pulled carts out of line, racing for Gourmet Foods. Suddenly I was face to face with the checker. She'd been listening too, and I had to beg her to take my money before she ran after them.

All the same I was late. I almost trotted the last couple of blocks to Mitzi's place. The smog and exertion had me gasping and sweating by the time I got there—good-by LuvMe.

When I got past the doorthing I was startled to see what kind of a pad Mitzi lived in. I don't mean that it was fancy—I would have expected that, considering her current credit rating. On the contrary, what hit me in the eye when Mitzi let me in was its starkness.

It certainly was not poverty that made it so peculiarly bare. You don't get a four-hundred-square-foot flat in a building with twenty-four-hour reflex-conditioned attack guards without paying through the nose for it—I would have known that even if I hadn't known about all that Veenie damage money. The surprising thing was that splurging had stopped with the pad itself. No RotaBath. No tanks of tropical fish. No—well, no anything at all to show her status. She didn't even have Nelson Rockwell's pathetic busts or commemorative medallions. A few pieces of furniture, a small Omni-V set in a corner—that was about it. And the decor was peculiar. It was all hot reds and yellows, and on one wall there was a huge static mural—not even liquid crystal—which I puzzled over for a moment before I recognized it. Sure enough, it was a rendering of that famous scene in Venusian history when they put the first big Hilsch tube on top of the tallest mountain in the Freysa range, to blow the noxious gases out into orbit as they began reducing the atmosphere to something people could stand.

"Sorry I'm late," I apologized, staring at the mural, "but there was a long line at the supermarket." I held up the Mokie-Kokes as explanation.

"Aw, Tenny, we don't need that swill." Then she bit her lip. "Come on in the kitchen while I finish dinner, and you can tell me how things are going for you."

To my surprise, she put me to work while I talked. To a surprise bigger still, the work was peeling potatoes! I mean, raw *vegetable* potatoes—some of them still had dirt on them! "Where'd you get these things?" I asked, trying to figure out what I was supposed to do to "peel" them.

"Money will get you anything," she said, shredding some other raw unprocessed vegetables, orange and green colored ones this time. It wasn't exactly an answer, since I hadn't really wondered where, or even how, but why?

I was brought up polite, though. I really did eat quite a lot of her dinner, even the raw roots and leaves she called salad, and I didn't say anything critical at all. Well, not *critical*. I did, after a while, when the conversation seemed to be limping along, ask if she really liked that stuff.

Mitzi was chomping away with a faraway look in her eyes, but she collected herself. "Like it? Of course I like it! It's—" She paused, as though something had occurred to her. "It's *healthy*," she said.

"I thought it must be," I said politely.

"No, really! There are some new, uh, studies, not yet published, that show that. For example, did you know that processed foods may cause memory deficiencies?"

"Aw, come on, Mitzi," I grinned. "Nobody would sell consumers things that did them harm."

She gave me a quizzical look. "Well, not on purpose," she said, "maybe. But these are new studies. Tell you what. Let's test it out!"

"Test what out?"

"Test out whether your diet has screwed up your memory, damn it," she flared. "We'll try a little experiment to see how much you remember about something and, uh, I'll tape it so we can check it over."

It did not sound like a very fun game to me, but I was still trying to be polite. "Why not?" I said. "Let's see. Suppose I give you the annual billings of the Agency for the past fifteen years, broken down for—"

"No, nothing that dull," she complained. "I know! Let's see how much you remember about what was going on in the Embassy on Venus. Some particular aspect—I don't know—sure! Let's hear everything you remember about the spy ring I was running."

"Ah, but that's not fair!" I protested. "You were doing the actual running, all I know is bits and pieces."

"We'll make allowances for that," she promised, and I shrugged.

"All right. Well, for a starter, you had twenty-three active agents and about a hundred and fifty free lancers and part-timers—most of them weren't actual agents, at least they didn't know who they were working for."

"Names, Tenny!"

I looked at her in surprise—she was taking this pretty seriously. "Well, there was Glenda Pattison in the Park Department, she was the one who got the defective parts in the new powerplant. Al Tischler, from Learoyd City—I don't know what he did, but I remember him because he was so short for a Veenie. Margaret Tucsnak, the doctor that put anticonception pills in with the aspirins. Mike Vaccaro, the prison guard from the Pole—say, should I count Hamid or not?"

"Hamid?"

"The grek," I explained. "The one that I tricked old Harriman into taking as a bona-fide political refugee. Of course, you left before he got to make contact, so I don't know whether I should include him on the list. But I'm surprised you don't remember him." I grinned. "You'll be saying you don't remember Hay next," I ventured. Bafflingly, she looked puzzled even at that. "Jesus Maria Lopez, for God's sake," I said, exasperated, and she looked at me opaquely for a moment.

Then she said, "That's all back on Venus, Tenny. He's there. We're here."

"That a girl!" Things were looking up. I moved closer to her, and she looked at me almost invitingly. But there was still the ghost of a scowl on her face. I reached up and touched her frown lines; they seemed actually sculpted into her brow. "Mitzi," I said tenderly, "you're working too hard."

She flinched away almost angrily from my hand, but I persisted. "No, really. You're—I don't know. More tired. More mellow, too." She was; my brassy lady was bronze now. Even her voice was deeper and softer.

And, as a matter of fact, I liked her better that way. She said, "Keep going with the names, please?" But she smiled when she said it.

"Why not? Theiller, Weeks, Storz, the Yurkewitch brothers— how'm I doing so far?"

She was biting her lip—vexed, I thought, because my memory was pretty good after all. "Just go on," she said. "There's plenty more."

So I did. Actually I only remembered about a dozen names, but she agreed to accept my remembering some of the agents just by where they worked and what they did for her, and when I wasn't just sure of something she helped out by asking questions until I got it straight. But it went on so long! "Let's try something else," I offered. "For instance, let's see which of us can remember more about the last night we spent together."

She smiled absently. "In a minute, Tenn, but first, this person from Myers-White who spoiled the wheat crop—"

I laughed out loud. "Mitzi dear," I said, "the Myers-White agent was growing rice; it was at Nevindale that they messed up the wheat crop! See? If diet messes up memory, maybe you ought to switch to Kelpy Crisps!"

She was biting her lip again, and for a moment her expression was not friendly at all. Funny. I'd never thought of Mitzi as a sore loser. Then she smiled and surrendered, clicking off the recorder. "I guess you've proved your point, dear," she said, and patted the couch beside her. "Why don't you come over here and collect your winnings?" And so it turned out that we had a nice time after all.

III

The nice time didn't get repeated very rapidly, though. Mitzi didn't leave any more messages for me. I called her a few times—she was friendly enough, to be sure—she was also, she explained, *really* busy, and maybe some time next week, Tenn, dear, or anyway right after the first of the month—

Of course, I had plenty to keep me busy. I was doing very well on the Religion account, and even Desmond Haseldyne was flattering. But I wanted to see Mitzi. Not just for the sake of, well, you know, the things for the sake of which I'd got interested in her in the first place. There were other things.

A couple of times when I went into Haseldyne's office, he was making mysterious private calls, and I had the funny idea that some of them were to Mitzi. And I saw him, along with Val Dambois and Mitzi and the Old Man himself, in a huddle in a fast-food place a long way from the Agency. It wasn't a place where executives went for dinner. It wasn't even a place where junior copy trainees like me went for dinner very often, but it happened to be near Columbia Advertising & Promotion University. When they saw me it obviously shook them up. They were all in on something together. I didn't know what. None of my business, maybe—but it hurt me that Mitzi didn't tell me what it was. I went on to my Columbia class—that was the creative writing one—and that whole evening I'm afraid I didn't pay much attention.

That was the best of the courses I was taking, too. Creative writing is really—well—creative. At the beginning of the course the professor told us that it was only in our time that the subject had been taught in a reasonable way. In the old days, she said, creative-writing students would just sort of make things up themselves, and the teachers would have to try to distinguish how much of what was good, or bad, about a paper was the idea or how the ideas were expressed. And yet, she said, they had the example of art courses for hundreds of years to show them the right way to do it. Aspiring artists had always been set to copy the works of Cézanne and Rembrandt and Warhol in order to learn their craft, while all aspiring writers were urged to create was their own blather. Handy word-processors changed all that, and so the first assignment she gave us was to rewrite *A Midsummer Night's Dream* in modern English. And I got an A.

Well, from then on I was teacher's pet, and she let me do all sorts of extracredit themes. There was a good chance, she said, that I would pass her course with the highest mark ever attained, and you know that sort of thing can do you nothing but good when it comes time to add up your degree credits. So I took on some pretty ambitious projects. The hardest one, I guess, was to rewrite all of *The Remembrance of Things Past* in the style of Ernest Hemingway, changing the locale to Germany in the time of Hitler and presenting it as a one-act play.

That sort of thing was well beyond the capacity of any equipment I had in my little shared-time condo, not to mention that my roomies were likely to interrupt me, so I took to staying after work now and then to use the big machines in the copy consoles. I had set sentence length for not more than six words, dialed introspection down to 5 percent and programmed playscript format, and I was just getting set to run the program when I ran out of Mokes. The soft-drink machine had nothing but our own Agency brands in it, of course. I had tried them before; they didn't satisfy the craving. I had the idea that I'd seen a Mokie-Koke bottle in the wastebasket in Desmond Haseldyne's office once—I suppose it was just my imagination—so I wandered over in that direction.

Somebody was in his office. I could hear voices; the lights were on; the data processors had their hoods off and were running some sort of financial programs. I would have turned quietly away and gone back to my copy console, except that one of the voices was Mitzi's.

Curiosity was my undoing.

I paused to look at the programs running on the machines. At first I thought it was a projection for some sort of investment plan, for it was all about stock holdings and percentages of total shares outstanding. But it seemed to make a pattern. I stood up, deciding to get out of there—

And made the mistake of trying to leave inconspicuously through the darkened offices on the other side of the processors. They had been locked for the night. Nothing kept me from entering, but the break-in trap had been set. I heard a great, hollow hissing, like the sound of the Hilsch tubes around Port Kathy, and a huge cloud of white blew up around me. I'd been foamed! I could see nothing at all. The foam allowed me to breathe, but it did not allow me to see, not anything at all. I stumbled around for a moment, bashing into chairs, bumping over desks.

Then I surrendered to the foam and just stood there, waiting. And while I waited, I thought.

By the time I heard someone approaching I had figured it out.

It was Mitzi and Haseldyne, spraying the foam with a dispersant chemical as they came—I could hear the hiss. "Tenn!" Mitzi cried. "What the hell are you doing here?"

I didn't answer, not directly anyway. I wiped the last of the foam off my face and shoulders and grinned at her.

"I'm onto you," I said.

What I said had a curious effect on them. Naturally they were startled to see me there. Mitzi was holding the dispersant spray like a weapon, and Haseldyne was fondling a heavy tape dispenser as though he'd brought it along to bash someone's head in with it—not so very surprising, I suppose, since I had set off the burglar alarm and foam. But both of them went absolutely expressionless. It was as though their faces had become dead, and they kept that queer immobility for seconds.

Then Mitzi said, "I don't know what you mean, Tennison."

I chuckled. "It's perfectly obvious. I saw the programs you're running. You're planning a takeover bid, aren't you?"

Still no expression. "I mean," I clarified, "the two of you, maybe Dambois too, are planning to take over control of the Agency with your investments. Isn't that right?"

Slowly, glacially, expression returned to Haseldyne's face, and then to Mitzi's. "I'll be darned," rumbled Haseldyne. "He's caught us fair and square, Mitzi."

She swallowed, and then smiled. It was not a very good smile— too much tension in the jaw muscles, too much narrowing of the lips. "It certainly looks that way," she said. "Well, Tenn, what are you going to do about it?"

I had not felt this good in a long time. Even Haseldyne looked like a harmless and friendly fat man to me, not a ravening monster. I said amiably, "Why, nothing you don't want me to, Mitz. I'm your friend. All I want is a little friendliness from the two of you."

Haseldyne glanced at Mitzi. Mitzi looked at Haseldyne. Then both of them turned to me. "I guess," said Haseldyne, choosing his words with care, "what we ought to do now is talk about just how friendly you want us to be, Tarb."

"Gladly," I said. "But first—have you got a Moke on you?"

IV

The next day at the Agency the climate had thawed. By midafternoon it was downright tropical, because Mitzi Ku had smiled on me. What made Mitzi Ku so suddenly great a power no one exactly knew, but the water-cooler gossip had made it clear that she was. There was no talk about putting me back on the pedicab run.

Even Val Dambois found me worthy of love. "Tenny, boy," he boomed, making the long trek down to my little cubicle in Intangibles, "why'd you let them put you in a hole like this? Why the hell didn't you *say* something?" I didn't say anything because I couldn't get past his sec^3, was the answer, but there was no sense telling him what he already knew. Bygones could be bygones—for now, anyway. Forgiveness, no lingering grudges, a truly sales-fearing spirit, that was what Tennison Tarb was like these days. I grinned back at Dambois and let him throw his arm around me as he conducted me back to Executive Country. There would be a time, I knew, when his throat would be exposed to my fangs—until then it was forgive and forget.

They even, without saying a word about it, arranged to put a Moke dispenser in my office. There was no official ruling. It just appeared that afternoon.

And that made me do some hard thinking. Swigging Mokes was surely harmless enough—hell, I'd proved that!—but did it really suit the star-class image I ought to present to the world? It was such a consumer kind of thing to do—and a consumer, moreover, of a competing Agency's account. I pondered over it all the way home in my company car. When I tipped the pedaler the thought crystallized, because I got a look at the black resentment in his eyes before he covered it up and touched his cap to me. Three days earlier, we'd shared the same tandem pedicab run. I could understand his resentment. What that resentment implied was that if I got cast down into the lower depths again, he and the other sharks would be waiting.

So I marched in and rapped on the sleeping tank. "Rockwell," I shouted. "Wake up! I want to ask you something!"

He wasn't a bad guy, old Nelson Rockwell. He had nearly six more hours coming to him in the tank before it was my turn, and every right in the world to bite my head off when I dragged him out of it. But when he heard what I wanted he was kindness itself. A little puzzled, maybe. "You want to go dry, Tenny?" he repeated, still half-asleep. "Well, sure, that's the smart thing to do, you don't want to screw up your big chance. But I don't honestly see what it's got to do with me."

"What it's got to do with you, Nels, is, didn't you tell me once you were in ConsumAnon?"

"Yeah, sure. Years ago. Gave it up, though, because I didn't need it once I straightened myself out and got into collectibles—oh!" he said, eyes lighting up. "I get it! You want me to tell you about ConsumAnon so you can decide if you want to try it."

"What I want, Nels, is to go to ConsumAnon. And I want you to take me."

He glanced wistfully at the warm, inviting sleep box. "Gosh, Tenny. It's open to anyone. You don't need to be taken."

I shook my head. "I'd feel better if I went with someone," I confessed. "Please? And soon? Tomorrow night, even, if there's a meeting—"

He laughed at that. When he was through laughing, he patted my arm. "You've got a lot to learn, Tenny. There's a meeting *every* night. That's how it works. Now, if you'll just hand me my socks. . . ."

That's the kind of guy Nels Rockwell was. All the time he was dressing I was thinking of ways to return the favor. I'd have to be moving out of this shared-time dump, of course. What was to stop me from, say, prepaying two or three months of my share and letting him have it, so he could pick his own time to sleep? I knew he had to take the lobster trick at the grommet works because of his sleep schedule; he could probably get a different shift, maybe even more money. . . .

But I got a grip on myself. It wasn't doing a consumer any favor, I told myself, to give them ideas above their station. He was getting along all right the way he was. I might mess him up badly by interfering.

So I kept my mouth shut about prepaying the rent, but in my heart I was truly grateful.

ConsumAnon turned out to be a bad idea. I knew that in the first two minutes. The place Rockwell had taken me to was a *church*.

Now, that's not so bad in itself. In fact, it was kind of interesting —I'd never seen the inside of one before. Besides, you could look at it as a kind of research for my Intangibles work, which meant I could put in a chit for my and Rockwell's pedicab fare (even though he'd insisted we take the bus).

But—these *people!* I don't just mean they were consumers. They were the dregs of the consumer class, shriveled up little old men with facial tics; fat, frowning girls with the kind of complexions you get from solid soy and not much of that. There was a young couple whispering jitterily to each other, with a small child crying itself frantic unnoticed in the seat between them. There was a weasel-faced man skulking by the door as though he couldn't make up his mind, stay or run—well, I couldn't either, really. These people were *losers*. A well-trained consumer is one thing. They were all of that. They had been bred and trained to do what the world needed from them: buying what we Agency people had to sell. But, oh, what stolid and stunned faces! What made for a good consumer was boredom. Reading was discouraged, homes were no joy to be in— what else did they have to do with their lives but consume? But these people had made a travesty of that noble—well, fairly noble—calling. They were *obsessed*. I almost ducked out for a Moke to ease the jangly shudders they gave me, but as long as I'd come this far I decided to stay for the meeting.

That was my second bad mistake, because the proceedings rapidly became disgusting. First, they started with a *prayer*. Then they began singing *hymns*. Rockwell nudged me to join in, grinning and croaking away at the top of his voice, but I couldn't even look him in the face.

Then it got worse. One by one, these misfits stood up and sobbed out their tawdry stories. Talk about sickening! This one had blighted her life by popping NicoChews, forty packs a day, till her teeth came out and her bosses fired her because she couldn't handle her job—her job was phone operator. This other one was into deodorants and breath-fresheners, and had so thoroughly scoured away every trace of natural body exudates that his skin was chapped and his mucous surfaces dried out. The jittery young couple—why, they were Moke-heads like myself! I stared at them in amazement. How could they let themselves sink so low? Sure, I had a Moke *problem*. But just being here meant I was *doing* something about the problem. No way would I let myself turn into such raddled wrecks as they! "Go on, Tenny," muttered Rockwell, nudging me. "Don't you want to testify?"

I don't know what I said to him, except that it included the word, "Good-by." I squeezed past him and out the door, yearning for the open air. As I stood in the entrance, wheezing and clearing my lungs, the weasel-faced man crept out after me. "Gee," he said grinning slyly, "I heard what your friend said. Sure wish I had your monkey instead of my own."

No one likes to hear that the trouble that blights his life is less awful than some stranger's. I was not cordial. I said stiffly, "My, ah, problem is bad enough to suit me, thanks." For some reason my mind was fluttering just then. I had half a dozen separate yearnings and loathings filling my head at once—the desperate need for a Moke, the contempt for those ConsumAnon dummies inside, the more acute dislike for Weasel-face himself, the itchy yearning for Mitzi Ku that came over me every now and then . . . and, under them all, something else that I couldn't quite identify. A memory? An inspiration? A resolve? I couldn't quite put my finger on it. It had something to do with what was going on inside—no, with something before that, something Rockwell had said?

Weasel-face, I suddenly realized, was hissing rapidly in my ear. "—What?" I barked.

"I said," he repeated behind his hand, glancing about, "I know a guy's got what you need. Moke-Eeeze pills. Take three a day, one each meal, and you'll never need a Moke again."

"My God, man!" I roared. "Are you offering me *drugs?* I'm no consumer. I'm Agency personnel! If I could find a cop I'd have you locked up—" And I actually looked around for a familiar Brinks or Wackerhut uniform; but you know how it is, there's never a policeman when you want one, and anyway when I looked back Weasel-face was gone.

And so was my idea. Whatever it had been.

The human kidney is not meant to handle forty Mokie-Kokes a day. There were times over the next twenty-four hours when I wondered if Weasel-face hadn't had a good idea after all. Some cautious inquiries at the Agency clinic (oh, how sweet they were to me now!) solidified the vague notions I'd had. The pills were bad news. They worked, but after a time—maybe six months, maybe more or less— the stressed nervous system faltered and ultimately broke. I didn't want that. True, I was losing weight and the view in the mirror when I depilated showed new strain lines on my face every morning; but I was functioning well enough still.

No, hell, let's tell the truth: I was functioning *magnificently*. Every new set of hourlies showed that Religion was uptrending. Joss sticks, up 0.03; prayer candles, 0.02; exit polls from three hundred and fifty randomly chosen Zoroastrian temples showed a nearly one percent increase in first-time worshippers. The Old Man called me himself. "You've established a lot of credibility with the Planning Committee," he boomed. "Tarb, my hat's off to you! What can I do to make your work easier? Another assistant?"

"Great idea, sir!" I cried, and added carelessly, "What's Dixmeister doing now?"

So my old trainee was back on my team. Apprehensive, placatory, desperate to please—consumed by curiosity. Just the way I wanted him.

He wasn't the only one devoured by curiosity, because everybody in the Agency knew something big was going on, and none of them knew exactly what. The gravy was that none of them knew how little I myself knew. Account executives and copy chiefs, on the way from level nine to level fifteen, a dozen times a day decided to take the shortcut through my office. Common courtesy made them stop in to slap me on the back and tell me what a great job everybody knew I was doing . . . and tell me that we really ought to get together for lunch or a drink, or a round of bumper pool at the country club. I smiled, and accepted no invitations. I declined none, either, because if they pressed me too hard they'd find out how ignorant I really was. So, "Sure thing," I'd say, and, "Real soon!" And then if they lingered I'd pick up the phone and whisper into it until, smiling but eaten up inside, they went away. While Dixmeister, in his cubicle outside my office, would have his eyes on me, worried and glowering until he caught me looking at him, and then there'd be that hangdog, whimpery smile.

Ah, I loved it!

Of course, common sense reminded me not to push too hard. I was only a tiny cog in the takeover bid Haseldyne and Mitzi were putting together. I was tolerated more than needed. No. I wasn't needed at all, except that it was easier for them to cut me in than to shut me up.

All I had to do was keep on making it easier for them to cut me in than cut me down . . . and then . . . and then the time would come when the takeover would go through, and Mitzi and Haseldyne would be owners. And, with a little luck, Tenny Tarb would be right on their team. An account executive—no, I thought, swigging a Moke, better than that. A C.E.O.! And that was a dream of splendor. You know what a king is? I'll tell you what a king is. Compared with a Chief Executive Officer of a major ad Agency, a king is *nothing*.

And, then, I thought, opening another Moke, what about the future? What if Mitzi and I got back together again on a full-time basis? What if we even got *married*? What if I were not just C.E.O. but a community-property coowner of the Agency? Intoxicating dreams! They made my little Moke problem seem pretty small potatoes. With that kind of money I could afford the best detoxing in the world. I could even . . . wait a minute . . . what was it? The idea that had been poking around in my subconscious at the Consum-Anon meeting?

I sat up straight and almost dropped the Moke. Dixmeister came rushing in, scared. "Mr. Tarb? Are you all right?"

"I'm *fine*, Dixmeister," I told him. "Listen, didn't I see the Old Man going down the hall a minute ago? See if you can find him—ask him if he'd like to drop in for a minute."

And I sat back and waited, while the idea formed itself into perfect shape in my mind.

You don't get the Old Man without his gaggle of droogs, three or four of them tagging along and clustering in the doorways while he paid his calls. They all had big titles, and any one of them made four times as much a year as I did, but they were stooges. I ignored them. "Thanks a lot for dropping in, sir," I beamed. "Sit down, won't you? Here. Take my chair!"

You don't get the Old Man without five minutes of preliminary chitchat, either. He sat down and began to tell me about the old days and how he'd made his pile, averting his eyes from my Mokie-Koke dispenser as though it were false teeth I'd left on the dresser. I heard all over again the saga of how he'd come back from Venus with his lucky millions and bet it all on the forlorn hope of turning two dead Agencies into one towering success. "It worked, Tenn," he rasped, "because of product! That's what T., G. & S. is built on, *product*. I'm not saying anything against Intangibles, but it's *goods* that people need to be sold, for their own sakes and the sake of humankind itself!"

"Right, chief," I said, because no other response is allowed when power speaks, "but I've got a little idea I'd like to bounce off you. You know ConsumAnon?"

He gave me a frown like thunderclouds. His vertical lines were as deep as Mitzi's, and there were a lot more of them. "When I see ConsumAnon people," he declared, "I always think I'm looking at dupes of the Venusians. They're crackpots at best!"

"You bet they're crackpots, but there's a market potential there that I don't think we've tapped. You see, these ConsumAnon people have gone out of control. It's Coffiest fifty times a day, a Mementoes habit that would bankrupt a star-class time-buyer, every sort of mega-hypertrophy of normal, decent consuming. So they go to C.A. Then what happens? Why, most of them stay clean about two days. If that. Then they slip. In a week they're worse off than ever. They become institutional cases, as like as not, lost to consuming forever. And the successes are even worse. They're brainwashed into *economizing*. Even *saving*."

"I've always said," the Old Man announced gravely, "that C.A. is the next thing to Conservationism."

"Right! But we don't have to lose these people. All we have to do is redirect them. Not abstinence. Substitution."

The Old Man pursed his lips. Naturally all of the droogs followed suit. Not one of them had grasped the idea, and not one of them would admit it.

I let them off the hook. "We set up a self-help group for each kind of overconsuming," I explained, "and we train them to *substitute*. If they're Coffiest addicts, we switch them to Nic-O-Chews. Nic-O-Chews to the San Jacinto Mint—"

Clearing of throat from the doorway. "The San Jacinto Mint isn't one of our clients," said Droog No. 2.

I said stonily, "Then to someone who is our client, *of course—*

we're a full-range Agency, we've got something for every consuming niche, don't we? I would estimate that a consumer who's five years into, say, a Coffiest habit and just about on the skids still has years of useful life with, say, Starrzelius Diet-Aids." The Old Man glanced once at his droog, who shut up instantly. I pressed on. "The next part," I said, "is where I think the real money is. What about these self-help groups? Why shouldn't they be actual clubs? Like lodges. They could charge dues. They could have to buy regalia and paraphernalia—watches, rings, tee shirts. Ceremonial robes. A different design for each degree as they move up, and so constructed that they can't be passed on as second-hand goods—"

"*Product*," whispered the Old Man, and his eyes gleamed.

It was the magic word; I had won him over. The retinue knew it before I did, of course, and the air was thick with congratulations and plans. A whole new department within Intangibles. First a two-week crash feasibility survey, just to make sure there were no roadblocks and to identify the main profit areas. That would have to go to the Planning Committee, but then—"When it happens, Tenny," the Old Man beamed, "it's all yours!" And then he did the ritual act that generations of ad execs have done to show their whole-hearted admiration. He took off his hat and placed it on the table.

It was glory time. My heart was full. And I could hardly wait for them to get out of the office because it was a grand scheme that would benefit its inventor very little. Money, yes. Promotion and prestige, yes. But substitution could not cure Campbellian limbic compulsion . . . and, God, how I wanted a Moke!

I even got to see my brassy lady once in a while, though not very often. She did show up in my office in response to the memo I flashed her about my new project, looking around abstractedly while I apologized for going to the Old Man with it instead of waiting until, uh, *after*. "No problem, Tenny," she said cheerfully—and absentmindedly. "It won't affect our, uh, *plans*. See each other? Why, certainly—real soon—we'll be in touch—bye!" Real soon it was not. She wouldn't come to my place and didn't invite me to hers, and when I tried to get her on the phone she was either out or too rushed to talk. Well, that wasn't unreasonable. Now that I knew what she was up to I could see that there wasn't time in her life for everything just now.

But I still wanted to see her, and when I got a surprise call in my office just before quitting time I raced right up to her office, waited out the sec³, breezed past the sec² and was allowed to call Mitzi herself from the sec¹'s desk. "I was just on the phone with Honolulu," I said. "Your mother. I've got a message from her."

Silence from the other end of the line. Then, "Give me an hour, will you, Tenny? Then let's have a drink in the Executive lounge."

Well, it wasn't an hour, it was a lot nearer two, but I didn't mind waiting. Although I was well on the way to being a fair-haired boy, my official status had not yet improved to the point of full Executive privileges. I was glad to be admitted on Mitzi's invitation and sit with my Drambuie, gazing out over the cloudy, smoggy city with all its wonderful wealth and promise, in the company of my peers—well, almost peers. They didn't snub me, either. In fact when Mitzi at last appeared and frowned around the room, looking for me, I had trouble disengaging myself to find a quiet table for two.

She was frowning—she was always frowning these days—and she looked flustered. But she waited until I had ordered drinks, her favorites, Mimosas, with nearly real champagne and reconstituted orange juice, before she demanded, "Now, what's this about my mother?"

"She called me, Mits. She said she'd been trying to reach you ever since you got back, and no luck."

"I did talk to her!"

"Once, right," I nodded, "the day after you landed. She says for three miutes—"

"I was busy!"

"—and then you never returned her calls after that."

There were at least half a dozen of the frown lines warning me, and her voice was chilly: "Tarb," she snapped, "get straight. I'm a big girl. What's between my mother and me is none of your business. She's an interfering old busybody who's half the reason I left for Venus in the first place, and if I don't want to talk to her I don't have to. Got it?" The drinks arrived, and she grabbed for hers. Halfway to her lips she added, "I'll call her next week." And poured half the Mimosa down her throat.

"It's not really bad," she admitted grudgingly.

"I can make them better myself," I offered. Thinking: Damn it, I'd better get out of that shared-time condo fast, can't expect Mitzi to offer her place every time. And it was as though I'd spoken out loud. She leaned back in her seat, regarding me thoughtfully. Most of the frown lines had gone from her brow, bar the two that now seemed semipermanent, but her gaze was more analytical than I would have hoped for.

"Tenny," she said, "There's something about you that appeals very strongly to me—"

"Thank you, Mits."

"Your dumbness, I think," she went on, not paying attention to what I said. "Yes. That's it. Dumb and helpless. You remind me of a lost pet mouse."

I essayed, "Only a mouse? Not at least a kitten to cuddle?"

"Kittens grow up to be cats. Cats are predators. I think what I really like best about you is that you've lost your fangs somewhere." She wasn't looking at me now, staring past me out the window at the smoggy lights of the city. I would have given a lot to know what sentences were forming in her mind just then, that she had vetoed before they came out of her mouth. She sighed. "I'd like another of these," she added, coming back to the world I was in.

I signaled the waiter and whispered in his ear while she exchanged smiles and nods with a dozen others from Executive country. "I'm sorry I stuck my nose in about your mother," I said.

She shrugged absently. "I said I'd call her. Let's forget it." She brightened. "How's the job going? I hear your new project's looking good."

I shrugged modestly. "It'll be a while yet before we know if it will amount to anything."

"It will, Tenn. So until then are you going to stay with Religion?"

I said, "Well, sure, but that's pretty well in hand. I thought I'd take a few extra classes, see about speeding up that master's degree."

She nodded as though she were agreeing, but said: "Did you ever think of switching to Politics?"

That startled me. *"Politics?"*

She said thoughtfully, "I can't tell you much right now, but it might be useful if you got your feet wet in that."

There was a little tingle down my backbone. She was talking about *after!* "Why not, Mits? I'll turn Religion over to my Number Two tomorrow! And now—we've got the whole evening before us—"

She shook her head. "You do, Tenny, I've got something else I've got to do." She saw how my face fell. It seemed to depress her too. She watched the waiter bring the second round of drinks before she said: "Tenny, you know I've got a lot on my mind right now—"

"I understand perfectly, Mits!"

"Do you?" The thoughtful look again. "You understand, anyway, that I'm busy. I don't know if you understand how I feel about you."

"Good, I hope."

"Both good and bad, Tenny," she said somberly, "both good and bad. If I had any sense at all—"

But she didn't say what she'd do if she had any sense at all and, since I had a numbing suspicion that I knew what it would have been, I let the sentence hang in air. "To you," she said, examining the new Mimosa as though it were medicine before she sipped it.

"To us," I said, lifting my own drink. It wasn't a Mimosa. It wasn't an Irish Coffee, either, though it looked like one. On top was the regulation puff of whipped NeerKreme, but what was underneath it was what I had sent the waiter scurrying down to my office to get: four ounces of pure Mokie-Koke.

V

The next morning, first thing, I snapped my fingers. Dixmeister materialized in the doorway at once, waiting for either orders or an invitation to come in and sit down. I gave him neither. "Dixmeister," I said, "I've got Religion pretty straight now, so I'm turning it over to—what's his name—"

"Wrocjek, Mr. Tarb?"

"Right. I've got a couple days free, so I'm going to get Politics on the right track."

Dixmeister shifted position uncomfortably in the doorway. "Well, actually, Mr. Tarb," he said, "since old Mr. Sarms left I've been pretty much running Politics myself."

"That's exactly what we're going to straighten out, Dixmeister. I want all current sitreps and plan outlines fed to my monitor for approval and action, and I want them this afternoon. No, in one hour . . . no, come to think of it, let's do it now."

He stammered, "But—but—" I knew the problem; there were at least fifty separate stores of data to be tapped and digested, and preparing a decent synoptic was half a day's work. About that I cared little or not at all.

"Do it, Dixmeister," I said benignly, leaned back in my chair and closed my eyes. Ah, how good it felt!

I had almost forgotten I was a Mokie.

They say that Mokie-Koke gets you so wired up after a while that your decisions suffer. It isn't that you can't make the decisions. It isn't even that they're wrong when you make them. What it is, you're so hyper, so strung out, that one decision isn't enough for you. You make one, and then another, and then another, bing-bang-biff, and when the ordinary human being can't keep up with you, which is always, you lose your cool. Dixmeister probably would have thought that was going on with me, because I guess I gave him the sharp part of the tongue pretty often. But I wasn't worried. I knew that was *supposed* to happen, but I did not fear its happening to me. Oh, sure, maybe after a long time—ten years, five years—far enough in the future, anyway, so that I didn't have to worry about it, since I was going to give the stuff up any day. First chance I got. And meanwhile, actually, I was touching all bases and swinging the old home-run paddle. Even Dixmeister had to admit it. I spent two days on current projects and plans, and, man, how I made the old place hum!

The first thing I got into was the PAC department. You know what a Political Action Committee is. It's a group of people with a special interest who are willing to put up money to bribe—well, strike that, to *influence*—officials to enact laws and regulations that favor whatever it is they care about. In the old days the PACs belonged mostly to businessmen and what they called labor unions. I remembered seeing those great old historical romances with the American Medical Association and the used-car dealers—eager young doctors winning tax exemption for conferences in Tahiti; antic car salesmen battling for the inalienable right to put sawdust in a transmission. That sort of show is fun when you're young, but as you get older and more cynical you stop believing people are so goody-goody. . . . Anyway, those battles are of course long won, but PACs are still around. They're almost as good as religion. You set them up and collect their money, and what do they spend it on? In the long run, advertising! Either their own, or for the campaign ads for the candidates they like. So in one long day I set up a dozen new PACs. There was an Objet-d'art PAC (I got the idea from Nelson

Rockwell), a Swiss Army Knife PAC ("We need them to clean our nails—is it our fault that criminals use them for other purposes?"), a Pedicab-Pumpers PAC, a Tenants' PAC to legislate longer sleeping hours before the daytime users of the space moved in—oh, I was knocking them out!

It was almost too easy. I had more energy left at the end of a hard day than I knew what to do with. I could have gone on with school, but what was the point? How much higher in the world would a graduate degree get me? I could have moved to a better place, but the thought of hunting one out and moving into it depressed me . . . and there was one other thing. I *felt* secure. The way things were going I had every reason to *be* secure. But I had been real secure once before and out of a cloud no bigger than a man's hand Destiny had reached down to smite me. . . . I stayed in the shared-time condo. And talked with Nels Rockwell when we happened to be awake together, and watched the Omni-V until all hours when we were not. I watched sports events and soaps and comics, and most of all news. The Sudan had just been reclaimed for civilization, using the same Campbellian techniques that had been used on me—glow of pride at the world bettering itself every day; little nagging itch of resentment, because the Campbellian techniques had, after all, not bettered my own world a hell of a lot. A whale had been sighted off Lahaina, but further investigation showed it was just a lost tank of jojoba oil. The spring Olympics were going on in Tucson, and there was a big upset in the unicycle event. Ms. Mitzi Ku, interviewed at the entrance to T., G. & S. Tower, denied reports that she was leaving the Agency—

And she looked so sweet and so tired on the little screen; and I wished for . . . No. I didn't wish "for" anything. I just wished. There was too much involved between me and Mitzi to wish for anything specific.

She didn't answer when I tried to call her at home.

The way to make all my wishes true with Mitzi, I told myself, was to do the best possible job on politics; and so I made the next morning hell for poor little Dixmeister. "The work's *wasted*," I yelled at him, "because Casting's lying down on the job!" He was directly responsible for Casting, of course.

"I do my best," he sulked, and I just shook my head.

"Candidate screening," I explained, "is one of the most important functions of a political campaign." He was still sulking, but he made the pretense of an eager nod. Well, of course, everyone knew that. It had been established way back in the mid-twentieth century that a candidate shouldn't sweat much; he had to be at least five per cent taller than average so he didn't need a box to stand on in a debate. His hair could be gray, but he had to have plenty of it. You didn't want him too fat (but not too skinny, either), and above all he had to be able to deliver his lines as though he really believed them.

"Absolutely, Mr. Tarb," Dixmeister said indignantly. "I always tell that to Central Casting, the whole list—"

"It isn't good enough, Dixmeister. From now on I'll do the first cut myself."

His jaw dropped. "Gee, Mr. Tarb, Mr. Sarms always used to let me handle that."

"Mr. Sarms isn't here any more. Casting call is nine A.M., in the big room. Fill it." And I waved him out of the room and closed the door, because I was half an hour behind on my next Moke.

Fill the big room he did, all nine hundred seats except for the first row. That was mine—mine and my secretary's and my makeup guy's and my director's. I came down the center aisle, not looking to the left or right, waved the entourage into seats and jumped up onto the stage. At once Dixmeister came bounding in from the wings. "Quiet!" he yelled. "Quiet for Mr. Tarb!"

I stood there, looking over them, waiting for the feel of the audience to reach me. Actually, they were quiet enough already, because they knew where they were. This hall was where the Old Man held his all-exec pep rallies, where major presentations were made and new accounts solicited us. Every one of the nine hundred seats had its own back, arm, cushion and phone jack—the Agency executives traveled first class! And the nine hundred people from Central Casting were nearly all consumer class in their origins.

So they were quiet with awe, and as I perceived their feelings I knew how to pitch to them. I waved an arm around the vast auditorium. "Do you like what you see here?" I demanded. "Do you want this sort of thing for your own lives? It's easy! *Just make me like you.* You're each going to be called up here on the stage and given ten seconds to make a presentation. Ten seconds! It's not much, is it? But that's all the seconds there are in a flash spot, and if you can't make it here in this auditorium you can't do the job for T., G. & S. in prime time. Now, what do you do with your ten seconds? That's up to you. You can sing. Tell a story. Say what your favorite color is. Ask for my vote—anything! But what you say doesn't matter, just so you make me care about you and want to help you get elected—make me *like* you!"

I nodded to Dixmeister. As the makeup guy helped me down to my seat Dixmeister sprang forward and barked: "First row! Start from the left! You on the end there—onstage!"

Dixmeister jumped down into the seat beside me, anxiously dividing his glances between my face and the actor before us. The actor was a big one, shaggy-haired, bright eyes under shaggy brows. A likeable face, all right. He'd thought about his bit, too. "I trust you all!" he boomed, "and you can trust Marty O'Loyre, because Marty O'Loyre *loves* you. Please help Marty O'Loyre with your vote on Election Day!"

Dixmeister stabbed the timer with his finger, and the result blinked up from the monitor: 10.0 seconds. Dixmeister nodded. "Great timing, and three name repetitions." He studied my face, trying to jump the right way at the right time. "Good sheriff candidate?" he guessed. "Solid, strong, warm—"

"Look at the way his hands are shaking," I said kindly. "Not a chance. Next!"

Tall outdoorsy blonde, with the forearm muscles you get from long hours of table polo: "Too upper-class. Next!"

Elderly black woman with plump, permanently pursed lips: "Maybe probate judge, but get her a haircut. Next!"

Twin brothers with identical heart-shaped birthmarks over their right eyes: "Sensational reinforcement there, Dixmeister," I lectured. "Have we got two alderman-at-large spots? Right. Next!"

Slim, pale, a faraway look in her eyes, no more than twenty-three. "I know what it is to be unhappy," she said—sobbed, almost. "If you help me I'll try my very best to take care of you too. . . ."

"Too sappy?" asked Dixmeister.

"There's no such thing as too sappy for Congress, Dixmeister. Take her name. Next!"

The find of the day was a callow, sharp-featured youth who grunted his lines while his eyes darted fearfully in all directions. Heaven knows how he got listed with Central Casting in the first place, for he was surely not a pro, and his "presentation" was a stumbling account of a boyhood trip to Prospect Park. Way over time, at that. Dixmeister cut him off in midsentence and glanced at me, eyebrows raised in amused contempt. As he was lifting a hand to wave the kid away I stopped him, for something was stirring in my mind. "Wait a minute." I closed my eyes, trying to recapture the vagrant image. "I see. . . . Yes. Got it! The unicycle races yesterday—one of the winners had just that look of eager stupidity. The jock look."

"Actually, Mr. Tarb," the kid called down, "I'm not much into sports. I'm a clip sorter in the Starrzelius mailroom."

"You're a unicyclist now," I told him. "Report to Wardrobe for costumes and Mr. Dixmeister here will find you a coach for the cycle. Dixmeister, take a copy theme note: 'My friends thought I was sort of peculiar for taking up the unicycle, but I don't see it that way. Stubborn, maybe. Willing to pay the price to do the hard job, whether it's on the unicycle or in the office of—' Let's see whether it's—"

"Congress, Mr. Tarb?" Dixmeister ventured, holding his breath.

I said generously, "Right, Congress. Maybe." Actually the wimp was too good for Congress; I was thinking of a lot higher, maybe Vice-President. But I could straighten out the casting later, and meanwhile it cost nothing to let Dixmeister feel good for a moment. "And, oh, yes," I said, remembering, "call up the unicycle club and arrange for him to win a couple of races."

"Well, Mr. Tarb," dithered Dixmeister, "I don't know if they'll want to go along with fixing a—"

"Tell them, Dixmeister. Tell them what a good tie-in promotion for unicycling this is going to be. *Sell* them. Got it? Good. Then next!"

And next. And next, and next. Nine hundred nexts. But we needed a lot of candidates. Although there were nearly a dozen Agencies with strong political divisions, there was plenty of work for all of us. Sixty-one state legislatures. Nine thousand cities and towns. Three thousand counties. And the federal government. Put them all together and, on the average, there were a quarter of a million elective posts to be filled a year. (Of course, only a fraction of them were important enough—by this I mean expensive enough —to warrant the time of T., G. & S.) About half the time we could recycle incumbents, but we still had to find every year five or ten thousand warm bodies to teach and dress and make up and rehearse and direct . . . and maybe elect. *Usually* elect. It didn't particularly matter who won any election in any real sense, but T., G. & S. had a reputation to protect as a can-do Agency. So we battled for our candidates as hard as though winning or losing made some actual difference.

By the time we got to the end of the nine hundred the "coffee" thermos on my chair arm had been refilled twice with Mokes and my stomach was beginning to growl its first pangs of hunger. We had reduced the nine hundred to eighty-two possibles and sent the losers home. I mounted the stage again, beckoning to the survivors. "Come up front," I ordered. Briskly they obeyed; they knew they were on a streak. I reinforced that knowledge. "Let's talk about money," I said, and dead silence said they were listening intently. "The job of congressman pays as much as a junior copysmith. Even alderman pays not much less." There was a sound—not a gasp, but a sort of suspension of breathing as each one of them contemplated the kind of wage that would lift them right out of the consumer class in a single bound. "That's just *salary*. That's only the beginning. The gravy part is the retainers and the consultancies and the director-ships—" I didn't have to say the bribes—"that go along with the position. They can be really big. How big? Well, I happen to know of two senators that sock away as much pay as an account executive." Thrill from the crowd, and this time the gasps were real. "I'm not going to ask you if you want that, because I don't think there are any crazy people in this room today. I'm going to tell you how to get it. Three things. Keep your noses clean. Work hard. Do what you're told. Then, if you're lucky—" I let the thought float in the air for a moment before grinning at them: "For now, go on home. Report at nine A.M. tomorrow for processing."

I glanced at my watch as they filed out. The whole thing had taken four hours and a bit, and Dixmeister was fawning all over me. "What a great day's work, chief! Sarms would have dawdled a week over this bunch. Now," he twinkled, "if I'm not being too forward, I know a place where they serve real meat and just about any kind of grain neutral spirits you can name. What would you say to a good old-fashioned three-martini—"

"Lunch," I finished for him, "will be a sandwich in my office and you're going to have the same in yours. Because I want this hall filled up again in ninety minutes!"

Well, it was, or just about, and we got seventy-one more candidate possibles. But when I ordered the same thing for the following morning, Central Casting could only send over about a hundred and fifty. We were eating up their pool faster than they could replenish it. And so I went out and roamed the streets, from one Mokie-Koke dispenser to the next, studying faces, walks, gestures. I eavesdropped on conversations. I started an argument, now and then, to see how the prospect would react. Then I went home or back to my office and watched the Omni-V news, looking for talent in a traffic victim or the weeping mother of someone who had just been mugged—someone who had just been doing the mugging, even, because I found one of my best New Jersey congressman candidate prospects in the police line-up after an attempted smash-and-grab. And I rode hard on Dixmeister to see that he kept the loose ends tied up. He made me up a tape of the Agency's present incumbents, and I cursored through the scenes to mark a good bit of business or a mannerism that they'd have to get rid of if they wanted us to run them again.

One gave me trouble. It was our President of the United States, a sweet-looking old man with turkey wattles strung from the point of his chin to his collarbone and the mummy of a face that three-quarters of the voters had grown up on. He'd played the daddy in the kiddyporn remake of *Father Knows Best*—you know, the one that's always stepping in the dog excrement or breaking wind when he bends down to pick up a dropped handkerchief. He'd been on the news interviewing the new High Chief Secretary of the Free-Market Republic of the Sudan. No more than a twenty-second clip, but the Sudanese managed to light two Verily cigarettes, drink a cup of Coffiest and spill half of it over his new Starrzelius suit while he coughed out, "Oh, yis, Mister Pres'nt, mony thoun thank-us for saving us!" I felt a warm rush of patriotism and love in the pit of my stomach as I thought of that little gook and all his people now blessed with a true mercantile society . . . but I felt something else, too. It wasn't the Sudanese. It was the President. He hadn't moved fast enough, and half the Coffiest had drenched his formal daywear short-suit . . . and I had the idea.

"Dixmeister!" I yelled, and in three seconds he was hanging in the doorway, waiting on orders. "The unicycle jerk. How's he doing?"

"Fell off five times this morning," said Dixmeister gloomily. "I don't know if he'll ever master it. If you want to go ahead with this—"

"Damn sure I do!"

He gulped. "No problem, Mr. Tarb, I've got that under control. We'll just take a couple of other unicyclists and matte his face in—"

"Ten minutes," I ordered, and it was even so. In nine minutes and thirty seconds he was back in my office to say that the clips were ready. "Display," I commanded, and proudly he keyed his selection of races.

They were all good, I had to admit. There were four of them. In each of them the winner was close enough to our jerk's appearance for a close simulation match, and in each of them the winner, grinning and gasping, came full-face into the camera so we could patch in our jerk's face delivering the commercial for his election. But one was better than the others, because it was just what I was looking for.

"Do you see it?" I asked. Of course he didn't. I shook my finger at him. "The crash," I said paternally. In one of the clips the fourth unicyclist at the finish had swerved desperately to miss colliding with the third. Yards short of the tape, he had come tumbling down in a splatter of arms and legs. The camera had zoomed in for a quick look at his face, sullen and humiliated, before whisking back to catch the winner.

And he still didn't see it. "We're going to run the wimp in the presidential primaries," I announced.

That took his breath away. "But he hasn't—He isn't—There's no way—"

"That's what we're going to do," I explained, "and there's something else. Notice the cyclist who fell down? Remind you of anybody?"

He zipped back, froze the image, stared. "No," he confessed. "Not really, except—" He caught his breath. "The *President?*" I nodded. "But—but he's *ours.* We don't want to defeat our own man—"

"What we don't want, Dixmeister," I snapped, "is to have our own man lose—whichever man it is. I said 'the primaries.' If the President wins out, fine, he gets another chance. But if this unicycle jerk can take him, why not? And we'll use this tape! Matte the President's face onto the one that falls down—just a flash—just enough to suggest him flopping at the finish line—then we go into the kid's commercial."

Dixmeister stared at me incredulously for a moment. Then it began to penetrate, and the expression melted into hero worship. "Subliminalwise," he glowed, "it's a masterpiece, Mr. Tarb."

Well, it was. Pedaling on both legs, I was.

And yet it didn't make me happy.

By Friday I was feeling very frayed. When Mitzi passed me in the hall she looked shocked. "You're losing weight, Tenny! Get more sleep. Eat more decent food—" But then Haseldyne tugged irritably at her elbow and she was gone into the downlift, peering worriedly up at me.

It was true that I was losing weight. I wasn't getting much sleep. I could feel that my temper was getting short, and even Nelson Rockwell didn't seem to want to talk to me much any more.

I should have been happy. The fact that I wasn't puzzled me very much, because never in my life had my prospects been so bright. Mitzi and Haseldyne were getting ready to make their move. I was proving every hour that I was the right stuff for them to take along in their takeover. I forced myself to daydream of the time when I'd be up there on the fifty-fifth floor, with a *window* in my *corner office*, and maybe a *stall shower* . . . and then, at last, they did it. They made their move. They made it that very Friday, at a quarter past four in the afternoon. I was out at a halfway house for recovering psychoneurotics, looking for an appellate court judge candidate, and when I got back to the Tower it was in an uproar. Everybody was whispering to everybody else, and everybody's face was thunderstruck. On the way up I heard from the rungs below me the name "Mitzi Ku." As I got off I waited for the junior AE who'd been talking and smirked to her, "Mitzi's the new boss here, right?"

She didn't smile back, only looked at me strangely. "New boss, yes. Here, no," she said, and pushed past me.

Shaking, I finally made it to Val Dambois's office. "Val, baby," I begged, "what's happening? Was it the takeover?"

He frosted me with a look. "The hands," he said. "Get them off my desk. You're smudging the polish."

Yes, there had been a big change! "Please, Val, tell me!" I begged.

He said bitterly, "It was your girl friend Mitzi and that heavyweight Haseldyne, all right, but it wasn't a takeover. Fooled everybody, though. It was the old Icahn maneuver."

"Icahn!" I gasped. He nodded.

"A textbook case, just like old Carl Icahn himself. Scared the Old Man into thinking it was a takeover bid—got the stockholders to buy them out at ten times what their stock was worth—took the money and bought another Agency!"

And I hadn't suspected a thing.

I reeled blindly toward the door, hardly aware of what I was doing, until from behind me Dambois said the magic words:

"One more thing. You're fired."

That turned me right around. I gasped. "You can't do that!" He sneered. "No, really! My ConsumAnon project—"

He shrugged. "In good hands. Mine as it happens."

"But—But—" Then I remembered, and brought it out as a drowning man might produce the only lifesaver in the ocean: "Tenure! I'm star class—I've got tenure—you can't fire me!"

He glared at me irritably, then pursed his lips. "Hmmm," he said, and sucked his teeth. He punched out my personnel code and studied the screen for a moment.

Then his expression cleared. "Why, Tarb," he said warmly, "you're a patriot! I had no idea you were in the Reserves. I can't fire you, no, but," he explained, "what I *can* do is furlough you to the services for a year or two—there's some kind of call-up going on—"

I got up, a hollow feeling in my stomach. "This is preposterous! I've still got tenure, you know. When this military call-up is over—"

He shrugged winsomely. "I always look on the bright side, Tarb," he told me. "After all, you may never come back."

Tarb's Downfall

· · ◆ · ·

I

I knew I shouldn't have signed those Reserve papers in college, but who knew they'd take it seriously? When you're ten years old you join the Junior Copywriters. When you're fifteen it's the Little Merchandising League. In college it's the Reserves. Everybody does it. It's two course credits a semester, and you don't have to take English lit. All the smart students spotted it for a snap course.

But for somebody who'd got the bad breaks, somebody like me, it wasn't all that smart.

If I'd kept my wits about me I'd have seen a way to escape—maybe find Mitzi and grovel for a job—maybe find a friendly medic to help me fail the physical. Maybe suicide. What I actually did was closest to Option 3. I went on a Moke binge, lacing the stuff with Vodd-Quor, and woke up on a troop transport. I had no memory at all of reporting for duty, and not much of what turned out to be the forty-eight hours before that. Total blackout.

And total hangover. I didn't have time to appreciate the sordid miseries of traveling military style because I was too absorbed in the internal miseries of my own head. I was just beginning to be able to open the eyes without instant death when they dumped me, and five hundred others, at Camp Rubicam, North Dakota, for two weeks of the officers' refresher course. It consisted mostly of being told that we were doing society's most honorable work, plus close-order drill. Then it was pack your keyboard, sling your disk bag on your shoulder, all aboard for a field exercise.

Field exercise. I'd hate to get involved in the real thing.

The first troop transport had been plain hell. This one was nearly identical, except that it lasted many hours longer and I had to face it cold sober. No food. No toilets. No place to go outside the cocoon you were supposed to "rest" in. Nothing to drink but water —and the "water" was as close to purest ocean brine as you could get without actually breaking the law. The worst was we didn't know how long it was going to last. Some people thought it was all the way to Hyperion, to teach the gas miners a lesson. I might have thought so myself except that the transport had only wings and jets. No rockets. No space travel, therefore; so it had to be somewhere on Earth.

But where? The rumors that floated through the fetid air from bunk to bunk were Australia—no; Chile—no, positively; the watch officer had been heard to tell the flight engineer definitely Iceland.

We wound up in the Gobi Desert.

We piled out of the transport with our kits and our bursting bladders and lined up to be counted. The first thing we noticed was it was hot. The second thing was it was dry. I don't mean your average summer hot-spell dry, I mean *dry*. The wind blew fine white dust everywhere. It got between your fingers. If you kept your mouth closed it even got in between your teeth, and when you moved your jaw it crunched. They took an hour for the head count and then loaded us up into ten-trailer troop transports and dragged us along those dusty white roads to our billets.

The place is technically known as the Xinjiang Uygur Autonomous Region, but everybody called it the Reservation. It was where one of the last remaining batches of unconsolidated aboriginals lived, Uygurs and Hui and Kazak, the ones that never made the transition to the market society when the rest of China joined in. There's civilization all around them. There's RussCorp to the North, Indiastries South and all the China-Han complex at their gates. But the Eager Weegers just sit there and do their own thing. As we dragged along, coughing and choking, we'd see the men squatting in a circle in the middle of the side roads, never looking up at us. The squalor was shocking. Their mud houses were crumbling around them, with a stack of mud bricks in the backyard drying to be ready for building the next house when that one fell down. In the front there was a rusty old satellite dish that couldn't get a decent picture any more . . . and always there would be the kids, hundreds of them, laughing and waving to us—what did they have to be happy about? Not their housing, surely. Certainly not after we came along and requisitioned the best of it—what I guess had been a row of tourist motels (imagine anybody going there voluntarily?), with real air conditioners in the windows and a real fountain in the courtyard. Of course, the fountain was turned off. So, it turned out, were the air conditioners. So was all the power there was, so we ate (if you could call it eating—soy steaks and nondairy milkshakes!) by the light of *candles*. They promised the officers among us better quarters in the morning, after the commanders sorted us out, but for now, if we wouldn't mind—

Whether we minded or not made no difference, because there was nowhere for us to go but into the motel rooms. They might not have been so bad if the quartermaster had got mattresses onto the beds before we had to sleep on them. So we all spread out as much of our clothing as we could and tried to sleep, in the heat, in the dust, with everyone coughing around us and strange sounds coming from outside. The worst was a kind of mechanical honking noise— "Aaaah," and sometimes "Aaaah-*ee!*" I fell asleep wondering what sort of primitive machinery they kept going all night. Wondering what I was doing there. Wondering if I'd ever get back to the Tower, much less to the fifty-fifth floor. Wondering, most of all, what a guy's chances were of scoring a couple of Mokes around here in the morning, since the twelve-packs I'd put in my kitbag were just about running out.

"You Tarb?" grated a harsh voice in my ear. "Out of the sack! Chow's in five minutes and the colonel wants to see you in ten."

I propped one eye open. "The what?"

The face leaning down to mine didn't retreat. "Up!" it roared, and as my eyes focused I perceived that it belonged to a dark, scowling man with major's stripes and a row of ribbons on his camouflage suit.

"Right you are," I mumbled, and managed to remember to add, "sir." The face didn't look pleased, but it went away. I edged myself to the side of the bed, trying to avoid the sharpest and rustiest of the springs—half my body was covered with punctures from where I had tossed and turned in the night—and attacked the problem of getting into my tee and culottes. That problem proved soluble, though I think I carried it out in my sleep. The problem of where "chow" was was no problem at all, because I only had to follow the slow migration of red-eyed, unshaved, blinking troops to what was marked Dining Hall A. At least there was Coffiest. Better than that, there were Mokes, though these were not government issue and I wasted precious moments wheedling change from the one or two slightly familiar faces doggedly attacking their Om'Lets and Bredd. Naturally the vending machine ate my first three coins without spitting out a Moke in return, but on the fourth try I got one—warm, to be sure—and faced the blinding outdoor sun a little more bravely.

Finding the colonel's office was a lot harder. None of the new replacements like myself seemed to have a clue. The wiser regulars were, it appeared, still happily asleep in their bunks, waiting out the press of new boys in the mess hall so that they could enjoy their breakfast in a more leisurely way later on. The couple of natives wandering around, bearing brooms or pails of gray, scummy water —though showing no signs of using either—were glad to give me directions; but as we had no language in common I had no notion of what they were directing me to. I found myself on the edge of the compound, passing through a gate, when a repellent odor filled my nostrils and, at the same moment, that raucous Aaaah-*ee!* blasted in my ear.

The mystery of the machine noises in the night was cleared up. To my infinite disgust I discovered that the machines were no machines. These people had *animals*. Living animals! Not in a zoo or properly stuffed in some museum, but standing on the streets, pulling carts, even *defecating* right where people might walk. I had blundered into what was a kind of parking lot for the creatures. I tell you, for a minute there it was touch and go whether I would retain the hard-won Moke I had just swallowed.

By the time I finally found the colonel's office I was, of course, at least twenty minutes late, but I had learned some sobering facts about this new world I had been thrust into. The particular animals with the loud bray were called donkeys. A smaller, horned kind of donkey they called goat, but they also had chickens and horses and yaks. And each one smelled fouler, and had habits more disgusting, than the next. When at last I stumbled into the mud-brick structure marked 3d Bn Hq & Hq Cy I knew I was well on the way to earning my first reprimand, but I didn't care. It was air-conditioned, and the air conditioning actually worked, and when the first sergeant told me, scowling, that I would have to wait and the colonel would eat me out, I could have kissed him, for the air was cool, the sickening sounds from outside were muffled—and there was a Moke dispenser by the door.

The sergeant was a true prophet. The colonel's first words were, "You were late, Tarb! A bad beginning! I tell you true, you admen make me sick!"

In normal times that kind of talk would have had me up and fighting, but these were not normal times. I could read the colonel like a book: grizzled old campaigner, chest full of ribbons for the Sudan and Papua New Guinea and the Patagonian campaign. No doubt up from the ranks, with all the former consumer's hatred of the upper classes. I swallowed the words that rose to my lips, held the tightest brace at attention I could manage and said only, "Yes, ma'am."

She looked at me with the same sort of unbelieving dislike that, I am sure, I gave to the donkeys. She shook her head. "So what am I going to do with you, Tarb? You got any skills that don't show on your personnel record—cooking, plumbing, running an officers' club?"

I said indignantly, "Ma'am! I'm a copysmith, star class!"

"You were," she corrected. "Here you're just another casual officer that I've got to find a job for."

"But surely—my skills—my ability to create a promotional campaign—"

"Tarb," she said wearily, "all that stuff's done back in the Pentagon. We don't make strategy here in the field. We're just the dogfaces that carry it out." She flicked gloomily through the data stores—hesitated—went on—turned back and cursored one line in the Table of Organization.

"Chaplain," she said with satisfaction.

I goggled at her. "Chaplain? But I never—I mean, I don't know anything about—"

"You don't know anything about anything, Lieutenant Tarb," she said, "but chaplaining's easy work. You can get the hang of it in no time. You'll have an assistant who knows the ropes—and, as far as I can see, it's a place where you can't do much harm. Dismissed! And try to keep your nose clean till this campaign's over so you'll be somebody else's problem."

So I began my career as chaplain to the Third Battalion Headquarters and Headquarters Company—heavy limbic projectors and skyscreens—not the best duty in the world, but a long way better than going door-to-door with the infantry. The colonel had promised me an experienced chaplain's assistant, and I got one. Staff-Sergeant Gert Martels wore the ribbons of campaigns as far back as Kampuchea on her rather prominent chest.

She greeted me as I entered my domain for the first time with a sloppy salute but a fully accomplished smile. "Morning, Lieutenant," she sang out. "Welcome to the Third!"

I saw at once that S/Sgt Martels was going to be the best thing about my chaplaincy—well, the second best thing, anyway. The office itself was drab. It had been a laundry room in the motel, and you could still see the stains of bleach and soap powder outlining where the washing machines had been. Capped-off pipes were still present along the wall. But it was air-conditioned! It was located in that handsome motel with the fountains and shady arbors, only now the fountains were working—and we casuals had been moved out to "regular" housing, so that the space could become headquarters offices. I guess the air conditioning was the third best thing; the very best was a Moke vending machine, and the way it purred told me that the Mokes would be coming out ice-cold. "How did you know?" I demanded, and the handsome, scarred face lit up with another of those excellent smiles.

"It is," she said, "a chaplain's assistant's *business* to know such things. Now, if the lieutenant would care to sit at his desk I'll be glad to answer the lieutenant's questions. . . ."

It was better than that. I didn't even have to ask any questions, because S/Sgt Martels knew what the lieutenant needed to know better than the lieutenant did. This was the way to the officers' club. These were the blank passes I had the authority to sign. That on the wall was the intercom, used only by a friend in the colonel's office to warn us when the colonel was coming this way. And, in case the lieutenant didn't much care for the food in the mess hall, the lieutenant always had the privilege of declaring that he had been too busy with emergency duties during regular meal hours to get there, and so avail himself of between-meals "snacks" in the private dining room of the field-officers' mess. The lieutenant, she added innocently, had also the privilege of taking his assistant at such times if he cared to.

And why, I wondered starrily, had I been so reluctant to give up the Mad. Ave. rat race to come to this earthly paradise?

Well, paradise it was not. Nights were still hell. "Regular" housing turned out to be foam pop-ups, with slit trenches. The only "air conditioning" they had were tiny solar-battery fans, and the foam walls soaked up every calorie of the Gobi's blazing daytime sun to give back to us all night. There were also *bugs*. There was also the all-night braying of the animals in the stockades outside the walls. There were also the sleepless hours, miserably wondering what Mitzi was up to, who was taking over my job at Taunton, Gatchweiler and Schocken. There was also the fact that the desert heat was boiling the Mokes out of my body as fast as I could swallow them, and every day I got gaunter and shakier. On the second day Gert Martels looked at me in alarm. " The lieutenant," she said, "is working too hard." Palpable lie, of course; I had yet to see my first soldier coming in for solace or help. "I suggest the lieutenant write himself a pass and take the rest of the day off."

"Pass to where in this hellhole?" I snarled, and brought myself up short. Hadn't I had a conversation like this once before—on Venus—with Mitzi? "Well," I said, reconsidering, "I suppose that ten years from now I'll regret it if I don't see whatever sights there are. Only you come along."

So twenty minutes later we were sitting back-to-back on a sort of four-wheeled cart with an awning over our heads, clop-clopping along the white-dust road to the metropolis of Urumqi. Military trucks roared by, raising a six-foot wake of dust. What fun! Conversation was pretty nearly impossible, not only because we were facing away from each other but because we spent half our time coughing the dust out of our lungs until Gert produced some sort of white surgical masks to tie over our noses and mouths.

Fortunately Urumqi—they pronounced it "Oo-ROOM-chee," which tells you a lot about the Uygurs—wasn't far away. It also wasn't much when you got there. The main street had real trees, a double row of them, but there was nothing but bare yellow dirt under the trees. No grass. No flowers. What there was was about a dozen Uygurs with gauze masks of their own, sweeping leaves off the bare ground. You'd think there was already enough dust in the air for any normal person, but, no, there the Weegs were, sweeping great clouds up in case we might run out. "I wish I had a Moke," I gritted out, and Gert twisted around to say:

"Hang on, Lieutenant—"

"My name's Tenny."

"Hang on, Tenny, we're almost there. See it down the block? Divisional R&R, and they've got all the Mokes you want."

And so they did; and not only that, they had a bar, and an all-ranks coffee shop where you could get brand-name food, and an officers' lounge with satellite Omni-V. And flush toilets! And—I'll give you an idea of what heavenly luxury this was after my forty-eight hours in the field—it wasn't until after I'd noticed all those things that I noticed that the whole building was air-conditioned. "How many passes can I give myself?" I demanded.

"All you want," said Gert gratifyingly, and we headed first for the coffee shop. When I said it was my treat she looked amused but didn't argue, and we washed down Turr-Kee salad sandwiches on real Bredd with half a dozen Mokes and sat comfortably at our windowside table, gazing disdainfully at the Weegs outside. "There's worse duty than this, Tenny," Gert announced, ordering another Coffiest.

I reached over and touched her ribbons. She didn't draw back. "I guess you've seen some, right?" I offered.

Her expression clouded. "I guess Papua New Guinea was about the worst," she said, as though the memory pained her.

I nodded. Everybody knew about Papua New Guinea, and the way hundreds of natives had died in the riots when the Coffiest and Reel-Meet ran out.

"It's good work, Gert," I said consolingly. "There aren't many abo reservations left. Cleaning up the holdouts has to be done—a dirty job, but somebody has to do it." She didn't answer, just took a sip of her Coffiest without meeting my eyes. I said, "I know what I've done isn't in the same league as you veterans. Still, I spent six years on Venus, you know."

"Vice-consul and morale officer," she nodded. She knew.

"Well, then you know that the Veenies aren't really much better than these Weegs. Salesless, bigoted, antiprogress—why, take away a little superficial technology and they'd fit right in on this reservation!" I waved my hand at the street outside. A bunch of enlisted personnel were loafing around the hotel steps, trying to tempt the Uygurs with Mokes and pocket viewers and Nic-o-Chews, but the tribesmen just smiled and shook their heads and moved on. "I doubt most of these aboriginals even know that civilization exists. They haven't changed for a thousand years."

She gazed out at the street, her expression hard to read. "More than that, Tenny. We're not the first invaders they've seen. They've had the Manchus and the Mongols and the Hans and outlived them all."

I coughed—it wasn't dust in my throat. "*Invaders* isn't exactly the word I would have chosen, Gert. We're *civilizers*, you know. What we're doing here is an important mission."

"Important is right," she snapped, and there was an edge to her voice that caught me unaware. "The last one before the big push, eh? Did you ever think that there's a logical progression here, New Guinea, the Sudan, the Gobi? And then—" Suddenly she faltered and looked around the room, as though wondering who might have heard.

That I could understand, for she was saying things that would cost her if the wrong people were listening. I was sure she didn't mean them. Not deep down inside, that is. The combat troops at the spearhead of civilization couldn't be blamed if, now and then, strange ideas crossed their minds. Back in civilization that kind of talk could get you in a lot of trouble. Here—"Here," I said kindly, "you're under a strain, Gert. Have another Coffiest, it'll soothe you."

She looked at me in silence for a moment, then laughed. "All right, Tenny," she said, beckoning to the Weeg waitress. "You know what? You're going to make a *great* chaplain."

It took me a moment to respond to that—somehow it hadn't sounded like a compliment. "Thank you," I said at last.

"And in order to make you one," she said, "I guess I'd better fill you in on your duties. Now, you're going to get two kinds of people coming to you for help. The first kind will be the ones that are worried about something—they've received a Dear Jane letter or they think their mother's sick or they're convinced they're going crazy. The way you handle them is to tell them not to worry and give them a twenty-four-hour pass. The second kind will be the foul-ups. They're missing formations or oversleeping roll call or failing inspection. What you do with them is send a chit to the first sergeant cutting off their passes for a week, and you tell them they better *start* worrying. Now, sometimes there'll be somebody with a real problem, and what you do—"

So I listened, and I nodded, and, actually, I was quite enjoying myself. I didn't then know that there were two of those people with real problems in my company.

Or that both of them were sitting at my table.

Chaplaincy wasn't arduous. It left me plenty of time for long, late lunches in the field officers' mess and evening passes to Urumqi. It also left me time to wonder, rather frequently at first, just what I was doing there, because the operation that we'd all been hustled from hemisphere to hemisphere to perform didn't seem to be happening . . . whatever it was that was supposed to happen. When I asked Gert Martels, she shrugged and said it was just the good old tradition of hurry up and wait, so I stopped worrying about it. I took what each day offered. The old Urumqi hotel that had been commandeered for divisional R&R became as familiar to me as my official pop-up sleeping tent—in fact, the hotel was where I spent nights when I could, not only because of the air conditioning but because each of the tatty old guest rooms had its own flush toilet and tub and shower. Often all three of them worked. And in the officers' lounge there was the Omni-V.

That wasn't all joy. For one thing, what I really wanted was news. In order to get it I had to fight off the civilization-starved officers, most of them with more rank than I had, who were desperate for sports, variety shows, sitcoms and commercials—mostly commercials. The kind of news I wanted wasn't the usual thing—the goggling, blinking, grinning couple who'd won "Consumer of the Month" in Detroit, or the President's speeches, or the story of six pedicabs destroyed, with loss of eleven lives, when the spire fell off the old Chrysler Building and flattened half a block of Forty-second Street. I mean the *real* news, the "World of Advertising" report and the daily lineage and spot-time charts. That news came on at six o'clock in the morning, because of the fact that we were halfway around the world, and so I had no hope of seeing it unless I pressed my luck and took yet one more night in the divisional R&R—and, of course, managed to wake myself up in time to get down to the lounge. That wasn't easy. Every morning waking up got harder and harder. The only thing that could get me out of bed, finally, was to not have any Mokes in the room, so as soon as my eyes opened I had to get up and out to find one.

And then what I saw wasn't all joy. There was a whole ten-minute spot, one morning, given to my ConsumAnon plan. It had been launched with a sixteen-megabuck promotion budget. It was a great success. But it wasn't mine.

For that I was prepared. What I wasn't prepared for was the commentator, with that sickly, covetous smile people get when somebody's pulled off a coup, finishing up by giving credit to that dynamic new agency that came from nowhere to challenge the giants . . . Haseldyne and Ku.

The captain who came into the lounge just then, swinging his weights and all ready for his morning setting-up exercises, didn't know how lucky he was. I let him live. If I hadn't startled him so with my blast of rage when he tried to change the channel he would surely have had me in for conduct unbecoming an officer, but I don't think he'd ever seen so much violence on a face. I clung to that channel selector. I didn't even look around when he slunk away, his weights hanging straight at his side. I was spinning that dial, hunting for news, starving for crumbs of information. With two hundred and fifty channels coming down from the satellites it was like looking for the winning boxtop in a trash can. I didn't care about the odds. Flick, and I was getting a Korean weather report; flick, a commercial jockey; flick, a kiddyporn audience-participation show; flick—I flicked on. I caught the tail end of the BBC's late-night wrap-up and RussCorp's early morning newscast from Vladivostok. I didn't get the whole story. I was not sure all the pieces fit together. But Haseldyne and Ku was news worldwide, and the outline was clear. Dambois hadn't told me all the truth. Mitzi and Desmond Haseldyne had taken their profits and started their own agency, right enough. But they hadn't taken just money. They'd taken the whole Intangibles department from T., G. & S. with them—raided the staff—pirated the accounts—

Stolen my idea.

The next time I knew what I was doing I was halfway back to headquarters along that mean, hot, dusty road, and I was walking.

I have never felt such fury. It was the next thing to madness—close enough, really, because what other than insanity would have gotten me walking through that inferno, where even the Weegs let their donkeys or yaks carry them from place to place? I was thirsty, too. I'd been hitting the Mokes hard—not just plain Mokie-Kokes, but spiking them with anything alcoholic the officers' lounge could supply. But it had all boiled out of me along the way, and the residue that was left was concentrated, crystalline rage.

How could I get back to civilization?—get back and get justice; get what I was owed from Mitzi Ku! There had to be a way. I was a chaplain. Could I give myself compassionate leave? If I couldn't do that, could I fake a nervous breakdown or get some friendly medic to supply me with heart-palpitation pills? If I couldn't do any of those, what were the chances of stowing away on the return flight of the next cargo plane that landed? If I couldn't do that—

And, of course, I couldn't do any of them. I'd seen what happened to the whimpering feebs who'd come into my office, with their cock-and-bull stories of errant wives or intolerable lower-back pain; there were no compassionate leaves given out from the Reservation, and no chance of stowing away.

I was stuck.

I was also beginning to feel really bad. Heavy drinking and sleepless nights hadn't done a thing to help my Moke-raddled body. The sun was merciless, and every time a vehicle went by I thought I'd cough my lungs out. There were plenty of vehicles, too, because the word was that our operation was going to come off at last. Any time now. The heavy attack pieces were in place. The troops had been given their designated assault targets. The support logistics were operational.

I stopped dead in the middle of the road, swaying dizzily as I tried to collect my thoughts. There was a meaning there, a hope . . . of course! Once the operation was complete we'd all be rotated back to civilization! I'd still be in the service, sure, but in some stateside camp where I could easily wangle a forty-eight-hour pass, long enough to get back to New York to confront Mitzi and her nasty sidekick—

"Tenny!" cried a voice. "Oh, Tenny, thank heaven I found you—and, boy, are you in trouble!"

I squinted through the blinding dust and glare. A two-wheel Uygur "taxi" was pulling up alongside me, and Gert Martels was hopping off, the lean, scarred face worried. "The colonel's on the warpath! We have to get you cleaned up before she finds you!"

I staggered toward the sound of her voice. "Hell with the colonel," I croaked.

"Aw, please, Tenny," she begged. "Get on the taxi. Scrunch down so if any MPs come by they won't see you."

"Let them see me!" The funny thing about S/Sgt Martels was that she kept *blurring.* Part of the time she was a foggy figure of black smoke, opaque against the blinding sky. Part of the time she was in sharp focus, and I could even read the expression on her face—worry; revulsion; then, curiously, relief.

"You've got *heatstroke!*" she cried. "Thank heaven! The colonel can't argue with *heatstroke!* Driver! You savvy Army hospital, yes? You go there quick-quick, yes?" And I found myself being dragged aboard the cart by Gert Martels's strong arms.

"Who wants a hospital?" I demanded belligerently. "I don't need any damn hospital! All I need is a Moke—" I didn't get it, though. I didn't get anything. If I had I wouldn't have been able to do anything with it, because just then the sky darkened and wrapped itself around me in a black-wool cocoon, and I was out of it for the next ten hours.

II

They were not idle hours. The prescription for heatstroke was: rehydrate; keep cool; bed rest. Fortunately, it was the same prescription for acute hangover. I got what the doctor ordered. True, I didn't know it at the time, because I was unconscious at first, drugged asleep after that. I had hazy memories of the needles with saline and glucose going into my arm now and then, and of being coaxed awake to swallow immense doses of liquid. And of dreams. Oh, yes, dreams. Bad dreams. Dreams of Mitzi and Des Haseldyne pigging it in their deluxe penthouses and laughing themselves silly when they thought of poor, dumb old Tennison Tarb.

And when I did wake up at last I thought it was still a dream, because the first sergeant was bending over me, a finger to his lips. "Lieutenant Tarb? Can you hear me? Don't make any noise—just nod your head if you can—"

The mistake I made was in doing what he said. I nodded. The top of my head shook loose and rattled on the floor, exploding with pain at every bounce.

"I guess you've got a pretty bad hangover, right? Too bad . . . but listen, there's a problem."

The fact that there was a problem was not news to me. The only question was, which problem did he mean? Surprise; it wasn't any of the ones I was aware of. It was something brand new, and not so much my problem as Gert Martels's. One eye cocked for the floor nurse, whispering with his lips so close to my ear that his breath tickled my ear-hairs, he explained, "Gert's got this one bad habit, I guess you know—"

"What habit's that?" I asked.

"You don't know?" He looked surprised, then actually embarrassed. "Well," he said reluctantly, "I know it sounds real lousy, but a lot of the guys, you know, out in the field, exposed to all sorts of influences—"

Against all wisdom and desire, I pushed myself up. "Sergeant," I said, "I don't have clue one to what you're talking about. Spell it out for me."

He said, "She's off with the Weegs, Lieutenant. And she hasn't got her protective equipment. And it's T minus two hours and counting."

That got me. "You mean the operation's on tonight?" I yelled.

He winced. "Please, keep your voice down. But yes. It goes at midnight, and it's ten o'clock right now."

I stared at him. "Tonight?" I repeated. Where had I been? How had I missed the warning? Of course, it was technically secret information, but surely every trooper in the camp must have known hours before.

The first sergeant nodded. "They moved it up because the weather's perfect." Now that I knew what to look for I could see the polarized fabric hood slung over his shoulders and the huge sound-deadening earmuffs hanging down below his chin. "The thing is—"

Sound at the end of the ward. A door opening. A light.

"Oh, hell," he snapped. "Listen, I've got things to do. Go get her, will you, Lieutenant? There's a Weeg waiting for you downstairs, with protective gear for both of you—he'll take you to her—he—" Footsteps coming nearer. "Sorry, Lieutenant," he panted. "I've got to go."

And went.

So, as soon as the nurse had made her rounds and gone, I slipped out of bed, slid into my clothes, sneaked out of the ward. My head was hammering and I knew that the last thing I needed was to get an AWOL-from-hospital mark on my record to add to all the other black marks. The funny thing was, I didn't hesitate for a minute.

I didn't even hesitate long enough to realize that it was strange. Only later did it occur to me that there had been plenty of times in the past when someone or other had put his tail in a crack to save me from something. Never before had I had any trouble forgetting that when a chance came to pay the favor back. All that was in my mind was that I owed Gert, and she needed me to bail her out. So I went . . . pausing only once, at the hospital door, to score a couple of Mokes from the vending machine. And I actually think that if the machine hadn't been right there and available, I might well have gone even without them.

The Weeg was waiting as advertised, not only with complete gear for two but even with a donkey and a two-wheel cart. The only thing missing was his knowledge of English. But, as he seemed to know where to go without any instructions from me, that didn't appear to be a problem.

It was a hot, dark night, so dark that it was almost scary. You could see the sky! I don't just mean a daytime sky, or even the night sky when the lights from below give it that dull reddish kind of glow, I mean *stars*. Everybody's heard of stars, but how many people have actually seen one? And here were *millions* of them, spanning the sky, bright enough to see by—

Bright enough, anyway, for the donkey to see by, because it didn't seem to have any trouble finding its way. We were off the main roads, heading for the nearby hills. Between us and the hills was a valley. I'd heard of it; it was kind of a curiosity in those parts, because it was fertile. What makes the Gobi a gobi—that is, a gravelly desert—is dryness and wind. Dryness turns the soil into dust. Wind blows the dust away, until all that's left is endless square miles of stony desert. Except that now and then in a few isolated places—a valley, the sheltered side of a hill—there's a little water, and those places trap the soil. Other officers had told me that this one was almost like an Italian vineyard, with trellised grapes and even murmuring streams. I hadn't thought it worth the trouble of visiting. I hadn't planned to visit it now, especially at night, especially when all hell was supposed to break loose in—I sneaked a look at my watch, brilliant in the dark night—about an hour and five minutes. And actually we didn't visit it this time. The Weeg took a path around the vineyard, stopped the cart, motioned me to get out and pointed up a hill.

In the starlight I could vaguely see a structure of some sort, shedlike, all by itself. "You mean I should go up there?" I asked. The Weeg shrugged and pointed again. "Is Sergeant Martels in that shack?" Another shrug. "Hell," I said, turned around and, sighing, started up the hill.

The starlight was not quite enough to see by after all. I stumbled and fell a dozen times trying to climb that feeble excuse for a path— that damn, dirty, dusty path, so dry that when I slipped I was likely as not to slide a yard or two backward. I gashed myself at least twice. The second time as I clambered back to my feet something beyond the hills coughed *whump*, and a moment later *whump* . . . *whump* . . . *whump* came from all around the horizon, and in a score of places the stars were stained by slow, spreading clouds of darkness. I didn't have to be told what they were: sky screens. The operation was about to begin.

I smelled the shed yards before I reached it. It was used for drying grapes into raisins, and it was heavy with a winy stink. But over and above that sickening fruit stench there was something stronger—not just stronger. Almost frightening. It was a little like food—ReelMeet, maybe, or TurrKee—but there was something wrong with the smell. Not spoilage. Worse than spoilage. My stomach had been reminding me for some time that I'd given it a hard life recently; the smell almost pushed it into revolt. I swallowed and groped my way into the shed.

Inside there was a sort of light. They had built a fire—to see by while they ate stolen rations, I assumed. Wrong assumption. As wrong as the other assumption, which was that Sergeant Martels's "one bad habit" was something like shacking up with the natives, or maybe getting drunk on home-brewed popskull. How naive I had been! There were half a dozen troopers gathered around the fire in the shed, and what they were doing with the fire was desiccating an *animal* over it. Worse than that, they were *eating* the dead animal. Gert Martels stared up at me open-mouthed, and in her hand was a part of its limb. She was holding it by its skeleton—

That finished my stomach. I had to blunder outside.

I barely made it. When I had finished heaving everything I'd swallowed for twenty-four hours I took a deep breath and went back inside. They were scared now, looking at me with pale, fearful faces in the firelight.

"You're worse than gooks," I told them, my voice shaking. "You're worse than *Veenies*. Sergeant Martels! Put this on. The rest of you, get your heads down, put your fingers in your ears, don't open your eyes for the next hour. The operation's in ten minutes!"

I didn't wait to hear their anguished complaints, or even to see if Gert Martels was doing as I had ordered. I got out of that hellhole as fast as I could, slipping and skidding a dozen yards down the path before I paused long enough to put the earmuffs in place and the hood over all. Of course, then I could hear nothing at all, least of all Gert Martels coming up beside me. Conversation was impossible. That was just as well. There was nothing I wanted to say to her just then. Or hear. We picked our way down the hill to where the Weeg was waiting with his donkey, squeezed into the cart pointed back toward the encampment. The Weeg picked up the reins—

Then it began.

The first step was fireworks—plain, simple old pyrotechnics. Starbursts. Golden rain. Showers of diamond-bright waterfalls. They weren't quite bright enough to actuate the quick-response dimmers in our hoods, but they were bright enough to be startling —our Weeg driver almost dropped the reins, gazing pop-eyed at the sky—and all of it punctuated with bombs bursting in air, muffled and dim through our cutouts, but the sound rolling off the hills. The landscape was bright with the aerial bursts; and that was only the come-on. That was to wake the Weegs up and get them out in the open.

Then the Campbellian brigades went into action.

There weren't many blasts of sound now, but the ones there were sounded like a sonic boom happening between your shoulder and your ear. Incredibly loud. Even through the earmuffs, *painfully* loud—if we hadn't had the big cutouts half the troops would have experienced hearing loss. For the Weegers, I suppose there was. I found out later that in those booms two glaciers on the distant mountains had calved, and an avalanche of loosened snow had caught the population of one Uygur village staring at the sky. But the noise was only half of it. The other half was *light*. It strobed in your eye—even through the quick-response hoods. Even through closed lids. There was never a show like it. Even protected, it shocked the senses numb.

And then, of course, the speaker balloons bellowed their commands and our projector battalion filled its vapor screens with the vivid, luscious, compelling images of steaming mugs of Coffiest and Cari-O candy bars and Nic-O-Chews and Starrzelius Verily pants suits and athletic supporters—and sizzling, juicy cubes of Reel-Meet with slices curling off them, so rich and rare that you could almost taste them—could in fact smell them because the Chemical Reinforcement Team from the 9th Battalion had not been idle, and their generators poured out whiffs of Coffiest and aromas of Reel-Meet Burgers and, worst of all for me, the occasional chocolaty tang of a Moke—and always and above all the deafening sounds, the blinding strobe lights. . . . "Don't look!" I shouted in Sergeant Martels's ear. But how could she help it? Even protected from the limbic stimuli by earpieces and hoods, the images themselves were so appetizing, so heart's-desire demanding, that my mouth watered and my hands reached as by themselves into my pockets for credit cards. Most of the basic compulsion of the campaign passed us by, of course. We were spared the Campbellian reinforcers. The verbal messages that boomed from hill to hill were in the Uygur dialect, which we did not understand. But our driver sat rapt, head thrown back, reins loose in his lap, eyes shining, and on his face a look of such unutterable longing that my heart melted. I reached in my pocket and found half a Cari-O bar; and when I gave it to him he responded with such a profusion of gratitude that, without understanding a word, I knew that I had earned his lifelong devotion. Poor Weegs! They didn't have a chance.

Or, to put it more properly, I corrected myself primly, at last they had entered the rich and rewarding comity of mercantile society. Where the Mongols and the Manchus and Hans had failed, modern cultural imperatives had triumphed.

My heart was full. All the worries and tragedies of the last few days were forgotten. I reached out for Gert Martels as we sat in that unmoving cart, with the last of the sky display fading and the echoes of the acoustics fading away, and put my arm around her shoulders.

To my astonishment, she was crying.

By eleven the next morning the trading posts were stripped bare. There were Kazaks and Uygurs and Hui begging at their empty shelves for the chance to buy Popsies and Kelpy Krisps. The entire operation was a flawless triumph. It meant a unit citation for everyone involved, and an Account-Exec citation for some.

It meant—it might even mean—a chance at a fresh start for me.

III

But, it turned out, it wasn't going to mean that right away. I got Gert, red-eyed and still mysteriously sniffling, back to her NCO quarters and sneaked back into the hospital with no trouble—half the patients, and nearly all the orderlies and medical staff, were still outside with their hoods thrown back over their shoulders, chattering excitedly about the attack. I mingled for a moment, worked my way through the crowd, found my bed and was asleep again; it had been a hard day.

The next morning replayed my first day, as the major came poking through the ward with the medics in tow to tell me that I was discharged from the ward and due at headquarters in twenty minutes. The only good thing was that the colonel wasn't there; she'd ordered herself to the fleshpots of Shanghai as soon as the exercise was over to report to General HQ. "But that doesn't let you off the hook, Tarb," lectured the lieutenant colonel who was second in command. "Your conduct is *shocking*. You'd be a disgrace to the uniform even as a consumer, but you're an adman. Watch your step, because I'll be watching you!"

"Yessir." I tried to keep my face impassive, but I guess I didn't succeed because he snarled: "Think you're going home, do you, so you won't have to worry about this sort of thing any more?"

Well, that was exactly what I'd been thinking. The word was that troop redeployment would start that very day.

"No way," he said positively. "Chaplains are part of Personnel. Personnel get the job of getting everybody else out before they can go home. You're not going anywhere, Tarb . . . except maybe to the stockade if you don't straighten out!"

So I crept back to my office and my shamefaced S/Sgt Gert Martels. "Tenny," she began in embarrassment.

I snapped, "Lieutenant Tarb, Sergeant!"

Her face flushed dark red and she came to a hard brace. "Yes, *sir*. I only want to offer to apologize to the lieutenant for my, uh, my—"

"Your revolting behavior, you mean," I lectured. "Sergeant, your conduct is *shocking*. You'd be a disgrace to the uniform even as —ah—as a private, but you're a noncommissioned officer. . . ." I stopped, because there was an echo in the room. Or in my head. I stared at her in silence for a moment, then collapsed heavily into my chair. "Aw, hell, Gert," I said. "Forget it. We're two of a kind."

The flush drained out of her face. She stood there uncertainly, shifting from foot to foot. Finally she said in a low voice, "I can explain about that business on the hill, Tenny—"

"No, you can't. I don't need to hear it. Just get me a Moke."

Lieutenant Colonel Headley may have meant to keep an eye on me, but he only had two eyes. Redeployment took both of them. All the heavy limbic equipment was packed up and loaded onto transports and the assault troops marched into the bays after it and were gone. The returning transports weren't empty, though. They were full of Services of Supply troops and, most of all, merchandise. And the merchandise melted like the snow. Every morning you'd see the Weegs lined up at the trading posts waiting for them to open, and staggering away to their yurts with their arms full of candy bars and food snacks and Thomas Jefferson Pure Simulated Silver amulets for the wives and kiddies. The operation had been a total triumph. You never saw such a dedicated bunch of consumers as the Eager Weegers, and I would have taken pride in my participation in the great crusade if my spirit had any pride left in it. But that commodity the Services of Supply could not provide.

If I had had anything to do it might have been easier. The chaplain's office was the quietest place on the Reservation. The old troops had nothing to come and complain about because they were on their way home anyway; the Supply forces were too busy. Gert Martels and I, without ever spelling it out, worked out an ad hoc division of labor. Each morning I would sit alone in the empty office, guzzling Mokes and wishing I were—anything—anything but what and where I was. Even dead. And in the afternoon she would take over and I would be off to the officers' lounge in Urumqi, squabbling over what channels to watch on the Omni-V and waiting fruitless hours in my endless attempts to get a call through to Mitzi, or Haseldyne, or the Old Man . . . or God. I even dared the lieutenant colonel's office a couple of times, trying to get myself turned loose. The time to go home a hero is before everybody forgets what you were being heroic about, and already the Gobi operation was disappearing from the Omni-V newscasts. No luck. And it kept on being *hot*. No matter how many Mokes I swilled I seemed to sweat them out faster than I could pour them down. I didn't weigh myself any more, because the numbers that were coming up were beginning to be scary.

Fridays were the worst, because we didn't even try to keep the chaplain's office open. I fought my way up to Urumqi through the masses of Weegs in their wagons and carts and bicycles, all with the consumer light glowing in their eyes as they headed for the bazaars of the big city, reserved a room, stocked up on Mokes, headed for the officers' lounge and my unending squabbles about Omni-V and phone calls—

But Gert Martels was waiting for me outside the lounge. "Tenny," she said, glancing around to make sure no one was near enough to listen, "you look like hell. You need a weekend in Shanghai. So do I."

"Out of my pass authority," I said gloomily. "Go try with Lieutenant Colonel Headley if you want to. He might let you go, maybe. Not me. I'm sure." I stopped, because she held up two pass cards before my eyes. Over the magnetic striping was Headley's signature.

"There's no use," she said, "in being friends with the first sergeant if he can't slip a couple of passes into the colonel's signature box when he wants to. The plane leaves in forty minutes, Tenny. Want to be on it?"

Shanghai! Jewel of the Orient! By ten o'clock that night we were in a floating bar along the Bund. I was getting down the tenth, or maybe it was the twentieth, well-spiked Moke, checking out the dark-haired little bar girls with their flapper haircuts, wondering if I ought to try connecting with one before I got too paralyzed to do anything about it. Gert was drinking straight GNS, and with every shot getting more and more upright and careful in her speech, and glassy-eyed. That was a funny thing about Gert Martels. She was not a bad-looking woman, not counting the scars that slashed down the left side of her face, from ear to jawbone. But I had never come on to her, nor she to me. A lot of it had to do, I guess, with the military code and the trouble you could get into fraternizing between officers and enlisted personnel, but lots of other Os and EPs had taken their chances and gotten away with it. And it had been a long, long time since Mitzi. "How come?" I asked, waving to the waitress.

She hiccoughed in a ladylike fashion and turned her eyes on me. It took a second or two; she seemed to be having trouble focusing. "How come exactly what, Tennison?" she asked with careful articulation.

I would have answered her question except that the waitress came by and I had to order another Moke-and-Djinn and a grain neutral spirits for the lady. It took a moment for me to remember. "Oh, yeah," I said, "what I wanted to ask was how come you and I never made it."

She gave me a dignified smile. "If you want to, Tennison."

I shook my head. "No, I don't mean if I want to, I mean how come we've never, you know, sort of, like, *emanated* to each other." She didn't answer right away. The drinks came, and when I finished paying the waitress and handed the GNS to Gert I saw that she was crying.

"Aw, listen," I said, "I wasn't pulling rank or anything. Was I?" I demanded, looking around the table for confirmation. I didn't remember exactly how it had happened, but there seemed to be four or five other people who had joined us. They all smiled and shook their heads—meaning maybe no I wasn't and maybe no, we don't understand English. But one of them did, anyway. The civilian. He leaned across and shouted over the noise of the bar:

"You let me buy next lound, okay?"

"Why not?" I gave him a thank-you smile and turned back to Gert. "Excuse me, but what did you say?" I asked.

She reflected over that for a moment, and the civilian leaned back to me:

"You guys from Ooloomoochee, light?" It took me a moment to realize he was trying to say Urumqi, but then I admitted he was right. "Can always tell! You guys tops. I buy two lounds!" And the sailors from the Whangpoo River Patrol all grinned and applauded; that much English they knew too.

"I guess," said Gert reflectively, "I was going to tell you the story of my life." She accepted the next drink, nodded courteously and knocked it back between sentences without missing a beat. "When I was a little girl," she said, "we had a happy family. What Mom could do with Soya-tem and CelloWheet and a couple pinches of MSG! And then on Christmas we'd have Turr-Kee—real reconstituted meat, and cranberry-flavored Jellatine Dessert and all."

"Chlistmas!" cried the civilian in delight. "Oh, you guys *tops* with you Chlistmas!"

She gave the man a polite but distant smile and reached out for the next drink. "When I was fifteen Daddy died. They said it was bronchio-something. He coughed himself to death." She paused to swallow, and that gave the plump old civilian a chance.

"You know I went to missionary school?" he demanded. "Had Chlistmas there, too. Oh, we owe you missionary guys big debt!"

It was not easy for me to follow one life story, much less two. The bar had gotten a great deal noisier and more crowded and, although the old excursion steamer was moored tightly to the Bund pilings, I could have sworn it was swaying in the waves. "Go on," I said in general.

Gert was faster on the uptake. "Did you know, Tenny," she asked, "that once factories had smoke-scrubbers in their stacks? They scrubbed out the sulfur and fly ash. The air was clean, and the average life expectancy was eight years longer than it is today."

"Here, too!" cried the civilian. "When I young boy in missionary school—"

But she rode right over him. "Do you know why they stopped? Death. They wanted more death. There's big money in death. Partly it's the insurance-company accounts—the actuaries figured out it cost less to pay off life policies than annuities. Then there's all the dollar volume from hospitalization insurance, and a fifty-year-old who's lived all his life in smog knows he's going to spend a lot of time sick, so he has to buy—then, if he dies quickly, it's nearly all profit. Of course, there's the morticians, too. You wouldn't *believe* the profits in burying the dead. But mostly—" she looked around the table, smiling gently—"mostly, well, hell. When a consumer gets to be past working age how much money does he have to buy things? Damn little. So who needs him?"

I said nervously, "Gert, honey, maybe we ought to get some fresh air." The old civilian was grinning and bobbing his head; he'd had enough to drink himself that he didn't care what anybody said. But one of the Whangpoo sailors was frowning as though he understood a little English after all. It didn't seem to faze Gert.

"If there was any fresh air," she explained, "probably Daddy wouldn't have died that way, would he?" She extended her empty glass with a sweet, little-girl smile. "Could I have just a little more, please?" she asked.

God bless the old civilian. He had the waitress there with another round in a minute, and the Whangpoo sailor's face relaxed as he got his refill.

I was a long way from sober, but not so far that I didn't realize Gert was in worse shape than I was. I made an effort to change the subject. "So you like the missionaries, eh?" I offered genially to our benefactor.

"Oh, damn good guys, yes! Owe them plenty."

"For bringing Christianity to China, you mean?"

He looked puzzled. "What Chlistianity? For *Chlistmas.* You know what Chlistmas mean? I tell you! My business—wholesale dless goods, all kinds—Chlistmas sales mean fi'ty-four percent annual letail volume, almost fi'ty-eight percent of net. *That* what Chlistmas mean! Buddha, Mao, they never give us anything like that!"

Unfortunately he had set Gert off again. "Christmas," she said dreamily, "wasn't the same after Daddy died. Fortunately he had an old gun. So I'd go out in the garbage dumps—we were living in Baltimore at the time, down by the harbor—and I'd shoot seagulls and sneak them home. Of course, they weren't like TurrKee, but Mom—"

I almost spilled my drink. "Gert," I cried, "I think we'd better go now!" But I was too late.

"—Mom would cook up those seagulls so you'd think they were ReelMeet and we'd just eat ourselves sick, and—"

She never finished. The Whangpoo sailor leaped to his feet, his face working in rage and disgust. I didn't understand the words he said, but the meaning was clear enough. *Animal eater.* And that was when it all hit the fan.

I don't remember the fight very clearly, only the MPs pouring in along about the second time I pulled myself out from under the table. Adrenalin and panic had boiled a lot of the booze out of me, but I thought I was still drunk, hallucinatory drunk, DTs drunk, when I saw who was leading them. "Why, Colonel Heckscher!" I murmured. "Fancy seeing you here."

And that was when I passed out.

Well, it was one way of getting home. Almost home. Arizona, anyway. That was where Colonel Heckscher was going and, as we were still nominally members of her command, she had no difficulty getting us transferred along with her for the court-martial.

So I went from one dusty desert to another. It seemed like half the assault troops from Urumqi had gotten there before me. From my lonely room in the BOQ—Gert was in the stockade but, being an officer, I was just under house arrest—I could see their pop-ups in neat rows stretching to the horizon, and at the very edge of the camp a line of space shuttles. I didn't spend much time looking at them. I spent most of my time with the law officer the court had assigned me for defense. Defense! She was no more than twenty, and her principal credential was that she'd served in the Copyright & Trade Mark Division of a minor Houston agency while waiting to be accepted to law school.

But I had a powerful friend. The Chinese civilian didn't forget his old drinking buddies. He wouldn't testify against us, and it appeared he'd paid off the whole Whangpoo fleet, because when they were called on the person-to-person video for depositions they one and all testified that they didn't speak English, didn't know what if anything Gert or I had said, wasn't even sure we were the Westerners who'd been in the bar that night. So all they could get me for was conduct unbecoming an officer and that meant no more than a dishonorable discharge.

It meant no less, either. Colonel Heckscher saw to that. But I was lucky. Gert Martels got the same DD, but as she was enlisted personnel and a career noncom they had a long file on her; and just to make the dishonorable discharge a little nastier in her memory they gave her sixty days' hard first.

Tarb in Purgatory

· · ◆ · ·

I

When I went to Taunton, Gatchweiler & Schocken to ask about getting my old job back I was afraid Val Dambois wouldn't even see me. I was wrong about that. He saw me. He was glad to. He laughed all the way through the interview. "You poor fool," he said, "you poor, shaking, demoralized wreck. What makes you think we need pedicab pushers bad enough to take you on?"

I said, "My tenure—"

"Your tenure, Tarb," he said with pleasure, "ended with your dishonorable discharge. Terminated for cause. Get lost. Better still, kill yourself." And, walking down forty-three flights of stairs to the back exit—Dambois hadn't seen fit to give me an elevator pass—I wondered how long it would be before that seemed a logical option.

There was a body of opinion which said that was what I was doing already, for at my final separation physical from the service the medic had read her dials and gauges with an increasingly worried look until she punched up my discharge papers and saw I was a DD. "Ah, well," she said then, "I guess it doesn't matter. But I'd say you're headed for total physical and mental collapse in the next six months." And she scribed in great red letters across the long list of my deteriorating physical traits the legend *Not Service Connected,* so that not even the Veterans Administration was likely to take an interest in what became of Tennison Tarb. Would Mitzi? Pride kept me from asking—for five days. Then I sent her a message, bright and positive, how about a drink for old time's sake? She didn't answer that. She also didn't answer the less bright and far from positive messages of the tenth day, the twelfth, the fifteenth. . . .

Tennison Tarb didn't have any friends any more, it seemed.

Tennison Tarb didn't have a whole lot of money any more, either. Dishonorable discharge included forfeiture of all pay and allowances, which meant, among other things, that all my bar bills from the officers' lounge in Urumqi got passed on to a collection agency. The rest of the world had forgotten I was alive, but the knee-breakers had no trouble finding me and what remained of my bank account. By the time they went away with the amount due plus interest plus collection fees plus tax—plus tip!—because they explained that customers *always* tipped the collectors, swinging their hard-rubber batons as they explained—there wasn't much more left of Tennison Tarb financially than in any other way.

And yet I still had my bright, original, creative mind! (Or had my mind so deteriorated with the rest of me that trivial insights and dumb ideas seemed brilliant?) I read *Advertising Age* every time I got a chance to pick an Omni-V channel, waiting in some hiring hall for interviews for jobs I never got. I nodded approvingly over some campaigns, frowned with disgust at others—I could have done them so much better!

But nobody would give me the chance. The word was out; I was blacklisted.

Even the cheapest shared-time rental was more than I could afford, so I took a futon with a consumer family in Bensonhurst. They'd advertised space to share and the price was right. I took the long subway ride, found the building, climbed down the steps to the third sublevel and knocked on the door. "Hello," I said to the tired, worried-looking woman who answered, "I'm Tennison Tarb," and at the end of the sentence I took a breath. Oh, wow! I had forgotten! I had forgotten how consumers lived, and most of all I had forgotten what a consumer diet turned into in the digestive system. It is true that textured vegetable protein does resemble meat—a little like meat—like the ReelMeet from the cell cultures, anyway—but even if the taste buds are deceived the intestinal flora are not. They know what to do with the stuff. Get rid of it—a lot of it as gas. The best way I can describe the atmosphere of that suburban consumer household is like when you're caught short in a bottom-class neighborhood and have to use the communijohn, and it's in the last half hour before the morning or evening flush. Only now I had to live in it.

They weren't all that happy to see me, either, because my little shoulder bag of Moke containers added a new worry to the lines on the woman's face. But they needed the money, and I needed the space to sleep. "You can have meals with us, too," she said hospitably, "just eat right with the family, and it wouldn't cost you much."

"Maybe later," I said. They'd already put the kids to sleep in their over-the-sink cribs. With their help I tugged the furniture around to make space to roll out my futon, and as I fell asleep, my bright, original, creative mind was finding inspiration even in adversity. A new product! Antigas deodorizers to put in the food. The chemists could cook something up in no time—whether it actually worked or not, of course, mattered very little, just so we had a strong theme campaign and a good brand name. . . .

When I woke up in the morning the campaign was still clear in my mind, but something was wrong. Where was the pong? I didn't smell it any more! And I realized that consumers don't perceive their own stink.

Of course, I told myself that only meant they had to be told about it. That's the glory of advertising—not just to fill needs, but to *create* them.

I learned something that morning on my way to the next employment agency. I learned that brilliant ideas aren't worth a snake's sneeze if the wrong people get them. Back at T., G. & S., when I had easy access to the Old Man's office and the planning committee, that brainstorm would have turned into a ten-megabuck account in ninety days. Hanging onto the subway car en route to a job interview, unemployed, nearly broke, all my network of associates and connections evaporated, it wasn't a brainstorm. It was a fantasy, and the sooner I stopped fantasizing and reconciled myself to my new station in life the better, or anyway the less worse, it was going to be.

But, oh! Pride or no pride, how I missed my brassy lady, Mitzi Ku.

That night I made a decision. I didn't go back to my consumer family for dinner. I didn't eat dinner at all. I sat outside Nelson Rockwell's shared-time condo, swigging Mokes and waiting for him to wake up. A tired old man with a tray of Kelpy-Krisp samples traded me snacks for Mokes; a nasty young Brinks beat cop moved me on twice; a thousand hurrying consumers scowled their way past, ignoring me even when they tripped over me—I had plenty of time to think, and not much pleasant to think about. I was a long way from Mitzi Ku.

When at last Rockwell came out and spotted me leaning against the garbage disposal his jaw dropped—not far, because it was wired shut. And his head was covered with bandages; as a matter of fact he looked like hell. "Tenny!" he cried. "Gee, it's good to see you! But what've you been doing to yourself; you look like hell!" When I returned the compliment he gave an embarrassed shrug. "Aw, nothing serious, I just got a little behind in my payments. But what're you doing out here? Why didn't you come right in and wake me up?"

Well, actually the reason was I didn't want to see whoever it was that had taken over my ten-to-six shift in the sleepy box. I passed the question by. "Nels," I said, "I want to ask you another favor. Well, I mean the same favor over again. Would you take me to that ConsumAnon place again?"

He opened his mouth twice, and closed it twice without saying anything. He didn't have to. The first thing he was going to say was that I could go by myself, but he'd already said that. The second thing, I was pretty sure, was that maybe I'd left it a little too late for ConsumAnon to do me any good; maybe a hospital was a better idea right then. On the third try the censor passed what he wanted to say: "Well, gee, Tenny, I don't know. The group's kind of fallen apart—there's this new self-help franchise deal, see, and a lot of the members are into substitution instead of abstinence." I kept my mouth closed and my face expressionless. "Still," he said—and then, sunnily, "Well, hell, Tenny, what are friends for? Sure I'll take you!" And, this time, he insisted on a tandem pedicab, and insisted on paying the pullers himself.

See, I hadn't looked for that sort of kindness from Nelson Rockwell. All I wanted from him was one little favor, so little that he wouldn't even know exactly what it was. Consideration, tact, generosity—they were more than I wanted, and more than I really cared to accept; if you take more kindness than the giver can afford there's a debt that I didn't want to repay. So I let him spend his tact on a blank wall—smiling, cordial, reserved, off-handed; and I turned away his generosity. No, thanks, I didn't need twenty until I got myself straightened out. No, really, I'd just eaten, no sense stopping for a quick soyaburger anywhere. I gave polite but dismissive answers to his overtures, and all I volunteered was comments on how the neighborhoods we were passing through had run down, or how the off-puller was limping in her left leg as she struggled up a not very steep hill. (And wondering inside of me if she'd have to quit the job, and if so whom to apply to for the vacancy.)

The church was as dismal as before, and the congregation far more sparse; my little scheme had obviously cut into their membership. But my luck wasn't entirely out. The one person I had hoped to find there was there. After ten minutes of exhortations from the pulpit and fevered vows of abstinence from the wimps, I excused myself for a moment, and when I came back I had what I needed.

All I wanted then was to get away. I couldn't do it. I hadn't voluntarily incurred the debt of courtesy to Nelson Rockwell. But there it was on the books.

So I stayed with him to the grisly, tedious end, and even let him buy the soyaburgers when it was over. I guess that was a mistake. It emboldened him to offer help all over again. "No, honestly, Nels, I don't want to borrow any money," I said, and then something made me add, "especially since I don't know when I could pay it back."

"Yeah," he said gravely, licking burger juice off his fingers. "Good jobs are hard to get, I guess." I shrugged as though the problem was in making up my mind which offer to accept. There'd been only one. Attendant in a custodial-care institution for the brainburned, and I hadn't had any problem turning *that* down—who wants to change the diapers of a forty-year-old contract-breach criminal? "Listen," he said, "I maybe could get you in at the grommet works. Of course, it's not such good pay, I mean, for somebody with your background—"

I smiled in a forgiving fashion. He looked abashed. "I guess you've got Agency prospects, hey, Tenny? That girl friend of yours. I hear she's got her own Agency now. I guess now that you're into CA and getting that problem under control, pretty soon you'll be right up there again."

"Of course," I said, watching him dunk the last crust of his soyaburger roll into his Coffiest. "But for now—what kind of money, exactly, do they pay in grommets?"

And so by the time I was in the subway on my way back to Bensonhurst I had the promise of a job. Not a good job. Not even a passable job. But the only job in sight.

In the dim light from the flickering subway tunnel lamps, I pulled out the flat plastic box I'd bought from the weasel-faced man outside the church. The wind was streaming through my hair, and I opened it carefully. The contents had cost too much to let them blow away.

With them, I probably did have that problem under control, I thought. At least for a while.

I looked at the little green tablet for a long time. They said in six months you went psycho, in a year you'd be dead.

I took a deep breath and popped it down.

I don't know what I expected. A rush. A feeling of liberation. A sense of well-being.

What I got was very little. As best I can describe it, it was like novocaine all over my body. Faint tingle, then a total absence of feeling. Although I was three hours past my last Moke, I didn't want one.

But, oh, the world was gray!

"We make grommets *cheap*," said Mr. Semmelweiss. "That means *no rejects*. That means we can't take chances on stumblebums in this industry, there's too much at stake." He glared disapprovingly at my personnel record. I couldn't see the screen from where I stood, but I knew what it said. "On the other hand," he conceded, "Rockwell's one of my best men, and if he says you're all right—"

So I had the job. For that reason, and for two others. Reason 1: The pay was lousy. I would have done better with the brainburned, financially speaking, although in the grommet plant of course I didn't have to risk my fingertips spoon-feeding the patients. Reason 2: It gave Semmelweiss a thrill to point out his adman employee to visitors. I'd be lugging away full boxes and sliding empties into place, and I'd see him inside his glass-enclosed cubicle at the end of the floor pointing toward me. And laughing. And the people with him, customers or stockholders or whatever, grinning incredulously at what he said.

I didn't care.

No, untrue, I did care, cared a lot. But not as much as I cared about holding onto the job, any job, until I could figure out how to get back to my life. The little green pills were maybe a first step. Maybe. True, I didn't swig Mokes any more. That was all you could say. I didn't gain back any weight, didn't get rid of that hair-trigger tension that made my fingers want to twitch and kept me tossing and turning on my futon until, sometimes, I woke one of the kids and the parents glowered and muttered to themselves. But most of that was inside, where it didn't show, and my mind was busier, quicker than ever. I dreamed up great slogans, campaigns, product categories, promotions. One by one I went down the list of Agencies, printing up résumés, begging for interviews, calling on personnel managers. The résumés drew no answers. The phone calls were hung up. The visits ended when they threw me out. I tried them all, the big and the little. All but one.

I came close. I got as far as the sidewalk outside the rather undistinguished little building near the old Lincoln Center that held the brand-new Agency of Haseldyne & Ku. . . .

But I didn't go in.

I'm not sure what kept me going, because it certainly wasn't ambition and it was positively not the rewarding quality of my life. The gray numbness kept pain and want out, but it was just as good against pleasure and joy. I slept. I ate. I worked on my résumés and sample books. I pulled my trick at the grommet works. One day followed another.

There certainly was nothing inspiring about the grommet works. The job was dull, and the industry appeared to be dying. We never saw the finished product. We turned out the grommets and they were shipped to places like Calcutta and Kampuchea to be used in whatever they were used in—it was cheaper for the Indians and Kampucheans to buy from us than to make them locally, but not *much* cheaper, so business was not thriving. My first week there they closed down the wire-plastic division, though extruded-aluminum and enamel-brass were still going well enough. There was lots of unused space on the upper floors of the plant, and when things were slow I went poking around. You could see the history of industry written in the stratigraphy of the old plant. Bolt holes in the floor where once the individual punch presses had stood . . . overlaid by the scars of the high-speed extrusion lines . . . buried under the marks of the microprocessor-controlled customized machines . . . and now again outmoded by the individual punch presses. And covered all by dust, rust and must. There were lights on the upper floor, but when I pressed the switch only a handful came on, old fluorescents, most of them flickering wildly. A regiment of stair-sleepers could have found homes here, but Mr. Semmelweiss was pursuing the fantasy of "more desirable" tenants . . . or the even more fantastic hope that somehow grommets would boom again and all the old space would be bustling.

Fantasies, I sneered—enviously, for the little green pills had not only taken away my Moke-hunger, they had punctured my own fantasies as well. It is a terrible thing to wake up in the morning and realize that the day just dawned will be no better than the last.

II

What changed things? I don't know. Nothing changed things. I made no resolve, settled no unanswerable questions. But one morning I got up early, changed trains at a different station, got out where I had not been in a long, long time and presented myself at Mitzi's apartment building.

The doorthing opened its jaw to sniff my fingertips and read my palm print. Medium success. It didn't admit me, but it didn't clamp down to hold me until the cops came either. In a minute Mitzi's sleepy face appeared on the screen. "It really is you," she said, thought for a minute and then added, "You might as well come on up."

The door opened long enough for me to squeeze through, and all the way up on the hang-on lift I was trying to figure out what had been odd about the way she looked. Hair tousled? Sure, but obviously I'd got her right out of bed. Expression peculiar? Maybe. It was clearly not the look of someone glad to see me.

I pushed that question to the corner of my mind where the growing mountain of unanswered questions and unresolved doubts was locked away. By the time she let me in to her own place she'd washed her face and thrown a kerchief over her hair. The only expression she wore was polite curiosity. Polite *distant* curiosity. "I don't know why I'm here," I said—"except that, really, I've got nowhere else to go." I hadn't planned to say that. I hadn't planned anything, really, but as the words came out of my mouth and I heard them I recognized them as true.

She looked at my empty hands and unbulging pockets. "I don't have any Mokes here, Tenny."

I brushed it aside. "I'm not drinking Mokes any more. No. I haven't kicked them; I'm just on replacements."

She looked shocked. "Pills, Tenny? No wonder you look like hell."

I said steadily, "Mitzi, I'm not mad and I don't think you owe me anything, but I thought you'd listen to me. I need a job. A job that'll use my skills, because what I'm doing now is so close to being dead that one morning I just won't wake up because I won't be able to tell the difference. I'm blacklisted, you know. It's not your fault; I'm not saying that. But you're my only hope."

"Aw, Tenny," she said. The polite curiosity face broke, and for a minute I thought she was going to cry. "Aw, *hell*, Tenny," she said. "Come on in the kitchen and have some breakfast."

Even when the world is all gray, even when the circumstances are so wildly unlike anything you've ever done before that part of your mind is chasing its tail in baffled circles, your habits and training carry you through. I watched Mitzi squeeze oranges (real fruit oranges! *Squeezed* them!) for juice, and grind coffee beans (real coffee beans!) to make coffee, and all the while I was pitching her as confidently and strongly as ever I'd done for the Old Man. "Product, Mitzi," I said. "That's what I'm good at, and I've worked out major new product campaigns. Try this: Did it ever occur to you that it's a lot of trouble to be using disposable pocket tissues, razors, combs, toothbrushes? You have to keep a supply on hand. Whereas if you had permanent ones—"

She wrinkled her brow, the frown lines very deep and very conspicuous. "I don't see what you're getting at, Tenny."

"A permanent replacement for, say, pocket tissues. I've researched it; they used to be called handkerchiefs. A luxury item, don't you see? Priced for prestige."

She said dubiously, "There's no repeat business, though, is there? I mean if they're permanent—"

I shook my head. "Permanent's only as long as the consumer wants to keep it. The key is fashion. First year we sell square ones. Next year triangular, maybe—then with different designs, prints, colors, maybe embroidery; the numbers say there's bigger grosses in that than in disposables."

"Not bad, Tenny," she conceded, putting a cup of this peculiar coffee in front of me. Actually it didn't taste bad.

"That's only one little one," I said, swallowing my first sip. "I've got big ones. *Very* big ones. Val Dambois tried to steal my self-help substitution groups from me, but he only got part of it."

"There's more?" she asked, glancing at her watch.

"You bet there's more! They just never let me work it all out. See, after the groups are formed, each member goes out and digs up other members. He gets a commission on the new ones. You get ten new members at fifty dollars a year each, and you get a ten percent commission on each one—that pays your dues."

She pursed her lips. "I suppose it's a good way to expand."

"Not just expand! How do you recruit these new members? You have a party in your condo. Invite your friends. Give them food and drinks and party favors—*and we sell them the favors*. And then—" I took a deep breath—"the beauty part, the member that signs up new members gets promoted. He becomes a Fellow of the group, and that means his dues go up to seventy-five a year. Twenty members, he becomes a Councilor—dues, a hundred. Thirty he's a, I don't know, Grand Exalted Theta-Class Selectman or something. See, we always stay ahead of them, so no matter how many membership he peddles he pays half of it back—and we go on selling him the merchandise."

I sat back with my coffee, watching the expression on her face. Whatever that expression was. I had thought it might be admiration, but I could not really tell. "Tenny," she sighed, "you are one hell of a true-blue huckster."

And that broke through the well-trained reflexes. I set the coffee cup down so hard that some of the coffee spilled into the saucer. Once more I listened to the words coming out of my mouth and, although I had not planned to say them, I recognized they were true. "No," I said, "I'm not. As far as I can tell I'm not a true-blue anything. The reason I want to get back into the ad business is that I have a notion I *ought* to want it. What I really want is only—"

And I stopped there, because I was afraid to finish the sentence with the word "you" . . . and because the other thing I noticed was that my voice was shaking.

"I wish," I said despairingly, and thought for a minute before going on: "I wish this was a different world."

Now, what do you suppose I meant by that? That's not a rhetorical question. I didn't know the answer to it then and don't now; my heart was saying something my head hadn't considered at all. I guess the meaning of the question isn't that important. The feeling was what counted, and I could see that it reached Mitzi. "Oh, hell, Tenny," she said, and her eyes dropped.

When she raised them again she stared at me searchingly for a moment before she spoke. "Do you know," she said—funny, but as much to herself, I thought, as to me, "that you keep me awake at night?"

Shocked, I began, "I had no idea—" But she pressed on.

"It's foolish," she mused. "You're a huck. True, you're down right now, and you're thinking things you wouldn't have let yourself think a few weeks ago. But you're a huck."

I said—not quarrelsomely, just making my point, "I'm an adman, yes, Mitzi." It wasn't like her to use that kind of language.

She might as well not have heard. "When I was a little girl Daddy-san used to tell me that I'd fall in love and I wouldn't be able to help myself, and the best and only thing for me to do was to stay away from the kind of man I wouldn't be able to help myself with. I wish I'd listened to Daddy-san."

My heart swelled inside me. Hoarsely I cried, "Oh, Mitzi!" And I reached out for her. Didn't touch her though. Easily, not hurrying a bit, she stood up, just fast enough for my reaching hands to miss her, and stepped back. "Stay here, Tenny," she ordered calmly and disappeared into her sleep room. The door slid locked behind her. In a minute I heard the shower begin to run, and there I sat, studying Mitzi's queer ideas of interior decoration, trying to see what anybody would like about the painting of Venus on the wall—trying to make sense of what she had said.

She gave me plenty of time. I didn't succeed, though, and when she came out she was fully dressed, her hair was neat, her face was composed, and she was somebody else entirely. "Tenny," she said directly, "listen to me. I think I'm crazy and I'm sure I'm going to have trouble over this. But still, three things:

"First, I'm not interested in your product ideas or your Consum-Anon scams. That's not the kind of Agency I'm running.

"Second, at this moment I can't do a thing for you. Probably I shouldn't even if I could. Probably in a day or two I'll come to my senses and then I won't see you at all. But right now there's no space for another adman in our offices—and no time in my life, either.

"Third—" she hesitated, then shrugged—"third, there *might* be something for us to talk about later on. Intangibles, Tenny. Political. A special project. So hush-hush I shouldn't even be saying it exists. Maybe it never will. It won't unless we can get a lot of things straight —we even need a place to house it, out of sight, because it's *really* hush-hush. Even then maybe we'll decide the time isn't ripe and we shouldn't go ahead with it now anyway. Do you hear how iffy all this is, Tenn? But if it does happen, then maybe, just maybe, I can find a place for you in it. Call me in a week."

She stepped briskly toward me. With my heart in my eyes I reached out for her but she sidestepped, leaned forward to kiss me chastely and firmly on the cheek and then went to the door. "Don't come with me," she ordered. "Wait ten minutes, then leave."

And she was gone.

Although those little, flat green tablets seemed to be clarifying my thoughts, they didn't make what I was trying to think about Mitzi clear at all. I rehearsed every word of our conversation in my mind, tossing on my futon while the babies whimpered and the parents snored or bickered softly between themselves in the same room. I could not make sense of it. I couldn't figure out what Mitzi felt about me (oh, she'd all but said the word "love"—but surely she never acted it!). I could not square the Mitzi I had known so casually and carnally on Venus, her only secrets Agency ones, with the increasingly mysterious and unpredictable one on Earth.

I couldn't understand anything at all—except for one thing that rang clear in my memory. And so I finished my shift at the grommet works, cleaned myself up, combed my hair and presented myself at the glass cubicle at the end of the floor. Semmelweiss wasn't alone; the man with him was there at least once a week, staying for hours sometimes, going out to lunch with him and coming back with that three-martini lurch. I knew what they talked about: nothing. I coughed from the doorway and said: "Excuse me, Mr. Semmelweiss."

He gave me the exasperated can't-you-see-I'm-in-conference growl: "In a minute, Tarb!" And went back to his friend. The conference was about their pedicars:

"Acceleration? Listen, I had an old Ford with the outside pushoff, first pedicar I ever owned, secondhand, real clunker—but when I'd be waiting for a light to change I'd just stick that old right foot outside and *zoom!* I'd cut right in front of the pedicabs and all!"

I coughed again. Semmelweiss cast a despairing glance at heaven and then turned to me: "Why aren't you at your machine, Tarb?"

"My shift's over, Mr. Semmelweiss. I just wanted to ask you something."

"Tchah," he said, glancing at his friend, eyebrows raised in scorn—scornful of me, who had once owned a battery-powered bike! But he said, "What the hell is it, then?"

"It's about that extra space, Mr. Semmelweiss. I think I know someone who might rent it. They're an Agency."

His eyes popped. "Hell, Tarb! Why didn't you say so?" And then everything was all right. It was all right for me to show Mitzi and Haseldyne the space. It was all right to take off work the next day to bring them there. It was all right to interrupt him, hell, Tarb, sure it was, any time! Everything in the world was all right . . . except maybe me, and all the worries and fears and puzzles that I couldn't even put a name to.

III

When I finally got Mitzi on the phone she was very irritable, exactly as though she was mad at herself for encouraging me at all—which, I was sure, was exactly the case. She demurred, and hesitated, and finally admitted that yes, she had said they needed hideout space. She'd have to check with Des Haseldyne, though.

But when I called her back, on her instructions, ten minutes later, she said, "We'll be there." And so they were.

When I met them on the filthy sidewalk outside the grommet plant Haseldyne looked far more irritated than Mitzi had sounded. I put out my hand. "Hello, Des," I said civilly.

Uncivilly he ignored my hand. "You look like hell," he said unsympathetically. "Where's this rathole you're trying to sell us?"

"This way, please," I said, usherlike, and bowed them in. I didn't tell them to watch out for the dirt. They could see the dirt themselves. I didn't apologize for it, or for the coughing, barking, sometimes machine-gun noise of the machines spitting out their million grommets an hour; or for Semmelweiss waving greasily to us from his cubicle; or for the smells; or for the neighborhood. Or for anything. It was their decision to make. I wasn't going to beg.

Once we got upstairs it was a little better, anyway. Those ancient buildings were put together solidly; you could hear the machines below, but only as a distant and not unpleasant mutter. The lights were still flickering madly, and the dust made Mitzi wheeze and sneeze. But they didn't seem to notice. They were more interested in the back stairs and the freight elevator and all the unused ratholes marked Exit that no one had opened in decades. "Plenty of ways in and out, anyway," said Desmond ungraciously. I nodded, but I hadn't actually heard him. I was adrift in my own head. Funny. With Mitzi actually in the same room wth me I seemed farther away from her than ever. I supposed I was just strung out. The pills were not without cost, and although my weight loss had slowed, it had not stopped, nor had my insomnia come to an end. And yet there was something very strange—

"Tarb!" Haseldyne called crossly. "Are you nodding off on us? I asked you about transportation."

"Transportation?" I counted off on my fingers. "Let's see, there's two subway lines, all the north-south buses, the crosstown buses, the crosstown pedstrip. And pedicabs, of course."

"And power availability?" Mitzi put in, sneezing.

"Sure, there's power. That's how they make the grommet machines go," I explained.

"No, damn it, I mean is it *reliable?* No interruptions?"

I shrugged. I hadn't really noticed. "I guess not," I said.

I hadn't realized she was more on edge than I. "You *guess?*" she flared. "God, Tenny, even for a Moke-head you're—ah, ah—you're pretty stupid—ah—"

When the *choo* came it was violent. She clapped her hands to her face. "Oh, *hell!*" she growled. Down on her hands and knees, scrabbling at the dusty floor, she looked up ferociously, and one of Mitzi's blue eyes was brown.

I suppose that if I hadn't been a Moke-head I would have figured it out long before. Eating salads. Contact lenses to hide her eye-color. Dodging the mother who desperately wanted to see her daughter. Calling me a "huck" when she got mad. A dozen different incongruous things.

And only one explanation to fit them all.

I suppose if I hadn't been first a Moke-head, then a pill-popper, I would have reacted in a different way entirely. Called the cops, I guess. Or tried to, even though that might easily have cost me my life. But I'd been through the wringer. What she was doing might be terribly wrong. But I hadn't anything left that I was sure was right.

I seemed to have all the time in the world. I pulled my notepad out of my pocket, wrote swiftly, then ripped out the page and folded it over. "Mitzi," I said, stepping forward, careless of her lost contact lens, "you're not Mitzi, are you?"

Freeze-frame. She stared up at me with one brown eye and one blue eye.

"You're a fraud, aren't you?" I asked. "A Veenie agent. A double for the real Mitzi Ku."

And Haseldyne exhaled a long, slow breath. I could feel him move toward me, tensing to act. "Read this!" I said, and shoved the note into his hand.

He almost didn't stop, but then he glanced at it, frowned, looked startled and read it aloud.

" 'To Whom It May Concern; I can't face life as an addict any longer. Suicide's the only way out.' Signed, Tennison Tarb. What the hell's this, Tarb?"

I said, "Use it if you want to get rid of me. Or let me help you. I'll help the best I can, every way I can, whatever you're doing. I don't care what it is. I know you're Veenies. It doesn't matter."

And I added:

"Please."

The False Mitsui Ku

· · ◆ · ·

I

Once upon a time there was this man Mitchell Courtenay, the one half the streets on Venus seem to be named after. They think he is a hero, but when my grade school teacher told us about him in history class she spat his name with loathing. Like me, he was a star-class copysmith. Like me, he got caught up in a crisis of conscience that he never wanted and didn't know how to handle.

Like me, he was a traitor.

That's the kind of a word that you don't want to hear, when it is you it is applied to. "Tennison Tarb," I yelled at the top of my voice —into the thunder of the subway tunnel as I took the late local to my Bensonhurst flop, where no one could hear the word, not even me— "Tennison Tarb, you are a traitor to Sales!"

Not even an echo answered. Or if it did it was drowned in the subway roar. I felt no pain from the word, though I knew it was fair, and damning.

I suppose it was the long green pills that dulled that pain, along with all the other pains I didn't feel any more. That was my good fortune; but if you flipped that coin, the other side was that I felt no joy at being an adman again, either. Up, down. Up, down. How long I would stay up this time I could not guess, but there I was. I would have exulted—if the world had not been so gray.

And, if the world had not been so gray, I might still have been shaking with fear, too, because it had been a very close thing, there in the loft over the grommet works. I could see the plans coming up, one after another, in Desmond Haseldyne's card-sorter mind: Bash his head in and stick him in a grommet press to hide the evidence. Drug him and toss him out of a high window. Get some Moke extract and OD him—that would have been the easiest and surest of all. But he didn't do it. Mitzi choked out that she wanted to give me my chance, and Haseldyne didn't overrule her.

He also didn't give me the "suicide" note back, though.

When I looked at the life ahead of me I could see two yawning chasms. On the one side, Haseldyne would, after all, use the suicide note and that would be the end of Tennison Tarb forever. On the other, discovery, arrest, brainburning. Between the two was a narrow knife-edge that I might hope to walk—leading to a future in which my name would forever be reviled by generations of schoolchildren to come.

It was a great blessing that I had the long green pills.

Since I was committed to the knife-edge, I went ahead with it. I shaved and pressed and spiffed up as far as I could manage on the money I had left and the facilities available in my Bensonhurst pad —when I could get past sleepwalking parents and cranky kids to get to them. The long, steamy subway ride soaked the new press out of my shorts and blew soot into my washed hair, but all the same I was reasonably presentable when I reported to the lobby of the Haseldyne & Ku building. There a Wackerhut cop checked my palm prints, pinned a temporary visitor's magnetic badge on my collar and whisked me up to Mitzi's office. To the door of Mitzi's office, anyway, where her new sec² stopped me. He was a stranger to me. I was not to him, for he greeted me by name. I had certain formalities to go through. The sec² had Personnel all primed; an employee-contract fax was ready for my thumbprint, and as soon as I had officially signed on he presented me with a permanent Agency I.D. and a two-week salary advance.

So it was with money in my credit store that I finally made it through the door into Mitzi's office. It was a first-class brainroom, as opulent and formidable as the Old Man's at T., G. & S. It was furnished with desk and conference couch, with a wet bar and vidscreen, with *three* windows and *two* visitors' chairs. What it wasn't furnished with was Mitzi Ku. In her place Des Haseldyne sat glowering behind the desk, and he never looked bigger. "Mitzi's busy; I'm handling this for her," he announced.

I nodded, though being handled by Des Haseldyne was not among my dearest dreams. "Can we talk here?" I asked.

He sighed patiently and waved a hand at the windows. Sure enough, windows and door all sparkled with the faint glimmer of a privacy curtain; no electronic buggery would go out of this room while it was on. "Fine," I said. "Put me to work."

He was oddly hesitant. "We don't really have a place for you," he grumbled at last.

That was obvious enough. I hadn't been any part of their calculations until I dumped myself on them. I didn't think anything I might offer would seem like a good idea to him; he might listen to Mitzi, but never to me. Still, I tried to make the pill easier to swallow. "Mitzi mentioned Politics—I can sell the hell out of that," I offered.

"*No!*" The bark was loud, angry and definite. Now, why did that upset him so? I shrugged and tried again.

"There are other Intangibles—say, Religion. Or any kind of product—"

"Not our line of work," he growled, the huge head shaking. He raised his hand to cut off any more useless suggestions from me. "It will have to be something a lot more significant than that," he said definitely.

Enlightenment! "Ah," I said, "I see. You want an overt act. You want me to put my neck on the line to prove loyalty. Commit an actual crime, right? So I can't turn back again? What is it you want me to do, murder somebody?"

I said that so easily! Maybe it was the grayed-out numbing of everything the pills had given me, but once I took his meaning the words came out without a qualm. Haseldyne had been taking no pills, though. The huge face assembled itself into a granite look of total revulsion. "What the hell do you think we are?" he demanded, loathing me. I shrugged. "We're not doing anything like that!" I waited for him to come down from the dudgeon. It took a while, because he seemed to be having trouble assembling his thoughts.

"There is one possibility," he said at last. "You were part of the limbic forces in the Gobi action."

"Chaplain, right," I agreed. "They fired me out with a DD."

"That's easy enough to reverse," he said impatiently. That was true enough, for somebody with the clout of an Agency partner. "Suppose we got you back in. Suppose we put you in a place where you had Campbellian equipment under your command—you do know how to use the stuff, I suppose."

"Not thing one, Des," I told him cheerfully. "That's technician stuff. You don't learn that, you hire it."

He said stubbornly, "But you could direct the technicians?"

"Of course. Anybody could. For what purpose?"

If I had been in any doubt that he was improvising as he went along, and not very well, he dispelled it then. "To promote the Venusian cause!" he roared. "To make the damn hucks leave us alone!"

I looked at him in real astonishment. "Are you serious? Forget it!"

Rumble lower and more dangerous: "Why?"

"Ah, Des, I can see now that you had to be a Veenie agent, for you certainly aren't an adman. Limbic stimulation isn't a technique in itself. It's only an intensifier. An expediter."

"So?"

"So it has to obey the basic laws of all advertising. You can only make people *want* things, Des. You can train knee-jerk buying patterns into them or create hungers, but you can't use advertising to make people *kind*, for God's sake!" I'd put my finger on the truth. Advertising-wise, the man was an ignoramus. How he'd kept his ignorance secret for so long at a major Agency was a miracle— although what I had just said was true: You didn't need to learn what you could hire from others. He glowered resentfully as I went on to explain. "For that kind of thing you need B-mod if you're in a real hurry, and that's out of the question except with small, captive audiences. You don't really want advertising at all, Des."

"I don't?"

"Publicity," I explained. "Word of mouth. You want to create an image. You start stories about the 'good Veenies' for openers. Get a couple of Veenie characters in sitcoms, and gradually change them from villainous clowns to sweet eccentrics. Do some tie-in commercials with a Venusian background—the 'Venus Loves Cari-Os' sort of thing."

"Venus damn it to hell *doesn't,*" he exploded.

"The exact details could be different, of course. Of course, you'd have to be supercareful of how you did it. You're tampering with deep-down prejudices, you know, not to mention maybe even bending the law. But it can be done, given the money and the time. I'd say five or six years."

"We don't *have* five or six years!"

"I didn't think you did, Des," I grinned. It was funny, but I found myself enjoying his aggravation just as much as though the thorn tearing his flesh wasn't me—and as though he didn't have the easy and obvious way to remove it that my "suicide" note had given him. It came down to the fact that I simply didn't care what happened to me. The whole thing was out of my hands. Mitzi was the only friend I had in the world. Either she would save me . . . or she wouldn't.

I left the glowering Des Haseldyne feeling as close to at ease as I'd been in many months, and that night I went out and spent a big chunk of my credit balance on new clothes. I picked them out as happily and carefully as though I were confident of being alive to wear them.

When the next morning's summons to Mitzi's brainroom came along, Mitzi herself was in it—red-eyed, looking as though she hadn't slept well, the frown lines deeper than ever between her eyes. She silently pointed to a chair, flicked on the secrecy screen and sat with her elbows on the desk and her chin in her elbows staring at me. At last she said, "How did I get into this with you, Tenny?"

I tipped her a wink. "I'm just lucky, I guess."

"Don't make jokes!" she snapped. "I didn't *ask* for you. I didn't want to fall in l— . . . in l—" She took a deep breath and forced it out: "In love with you, damn it! Do you know how dangerous all this is?"

I got up to kiss the top of her head before I said seriously, "I know exactly, Mits. What's the use of worrying about it?"

"Sit down where you belong!" Then, relenting as I retreated to my chair, "It's not your fault that my glands are messing me up, I guess. I don't want you hurt. But, Tenn, if it ever comes to a point where I have to choose between you and the cause—"

I raised my hand to stop her. "I know that, Mits. You won't ever have to do that. You'll be glad to have me aboard because, honestly, Mitzi, you clowns don't know what you're doing."

Hard stare. Then, sullenly, "It's true all this stuff revolts us too much for us to be really good at it. If you could supply some expertise—"

"I can. You know I can."

"Yes," she said reluctantly, "I guess I do. I told Des that limbic stuff was hopeless, but he didn't want to let you in on the real plan. All right. I'm taking the responsibility. What we're doing is political, Tenny, and you're going to do it for us. You'll run the whole campaign—under my direction and Des's."

"Fine," I said heartily. "Here? Or—"

She dropped her eyes. "For the beginning, anyway, here. Now are there any questions?"

Well, to begin with, there was the question of why it was going to be here instead of in the loft over the grommet works, but that didn't seem to be one of the ones she wanted to answer. I said slowly, "If you could just start by filling me in on what's going on—"

"Yes, of course." She said it as though I had asked directions to the men's room. "The big picture is, we're going to wreck Earth's economy, and the way we're going to do it is by taking over the governments."

I nodded, waiting for the next sentence that would make that all clear. When there wasn't any next sentence I asked, "The what?"

"The governments," she said firmly. "Surprises you, doesn't it? So obvious, and yet none of you hucks have ever had the wit to see it, not even the Conservationists."

"But Mits! What would you want to take over the government for? Nobody pays any attention to those dummies. The real power's right here in the Agencies."

She nodded. "So it is, de facto. But, de jure, the government still has eminent domain. The laws have never been changed. It's just that the Agencies own the people who write the laws. They get their instructions. No one ever questions them. The only difference is *we* will own them. The dummies will go right on taking our orders, and what we order will plunge this planet into the damnedest, worst depression the human race has ever seen—*then* let's see if they can still screw around with Venus!"

I goggled at her. It was about the craziest idea I had ever heard. Even if it worked, and all conventional wisdom swore to me it couldn't work, was that what I wanted? An economic depression? Mass unemployment? The destruction of everything I had been taught to revere. . . .

And yet—humility said—who was I, failure and addict, to criticize? Heaven knew my principles had been rocked and shaken so many times in the past few roller-coaster months that I couldn't pretend to know anything. I was floundering—and Mitzi seemed so sure.

I said, feeling my way, "Listen, Mits, since some of our Earth ways are so unfamiliar to you—"

"Not unfamiliar!" she flared. "Rotten! Criminal! *Sick.*"

I spread my hands, meaning, "No argument"—especially since I seemed to be changing sides in that argument. "The question is, how can you be sure this will work?"

She said fiercely, "Do you think we're illiterate barbarians? It's all been gamed and dry-run a hundred times. We've had input from the top brains on Venus—psychologists, anthropologists, poli-sci think tanks and war-plans strategists . . . hell," she finished glumly, "no. We don't know that it will work. But it's the only thing we've come up with that might."

I sat back and gazed at my brassy lady. So this was what I had committed myself to—an immense and lethal conspiracy, planned by eggheads, conducted by zealots. It was comically hopeless, baggy-pants farce, except that it wasn't very funny when you thought of what it meant. Treason, Contract Breach, unfair commercial practices. If it went sour, the best I could hope for was a return trip to the Polar Penal Colony, this time on the wrong side of the bars.

The expression on Mitzi's face might once have belonged to Joan of Arc. She seemed almost to glow, eyes lifted to the sky, the brassy-lady face transmuted through bronze to pure, warm gold, the twin frown lines harsh between her eyes. . . .

I reached across the desk and touched them. "Plastic surgery, I guess?" I inquired.

She came down fast, glowered at me (the frown lines reinforced now with real ones), pursed her lips. "Well, hell, Tenny," she said, "of course there had to be some plastic surgery. I only looked a *little* like Mitsui Ku."

"Yeah," I said, nodding, "I thought that was it. So the idea was," I added conversationally, "you'd kill both of us in the tram station, right? And then you'd announce that through Herculean efforts and the skill of Veenie surgeons you'd pulled at least Mitzi through? Only it would really be you?"

She said harshly, "Something like that."

"Yeah. Say," I inquired interestedly, "what's your real name, anyway?"

"Damn you, Tenn! What difference does that make?" She sulked for a minute, and then said, "Sophie Yamaguchi, in case it matters."

"Sophie Yamaguchi," I repeated, tasting the name. It didn't taste right. "I think I'll go on calling you Mitzi, if you don't mind."

"Mind? I *am* Mitzi Ku! I spent *seven months* practicing to be her, studying the surveillance tapes, copying her mannerisms, memorizing her background. I even fooled you, didn't I? Now I hardly remember Sophie Yamaguchi at all. It's like Sophie died instead of—"

She stopped short. I said, "I guess Mitzi's dead, then."

The false Mitzi said unwillingly, "Well, yes, she's dead. But she wasn't killed by the tram. And believe me, Tenny, I was glad! We're not assassins, you know. We don't want to hurt anybody, unnecessarily. It's just that the objective realities of the situation . . . Anyway, they hustled her away for, ah, retraining."

"Ah," I nodded. "The Anti-Oasis."

"Sure she went there! And she would have been all right there, too. Either she would have come around to our way of thinking or, at least, been kept there alive and out of sight. But she tried to escape. Ran out of oxygen or something in the desert. Tenny," she said earnestly, "it was nobody's *fault.*"

"Well, whoever said it was?" I asked. "Now, about what you want me to do . . ."

When you come right down to it, I guess nothing is ever anybody's fault, or anyway nobody ever thinks it is. You have to do what you have to do.

Yet, going back to Bensonhurst that night, I looked around me at the tired, sad-faced commuters hanging to their harnesses as the filthy tunnel walls flew past, the smoggy wind blowing us around, the lights flickering. And I wondered. Did I really want to make the hard life of these consumers harder? Wrecking Earth's economy wasn't an abstraction; it meant concrete things, a concrete loss of a job for a file clerk or a Brink's cop. A concrete downgrading for an adman. A concrete cut in the food budget for the family I lived with. Well, sure, I now believed that Earth was wrong in trying to sabotage and overpower Venus, and it was right to join forces with Mitzi, the false Mitzi, that was, and put a stop to that wickedness. But what degree of wickedness was appropriate to achieve that nonwicked end?

To all my troubles and worries and dilemmas I did not want to add the only one I hadn't much suffered from yet: guilt.

Nevertheless . . .

Nevertheless I did the job Mitzi had given me. Did it damn well, too. "What you're going to do, Tenny," she had ordered, "is *elect.* Don't try anything complicated. Don't try to get *principle* into the campaigns. Just do your huck damnedest to make our people win."

Right, Mitzi. I did—my damnedest, and tried not to let myself feel damned. One of the people she'd stolen from Taunton, Gatchweiler and Schocken was my old flunky, Dixmeister; he'd been jumped up to take my job and was gloomy, but resigned, to be jumped down again. He brightened when I told him he could have more authority this time; I let him set up all the casting calls, even let him pick possible candidates from the first screenings. I didn't tell him that I was keeping an eye on the screenings through the closed-circuit TV to my office, but then it wasn't necessary—left on his own, having had the benefit of my training, the kid was doing all right.

And I had more important things to do. I wanted *themes.* Slogans. Combinations of words that might or might not mean anything (that wasn't important) but were short and easy to remember. I put the Research Department to work, digging up all the themes and slogans that had ever been used in political campaigns, and presently my monitor was flooded with them. "The Square Deal." "54-40 or Fight." "The Moral Majority." "The Forgotten Man," "Mink, Stink and Pink." "Get Government off the Backs of the American People." "Cuba 90 Miles Away." "I Will Go to Korea." "Truth in Advertising"—well, no, that one didn't have the right ring. "I Am Not a Crook"—that one hadn't worked. "The War on Poverty." Better, though that one, it seemed, hadn't won the war. There were hundreds of the damned things. Of course, most of them had no bearing on the world we lived in—what could you make of "Tippecanoe and Tyler Too"?—but, what I used to tell my copy cubs, it isn't what a slogan says that matters, it's what people can read into it that somehow touches the subconscious. It was hard, slogging work, not made easier by the fact that I had lost something. What I had lost was the feeling that winning was an end in itself. It *was*, in this case—Mitzi had told me so. But I no longer *felt* that.

All the same I came up with some beauties. I called Dixmeister in to see them, all beautifully calligraphed and ornamented by Art, with theme music and multisensual background by Production. He gaped at the monitor, puzzled.

" 'Hands Off Hyperion'? That's truly superb, Mr. Tarb," he said by reflex, and then, hesitating, "but isn't it really kind of the other way around? I mean, we don't want to let go of Hyperion as a market, do we?"

"Not *our* hands off, Dixmeister," I said kindly. "*Veenies'* hands off. We want them left alone by *Veenies.*"

His expression cleared. "A masterpiece, Mr. Tarb," he said raptly. "And this one. 'Freedom of Information.' That means no attempts at censoring advertising, right? And 'Get Government Off the Backs of the People'?"

"Means abolishing the requirement to post warnings at Campbell areas," I explained.

"A work of genius!" And I sent him off to try the slogans on that day's crop of candidates, to see which of them could say them without stumbling or looking confused, while I got busy setting up a spy system to check out the other Agencies' candidates. So much to do! I was working twelve, fourteen hours a day, losing weight slowly but consistently, sometimes almost falling asleep and losing my grip on the hang-on in those long subway trips to Bensonhurst. I didn't care. I had made my commitment and I was going to see it through, whatever it cost. At least the pills were still working; I hadn't had even the desire for a Moke in a long time.

I hadn't had much of a desire for anything else, either—for almost anything else—for anything but the one thing, anyway, and that one thing was not the sort of famished physical craving the green pills anesthetized so well. It was a head-yearning. It was a memory-desire, a longing to feel again the sweet touch of bodies as we slept and the sound of breathing that came from a warm, soft body wrapped in my arms. It was Mitzi I wanted.

I didn't get much of her. Once a day I would report to her brainroom. Sometimes she was not there and it was Des Haseldyne who shifted his huge body irritably in the chair and scowled through my sitrep, never complete enough or fast-moving enough to please him, because Mitzi was off at some other meeting. Sometimes the meetings were far away. I knew there was much going on that I was not privy to, as they tried to patch and shore up the rickety scheme that I had committed myself to. It was just as well I was anesthetized. The pills didn't keep away entirely the sweaty nightmares about Fair Commercial Practices hit squads storming my office or Bensonhurst pad, but they let me live through them.

Even when Mitzi was there we didn't touch. The only difference between reporting to Mitzi and reporting to Des was that once in a while she called me "dear." The days went on. . . .

And then late one night I was rehearsing one of our candidates in the traditional moves of debate: the cocked eyebrow of humorous skepticism; the clenched jaw of resolution; the indignant thundercloud frown of disbelief—the sudden glance of astonishment and the edging away, as though the opponent had just, grossly and unforgivably, broken wind. As I was coaching the dummy in the various demeaning possible mispronunciations of his opponent's name, Mitzi came in. "Don't let me interrupt, Tenny," she called as she entered. And then, coming closer, she said softly in my ear so that the dummy couldn't hear: "But when you're through— Anyway, you're working too hard to take that long trip to Bensonhurst every night. There's plenty of room at my place."

It was what I would have prayed for, if I had prayed.

Unfortunately, it wasn't very satisfactory. The pills had not only grayed down the environment, they had grayed *me* down. I didn't have the passion, the zest, the overwhelming hunger; I was glad we were doing what we did, but it didn't really seem to matter all that much, and Mitzi was nervous and strained.

I guess old married couples go through times when both are tired or fretful—or, like me, strung out—and what they do, they do because they don't have anything better to do at the moment.

Actually, it seemed we did have something better to do. We talked. We talked a lot, pillow talk but not *that* kind of pillow talk. We talked because neither of us was sleeping very well and because, after some seldom very satisfactory sex, it was better to talk than to pretend to be asleep and listen to the person next to you pretending the same.

There were things we didn't say, of course. Mitzi never mentioned the secret bulk of the iceberg, the mysterious meetings I was not allowed to attend or know about. For my part I never again mentioned my doubts. That the Veenie conspirators were floundering in a ramshackle plan was clear. I'd known that from the moment

Des Haseldyne began asking about limbic compulsion. I didn't discuss it.

I did, now and then, think about brainburning. When Mitzi cried out and twitched in her sleep, I knew she was thinking about it too.

What I talked about mostly was confidences I could betray. I told Mitzi everything I could think of that might help the Veenies out, every Agency secret I'd ever heard, every Embassy covert operation, every detail of the Gobi Desert strike. Each time she'd sniff and say something like, "Typical merciless huck tyranny," and then I'd have to think of some other highly classified datum to betray. You know Scheherazade? That's what I was, telling a story every night to stay alive the next morning, because I hadn't forgotten how expendable I was.

Naturally it handicapped me in more intimately important areas. But it wasn't all like that, really. I told her about my childhood, and how Mom made my uniform with her own hands when I joined the Junior Copysmiths, and my school days and my first loves. And she told me—well, she told me everything. Well, at least everything about herself. Not so much about what my coconspirators were up to, but then I didn't expect that. "My Daddy-san came to Venus with the first ship," she would say, and I would know that she was telling me these things to avoid the risk of telling me something more risky.

It was interesting, though. Mitzi had a thing about her Daddy-san. He'd been one of old Mitchell Courtenay's gang of self-righteous revolutionary Conservationists that so hated the brainwashing and people-manipulating of the mercantile society that they jumped from the frying pan of Earth into Venus's pure hellfire. When she told me about Daddy-san's stories of the early days, it sounded like a clone of hell itself, all right. And her father hadn't been any big wheel. Just a kid. His main job appeared to be digging out holes for them to live in with his bare hands, and carrying slop outside of the ship to bury between work shifts. While the construction crews were putting together the first huge Hilsch tubes to tap the biggest asset Venus had—the immense energy in its hot, dense, wild winds—Daddy-san was changing diapers for the first generation of kids in the nurseries. "Daddy," she said, wet-eyed, "wasn't just an unskilled kid, he was also a physical wreck. Too much junk food when he was little, and something wrong with his spine that never got fixed—but he never let that keep him from doing his best!"

Along about the time they began nuking tectonic faults to make volcanos, he took time enough to get married and have Mitzi. That's when he got promoted, and subsequently died. The whole idea of the volcanos, of course, was that they were the best way the Veenies had of getting the underground oxygen and water vapor out where they could use them. That's where all the Earth's oceans and air came from, but Venus couldn't squander them the way the early Earth did because they couldn't afford to wait four billion years for the results. So the volcanos had to be capped. "That was hard and dangerous work," said Mitzi, "and when something went wrong and one of the caps blew, it blew my Daddy-san along with it. I was three years old."

Strung out, exhausted, worn as I was, she touched my heart. I reached out for her.

She turned away. "That's what love is," she said into the pillow. "You love somebody and you get hurt. After Daddy-san died I used up all my love on Venus—I never wanted to love another *person!*"

After a moment I got up unsteadily. She didn't call me back.

Dawn was breaking; might as well get into this next bad day. I put some of her "coffee" on and stared out the window at the smoggy, huge city, with its teeming hucks, and wondered what I was doing with my life? Physically the answer was easy; I was wrecking it. The faint reflection in the glass showed how every day my face got thinner, my eyes brighter and more hollow. From behind me she said, "Take a good look, Tenny. You look like hell."

Well, I was getting tired of hearing that. I turned. She was sitting up in bed, eyes fixed on me. She hadn't put her contacts in yet. I said, "Mits, honey, I'm sorry—"

"I'm getting tired of hearing *that!*" she snapped, as though she'd been reading my mind. "You're sorry, all right. You're about the sorriest specimen I've ever seen. Tenny! You're going to die on me!"

I looked out of the window to see if anybody in the dirty, old city was going to offer me an answer for that. Nobody did. Since what she said actually seemed like a likely possibility, the best plan appeared to be to let her remark alone.

Mitzi wouldn't let it alone. "You're going to die of those damn pills," she said furiously, "and then I'll have goddam *grief* to go with my goddam *worry* and goddam *fear.*"

I moved back to the bed to touch her bare shoulder soothingly. She wasn't soothed. She glared up at me like a trapped feral cat.

The anesthesia was wearing thin.

I reached for my morning pill and popped it down, praying that this once it would give me a lift instead of a numbness, that it would give me the wisdom and compassion to answer her in a way that would ease her pain. Wisdom and compassion didn't come. I did the best I could with what I had to work with; I said, placatingly, "Mits, maybe we better get dressed and go to work before we say something we shouldn't. We're both pretty ragged, maybe tonight we'll get some sleep—"

"Sleep!" she hissed. "Sleep! How can I sleep when every fifteen minutes I wake up thinking the Department of Fair Commercial Practices goons are breaking the door down!"

I winced; I had had the same nightmares; I thought about brainburning a lot. I said, my voice unsteady, "Isn't it worth it, Mits? We're really getting to know each other—"

"I know more than I want to, Tenny! You're an addict. You're a physical wreck. You're not even good in bed—"

And she stopped there, because she knew as well as I did what that meant. That was the mortal word. There was nothing to say after it but, "We're through." And in the special circumstances of our relationship there was only one way to terminate it.

I waited for the next words, which had to be, "Get out of here! Get out of my life!" After she threw me out, I thought abstractedly, the best plan would be go straight to the jetport, fly as far as my money would take me, lose myself in the seething mass of consumers in Los Angeles or Dallas or even farther. Des Haseldyne might not find me. I might just sit out the next few months, while the coup either succeeded or didn't. After that, of course, it got nasty— whichever side won, the winners would surely come looking for me. . . .

I noticed that she hadn't said those words. She was sitting up in bed, listening intently to a faint sound from the door. "Oh, my God," she said despairingly, "look at the time, they're here!"

Somebody was indeed at the door of Mitzi's apartment. It wasn't being broken down. It was being opened with a key, so it wasn't the Fair Practices stormtroopers.

It was three people. One of them was a woman I had never seen before. The others were two people who, I would have bet everything I owned, would be the last possible people to come into Mitzi's apartment in that way: Val Dambois and the Old Man.

When I saw them I was only startled. They were thunderstruck and, besides, furious. "Damn it, Mits!" raged Dambois, "you've really torn it now! What's that Moke-head doing here?"

I could have told him I wasn't a Moke-head, exactly, any more. I didn't try. I was spending all my shocked and horrified thoughts on what their presence here meant. I wouldn't have had a chance to tell him, anyway, because the Old Man held up a hand. His face was like granite. "You, Val," he ordered. "Stay here and keep an eye on him. You others, come with me."

I watched them go, Mitzi and the Old Man and the woman with them—short, dumpy, and what she had muttered when she saw me seemed to have had an accent. "She's RussCorp, isn't she?" I asked Dambois, and he gave me the answer I expected. He snarled:

"Shut up."

I nodded. He didn't have to confirm it. Just the fact that he and the Old Man were sneaking into Mitzi's apartment that way told me all I needed to know. The conspiracy was a lot bigger than Mitzi had admitted. And a lot older. How had the Old Man got his stake? From Venus. From a "lottery" that he had "happened" to win. How had Mitzi got hers? From a "damage settlement" for the "accident." How had Dambois? From "trading profits." All from Venus. All uncheckable by anyone on Earth.

All used for the same purpose.

And if RussCorps was in it, it wasn't just America; I had to assume it was worldwide. I had to assume that for every little crumb of information Mitzi had so reluctantly leaked out there was a whole hidden loaf behind. "There's some evidence you can trust me," I mentioned to Dambois. "After all, I haven't said a word to anybody so far." And, of course, he only replied with:

"Shut up."

"Yeah," I said, nodding. "Well, do you mind if I get myself some more coffee?"

"Sit still," he snapped, then thought it over for a moment. Reluctantly he added, "I'll get it for you, but you stay there." He went over to the pot, but he never took his eyes off me—heaven knows what he expected. I didn't move. I sat still, as ordered, listening to the rise and fall of furious voices from Mitzi's bedroom. I couldn't make out the words. On the other hand, I didn't have to; I was pretty sure I knew what they were discussing.

When they came out I searched their faces. They were all serious. Mitzi's was impenetrable. "We've made a decision," she said gloomily. "Sit down and drink your coffee and I'll tell you about it."

Well, that was the first ray of hope in a sunless situation. I listened carefully. "In the first place," she said slowly, "this is my fault. I should have got you out of here an hour ago. I knew they were coming for a meeting."

I nodded to show I was listening, glancing around to gauge their expressions. None of them were informative. "Yes?" I asked brightly.

"So it would be wrong, morally wrong," she said, every word coming out at spaced intervals, as though she were weighing each one, "to say that any of this is your fault." She paused, as though looking for a response from me.

"Thank you," I said, nervously sipping my coffee. But she didn't go on. She just went on watching me and, funny thing, the *expression* on her face didn't change, but her *face* did. It blurred. The features ran together. The whole room darkened and seemed to shrink. . . . It took me all that time to realize that the coffee had tasted just a tiny bit odd.

And, oh, how I wished I had never written that suicide note. I wished it hard and with all my being, right up to the point where my wishes stopped functioning entirely and so did my eyes, and so did my ears, and so—in the middle of a silent scream of terror, pleading for one more chance, begging to live one more day—so did my brain.

The world had gone away and left me.

II

Even then Mitzi must have fought hard for me. What they slipped into my coffee hadn't been lethal after all. It had only put me to sleep, deeply and helplessly asleep for a long time.

In my dream somebody was shouting, "First call—five minutes!" and I woke up.

I wasn't in Mitzi's apartment any more. I was in a tiny, Spartan cell with a single door and a single window, and outside the window it was dark.

Once I had come to believe in the odd fact that I was alive I looked around. I wasn't tied up, I found to my surprise, nor did I appear to have been recently beaten. I was lying quite comfortably on a narrow cot, with a pillow and a light sheet thrown over my somehow undressed body. Next to the bed was a table. On the table was a tray with some kind of cereal and a glass of Vita-Froot, and between them was an envelope like the tricky kind you use for top-secret Agency messages. I opened it and read it fast, working against the time limit. It said:

> Tenny, dear, you're no good to yourself or us as an addict. If you live through the detox we'll talk again. Good luck!

There wasn't any signature, but there was a P.S.:

> We've got people in the center to report on how you're doing. I ought to tell you that they're authorized to take independent action.

I mulled over what the words "independent action" might mean for a moment—a moment too long, because the trick paper scorched my fingers as it did what it was supposed to do and began to self-destruct. I dropped the smoldering ash hastily and glanced around the room.

There wasn't much information there. The door was locked. The window was shatterproof glass, and sealed. Evidently this center didn't want me walking away from this detox thing. It was all pretty ominous, and there wasn't any long green pill to numb the feelings. Still, there was food and I was starving. Evidently I had been asleep past a couple of mealtimes. I reached for the Vita-Froot just as all hell broke loose. The screaming voice from my dream was no dream. Now it was yelling, "Last call—everybody out!" It wasn't alone. There were sirens and klaxons to make sure I heard; the door lock snicked open, and running feet in the corridors accompanied a banging on every door. "Out!" yelled some individual live human being, glaring in and jerking a huge thumb.

I saw no reason to argue with him about it, since he was at least two sizes bigger than Des Haseldyne.

He was wearing a blue jogging suit. So were about a dozen

others, the ones doing all the yelling. I had found a pair of shorts and grabbed them at the last minute, feeling desperately under-dressed—but not alone; besides the jogging-suit tyrants there were a couple dozen other human beings streaming out of the building, all as inadequately clothed as myself and looking at least as un-happy. They chased us out into the sweaty, smoggy air, still dark although now there was a discouraging reddish glow in one corner of the sky, and we huddled there, waiting to be told what to do. It was, I thought, like the worst of basic training.

That was wrong. It was a lot worse than any basic training. Basic training at least usually starts with fairly healthy raw meat for its processing. There was nothing like that in sight among my com-peers. They came in all shapes and sizes but good. There was one woman who had to weigh over three hundred pounds, and a couple of others, both sexes, who probably weighed less but made up for it by being a lot shorter, so that they billowed grossly over their belts. There were scarecrows skinnier than me and at least as frazzled. There were elderly men and women who looked not hopelessly inhuman except that they had tics they couldn't control—hand to the mouth, hand to the mouth, over and over in endlessly repeated gestures of smoking, eating, drinking. But they had nothing in their hands. And, oh, yes, it was raining.

The joggers shoved and nagged us into a disorderly sort of clump in the middle of a wide cement quadrangle, surrounded by low barrackslike buildings. Over the door to the building we had just come out of was a sign:

Acute Addiction Facility
Detox Effort Division

One of the instructors blew a whistle close by my right ear. When the sound had stopped bouncing around inside my skull I saw that an Amazon in the same jogging suit as the others, but with a gold badge sewn to the jacket, was strutting toward us. She looked at us with revulsion. "God," she observed to the lunatic with the whistle, "every month they get worse. All right, you!" she bawled, climbing on a box to see us better and emphasizing her orders with a blast on her own whistle that neatly severed the top of my head and sent it spinning off over the barracks. "Pay attention! See that sign? 'Detox Effort Division.' The crucial word is *effort*. We'll make the *effort*. You'll make the *effort*, too, I promise you that. But in spite of all of our best *efforts* we're usually going to *fail*. The stats tell the story. Out of ten of you four will go out clean—and then readdict themselves within a month. Three will develop incapacitating physical or psychoneurotic symptoms and require extended treatment—extended has been known to mean the rest of your lives, which are often short. And two of you won't make it through the course." She grinned kindly—I guess she thought it was kindly. I was six hours behind my last pill and the Madonna wouldn't have looked kind to me just then.

Another shattering blast on the whistle. She had paused for a moment, and she didn't want us daydreaming. "Your treatment," she said, "comes in two phases. The first phase is the unpleasant one. That's when we cut you back to minimum dose, feed you up to build resistance, exercise you to develop muscle tone, teach you new behaviors to break up your body-movement patterns that reinforce your habit—and a few other things—and that starts right now. Down on your bellies, everybody, for fifty push-ups—and then it's clothes off and into the showers!"

Fifty push-ups! We stared at each other incredulously in that dark, sultry dawn. I had never in my *life* done fifty push-ups, and I didn't think it was possible . . . until I found out that there were no showers, no breakfast, no leaving the drill ground—above all, no pills—until they were done.

It became possible, even for the three-hundred-pounders.

The lady hadn't lied. Phase One was unpleasant, all right. The only way I could force myself through every miserable hour was by thinking about the blessed green pill that would come at the end of the day. They didn't take the pills away; they only made me earn them. And the horror was that the better I got at earning, the less the reward; by the third day they had begun to shave the end of the pills; by the sixth they were cutting them in half. Three of us had pill habits from Moke addiction. The others had every imaginable addiction. The fat lady, whose name turned out to be Marie, was junk-food; she wheezed like a calliope going over the obstacle course but she always went, because there was no other way to the mess hall. A dark little man named Jimmy Paleologue had been a Campbellian technician himself, borrowed from his Agency by the services to help teach the New Zealand Maoris civilized ways. He was far too sophisticated to be caught by Campbellian stimuli himself, but had inexplicably fallen for a free trial sample of Coffiest. "It was a lot-tery-ticket tie-in," he explained sheepishly as we lay on the muddy ground, panting between knee-bends and rope-climbing. "First prize was a three-room apartment, and I was thinking of getting married. . . ." Palsied and pitiful, barely dragging himself at the tail end of the three-mile runs, he wasn't thinking of it any more.

The center was in one of the outer suburbs, a place called Roch-ester, and it had once been a college campus. The buildings still had the old lettering carved into the cement walls—Psychology Depart-ment, Economics Section, Applied Physics and so on. There was a sludgy body of liquid lapping at the foot of the campus, and as far as the physical surroundings were concerned that was the worst part. They called it Lake Ontario. When the wind was from the north the stench would knock you down. Some of the old buildings were barracks, some therapy rooms, a mess hall, offices; but there were a couple at the edge of the campus that we were not allowed in. They weren't empty. Now and then we would catch glimpses of creatures as miserable as ourselves being shepherded in and out, but whoever they were, we did not mix. "Tenny," gasped Marie, leaning on me as we headed past them toward afternoon therapy, "what do you sup-pose they *do* in there?" A woman in a pink jogging suit—even their instructors were separate from ours—leaned out the door of one of the buildings to glare at us as she tossed something in the refuse bin. When she went back inside I tugged Marie over.

"Let's take a look," I said, glancing around to see that no blue suit was near. I didn't *think* there would be any discarded green pills among the trash, and I'm sure Marie didn't expect to dig up any extra morsels of food. Disappointingly, we were right. All we came up with was a couple of gold-colored booties and a cracked pseudoivory-handled toy gun. They meant nothing to me, but Marie let out a sudden squawk.

"Oh, my gosh, Tenny, they're *collectibles!* My sister had these! Those are from the Miniature Authentic Replicas of Bronzed Baby Shoes of Twentieth Century Gangsters—that one's Bugs Moran, I think—and I'm nearly sure the other is from the Lone Star Scrim-shaw Handgun Collection. That's aversion therapy they're doing in there—where first they make you stop needing it, then they make you hate it! Could that be Phase Two?"

And then the instructor's bellow from behind us: "All right, you two goof-offs, if you've got time to stand around and gossip you've got time for a few extra push-ups. Let's have fifty, now! And make it quick, because you know what happens if you're late for therapy!"

We knew.

When I wasn't doing jumps and jerks or having my head rebent I was eating—every ten minutes, it seemed. Plain food, healthy food, like Bredd and ReelMeet and Tangy-Joose, and no argument. I cleaned off my plate every time, or it was, you guessed it, another fifty push-ups for dessert. Not that fifty extra push-ups made that much difference. I was doing four or five hundred a day, plus squats and sit-ups and bendings-and-touchings, and forty laps a day in the pool strip. There was only room for three of us to swim abreast, and they handicapped us so we three were pretty even in skill—guess what the loser got? Of course he did. The forty of us dropped to thirty-one, to twenty-five, to twenty-two. . . . The one that hit me hardest was Marie. She'd actually lost forty pounds or so, and was beginning to be able to eat her "meals"—vitamins and protein bars, and not much of them—without whimpering, when on the twelfth day, scrambling up the nets, she gasped and choked and rolled to the ground. She was dead. She wasn't permanently dead, because they wheeled out the heart shocker and whisked her off in a pneumatic three-wheel ambulance, but she was too dead to come back to our group.

And all the time my nerves were crawling inside my skin, and what I wanted to do more than anything else was to conk the medication nurse over the skull, take away his keys and get into the locked cabinet of long green pills.

But I didn't.

The funny thing was that, after two weeks, down to one quarter-strength cap a day, I actually began to feel a little bit better. Not *good*. Just less bad, less strung out, less Jesus-I'd-*kill*-for-a-cap. "False well-being," Paleologue panted wisely when I said as much to him, just out of the pool, waiting to start our two-mile run. "You'll hit these temporary plateaus, but they don't mean anything. I've seen you Campbellian-syndrome people before—"

And I laughed at him. I knew better; it was my own body, wasn't it? I could even spare time for thinking about something beyond long green pills—even got as far as the line for the one public phone, once, with every intention of calling Mitzi. And would have, too, if one of those nausea fits hadn't driven me to the communijohn, and then there wasn't time to sweat the line again.

And two more weeks passed, and it was the end of Phase One. The unpleasant part.

Silly me. I hadn't asked our instructor what the second part was going to be like. I had happily, hopefully, assumed that if Phase One was described as *unpleasant* then Phase Two would be described best as something like at least *okay*.

That was before I encountered aversion therapy and final withdrawal, and found out that Phase Two certainly was not anything you would call *unpleasant*. It was way beyond unpleasant. The best term I can think of for it was just your ordinary plain hell.

I guess I don't want to talk any more about Phase Two because, every time I do, I start to shake; but I got through it. As the poisons got out of my body they seemed to get out of my head, too. By the time the director shook my hand and put me on a rocket back to the world—conscious, this time—I felt—still not good—more sad than good—more angry than sad—but, for the first time maybe in my life, *rational*.

The True
Tennison Tarb

· · ◆ · ·

I

You lose track of the seasons in Phase Two, because one is as bad as the next. When I got back to the city I was surprised to find that it was still summery, though the tree in Central Park had begun to turn. Sweat streamed down the back of my pedicab pusher. The ear-shattering traffic din of yells and squeals and crunches was underlaid with the pusher's hacking, sooty cough. There was a smog alert, of course. Of course my pedaler wasn't wearing a face-filter anyway, because you can't get enough air through a filter to keep your speed up in heavy traffic. As we rounded the Circle into Broadway, a six-man armored bank van swerved right in front of us; dodging them, the pedaler slipped on the greasy fallout and for a moment I thought the whole rig was going over. She turned a scared face to me. " 'Scuse it, mister," she panted. "Those damn trucks don't give you a chance!"

"As a matter of fact," I called, "it's such a nice day that I'm thinking of walking the rest of the way anyway." Of course she looked at me as though I were insane, especially when I ordered her to pace me empty in case I should change my mind about walking. When I paid her off with a big tip at the Haseldyne & Ku Building she was sure I was insane. She couldn't wait to get away. But the sweat had dried on her back and she was hardly coughing at all.

I had never done anything like that before.

I waved absently at the colleagues I recognized as I entered the building. They were looking at me with varying degrees of astonishment, but I was busy being astonished at myself. Something had happened to me at the Detox Center. I had come back with more than the bruises from the jabs of vitamin spray and the distaste for long green pills. I had come back with some new accessories inside my head. What they were exactly I didn't yet know, but one of them seemed to want to answer to the name "conscience."

When I walked into my office Dixmeister was as pop-eyed as anyone. "Gosh, Mr. Tarb," he marveled, "you look so *healthy!* That vacation sure must have done you a lot of good."

I nodded. He was only telling me what the scales and the mirror had been telling me the last few mornings. I'd gained back twenty pounds. I didn't shake. I didn't even feel shaky; even the flashing commercials and glitter-bang posters hadn't awakened any cravings on the way to the office. "Carry on," I told him. "I've got to report to Mitzi Ku before I take over here."

That was not easy. She wasn't there the first time I tried. She wasn't there the second, and when I caught her at last on the third round trip between her office and mine she was there all right, but just on the point of leaving. "Mr. Haseldyne's waiting," her sec[3] warned, but Mitzi tarried. She closed the door. We kissed. Then she stood back.

She looked at me. I looked at her. She said to me with wistful surprise, "Tenny, you are looking *fine.*"

I said to her, "Mitzi, you are looking fine, too," and added for truth's sake, "to me." For in fact Mitzi's morning mirror would not have been as kind as mine. She was looking terribly worn, in fact, but the subjective fact behind those facts was that I didn't care how she looked as long as she was there. With her complexion, the circles under her eyes were not emphatic. But they were there: she'd missed sleep, maybe even had missed some meals . . . and she still looked to me quite splendid.

"Was it awful, Tenny?"

"Middling awful." There had been a lot of throwing up, a lot of scrabbling around frantically to find something to cut my throat with. But I hadn't succeeded in that, and I'd only had the convulsions twice. I dismissed it. "Mitzi," I said, "I've got two important things to tell you."

"Of course, Tenny, but this is the damnedest busiest time right now—"

I cut her off. "Mitzi. I want us to get married."

Her hands clenched. Her body froze. Her eyes opened so wide that I feared her contacts would pop out.

I said, "I had plenty of time to think things over in the Detox Center. I mean it."

From outside came Haseldyne's peevish rumble: "Mitzi! Let's get going!"

Silently, automatically, she came to life again, picking up her bag, opening the door, staring at me the whole while. "Come *on*," barked Haseldyne.

"I'm coming," she called; and to me, heading toward the lift, "Dear Tenny, I can't talk now. I'll call you."

And then, two steps away, she turned and came back to me. And there, in the full view of God and everybody, she kissed me. Just before she disappeared into the descending lift she whispered, "I'd like that."

But she didn't call. She didn't call me that day at all.

Since I had never proposed marriage to anybody before, I had no personal experience to tell me if that was a reasonable response. It didn't feel like one. What it felt like was the way Mitzi herself had felt—well, not Mitzi herself; not *this* Mitzi, but the brassy other one back on Venus—the way *that* Mitzi had told me she felt when we first got it on together and I finished ahead of her, and she let me know that I'd damn well have to do better next time around or else. . . . Anyway, it felt bad. I was left hanging.

And I hadn't told her the other important thing.

Fortunately there was plenty to keep me busy. Dixmeister had kept things going as well as you could expect, but Dixmeister wasn't me. I kept him late that night, reviewing his mistakes and ordering changes. He was looking shop-soiled and grumpy by the time I let him go home. As to me, I flipped a coin about where I would spend the time and lost. I holed up in a private-drawer hotel a few blocks from the office and got to work early the next morning. When I went to Mitzi's office her sec^3 said her sec^2 had told her Ms. Ku would be out all morning, along with her sec^1. I spent my lunch hour—all twenty-five minutes of my lunch hour, because one day hadn't been enough to get things turned around and moving right—sitting in Mitzi's anteroom, using her sec^1's phone to keep Dixmeister on the hop. Mitzi didn't show. The all-morning engagements had been protracted.

That night I went to Mitzi's condo.

The door thing let me in, but Mitzi wasn't there. She wasn't there when I arrived at ten, nor at midnight, nor when I woke at six, and waited a while, and dressed, and went back to the office. Oh, yes, Mr. Tarb, her sec[3] told me, Ms. Ku had called in during the night to say that she'd been called out of town for an indefinite stay. She would be in touch with me herself. Soon.

But she wasn't.

Part of my head filed that fact without comment and went on with what it was doing. That was to carry out the orders given. What Mitzi wanted me to do was to elect candidates. It was already September and the "election" only weeks away. There was much to keep me busy, and that part of my head took advantage of every minute it had. It took advantage of every minute Dixmeister had, too, and everybody else in the Intangibles (Politics) department. When I stalked the halls people from other departments averted their eyes and stayed out of my path—for fear I'd draft them to twelve-hour days, I suppose.

The other part of my head, the new one that I'd seemed to discover at the Detox Center—that wasn't doing so well. It was hurting—not just for Mitzi, but for the pain of that other thing it was carrying that I hadn't told her. Then the interoffice mail-person darted into my office long enough to drop a flash-paper envelope on my desk and whisk away.

The note was from Mitzi. It said:

> Dear Tenny, I like your idea. If we get through this alive I hope you'll still want to, because I will, very much. But this isn't a time to talk about love. I'm under revolutionary discipline, Tenny, and so are you. Please hold that thought. . . .
>   With all the love I can only tell you about now—
>   Mitzi

Again it flared and scorched my fingers before I dropped it. But I didn't mind. It was an answer!—and the right answer, too.

There remained the question of the other thing I needed to say. So I kept badgering the sec[3], and when at last she told me that yes, Ms. Ku was back in the city that morning but going directly to an urgent meeting elsewhere, I couldn't wait.

Besides, I thought I knew where I could find her.

"Tarb," cried Semmelweiss—"I mean, Mr. Tarb, good to see you! You're looking really well!"

"Thanks," I said, looking around the grommet factory. The presses were chugging and rattling and thumping out their millions of little round things. The noise was the same, the dirt was the same, but something was missing. "Where's Rockwell?" I asked.

"Who? Oh, *Rockwell,*" he said. "Yeah, he used to be here. He got in some kind of accident. We had to let him go." His grin got nervous as he saw my expression. "Well, he really wasn't able to work any more, was he? Two broken legs, and then the way his face looked— Anyway, I guess you want to go upstairs? Go right ahead, Mr. Tarb! I guess they're up there. You never know, with all those entrances and exits—still, I always say if they pay their rent right on time, who needs to ask questions?"

I left him there. There was nothing else to say about Nelson Rockwell, and nothing I cared to say to satisfy his curiosity about his tenants. Poor Rockwell! So the collection agency had finally not been willing to wait any more. I vowed I would have to do something about Nelson Rockwell as I pushed open the door—

And then I didn't think about Nelson Rockwell for a while, because the door that once had opened into the dirty old loft now opened into a thieflock. Behind me the stair door slammed shut. Before me was a barred door; around me were steel walls. Light flooded over me. I could hear nothing, but I knew I was being observed.

A speaker over my head rumbled in Des Haseldyne's voice, "You'd better have a damn good reason for this, Tarb." The door before me slid open. The one behind me heaved me out of the cubicle with a thrust bar, and I was in a room full of people. They were all looking at me.

There'd been changes in the old loft. High-tech and luxury had come in. There was a telescreen monitor spitting out situation reports along one wall, and the other walls were draped more handsomely than the Old Man's office at T. G. & S. The center of the huge room was filled with an immense oval table—it looked like genuine wood veneer—and in armchairs around the table, each one with its own decanter and glass and scribe-screen and phone, were more than a dozen human beings, and what human beings they were! Not just Mitzi and Haseldyne and the Old Man. There were people there I'd never seen before except on the news screen, heads of Agencies from RussCorp and Indiastries and South America S.A. —German, English, African—half the might of the world's advertising was creamed off and poured into this room. At every step I had been dazzled by the constant revelations of grander scope, greater power to the Veenie moles organization. Now I had taken the last step and penetrated its core. It felt an awful lot like one step too many.

Mitzi must have thought so. She jumped up, face working in shock: "Tenny! Damn you, Tenny, why did you come here?"

I said steadily, "I told you I have something you need to know. It affects you all, so it's just as well I caught you. Your plan is down the tube. You don't have time. There's going to be a huck fleet heading for Venus any time now, with full Campbellian ordnance."

There was a vacant chair near Mitzi at the head of the table. I plumped myself down in it and waited for the storm to break.

It came, all right. Half of them didn't believe me. The other half might have had an opinion one way or the other on that, but the big thing on their minds was that I had entered into their most secret place. There was fury by the megaton in that loft, and it wasn't all aimed at me. Mitzi got her share—more than her share, especially from Des Haseldyne: "I warned you to get *rid* of him," he yelled. "Now there's no choice!" The lady from S.A.[2]: "I theenk you have got big problem here!" The man from RussCorp, pounding the table with his fist, "Is no question, problem! Is only question, how do we solve? Your problem, Ku!" The man from Indiastries, palms together and fingers upthrust: "One wishes not to take life, to be sure, but in certain classes of predicaments one can scarcely find alternatives which—"

I had had enough. I stood up and leaned into the table. "Will you listen?" I asked. "I know your easy way out is to get rid of me and forget what I said. That means Venus is gone."

"You be quiet!" grumped the woman from Germany, but she was alone. She looked around the table, a dozen human beings frozen in positions of rage, then said sulkily, "So tell then what you want, we will listen. A short time we will listen."

I gave them a big smile. "Thank you," I said. I wasn't feeling particularly brave. I knew that, among other things, I was on trial for my life. But my life no longer seemed all that valuable. It was not, for example, equal to the session at the detox farm; if ever I faced the need of that again, knowing now just what it was like, I would surely have Xed myself first. But I was fed up. I said:

"You've seen the news over the last few years, mopping up aboriginal areas to bring them into civilization. Have you noticed where the last few were? The Sudan. Arabia. The Gobi Desert. Does anything strike you about those places?" I looked around the table. It hadn't; but I could see that it was beginning to. "Deserts," I said. "Hot, dry deserts. Not as hot as Venus and not as dry—but the closest thing to Venus there is on the surface of the Earth, and so the best place to practice. That's point one."

I sat down, and made my voice conversational. When they court-martialed me," I said, "they kept me in Arizona for a couple of weeks. Another desert area. They had ten thousand troops there on maneuvers; as far as I could tell, they were the same troops they had had in Urumqi. And out in the boonies they had a fleet of rockets. Right next to the rockets were stockpiles: Campbell ordnance. Now, let's see if we can figure it out. They've been practicing in simulated Venus conditions; they've got trained combat troops rehearsing invasion tactics now; they've got Campbell heavy weapons ready to be loaded into shuttles. Add it up. What do you come out with?"

Total silence in the room. Then, tentatively, the woman from S.A.[2]: "It ees true, we have been told of very many shuttles formerly based in Venezuela now transferred for some purpose. We had assumed perhaps Hyperion was the target."

"Hyperion," sneered RussCorp. "One shuttle alone—plenty for Hyperion!"

Haseldyne snapped, "Don't get panicked by this pillhead! I'm sure he's exaggerating. The hucks are a paper tiger. If we do our job they won't have any time to worry about Venus—they'll be too busy sucking their thumbs and wondering what went wrong with the Earth."

"I am glad," said RussCorp gloomily, "that you are sure. I myself have doubts. Have been many rumors, all reported to this council—all dismissed. Wrongly, I now think."

"I personally suggest—" began the German, but Haseldyne cut her off.

"We'll talk this over in private," he said dangerously, and glared at me. "You! Outside! We'll call you back when we want you!"

I gave them a shrug, and a smile, and went out the door the man from Indiastries held open for me. It was no surprise to me to find that it led only to a short stairway and to an outside door—which was locked. I sat on the steps and waited.

When at last the inner door opened again and Haseldyne called my name I didn't try to read the expression on his face. I just politely slid past him and took the empty seat at the table. He didn't like it much; his face was reddening and his expression lethal, but he didn't say anything. He didn't have the right to. He wasn't the person in charge.

The person in charge now was the Old Man himself. He looked up to study me, and the face looked the same as it always had, pink and plump and wool-framed, except that it wasn't at all genial. The expression was bleak. And, wholly out of character for the Old Man I had known so long, he offered no small talk. He offered nothing at all for a long moment, just looked up at me, then back at his table-top screen, and his fingers busy tapping out new queries and getting bad answers. From the stairs I had heard a lot of noise—agitated rumbles and peremptory shrill squeals—but now they were silent. The stifling aroma of real tobacco came from the place where the RussCorp man was silently smoking his pipe. The SA^2 woman absently stroked something in her lap—a pet, I could see; possibly a kitten.

Then the Old Man slapped his board to clear his screen and said heavily, "Tarb, that's not good news you brought us. But we have to assume it's true."

"Yes, *sir,*" I cried, out of old reflex.

We have to act swiftly to meet this challenge," he declared. His pomposity had not gone the way of his good humor. "You will understand, of course, that we can't tell you our plans—"

"Of course not, sir!"

"—and you'll understand, too, that you have not yet proved yourself. Mitzi Ku vouches for you," he went on, his cold stare drifting across the table to focus on her. She was gazing at her fingertips and didn't look up to meet it. "Provisionally, we are accepting her guarantee." At that she winced, and I had a quick understanding of what the alternatives they had been discussing might be, *provisionally.*

"I understand," I said, and managed to omit the sir. "What do you want me to do?"

"You are ordered to continue with your work. That is our major project and it can't be stopped. Mitzi and the rest of us will now have to be doing—other things—so you'll be on your own to some extent. Don't let that make you sloppy."

I nodded, waiting to see if there was more. There wasn't. Des Haseldyne led me to the door and escorted me through. Mitzi hadn't spoken at all. At the foot of the stairs Haseldyne pushed me into another thieflock. Before he closed the door he snapped, "You looking for thanks? Forget it! We thanked you by letting you live."

As I waited for the outer door to open I heard the furious rumbles and squeaks begin again as they went at it once more. What Haseldyne had said was true: they'd let me live. What was also true was that they could reverse that decision at any time. Could I prevent that? Yes, I decided, but in only one way: by doing such a good job for them that I would become indispensable . . . or more accurately, by making sure they *thought* I was.

Then the outside door opened.

Des Haseldyne must have been operating the controls. That lock had thrust-bar capacities too; the door behind me hurled me out into the street. I stumbled and fell, skidding across the sidewalk under the feet of hurrying pedestrians. "You all right, mister?" quavered one old consumer, gaping at me with alarm.

"I'm fine," I snapped as I picked myself up. I don't think I have ever told a bigger lie.

II

It is a bad and worrisome thing to have lined yourself up with a bunch of felons as accomplice to brainburning crimes. It's a lot worse to realize that they're inept. That circle of Venusian master spies and saboteurs might, among the lot of them, have summoned up enough skill and villainy to sneak a bunch of forged discount coupons past a supermarket checker. For the task of preserving their world against the might of Earth they simply were not up to it.

Dixmeister had an easy time of it that afternoon. When I limped back into my office I snarled at him to go about his business and leave me alone until ordered otherwise. Then I locked my door and thought.

Without Mokes or little green pills to hide behind, what I saw when I opened my eyes was naked reality. It was not an attractive sight, for it was full of problems—three in particular:

First, if I didn't convince the Veenies that they needed me, and could even trust me, good old Haseldyne would know what to do about it. After that I wouldn't have any worries at all.

Second, if I did as I was told the future looked bleak. I hadn't been consulted in planning their great strategic campaign; the more I thought of it, the less sure I was that it would work.

Third and worst, if it didn't work, then we were all cooked. We would spend the rest of our lives living in playpens, wearing diapers, spoon-fed by attendants who didn't like us much and getting our chief intellectual stimulation from watching the pretty lights go by. All of us. Not just me. The woman I loved as well.

I didn't want Mitzi Ku brainburned.

I didn't want Tennison Tarb brainburned, either. My recently acquired clarity of thought soberly pointed out that there was a way out of that part of the fix, anyway. All I had to do was pick up the phone to the Fair Commercial Practices Commission and turn the Veenies in; I'd probably get off with the Polar Penal Colony, maybe even just reduction to consumer status. But that wouldn't save Mitzi. . . .

Just before the close of business Mitzi and Des called a top-level staff meeting in the boardroom. Mitzi didn't speak, didn't look at me, either. Des Haseldyne did all the talking. He said there were some, uh, unexpected expansion opportunities opening up and he and Mitzi would have to be out of the office to investigate them. Meanwhile, they had bought Val Dambois's contract from T., G. & S. and he would be coming in as temporary general manager; Intangibles (Political) would be directed independently by Tennison Tarb, that was me, and he was sure we'd carry on with full efficiency.

It was not a convincing performance. It wasn't received well, either. There were sidelong glances and worried looks in the audience. As we all got up to go I managed to get close to Mitzi long enough to whisper in her ear: "I'll stay on at the condo, all right?" She didn't answer that, either. She just looked at me and shrugged.

I didn't have a chance to pursue it, because at that point Val Dambois came up from behind and grabbed my shoulder. "A word with you, Tenny," he gritted, and led me to Mitzi's office—his office now. He slammed the door, slapped the privacy screen on and said: "Don't get too *independent*, Tarb. Remember I'll be right here, watching you." I didn't need to be reminded of that. When I didn't answer he looked at me closely: "Can you handle it?" he demanded. "Are you feeling all right?"

I said, in order, "I can handle it," which was a lot more hope than conviction, and, "I feel like somebody who's got two whole planets resting on his shoulders," which was true.

He nodded. "Just remember," he said, "if you have to let one of them drop, make sure it's the right one."

"Sure thing, Val," I said. But which was the right one?

Since Mitzi hadn't said I couldn't stay at the condo, I did. I didn't expect her to be there that first night, and she wasn't. I wasn't quite alone, though. Val Dambois made sure I had a certain amount of company. As I hailed a pedicab outside the office I noticed a muscular male type dawdling after me, and the same man was lounging around across from Mitzi's condo when I left in the morning. I didn't care. They left me alone in the office, although I might not have noticed if they hadn't. I was *busy*. I wanted that weight of two worlds off my shoulders, and the only way to do it was to win their war for them . . . somehow.

There were a dozen major theme commercials to prepare for the election and only days to do them in. I turned Dixmeister loose on lining up channel time and riding herd on the production department. I took over talent and script completely.

Now, normally when a project head says he takes over talent and script, what he means is he has about half a dozen headhunters searching out talent for him and at least that many copysmiths generating the scripts; what he does is mostly kick tail to make sure they're doing their jobs. With me it was a little different. I had the staff, and I kicked their tails. But I also had plans of my own. They weren't very clear in my mind. They were a long way from satisfactory, even to me. And there wasn't anybody I could bounce them off to see how high they climbed. But they were what kept me in the office for sixteen hours a day instead of the mere ten or twelve I might otherwise have spent. It wasn't so bad; what else did I have to do with my time?

I knew what else I *wanted* to do with my time, but Mitzi was—was

—what shall I say? Out of my reach? Not really; we bedded together every night she was in the city. Out of my grasp, though, because the bed was the only place I saw her, and not often there. I'd set the whole Veenie hive buzzing with my news, and they were zinging in all directions. When Mitzi was in the city she was at high-level, secret meetings every minute; when she wasn't in meetings here, she was somewhere else in the world. Or off it, because for a solid week she was on the Moon, trading furtive, coded messages with a freight-forwarder in Port Kathy on Venus.

One night I'd given up hope of her and gone to sleep when, in the middle of a really rotten dream about a Fair Commercial Practices strong-arm man creeping into the bed next to me, I woke to find someone really was, and it was Mitzi.

It took me a long time to get wholly awake because of exhaustion, and when I accomplished it, Mitzi was already asleep. I could see by looking at her that she was a lot more exhausted than I. If I'd had any compassion at all I'd have put my arms around her silently and let the two of us sleep through the night. I couldn't. I got up, and made some of that funny-tasting real coffee for her, and sat down on the edge of the bed until she smelled it and stirred. She didn't want to wake up. She was burrowed down under the blanket with just the top of her head and enough of her nose for breathing still visible, and there was a warm smell of sweet sleeping woman to mingle with the aroma of the coffee. She tossed herself petulantly over to the other side of the bed, muttering something—all I could understand were some words about "changing fuses." I waited. Then the rhythm of her breathing changed and I knew she was awake.

She opened her eyes. "Hello, Tenny," she said.

"Hello, Mitzi." I extended the coffee cup, but she ignored it for a moment, looking bleakly at me over it.

"Do you really want to get married?"

"You bet, if—"

She didn't expect me to finish that sentence. She nodded. "So do I," she said. "If." She put herself up against the pillows and took the cup. "Well," she said, postponing that subject for the duration, "how's it going?"

I ventured, "I've got some pretty hot new commercial themes. Maybe I should check them out with you."

"What for? You're in charge." That subject was dismissed too. I reached over and touched her shoulder. She didn't move away, but she didn't respond, either. There were a lot of other subjects I would have liked to discuss. Where we were going to live. Whether we wanted to have any kids, and what genders. What we would do for fun and, that subject always dear to the newly engaged, how much and in what particular ways we loved each other. . . .

I didn't say any of those things. Instead, I asked: "What did you mean about 'changing fuses,' Mitzi?"

She sat bolt upright, slopping coffee into the saucer, glaring at me. "What the hell are you asking, Tenn?" she snapped.

I said, "It kind of sounds to me as though you're talking about sabotaging equipment. Campbellian projectors, right? You're probably infiltrating people into the limbic units to screw up the machinery?"

"Shut up, Tenn."

"Because if you are," I went on reasonably, "I don't think that will work. See, they've got a long flight to Venus and there'll be standby crews kept awake in rotating shifts. They won't have anything to do but to keep checking and rechecking the equipment. Anything you bust, they'll have plenty of time to fix."

That shook her. She set the cup down by the side of the bed, staring at me.

"The other thing that worries me about that," I continued, "is that when they find out there's been sabotage they'll start looking for who did it. Sure, the huck intelligence services are fat, dumb and happy—they haven't had anything to worry about for a long time. But you just might wake them up."

"Tenny," she flared, *"butt out.* You do your own damn job. Let us worry about security!"

So I did what I should have done in the first place. I turned the light off and slipped into bed beside her and took her in my arms. We didn't talk any more. As I was drifting off to sleep I realized that she was weeping. I wasn't surprised. It was a hell of a way for a newly engaged couple to be spending their time, but it was the only way we had. We simply couldn't talk easily, for she had her secrets that she was obliged to protect.

And I had mine.

On the sixteenth of October the statutory ten-week-warning Christmas decorations appeared in the store windows. Election Day was getting very close.

It's the last ten days of a campaign that count. I was ready for them. I had done everything I had thought to do and done it real well. I was real well all over these days, barring a slight tendency to get the shakes when a can of Moke was in the room (that was aversion therapy for you), and a considerable loss of weight. People stopped telling me how well I looked. They didn't have to; I was looking as well as anybody could be expected to look when every night's sleep was maimed by dreams about brainburning. Dixmeister danced in and out of my office, thrilled by his new responsibilities, awed by the new themes I was unveiling. "They're really powerful stuff, Mr. Tarb," he told me uneasily, "but are you sure you're not going too far?"

"If I were," I smiled at him, "don't you think Ms. Ku would have stopped them?" Maybe she would have, if I had told her what they were. But the moment for that had passed. I was committed.

I stopped him as he turned to hurry out. "Dixmeister," I said, "I've had some complaints from the networks about degraded signals on our transmissions."

"Transmission fade? Gosh, Mr. Tarb, I haven't seen any memos—"

"They're coming along later. I got this head-to-head with the net people. So I want to check this out. Get me a wiring diagram of this building; I want to see where every signal goes from point of origin to the phone company mains outside."

"Right, Mr. Tarb! You mean just the commercial transmissions, of course?"

"I of course don't. I want everything. And I want it now."

"That'll take hours, Mr. Tarb," he wailed. He had a family, and he was thinking of what his wife would say when he didn't get home for First Gift Night.

"You've got hours," I told him. He did. And I didn't want him spending those hours looking for incoming memos that didn't exist or chattering with somebody else's staff about what Mr. Tarb was doing now. When he had the entire electronics circuitry displayed for me I froze a hard copy, jammed it in my pocket and made him join me on a physical inspection of the place where all the lines came together, the comm room in the basement.

"I've never *been* in the basement, Mr. Tarb," he whimpered. "Can't we leave that for the phone company?"

"Not if we ever want to get promoted again, Dixmeister," I told him kindly, and so the two of us took the lift down as far as it would go and then a freight elevator two more stories below that. The basement was damp, dirty, dim-lit, dingy—it was a lot of things beginning with *d* including deserted. There were hundreds of square yards of space here, but too nasty to rent out even to night-dwellers. It was just what I wanted.

The comm room was at the end of a long corridor, choked with dust. Next to it were three rooms of stored microfiles, mostly urgent FCC and Department of Commerce directives that, of course, had never been opened. I looked into every storeroom carefully, then stood at the door of the comm room and gave it one quick glance around. Every phone call, data-link message, facsimile and video transmission the Agency originated went through that room. Of course it was wholly automatic and electronic at that: nothing moved or flashed or clicked. There were manual override terminals for rerouting messages around a bad circuit—or cutting them off entirely—but there was no reason to man them. "Looks all right to me," I said.

Dixmeister gave me a glum look. "I suppose you're going to want to test all the circuits?"

"Nah, what for? The trouble's got to be outside." He opened his mouth to protest, but I closed it with, "And, listen, get all that junk out of those storerooms. I'm going to take them over for a brainroom."

"But, Mr. *Tarb!*"

"Dixmeister," I said gently, "when you're star class you'll understand the need for privacy at times like these. Right now, don't try. Just do it."

I left him to it and went back to Mitzi's condo, wanting very much to find her there. I had a problem or two still to solve. Mitzi was not the person to solve them for me, but she could give me, at least, the touch of beloved skin and the solace of body warmth . . . if this happened to be a night when she would be at home.

She wasn't. All there was of her was a flash-paper note on the pillow to say that she had to be in Rome for a few days.

It wasn't what I wanted but, as I sat staring out over the dirty, sleeping city with an ounce and a half of grain neutral spirits in my hand, I began to perceive that it might be what I needed.

III

My scripts were ready. The candidates to appear in them had been selected and stashed away in hideouts all around the city. It had not been hard to pick them, because I knew just what I wanted; getting them to the city and ready to go had been a lot harder. But they were there. From the condo I phoned in orders for two-man Wackerhut teams to round them up and deliver them to the recording studios, and by the time I reached the office they were there, too.

The actual recording was easy—well, comparatively easy. Compared to, say, six hours of brain surgery. It took all the skill I had and all my concentration, while I rehearsed my actors, and hung over the makeup people while they prepped them for the cameras, and ramrodded the production teams along, and directed every move and word. The easy part was that every one of the actors spoke the lines easily and convincingly, because I'd written them out of knowledge of just what they could do best. The hard part was that I could use only skeleton crews, since the fewer people who knew what was going on the better. When the last one was in the can I shipped the entire crew, production, makeup and all, to an imaginary "remote" in San Antonio, Texas, with orders to loaf around there until I arrived, which would be never.

But at least in San Antonio they wouldn't be talking to anybody else. Then I sent my actors down to the newly completed suite in the basement and got ready for the hard part. I took a deep breath, wished I dared swallow a pill to calm my nerves, exercised vigorously for five minutes so that I'd be out of breath and dashed into the office that once had been Mitzi's. Val Dambois jerked upright, startled, from the figures on his desk screen as I panted, "Val! Urgent call from Mitzi! You've got to get to the Moon! The agent's had a heart attack, the communication link's gone!"

"What the hell are you talking about?" he snarled, the chubby face quivering. In normal times Dambois might not have let me get away with it, but he, too, had been pushed past his strain limit in the last few weeks.

I gabbled, "Message from Mitzi! She said it was crucial. There's a cab waiting—you've got just time to get to the shuttleport—"

"But Mitzi's in—" He stopped, eyeing me uncertainly.

"In Rome, right," I nodded. "That's where she called from. She said there's a long priority order due in, and somebody's got to be on the Moon to receive it. So come on, Val!" I begged, grabbing his briefcase, his hat, his passport; hustling him out the door, onto the lift, into the cab. An hour later I called the shuttleport to ask if he'd boarded the flight.

They told me he had.

"Dixmeister!" I called. Dixmeister appeared instantly in the doorway, face flushed, half a soy sandwich in one hand, the other hand still holding his phone. "Dixmeister, those new spots I just taped. I want them aired tonight."

He swallowed down a mouthful of soy. "Why, yes, Mr. Tarb, I suppose we can do that, but we've got a group of other spots scheduled—"

"Switch the spots," I ordered. "New instructions from the top floor. I want those first spots on the air in an hour, full display by prime time. Kill all the others; use the new ones. Do it, Dixmeister." And he loped off, chewing, to get it done.

It was time to go to the mattresses.

As soon as Dixmeister was out of sight I got up and left, closing the door behind me. I would not open it again, at least not in the same world. Very likely I would never open it again at all.

My new office was a lot less luxurious than my old, especially because of where it was: down in subbasement six. Still, considering how little time I'd given them, Housekeeping had done their best. They'd put into it everything I'd asked for, including a wall of a dozen screens for direct display of any feed I chose. There were a dozen desks, all occupied by members of my new little task force. Best of all, Engineering had closed up a couple of old doorways and cut through some new ones, as ordered. There was no longer direct access from the corridor to the comm room. The only way to the Agency's nerve center lay through my new suite of former stockrooms. The little cubicle where the standby engineers had been accustomed to drowse through their duties was empty, and its door had a lock on it now. The engineers themselves were long gone, because I had given all of them a week off on the grounds that the system was automatic and foolproof and I wanted to try the experiment of having it completely unmanned for a while. They looked doubtful until I convinced them that nobody's job was threatened, then they left gladly enough.

The place was, in short, just what I had ordered, with everything I had been able to think of that was necessary to the success of my project. Whether it was also sufficient was another question entirely, but it was too late to worry about that. I put on my best and most confident grin as I approached Jimmy Paleologue at his "reception" desk in the corridor. "Got everything you need?" I asked genially.

He slid his desk drawer back just enough to show me the stun-gun nestling inside it before he grinned back. If there was a hint of strain in the grin you couldn't blame him; after he'd gotten through with the detox center he'd been promised his old job back as a Campbellian technician; then I found him and persuaded him to this unpromising exercise. "Gert and I rigged a tangle-net at the door and another one just inside your room," he reported. "Everybody's armed except Nels Rockwell—he couldn't manage to lift his arm enough to fire. He says he'd like a limbic grenade strapped to his body for, you know, last-ditch stuff—what do you think?"

"I think he'd be more dangerous to us than anybody else," I smiled, though actually it struck me that the idea had merit. Not limbic, though. Explosive. Maybe even a mini-nuke. If things got bad enough we might all welcome a nice clean vaporization instead of the alternative—I left that thought behind me and strode into the suite.

Gert Martels jumped up and grabbed me for a hug. She'd been the most difficult of my people to recruit—they didn't want to let her out of the stockade, even after I threw the Agency rank around; it had finally taken a job offer to the prison commandant—and she was also the most grateful for the chance. "Aw, Tenny," she chuckled—sobbed—it was actually some of both—"we're really doing it!"

"It's half done," I told her. "The first spots ought to be on any minute."

"They've started already!" called fat Marie from her couch by the wall. "We just saw Gwenny—she was great!" Gwendolyn Baltic was the youngest of my recruits, fifteen years old and with a harrowing story. I'd found her through Nelson Rockwell; she was the product of a broken home when her mother was brainburned for multiple credit frauds and her father committed suicide rather than

face detoxification for his Nico-Hype addiction. She'd been my
choice to run the March of Dollars campaign, soliciting funds for
more and better detox centers. I'd picked that to run first because it
was the entering wedge, the least likely to shock the network con-
tinuity-acceptance people into action. "She was *grand,*" beamed
Marie, and little Gwenny blushed.

If they had already started we could expect a reaction soon. It
came within ten minutes. "Company coming," called Jimmy Paleologue from the corridor, and when I saw who it was I ordered him let
in.

It was Dixmeister, hurrying down with urgent messages. "Mr.
Tarb!" he began, but was distracted by the crowded desks. Not by
the desks, exactly; by who was at the desks. "Mr. Tarb?" he asked
querulously. "You've got *talent* here? *Actors?*"

"In case we need them for some last-minute retakes," I said
smoothly, gesturing to Gert to take her hand away from the stun-
gun in her drawer. "You wanted me for something?"

"Oh, hell, yes—I mean, yes, Mr. Tarb. I've been getting calls
from the nets. They've screened your new promo themes, for the
candidates, you know—"

"I know," I said, with my most menacing scowl. "What the hell is
this, Dixmeister? Are you letting them get away with trying to censor
advertising?"

He looked shocked. "Oh, gee, Mr. Tarb, no! Nothing like that.
It's just that a couple of the Content Acceptance Division people
thought there was a, well, a kind of a hint of, uh, Co—Uh, Con—"

"Conservationism, you mean, Dixmeister?" I asked kindly.
"Look at me, Dixmeister. Do I look like a Conservationist to you?"

"Oh, gosh, no, Mr. Tarb!"

"Or do you think this Agency would put on Consie political
commercials?"

"Not in a million years! It's not just the commercials for the
candidates, though. It's this new charity drive, you know? The
March of Dollars?" I knew; it was my own invention, a fund drive for
expanding detox centers like the one I had been in.

"They're questioning that, too?" I asked, smiling my so-they're-
up-to-those-old-tricks-again smile.

"Well, as a matter of fact, yes, but that's not the part that I
wanted to ask you about. The thing is, I went through the files and I
can't find a topfloor order for that whole campaign."

"Well, of course not," I said, opening my eyes wide in surprise. "I don't suppose Val had time to finish it, did he? I mean, before he took off for the Moon like that. Flag it, Dixmeister," I ordered. "As soon as he gets back, I'll get on him. Good work noticing it, Dixmeister!"

"Thank you, Mr. Tarb," he cried—grinning, very nearly shuffling his feet. "I'll take another look for the order, though."

"Sure thing." Of course he would. And of course he wouldn't find it, there being none. "And don't take any gas from those network people. Remind them we're not playing for marbles here. We don't want to have to bring a charge of Contract Breach."

He winced and left, though he couldn't help one last, wondering glance at Marie and Gert Martels, clustered around Marie's desktop screen. "It's hotting up, isn't it?" asked Gert.

"Hotting up," I agreed. "Is that one of ours you're looking at? Display it for me, will you?"

Marie moved a stud on her control board, and the first of the wall screens lighted up with a network feed. It was the Nelson Rockwell commercial, eyes gleaming out of the bandage-swathed head as he delivered his pitch: "—severed patella, that's the kneecap, two broken ribs, internal bleeding and a concussion. That's what they did to me when I couldn't pay for the things I hadn't wanted in the first place—"

Gert giggled, "Doesn't he look cute?"

"Real lady-killer," I said genially. "Have you all got your stunguns where you can get at them in a hurry?" Gert nodded, the smile suddenly frozen on her face. It wasn't a smile any more. It was scary. I judged that the trouble it had taken to get her out of the stockade was well worth it.

Rockwell took his eyes off his own image on the screen and fastened them on me. "Do you think there's going to be trouble, Tenny?" he asked. His voice didn't shake but I noticed that his left hand, the one that wasn't in his whole-body cast, hovered close to the desk drawer. What could be in it? Not a gun; I hoped not a grenade—I hadn't quite made that decision yet.

"Well, you never know, do you?" I asked, strolling casually to his desk. "It's just best to be ready for it if it comes, right?" They all nodded, and I craned my neck to see what was in the drawer. It took me a moment to realize that it wasn't a grenade; it was one of his damned Miniature Simulated-Copper Authentic Death Masks of

Leading Male Undergarment Models. I almost choked with a rush of sympathy. Poor guy! "Nels," I said softly, "if we get out of this I *promise* you next week you'll be in Detox."

As far as you could tell under the bandages, his expression was scared but determined, and I think he nodded. Out loud I said to them all, "It's going to be a long night. We'd all better get some sleep—take it in shifts."

They all chorused agreement, and as I turned to my own office they went back to watching the end of the Rockwell spot: "—that's my story, and if you'd like to help me get elected please send your contributions to—"

I closed the door behind me and went right to my own desk. I punched up the latest *Advertising Age* and stared down at the screen. They hadn't waited for the hourly edition. They had a red-flashing special. The headlines were:

Shocking New Net Spots from H & K
FCC Orders Investigation

Things were hotting up, all right.

I hadn't been entirely honest with them. One did sometimes know when there was going to be trouble. I knew. And I knew it wasn't very far away.

I followed my own instructions, but not very successfully. Sleep didn't come easily. When it came it ended in a hurry—a worrisome noise from the outer room, a bad dream, most frequently of all an increasingly fretful call from Dixmeister up in the world. He had given up hope of getting home that night, and every hour he called with some new and more urgent Fair Commercial Practices complaint or network blast. I had no trouble with them. "Handle them," I ordered, every time, and handle them he did. He got Haseldyne & Ku's lawyers out of bed three times that night, to hire a tame judge to deliver a Freedom-of-Advertising injunction. They wouldn't stay enjoined. The hearings would all come due in a week or less, but within a lot less than a week, one way or another, it wouldn't matter.

When I peered out now and then I could see that my stalwart crew slept no better than I. They woke, startled, at odd noises— woke up fast and got back to sleep only slowly and uneasily, because they were having their bad dreams too. Not all of my dreams were nightmares. But none of them was really good. The last one I remembered was of Christmas, some improbable future Christmas spent with Mitzi. It was just like memories of childhood, with the sooty snow staining the windows and the Christmas tree chirping its messages of no-down-payment gifts . . . only Mitzi wouldn't stop ripping the commercials off the tree and pouring the kiddy-drug sweets down the toilet, and I could hear a banging on the door that I knew was Santa Claus's Helpers with guns drawn, ready to make a bust—

Part of it was true. Someone was indeed at the outer door.

If I had been of a wagering turn of mind, I would have bet that the first one banging on my door would have been the Old Man, because he would only have to come across town. I was wrong. The Old Man must have been in Rome with Mitzi and Des—more likely, already halfway back on the night rocket to put out this unexpected fire—because the first one was Val Dambois. Sneaky son of a gun! You couldn't even trust him to stay tricked when you tricked him, because he'd obviously tricked me right back. "You didn't get on the Moon ship after all," I said stupidly. He gave me an evil look.

The look wasn't half as evil as what he had in his hand. It wasn't a stun-gun, or even a lethal. It was worse than either. It was a Campbellian sidearm, definitely illegal for civilians to own at all, even more illegal to be used anywhere outside a posted area. And the worst part of it was that Marie had been left alone in the office and she'd drowsed off on her cot. He was past the tangle-net at the door before anyone could stop him.

I was shaking. That's surprising in itself, when you think about it, because I wouldn't have believed it was possible for anything to frighten a person who had as much to fear already as I did. Wrong opinion. Looking at the flaring muzzle of the limbic projector turned my spine to jelly and my heart to ice. And he was pointing it in my direction. "Huck bastard!" he snarled. "I *knew* you were up to something, hustling me away like that. Good thing there's always a Moke-head around the terminal you can bribe to take a free trip, so I could come back and wait to catch you in the act!"

He always talked too much, did Val Dambois. It gave me a chance to get my nerve back. I said, with all the courage I could find, forcing a grin, keeping the tone cool and assured—or so I hoped, though it didn't sound that way to me—"You waited too long, Val. It's all over. The commercials are on the air already."

"You'll never live to enjoy it!" he screamed, lifting the barrel of the Campbell.

I held the grin. "Val," I said patiently, "you're a fool. Don't you know what's going on?"

Faint waver of the gun; suspiciously, "What?"

"I had to get you out of the way," I explained, "because you talk too much. Mitzi's orders. She didn't trust you."

"Trust *me?*"

"Because you're a wimp, don't you see? Don't take my word for it—see for yourself. The next commercial will be Mitzi herself—" And I glanced at the wall screen—

And so did Val Dambois. He'd made mistakes before, but that one was terminal. He took his eyes off Marie. You can't altogether blame him for that, considering the shape that Marie was obviously in, but he had cause to regret it. *Zunggg* went her stun-gun, and the limbic projector dropped out of Val's hand, and Val dropped right after it.

A little late, the door to the storeroom flew open and the rest of my crew boiled in, wakened from their uneasy naps. Marie was propped on one elbow, grinning—her cot contained her mechanical heart and she couldn't move away from it, but she had a hand free for the stun-gun when it was needed. "I got him for you, Tenny," she said proudly.

"You surely did," I agreed, and then to Gert Martels, "Help me lug him into the storeroom."

So we tucked him into the room where once the engineers had dozed away their standby shifts, and left him to do the same. The limbic projector I turned over to Jimmy Paleologue. I couldn't stand to touch the thing, but I thought he might consider it a valuable addition to our limited arsenal. Another wrong guess. He darted out into the hall with it, I heard the sound of running water from the communijohn, and he came back with it dripping. "That one will never work again," he gritted, tossing it in a wastebasket. "What do you say, Tarb? Back to sleeping shifts?"

I shook my head. The sleeping room had now become a jail, and besides we were all good and wakeful. "Might as well enjoy the fun," I said, and left them brewing Kaf to jolt the drowsies away. I wanted a look at *Advertising Age,* and I wanted it in the privacy of my own office.

It wasn't reassuring. They were transmitting nothing but bulletins now, with headlines like:

FCC Head Vows Full Prosecution
and
Brainburn Seen Likely in H & K Case

I rubbed the back of my neck uneasily, wondering what it felt like to be a vegetable.

I didn't have long to spend on that unenjoyable task, because I guess Mitzi had caught the night rocket after all. There was a rattle and a squeal and a bunch of relieved guffaws, and when I got my door open there she was. Stuck in Gert Martel's tangle-net. "What'll we do with this one?" asked Nels Rockwell through his bandages. "There's still plenty of room in the storeroom."

I shook my head. "Not her. She can come in my office."

When Marie turned off the juice in the net, Mitzi stumbled and half fell. She caught herself, glaring up at me. "You fool, Tenn!" she spat. "What the hell do you think you're doing?"

I helped her up. "You shouldn't have given me the cure, Mitzi. It cured me."

Her jaw dropped. She let me take her arm and lead her into my office. She sat down heavily, staring at me. "Tenny," she said, "do you know what you've *done?* I couldn't believe it when they told me what you were putting on the air for political commercials—it's unheard of!"

"People telling the truth, yes," I nodded. "Never been done, as far as I know."

"Oh, Tenny! 'Truth.' Grow up!" she flared. "How can we win with *truth?*"

I said gently, "When I was being detoxed I had to do a lot of soul-searching—it was better than cutting my throat, you see. So I asked questions. Let me ask you one of them: In what way is what we're doing right?"

"Tenny!" She was shocked. "Are you defending the hucks? They've despoiled their own planet, now they want to do the same thing to Venus!"

"No," I said, shaking my head, "you're not answering the question. I didn't ask you why they were wrong, because I know why they were wrong. I wanted to know if we were right."

"Compared to the hucks—"

"No, that won't do, either. Not 'compared to.' You see, it isn't enough to be less bad. Less bad is still bad."

"I never heard such pious claptrap—" she began, and then paused, listening. Sudden sounds of a squabble from the anteroom: a man's furious bellow—Haseldyne's?; clipped orders in a higher voice—Gert Martels?; the sound of a door closing. She stared at me, wonderingly. "You'll never get away with it," she whispered.

"That's possible. Still," I explained, "I picked this place because it's next to the comm room. All Agency communications go through here, so the building's shut off, and the Wackerhuts have orders to let staff in, not out."

"No, Tenny," she sobbed, "I don't mean right now, I mean later. Do you know what they'll *do* to you?"

The flesh at the back of my neck crawled, because I did. "Brainburning, maybe. Or just kill me," I acknowledged. "But that's only if I fail, Mits. There are twenty-two separate commercials going out. Would you like to see some?" I turned to the monitor, but she stopped me.

"I've seen! That fat cripple you've got out there, whining about how she was made to eat junk food—the aboriginal that says his people's life-styles were destroyed—"

"Marie, yes. And the Sudanese." Finding him had been a bit of luck—Gert Martels had done it, once I bailed her out of the stockade and told her what I wanted. "That's only two of them, love. There's a real good one with Jimmy Paleologue about how Campbellian techniques work—on people like me as well as the natives. Nels Rockwell's good, too—"

"I've seen them, I tell you! Oh, Tenny, I thought you were on our side."

"Neither for you nor against you, Mits."

She sneered, "A real prescription for inaction." But I didn't have to say anything to that; inaction wasn't what I was guilty of, and she knew it as soon as she said the words. "You'll fail, Tenny. You can't defeat evil with namby-pamby piety!"

"Maybe not. Maybe you can't defeat evil at all. Maybe the world's social ills are too far along and evil's going to win. But you don't have to be an *accomplice* to it, Mitzi. And you don't have to give up, like your hero Mitch Courtenay."

"Tenny!" She wasn't angry now, just shocked at blasphemy.

"But that's what he did, Mitzi. He didn't solve the problem. He ran away from it."

"We're not running away!"

I nodded, "Right, you're fighting. And using the same weapons. And coming out with the same end results! The hucks turned the planet into ten billion mindless mouths—what you want to do is starve the mouths, just so you can be left alone! So I'm not on the huck side, I'm not on the Veenie side. I'm opting out! I'm trying something different."

"The *truth.*"

"The truth, Mitzi," I declared, "is the only weapon there is that doesn't cut both sides!"

And then I stopped. I was working myself up to a grand speech, and heaven knows what heights of oratory I might have reached for my one-woman audience. But the best parts of it I had already said, and I had them on tape. I fumbled on my keyboard to call up my own commercial and paused with my finger on the Execute button. "Look, Mits," I said, "there are twenty-two commercials altogether, three each for the seven people I'm using—"

"What seven?" she demanded suspiciously. "I only saw four out there."

"Two of them were kids, and I sent the Sudanese off with them to keep them out of trouble. Pay attention, Mits! Those first twenty-one are just to prepare the audience for the twenty-second. That's mine. At least, that's me delivering it—but it's really for you."

I hit the button. The screen jumped alive. There I was, looking serious and trouble-worn, with a stock shot of Port Kathy matted into the background. "My name," my recorded voice told us, and the professional part of my mind thought, *not bad, not too pompous, talking a little too fast, though,* "my name is Tennison Tarb. I'm a star-class copysmith, and what you see behind me is one of the cities on Venus. See the people? They look just like us, don't they? But they're different from us in one way. They don't like having their minds bent by advertising. Unfortunately that's made things bad all around, because now they have their minds bent in a different way. They've come to hate us. They call us 'hucks.' They think we're out to conquer them and force our advertising down their throats. This

has made them as mean as any agency man, and the terrible part is
that their suspicions are right. We sneak spies into their government. We send in teams of terrorists to sabotage their economy.
And right now we're planning to invade them with Campbellian
limbic weaponry, the exact same way I saw us do just a little while
ago in the Gobi Desert. . . ."

"Oh, Tenny," whispered Mitzi. "They'll brainburn you."

I nodded. "Yes, that's what they'll do, all right, if we fail."

"But you're bound to fail!"

Old habits die hard; much though I wanted to get straight with
Mitzi, I couldn't help casting a regretful glance at the screen—I was
just getting into the best parts! But I said, "We'll find that out pretty
soon, Mits. Let's see what they're saying." And, leaving the screen
to run through the rest of my spot unnoticed, I punched up the
headlines on my desk screen. The first half dozen were nothing but
dire threats and sinister portents, just as before—but then there was
one that made my heart leap:

City Stunned, Crowds Gather

And just below it:

Brinks Head Says Demonstration "Out of Control"

I didn't bother with the text. I threw open the door to the outer
office, where my trusty four were gathered around their desks.
"What is it?" I called. "Are we getting a play? Check the news
channels, will you?"

"A play! What do you think we're looking at?" called Gert
Martels, grinning. As the new wall panels flashed into life I saw what
she was grinning about. The local stations had knocked themselves
out with remotes to get reaction shots—and the reaction was huge.

"Jeez, Tenny," Rockwell shouted, "it's gridlock!" It just about
was. The cameras of the news stations were roving from intersection
to intersection—Times Square, Wall Street, Central Park Mall,
Riverspace—and every one looked the same. It was morning run
time, but traffic had come almost to a standstill while the city's
teeming millions listened on portables or watched the building-wall
displays, and every one of them was listening to one of our commercials.

I could hardly breathe with excitement. "The nets!" I called. "What's going on in the rest of the country?"

"The same thing, Tenny," said Gert Martels, and added, "Do you see what's happening there, in the corner?"

We were looking at Union Square, and, yes, in the far right corner, there was a group that wasn't just standing still with its jaws hanging. They were very busy indeed. They were methodically, brutally, ripping down a display screen.

"They're tearing down our commercials," I gasped.

"No, no, Tenny! That was a Kelpy-Crisp! And look over there—the limbic area? They've wrecked the projector!"

I felt Mitzi's hand creep into mine as I stood there, and when I turned she was smiling mistily. "At least you're getting an audience," she said; and from the door a new voice said solemnly,

"The biggest audience ever, Mr. Tarb."

It was Dixmeister. Gert Martels had already drawn a stun-gun and it was leveled right at his head. He didn't even look at her. His hands were empty. He said, "You'd better come upstairs, Mr. Tarb."

My first thought was my worst thought. "A Fair Practices squadron?" I guessed. "They're canceling the spots? They've got a counterinjunction—?"

He frowned. "Nothing like that, Mr. Tarb. Gosh! I've never *seen* such hourlies! Every one of the campaign spots is drawing optimum-plus-fifty responses, the March of Dollars is swamped with pledges—no, no, it's not a *bust.*"

"Then what, Dixmeister?" I cried.

He said uncertainly, "It's all those people. You'd better come up and see."

And so I did, and from the second floor of the Agency building I could look out over the street, the square, the windows opposite. And every inch was packed with people.

The funny thing is that even so I couldn't believe it at first. I thought they were a lynch mob—until I heard them cheering.

And the rest of the world? RussCorp, Indiastries, S.A.[2]—all of them? You begin to hear cheering there, too; and where it will end I know not. Old habits die hard for nations as well as individuals. Monoliths are hard to demolish.

But they've started unloading the shuttles in Arizona again, and the monolith has begun to crack.